Black Dog: The Long Dark Road

Matt Coleman

Cover Illustration and Design by Travis Gentry

ISBN: 1475246692
ISBN-13: 978-1475246698

DEDICATION

To all the lost and forgotten talespinners, legend-makers, raconteurs, and storytellers who have come before -- be they bards, tribal shaman, or favorite uncles.

Unsung prophets, all.

CONTENTS

ACKNOWLEDGMENTS

First, thanks to God for giving me the opportunity and drive to do what I love. Without Him, I'd be nothing.

Profuse thanks to Louis Skipper, who edited these stories *gratis*, as well as the stories to come. Thanks to him, I found out the easy way that I'm a comma-splicing sonuvagun. He's also one heck of a writer; check out his literary-horror mash-up of Charles Dickens' *Great Expectations* called *Pip and the Zombies* and see if I'm lying (I'm not, by the way.)

Travis Gentry is two steps away from artistically walking on water; his phenomenal cover brought Amos and the dog to life better than my own imagination. Thanks, Trav. You came cheap when you deserved a king's ransom.

Robert Bowden showed me the intricacies of formatting an eBook for publication and kept me from pulling out what's left of my rapidly-thinning hair; any mistakes or blunders in the formatting are totally mine. Check out Robert's sci-fi thrillers *Saving Concord* and *Reconciliation.*

Thanks also go out to the Initial Readers of BLACK DOG—they all know who they are. Without you guys, there would have been some serious wardrobe malfunctions in this book. Give yourselves a cee-gar. (Or a pudding pop if you don't smoke.)

Thanks to my parents and family, who all encouraged me to write since the age of seven and who have never given up on me. Having that kind of support system is a God-given boon, and every single writer out there knows what I'm talking about.

A gut-busting shout-out to the utterly fantastic crew at Starbucks #11379 in Pearland, TX, who kept me full of java and hitting the head every five minutes, and who basically rented me their corner counter as office space while I worked on the book. You guys rock and you *know* it.

And last but *always* first, my amazing wife Jessica. There are no words to describe her dedication, patience, and love during the long hours of wringing Amos's adventures from my noggin. She's always been on my side and always gave the best and most blunt advice on the stories and was right every time. I love you, sweetheart. Now and forever.

Thus did that poor soul wander in want and cheerless discomfort,

Bleeding, barefooted, over the shards and thorns of existence.

—Henry Wadsworth Longfellow
Evangeline, Part II

INTRODUCTION

Have you ever lost something important?

Not a matching sock, or a set of keys, or the remote control. Those things aggravate, but are easily replaceable.

No, I'm talking about something that once gone, leaves a hole in your very existence. Its absence nags you subconsciously, like the gap from a missing tooth that your tongue always finds itself exploring. It's something that you may not even have known *existed*, but once you learn of it, you wonder how you ever got along without it, how you could've missed it in the first place.

History is like that, in a way. Not everything makes it into the books, and some of what does is questionable. There are countless lost histories in the world, great and small.

Some were really insignificant—minor discoveries, petty feuds between forgotten families, marriages, divorces. But some, when discovered and plundered thoroughly, have had earth-shattering implications, leaving the researcher astounded as to why the event isn't plastered in every textbook and scholarly journal on the planet.

I discovered a lost history like that.

You're holding it.

* * * *

Ten years ago, I was researching an article for a blues magazine called *Ramblin' Soul* (it's gone belly-up since then; don't bother looking for it). The article was something I'd wanted to write since I inherited my grandparents' old Royal Saturn typewriter as a kid and heard Son House wail on the eight-track in my dad's El Dorado.

It centered on blues music, specifically Southern-born artists that were all but forgotten. There were some real gems: Lightnin' Hopkins, Blind Leroy Haines, Lil' Son Jackson, Archie "Outhouse" Collins, Johnny Copeland, Junior Davis, Augie Wright. All of them legends in their own right and to the lucky few that heard them work their magic.

The aim was to spotlight these lost treasures, to generate interest with a new generation and show the roots of most of the watered-down pablum they listen to. I had hoped the article would prove a success, maybe enough to get these forgotten legends into circulation and publication, some of them for the very first time.

It didn't work out that way.

Every person I spoke with, every smoke-filled backroom I sat in, every liquor-stained, scuffed-up bar I hunched over, one name kept cropping up over and over, with different emotions behind it--sometimes as just another name tossed out in a long string of the same, other times it was the conversation entire.

The name was Amos "Black Dog" Harlow.

I had never heard of him or his music. "'Course you ain't," was the common reply, maybe because I was a white man trying to move in a black man's world and history. But I learned later that it was more than that.

Way more.

Sometimes the name was just Amos Harlow, sometimes "Black Dog" Harlow, and other times just "Black Dog." But each time I pursued the name, pressed the point, or urged the interview in Harlow's direction, the conversation suddenly fell to the weather, and my ain't it hot, or pulled-pork and who had the best hereabouts, or the World Series and the Braves' chances of ever seeing another pennant.

Most times, the conversation just ended—once, with a gun in my face.

After *that*, I just *had* to know.

My research—which included five hundred dollars' worth of bought drinks and greased palms—led me to a back-alley pool room near Bellevue and Lamar in Memphis, and its scruffy owner, Easy Bake Rollins.

Easy was pushing eighty the hard way. He'd gotten his name from his tour humping a flamethrower through the jungles of Guadalcanal. "Baked enough Japs over there to make a casserole the size of Texas," he told me.

We met in the darkened grotto of the Corner Pocket, well out of the high heat of a Tennessee summer. Easy sat at the back of the shadowed hall watching two older men play nine-ball for small change, a halo of blue-white smoke circling his head in the still air, a highball half-full of ice and Johnny Walker sweating in one hand. He motioned with the hand holding the cigarette for me to sit.

I did, and he stared at me with blood-shot, jaundiced eyes and a deeply-etched, impassive face, sizing me up. A jagged scar ran down his right cheek, paused at the jaw line, and continued across his neck; it was hard not to stare at it. We continued the staring match, watching the tendrils of his smoke curl to the ceiling, the silence broken only by the occasional crack of the cue ball against one of its multi-hued brothers.

"I knew Black Dog Harlow," he said in slow, rough voice, paved with too much of the vices he currently was enjoying. "Reckon that's why you here, ain't it?" I was ecstatic. This was the first person willing to talk about Harlow in six months, much less admit that they'd *known* him personally.

"It is," I said, "I'd like to—"

"Wish I'd never *seen* the bastard," he cut me off, blowing another plume of smoke. I glanced at the other men. They'd stopped their game and were looking at me with hard eyes. After an uncomfortable moment, they returned to their game.

I wasn't sure how to proceed. Easy saved me the trouble, clearing his throat and spitting a wad of phlegm on the hardwood floor.

"This place used to be a gin joint back in the day," he said, gesturing with the cigarette. "White folks called 'em speakeasies. Granddaddy owned it, then. Used to make the sweetest, smoothest corn liquor you ever put in yo' mout'. Had all the John Laws for miles paid off—let 'em sample the goods, see, even the women he kep'.

"I was a boy back then, woulda been in high school if'n I cared about such a thing. But I didn't. Granddaddy pay me to haul in the barrels of hooch and jars of 'shine, and to keep 'em comin' all night. The place was a wonderland, I tell you true, full-up with all kindsa people—white and black—dressed to the nines, dancin' and shootin' pool, and the 'shine and cash flowed trew these doors like a river. Had live music, too. Memphis was lousy wit' music back then, bluesmen so thick you could swat 'em from yo' face like skeeters.

"So one night, Black Dog Harlow shows up wantin' to sit in with the band for some change, maybe a drink or two. Grandaddy says that's fine, and Harlow, he get up there on stage to pick with that ol' guitar he carry. Crusty ol' thing look like it would fall to pieces soon's he strum a chord. But it didn't, and the room got quiet. Folks respected the music back then, see?

"Lord, the sound that come outta that guitar and Harlow's throat… I ain't never heard as good before or since, an' I done heard my share. It was the closest damn thing to magic I'm ever gonna see or hear in this life. Every head in the place was facin' the stage. The women was lustin' after Harlow and the men was getting' pissed because of it.

"Round that time, Granddaddy whack me on the back of the head, woke me right up and tol' me to bring out another barrel and a box of jars, 'cause it was gonna be a good night, better than most. I run to do it. While I was back in the storeroom, Harlow finished up a set, and the roof was comin' off the struts with the folks' all clappin' and shoutin' for more. I grabbed a barrel and rolled it down the hall, tryin' to hurry up and get back in 'fore the next set. I was just about to open the door behind the bar when I heard the shots.

"Near on everybody back in them days was packin' heat; a body never knew what trouble folks could get up to back then. Whoever fired that gun nigh-on emptied it, no lie. Them shots sounded like the end of the world. I set the barrel upright and stood on it to see trew the door's window.

"A big ol' white man was holding the gun, one o' them 1911s, to my Granddaddy's head. Five, six dead people on the floor, the rest hidin' behind the bar, too scared to move. 'How many more got to die tonight, Black Dog?' the man yells. Harlow stood up on stage, froze right to the spot. He set his guitar on the floor and walked to stand three feet from the man holdin' Granddaddy."

"'Tess was a witch, Baker,' he said, "'an' she got what was comin' to her. Ain't nobody kill six young'uns and cut 'em up so bad they own folks cain't recognize 'em and 'spect to walk away.'"

"The old boy looked pissed, I tell you. 'You an' everybody in here's gonna die, Black Dog, startin' with this old man. I'm gonna bring Tess back, an' your blood's gonna be the way, 'long with the rest.' Then that sumbitch cocked the hammer on his pistol, and I done somethin' stupid that only a young'un would do -- I run through that door and threw two heavy–ass jars of 'shine at the bastard, screamin' the whole time."

"One jar hit the man in the leg and broke open and t'other hit him square in the head. The gun went off and Granddaddy's head rocked back and almost twisted right the hell around, brains leakin' right out a big ol' hole in his head. He hit the floor hard.

"I cain't remember much after that, 'cept me swingin' fists at the cracker and hollerin' like a crazy man, which I reckon I *was* at that point. Then the man snatched me up like he done Granddaddy an' brung the gun around."

"But Harlow was quick for an old timer. Somethin' shiny flashed in the air in front my eyes an' the big man screamed like a woman. He dropped me to the floor, next to Granddaddy. I held on to Grandaddy's waist and shut my eyes.

"The man kep' screamin', then started shoutin' in some crazy-ass language, one I ain't never heard, even across the sea in the Big One. His hand was bleedin' like a stuck pig, four fingers twitchin' on the floor like snails in salt. Harlow was standing over him with a straight razor. That was when I felt the pain."

Easy absently traced the scar on his face, cigarette between his fingers. "I started cryin' like a baby at the sight of m' own blood. The pain… I cain't even describe it. Sometimes I *still* feel it.

"Harlow tried to step in and finish the job, but the big man kicked him in the gut, sent him reelin' into some tables. The man stood up and finished whatever crazy shit he was yellin' and laughed out loud. 'Too late, Black Dog! She's a comin'! Ain't nothin' can stop that now!'

"Then Granddaddy moved underneath me. He starts to twitchin', his hands grabbin' at the air. At the time, I thought it was a miracle, but they ain't no miracles in Hell.

"Granddaddy starts to moanin', then opens his eyes. They was all white, no color in 'em a' tall. He reached out for me, grabs my shoulders and they felt like they was in a vice. I tried to talk to him, but he pulls me in tight, opens his mout' and tries to bite me, right where Harlow's razor done cut.

"I screamed and kicked him away. He flew backwards and landed in a heap. Then the rest of them dead folks what got shot started stirrin', gettin' up off the floor just like Granddaddy did, lookin' just the same, too. I scrambled on m' hands and knees, tryin' to get the hell out. Harlow and the man were tusslin', and Harlow tripped over Granddaddy and hit the floor. The big man was pushin' Harlow's own blade toward his face, gonna kill him. I pushed up off the floor, gonna run hit him, when my hand fell on somethin' hard and cold.

"The man's gun kicked like a pissed-off horse, damn near put me on my ass. Big ol' hole opened up in the man's head like the one he put in Granddaddy's. He fell on top of Harlow, who pushed him off. Soon's the man hit the floor, so did the rest o' them dead folks, Granddaddy, too.

"I kep' the gun pointed, arms shakin' so bad. Killed a lot of people in the War, but that was the first, and I reckon the worst. Don't recall how long I stood there, but I felt the gun bein' took from me, and a rough hand on my forehead.

"'Son?'" Harlow says. "'Son, you got to get outta here, now. You get on home, hear? I take care of this mess. Get on home 'fore the law come.' I did, and I ain't never seen nor heard from Harlow ever since.

"Ever'body heard 'bout the shootin'. Lawmen come and found all the bodies. Just another Saturday night gone bad, wasn't strange back then. Hushed it all up real good, less'n folks find out about they kickbacks. We buried Granddaddy soon after, an' I ain't never tol' nobody 'bout what happened -- leastways not 'til now. Grandmama thought I got myself hurt and I was lucky to be breathin'.

"But look here, this old scar," he gestured, "it ain't natural. Ever since I had dreams—bad ones, mind, right out the gates of Hell. All the shit I seen in the War ain't give none so bad. I learned to live with those, but I reckon them others'll scare me 'til I'm six feet under. Whatever that razor was, it weren't meant for nothin' but killin'. I wouldn't wish survivin' it on anybody."

I confess I was at a loss. I'd heard some wild tales, but this one was something else. Easy believed it and I found myself believing it, against better judgment. I started to ask him something else—I don't remember what—but he cut me off again with a raised hand.

"We done talkin'," he said. "I ain't never told nobody that story an' I ain't never gonna again. You wanted the truth 'bout Black Dog Harlow, you got it, far as I can say. That ol' bastard brought me more trouble and heartache in one night than the whole War did in four years."

He lit another cigarette and eyed me for a moment. "But there's others, one man in particular." He got up and went to the bar and grabbed a pencil and a napkin. He wrote something down, stopped to think, then wrote something else. He handed me the napkin, drained his drink in a single swallow, ice and all, then settled in to watch the pool match again.

I looked at the name and address on the napkin, then, for lack of words, I dug out my wallet and offered over a sheaf of bills—the last of my "research funds." Easy didn't even look at me as he shook his head and smoked.

"Don't want yo' money," he said. "Just a favor."

"All right," I said, tucking the money away.

"Walk out that door and don't come back. I hear you been talkin' to anybody 'bout this shit, I'll say I ain't never heard o' you." He looked at me pointedly. "An' I know some boys—big fellas, mind—that don't mind a little side work every now an' then to he'p with the rent, you catch me?"

I did indeed catch him. But, as you can see, it didn't stop me, and if those "big fellas" are on the hunt, I haven't seen them.

Still, I left Memphis that day and have not been back.

* * * *

I drove to Starkville, Mississippi to talk with a Professor Richard Burke—the name on Easy's napkin—at Mississippi State University. Burke was a folklorist and cultural anthropologist, and had apparently accumulated everything there was to know about "Black Dog" Harlow from eyewitness accounts. I looked forward to talking with him, maybe getting to the meat of Harlow's story, and comparing notes.

I had an appointment with him, but when I reached his office, his secretary, a severe-looking woman who never met my eyes, told me that Professor Burke had canceled the meeting and would not, under any circumstances, ever reschedule. As I stood gawking, she handed me a thick accordion folder and went back to typing. I tucked the folder under my arm and left.

The folder contained everything I ever could have asked about Amos Harlow, and a lot I never would have dreamed of asking. I spent at least three months analyzing, collating, and cross-referencing the data, trying to piece together something that would make sense of all that I'd learned.

The article I set out to write never happened. Black Dog Harlow became an obsession. In the file was a list of names and places—some with addresses and some that the shadow of the U.S. Postal

Service had never darkened. I visited them all, taking copious notes by hand and by digital recorder, when allowed. It cost me my life savings and more than a few friends and relationships.

This volume and the one to follow are the result. I have taken the stories down as they were told to me, cleaning up the narratives for easier reading, creating false names of real persons when none were given or known. What dates exist are at best vague recollections by the tellers. And while there is obviously no way for me to know the inner workings of Harlow's mind, I'm certain that what I wrote of them was an equal and honest reaction to his circumstances.

For me to claim that this work is a complete history of the lost legend is folly; there are almost certainly stories between the stories that are lost to us—for *now*, anyway. But what is here is as close as we may ever come to knowing the whole truth.

What truth is that? The truth behind the legends. The real story of the Great Depression and the horrors of the Dust Bowl and the evils that lurked beneath them, and how one broken man—called a prophet by some and a devil by others—was in fact, the savior of us all, and how it was that history never knew his name.

Some will call it fiction, and it is that, for how can such a thing be proven, aside from an anonymous file full of conjecture and tall tales? Others will call it the raving of a lunatic, and it may be that, too. In my darker hours, sometimes I *do* question my own sanity.

But then, when a storm is rolling in across the plains like a dark prophecy, or when the sun is deep in the west and red as a fresh wound, or when I hear the high lonesome whistle of a freight train roll through the woods near the house, the echo of the Black Dog's songs drift across time, reminding me of what was and what might have been, had he not existed.

And then I *believe.*

I hope you will, too. And maybe, just maybe, what was lost will be found once more.

Matt Coleman
Pearland, TX
October, 2011

HELL'S HALF-ACRE

A Song of the Black Dog

O black and unknown bards of long ago,
How came your lips to touch the sacred fire?

—James Weldon Johnson
O Black and Unknown Bards

When the Lord gave the earth its seasons, He apparently saw fit to give Southern Mississippi only one, and that was dead-balls summer. The heat was a thing *alive*, murky and heavy, like an old quilt in a musty room.

Amos Harlow sat at the edge of what used to be a cotton field, mopping sweat from his balding head with a well-used handkerchief and cursing the dust that billowed from the barren farmland in clouds three feet high. Some days were worse than others, and some were downright hell on earth.

Dust from Oklahoma, Texas, Kansas, and Missouri was caked in his nostrils and he figured he spent about three hours out of every day coughing up the stuff. He turned the handkerchief to his nose, trumpeted out a good one, and winced at the pale gray mucus he found in its folds.

Mississippi wasn't exactly in the Dust Bowl, but it was a damn sight near enough.

He'd been across the country and back now more times than most folks, but such was the life of a hobo. Not a bum; Amos worked for his keep, one of scores of wandering souls that walked, rode, and hitched across the American wasteland of the Great Depression looking for work, trying to survive, or just because they had no place else to go. Work came at the end of a shovel or a broom, other times from behind his guitar, and sometimes it came from places Amos was ashamed to speak of, but not sorry for. He was still alive, after all. He didn't kill people for their money and he didn't turn tricks, but he wasn't above filching and a little second-story work to get by when times got rough. And they were rough all the time.

The sun beat down like a hammer on the anvil of the dry earth, and he was the metal caught in between, shaped and wrought by sweat. He set his porkpie hat back on his head, which provided little relief, and stretched, listening to the dull pop his back was making more often of late.

"Gettin' on, Harlow," he said aloud. "Noontime in July ain't no place for an old man, nossir." The cicadas whined in reply, their familiar song in the pecan trees and milkweed bordering the dirt road's edge always put him in mind of times long laid to rest, where everything had seemed easier, better, and brighter.

He chuckled, shaking his head. He often spoke aloud on the road just to break the silence, to hear a human voice, even if it was his own. Living out of doors wasn't the easiest life and sometimes the want of another human being was so great it hurt. With so many on the road, throwing in with someone seemed to be the right idea. But distrust among strangers abounded, and Amos could hardly blame them. There were people and things loose in the world that sought the weak and downtrodden, stalking them over the land, hiding in their shadows and waiting to pounce. Evil wore many faces and was hard to spot in disguise. Best to keep to one's own and pass on by.

So Amos would sometimes talk to the road *itself*—that ancient wanderer with ancient secrets and miles of stories past and tales yet to be, winding into and out of innumerable lives, never stopping in one place long enough to grow moss or learn names, and no particular reason to care about one man over another. The road could be a surly companion, but sometimes it was the only companion you had, and so you chanced its mood if only to have an attentive ear.

He hadn't seen a car all morning, not since the grocery truck from Hattiesburg had dropped him off six miles east of where he stood now. The white man behind the wheel hadn't said boo to him, just stopped, motioned to the bed of the truck, and pulled off again before Amos had planted his tired old ass on the wheel well. The man hadn't turned around, hadn't acknowledged him at all. He just drove, the truck jouncing and bucking over every pothole and washout in the old road until Amos felt his teeth clacking.

After awhile, the man stopped the truck at a crossroads, the old Bearcat engine idling and coughing as if it had miner's lung. The man didn't look back when Amos jumped out and had ratcheted the old beast into gear and took off down the right hand road. Amos had barely enough time to snatch his guitar case from the tailgate before he was left in a cloud of dust, stinking of old cabbage and scraping rotten tomato off of his worn-out shoes.

That had been some good fortune. Most folks didn't pick up solitary vagrants, especially not black ones, and especially not in this part of the country. The man was either uneasy around coloreds, or he didn't want any of his neighbors seeing him give one a lift. Of course, there was always the off-chance that the man was earnest and just trying to help out a fellow man in need, but Amos knew those kinds of folks only existed in the dreams of a down man. Either way, he hadn't had to walk the bulk of the trip in the heat of the day, and Amos was grateful for small graces.

Realizing his good fortune was unlikely to repeat itself on this backstretch of nowhere, he thought it best to sit it out until night time when it would be easier to hoof it on down the road to Tylertown, out of the sun's caustic glare. He thought about settling in under one of the trees opposite him, but in the end decided against it. It didn't matter where he sat, he knew. The sun would shine right on down through the dead branches, past the once-green leaves, now brown and curling like bacon in the pan, and continue to cook him good-fashion.

He had a sudden fear that the sunstroke would get him, and that he'd be found in the juniper and sticker bushes, deader than Judas Iscariot, his eyes plucked out by the murder of crows that crowded the telephone lines like a dark congregation ready to partake of communion. Shoving the thought aside, he reached around the fallen tree and grabbed the one thing upon which he could always rely.

The old guitar case was black and cracked, but sturdy—much like himself. He sat the case across his knees and popped the latches on the side. The smell hit him like it always did—mink oil and metal strings, cheap whiskey and cheaper cigarettes.

It was the smell of before, of then, of always. It was the smell of juke joints on deserted crossroads, of nameless faces in countless boxcars, the train's high lonesome whistle carrying through the rain. It was the smell of loose women in rundown motels breathing promises of love above a sweaty pillow. It was burning trash in forgotten barrels in forgotten back-alleys. It was dreams never born and babies never grown. It was fist-fights and stale beer and broken hearts and broken lives. It was all that and more, and it was a heady mix.

Gently, almost reverently, he lifted the old acoustic from its bed of faded red faux fur and set the case aside. He wiped away a trickle of sweat from his dead left eye, its milky cataract his only medal from the Great War. He let his calloused, stubby fingers drift gently across the strings, which sighed almost in pleasure. He closed his eyes behind his bent spectacles and drew deep from that sorrowful well only men who've lived it could drink. He drew the pain up from the depths and it poured out of him in a rich tenor:

Sweep it clean,
Ain't going to tarry here!
I sweep my house with the gospel broom
Ain't going to tarry here!
Sweep it clean,
Ain't going to tarry here!
Gon' open my mouth to the Lord,
Ain't going to tarry here!
O-o-o Lordy,
Ain't going to tarry here!
'Cause he's digging down in the grave
Ain't going to tarry here
The big bell's tolling in Galilee
Ain't going to tarry here!
O-o-o Lordy
Ain't going to tarry here!

As he finished the song, he felt the weariness leave him and for all the heat, he might as well have been sitting in an icehouse. The music always had that effect on him, pushing him beyond himself and the troubles of the moment, if *only* for a moment. That feeling was worth all the hardships of Job.

The hairs at the base of his neck prickled and his every cell came alive with recognition. Slowly, he opened his eyes, and saw what he already knew was there.

Across the road, among the milkweed and the thickets of confederate jasmine, stood the black dog.

It was by-God enormous—a mastiff crossed with a Cadillac—and dark as the sin in a man's heart. Its fur was sleek and short, its eyes deep-set pinpricks of pale red. It stood panting and patient as always, its pink tongue lolling. Amos could hear its ragged breath, which sounded like a locomotive in the sullen stillness of the noonday heat.

For long moments they simply stared at each other. The dog made no move to charge or retreat. Slowly it dawned on Amos that the cicadas had ceased their droning.

The crows overhead sat silent, nervously moving from foot to clawed foot on the telephone line. In fact, there was no other sound in the world but the breathing of the massive dog, the stifling breeze, and the beating of his own ticker.

"Hmh," he said. With a sidelong, disgusted glance at the animal, he gently laid the guitar back in its case and closed it. Feeling around the log, he fetched his suit coat, natty as it was, and draped it over his shoulder. Sweat stains the size of dinner plates coated his underarms and he needed a shave and two fingers of whiskey more than he needed his next breath.

He hefted the guitar case in his right hand and walked across the dirt road to stand within three feet of the dog, which still stared, never moving, merely waiting.

"Alright, then," he said. "Let's be about it."

The dog turned and trotted into the woods without a backward glance.

Sighing heavily, Amos followed.

* * * *

Amos wasn't yet an old timer, but the road had made him one early, tacking years on his face, in his bones, and on his heart. His skin was brushed leather and the crow's feet spreading from his eyes were deep as mysteries. He'd made some bad choices in life and it showed on his face. Regret was a constant companion and lived in the slump of his shoulders, the hunch of his back, and the crease of his brow. His head hung perpetually forward to stare at the road, always the road, coming up only at the sound of an engine or to get his bearings. He was a hard fifty, and he'd earned every damned year.

The going was rough, as it usually was for Amos, and the ground itself seemed to drag at him, roots grabbing his shoes. The whole of nature seemed to oppose his every step.

The black dog wasn't far ahead, but it seemed anxious, stopping every so often, impatient for Amos to catch up. It sat on the edge of a steep ravine that dropped off into a creek. Amos noticed the dog had that same look in its eyes, a now-familiar look, like Amos was *its* burden, instead of the other way around.

"You in a race, ol' boy?" Amos shouted, dreading the precarious descent into the creek. The dog was silent, but seemed to have declared himself the winner in any case.

There were times he thought of running the dog off; he had, in fact, thrown rocks at it in the beginning, hoping for that very thing. In the end, though, Amos knew there was no escaping it. It haunted his dreams. It dug in its claws and teeth and refused to let go. He used to wonder if anyone else saw it but him, and soon learned to let that go, too.

Hell, he'd never heard the damned thing *bark*, and wasn't *that* a thing? It all didn't matter, though. The black dog was a constant in his life, in his misery, and after the life he'd led, he knew that he'd never be rid of it.

Hellhound on my trail, he thought.

Amos hefted the guitar case to port arms to pass through some particularly dense kudzu, cursing as he went. The case got stuck once, almost as if the tough vines were trying to snatch it from his weathered old hands. At one point in his life, Amos would have known better, but these were dark times, bad days, and by then, Amos had seen more than his fair share of the unusual.

He jerked the guitar case with all of his feeble might, and the vines gave way with terrible ripping sound. Threads of the stuff were laced in the guitar case's handle and latches. Then all at once, the woods went silent, save for the cracking of twigs and leaves under his feet. That was when the Feeling began.

It always started at the small of his back, right above his ass crack, climbing up his spine to hum and nest like angry wasps in the back of his head. Gooseflesh rippled across his back in waves as he turned and stood breathless, watching tendril after tendril of kudzu vines slither out of the trees of their own accord and snake across the ground and low-hanging branches.

Oh Lord, he thought, and started to run toward the nearby creek, but he was jerked to a halt and off his feet, struggling frantically as the vines coiled around his waist, legs, arms, and neck.

His windpipe closed to the size of a dime. He clawed at the devil-vine, which constricted around his throat like a python. Blue-white sparks danced at the edge of his vision and suddenly he wasn't sure if he was ready to see Heaven, since he thought that the *other* place might have a claim on him.

He struggled, choking on his own spittle. He looked this way and that, hoping to see someone—*anyone*—but knowing there was no one way out here in the barrens. He saw the black dog sitting on the opposite side of the ravine, that old pink tongue lolling as if to say, "This is *your* fix, Old Man. I'm just along for the ride."

You dumb shit, Amos thought bitterly. The dog never got him out of scrapes; just *into* them.

He reflected in those brief moments how much of a man's life *does* pass in front of him when death was knocking. The strangest scene came floating back up from his past, a scene he hadn't replayed in years. It was an odd, random thing to remember just then, but later, he would chide himself for being a fool.

There was *nothing* random about his life.

He remembered being garroted by a pimp in a Montgomery cathouse. The bastard had snuck up behind him while he was chatting up the man's hussies. He'd guessed later that the pimp was using his birds to snatch a few wallets. Amos had just finished a sit-in over to the Steel Aggie, one of a thousand juke-joints in that neck of the woods. His money roll was in his guitar case, back in the bar. He wasn't in the habit of keeping money on him, as he was already out of doors by then, and had learned to live smart or die stupid.

So this bastard had walked up quiet as you like and slipped that damn catgut around his throat. Would've killed him too, except one of the whores he was talking to raised her eyebrows just the slightest, and Amos got a hand up just in time and grabbed the string as the pimp pulled tight. Man had a *wicked* pull, a lot like the vines, and so Amos did now what he'd done then.

Reaching into his hip pocket with his free hand, he felt the worn, familiar bone handle. He whipped out Mean Sally, swearing a blue streak that would've made the Devil cringe. Sally flashed in the sun and cut through them sticker bushes like she'd cut through that shitkicker's throat, sweet and easy. The vines didn't fare any better than the pimp, Lord no, and for half a second, he was free.

The next half, though, he was falling sideways, tumbling ass over teakettle down the ravine. The world became a kaleidoscope of whirling browns and greens, slashed with a blinding yellow from the sun. Then his head smacked wetly into something harder than itself, and all went the color of evening. Amos dimly heard Sally clatter off some rocks and sploosh into the creek.

In the last moments before the black, he reached out blindly, arm flopping like a landed catfish, and felt the rough leather grip of his guitar case's frayed handle. Fighting unconsciousness, he pulled it in tight and draped his arm over it, clinging to it like a life raft, and knew no more.

* * * *

He came around much, much later. The sky had darkened in the east; it was getting on twilight. His head was pounding like a voodoo drum and he felt something sticky on his left temple. Gingerly, he lifted his head, the half-dried blood squelching as it tore away from the flat rock. A trickling sound filled his ears and he supposed it must be what was left of his brains spilling out. He soon realized that it was the creek bubbling over rocks like the one he'd tried to break with his head.

Sitting up was another matter. The world spun like a carousel and he could almost hear the calliope between his ears. He reeled and threw up all over himself and the rocks in the effort. When there wasn't anymore in him to lose, he looked around, steadier, and saw the black dog, sitting patient as ever, up the other side of the creek bed.

"Not a Christian then, I take it?" said Amos. "Nor a Samaritan, neither, I s'pose?" But the dog just pinned him with that look again, and Amos knew better than to expect more than what the old mutt ever gave.

Amos dragged himself over to the creek, leaned out over the bank, and splashed cold water all over his face. He was shocked at how cold it was, considering the land it ran through and the time of year, but he wasn't about to be fussy. He washed in the icy chill, the water running in rivulets down his shirt, soaking him, until he couldn't feel the dull throb in his head. His stomach growled and he obliged it, cupping his hands and draining two handfuls before he even tasted it.

He spat out the third like poison. The water was rotten, gamey, and nastier than all the flophouses in South Carolina. He looked upstream and gagged again, his stomach threatening to give up the goods one more time.

A little ways upstream—at first what he took for a rotten log in the middle of the creek—lay the corpse of the biggest deer he'd ever laid eyes on, bloated to the size of a dining room table and rotting in the summer heat. Even this deep in the woods, in the cold water, the sun managed to get in and do its dirty work.

He pulled out his handkerchief and tied it around his nose and mouth, wincing in pain as he cinched it tight around his injured head. Taking a few deep breaths, he managed to slosh upstream in the cold water to get a look-see.

No animal had been at it, like he first thought; there weren't any claw marks or bites. The gases inside it seeped out slow, and Amos could smell them even through the handkerchief. His stomach did another flip-flop, and he had to bend over to keep it from speaking again. He stole one more look at its head and saw the eyes were missing -- just *gone*. They simply weren't *there*, as if they'd sunk back into the skull and left two perfect black holes. He let his gaze drift further upstream and his breath hung up near his Adam's apple.

As far as the eye could see, there were corpses. Squirrels, 'coons, wildcats, boars, more deer, even a few armadillos, all with the same bloated bodies, the same empty eye sockets, as if they'd all come for a drink and died right on the spot. It was disturbing, to say the least, all those black eyes staring at him in the fading light. His rattled brain began conjuring images of the dead animals rising up, bloated and hollow-eyed, slogging through the creek toward him.

Amos hurried back downstream in the waning light, wanting to be a mile away at that very moment. For the next two weeks, those vacant eyes would haunt his dreams, even after what came next. All the 'shine in Appalachia couldn't drown them out.

He crossed the creek, careful not to slip on another rock and break a hip. Amos hated fretting about old man shit like that, but he'd waved "so long" to his twenties a while back. He looked around for Mean Sally, but it was too dark to see. Damn shame.

Sally'd been with him longer than most women, ever since that nasty business in New Orleans, and he could trust her better, too. Strange thing was, he'd never had to take the strop to her, nor the whetstone; she was as sharp as the day they'd met and had never rusted. Amos never found out who she belonged to or where she came from; he had been glad just to have her acquaintance.

At the bank, Amos bent his knees, heaved his guitar case up the bank and heard it thump on the grass. He crawled up the bank, almost falling back to the water from a dizzy spell, but it passed quickly, and soon he was on his hands and knees in the grass, panting like his four-legged friend.

After a time, he gathered his wits and headed up the sloping hill, the creek at his back. He could see the treetops thinning out toward the top of the incline and knew he'd find a clearing ahead. Sure enough, with the sun behind the trees leaving an angry bruise on the horizon, Amos broke through the last of the trees and stepped out into a clearing of desiccated weeds and grass. Across the clearing sat a house.

Truth be told, it wasn't much more than a bundle of leaning firewood waiting to be kindled. Another, smaller shack—maybe a woodshed—sat off to the side underneath what was once a great oak. It was the kind of tree that young'uns like to climb on a fall day, the wind whipping through their hair, to dare the Fates. Now, however, it was just a skeleton, something a man might've hung from once for crimes unknown. It stretched over the yard, a gaunt hand that held the old homestead in its grip, refusing to let loose.

The land rose up in a long, rolling hill behind the farm, and Amos could tell he was on the back end of a sharecropping. Most folks had done that to get by in those days, and the drought was stealing even *that* little bit of peace from them, leaving them with nothing but dust to fill their children's bellies.

But this… This was the worst Amos had ever seen in his travels. The grass was charred, curled in on itself, atrophied like a burned saint. The crops were blackened beyond recognition, shriveled carcasses of a former bounty. Even in the dust bowl, a body could still find an edible tater or two underneath the topsoil, maybe a carrot, but the land here was the color of rust, blighted beyond all salvation. It was as if all that was green, all that was life—all that was *real*— had been siphoned away, leaving only a sepia-toned photograph in a forgotten picture album.

The only sign of life was smoke wafting out of a leaning chimney. He debated with himself for a time, wondering whether it was worth the bother. Hell, from the look of things the place was dead, had been for a while. Mayhap that smoke belonged to fellow itinerants like himself, moving along the road, taking what shelter they could find.

He fancied approaching the shack, settling down into jug with a couple of travelers. There would be introductions all around and trading of information, the currency of the road. If things were friendly enough, why, he'd find himself a quiet corner of floor and roof, stretch out for the evening, and move on to Tylertown in the morning.

But Amos Harlow knew better. He knew this was merely another stop, another chore, another chit he owed someone, somewhere. This dead place was where the dog had brought him, like so many times before, like so many times hereafter. It was on Amos to see to whatever there was here to see and to do what he could—*if* he could—when the time arose.

He cast about for the dog, but it was nowhere to be seen or heard. He had vanished, as always, into the background, leaving Amos with the task at hand.

"Nah," muttered Amos, his eyes tired and watery. "This the place." He tucked his hat down a bit harder on his head, shifted his grip on the guitar, and made for the shack.

Right away, he could tell something was wrong. His hackles rose like Braille on the back of his neck. About halfway to the door, he eased his guitar case to the dirt and raised his hands above his head. In his experience, a black man walking up to a house in the middle of nowhere was asking for a round of buckshot in the breadbasket.

"Hello!" Amos called, trying to make his voice high and nice, like a pastor paying a call on a neighbor. "Hello, the house! Anybody home? I'm comin' up to the porch, see? Anybody to the house?"

He'd barely planted his foot on the first step when he heard an all-too-familiar sound: two dry clicks, twin hammers on a double-barrel.

"Tha's… far enough," croaked a voice that sounded like dry leaves in a fire, "lessen you want to be… fertilizer for them crops, yonder."

Amos squinted into the dark. The man was backlit by the fire in the hearth, and Amos couldn't make out his face. The screen door creaked on its hinges and the firelight glinted off the shotgun barrels sliding out the crack in the door.

Now, not many folks have ever been at the business end of a scattergun, but those twelve gauges seem like mountain tunnels at close range. Slowly, Amos stepped back off the porch steps, his head already ringing with the twin thunderbolts that could come from the barrels.

"Mister, I ain't about no trouble," said Amos, hands still grabbing for Heaven. "I got no weapon, just a buncha wet clothes and a guitar."

A cough, ragged and deep, broke up the man's speech. "What… what're you doin'…out here… on my land?" the voice rasped.

"Well sir, ain't trespassin', that's a fact," Amos said, slipping his hat off. It seemed sound logic to be deferential to a man with a gun. "I was headin' to Tylertown by way o' Hattiesburg an' I got lost, is all."

"You a long way from Tylertown, brown boy." He coughed again, harder this time, and the gun barrels wavered just a bit.

"Don't I know it," said Amos, smiling deferentially, though he doubted if the man could see his face. "Had me an accident by the creek back a-ways. Busted up m' head real good-fashion. I wandered around a bit, saw your smoke, and decided I'd give you a try, see if anybody might help. You know, a bandage or some'in."

"Ain't got… no bandages. Ain't got much…of anything useful. Not no more…" The man broke into a fit of coughing and hacked up something wet; Amos heard it smack the porch floor and cringed. Nerved up, he went for broke.

"Well, I don't mind choppin' some firewood to pay my way. Sounds like you ain't up to the chore, and I need a place to bed-down. Might be I could do it for you, maybe bunk out in the woodshed— "

"YOU STAY AWAY FROM THAT SHED, NIGGER! YOU HEAR ME?"

Amos flinched less from the word than the fear behind it. The weak, hacking whisper had been replaced by almighty thunder and for a second, Amos thought the man had gone and pulled the trigger.

"YOU HEAR ME, A'RIGHT, OR DO I NEED TO SPEAK A MIGHT LOUDER?" He brandished the shotgun, adding weight to his words.

"Nossir," Amos said, hands up. "I won't go anywheres near it, and that's a fact. I just need a place to sleep for the night, and I'll be gone at first light. I can bed down right here under the porch, if you like. An' if I might, sir, you sound like you could *use* the help."

The voice behind the shotgun pondered that for a moment, breath rattling in his lungs so loud it drowned out the crickets in the grass. For a long moment, Amos feared that might have the wrong place after all, that the old dog had finally had finally led him a merry chase, just for a change of pace.

"The…axe is behind the shed, next to the woodpile," he croaked. "But I'm…watchin' you, boy. You even… *touch* that shed, I'll...blow you to hell, you hear?"

"Oh, I do, sir." said Amos, backing down the steps. "Loud and clear." He hefted the guitar case and walked around the side of the house. He heard the screen door creak and then slam shut, then shuffling feet on the porch, and he knew the man was indeed watching him. He felt the twin stares of those barrels on the back of his neck and heard the man's muffled cough.

As he neared the shed, a chill stole through his body. He was afraid to tarry, for fear his very soul would freeze. He found an old kerosene lantern next to the shed, produced a small box of matches from a coat pocket, and lit the wick.

The old woodshed was a mite scarier than it looked from the woods. Set up off the ground on concrete, its planks were ancient gray things, like old papyrus ready to crumble in a good gust. A rusted tin roof barely clung to the frame and was peeled back in one corner, probably from a hurricane long past. A solitary window was set above the door, empty and black. The whole thing leaned toward Amos, like a great Cyclops hunkering down with a secret to whisper in his ear. The evening breeze moaned through the small window and the spaces between wall planks, giving the old shed a pair of lungs that heaved like a bellows.

Get this shit over wit', Harlow, he thought.

Amos shucked his coat, never taking his eyes off the shed. The evening breeze shifted, which normally was just the ticket for a summer night, but left Amos somehow colder.

He found the axe, a big double-bladed deal, next to a pile of dried up oak logs and a stump covered with hack marks. As he picked it up and placed a log on the stump, he heard a humming sound, felt a fuzzy bullet brush his cheek, followed by a sharp pinch at the back of his neck.

"Ah, *damn*!" Amos swore, slapping his neck and dropping the axe on his foot. "Dammit t' *hell*!"

He yelped and hopped on one foot, shaking his shirt, looking like the court jester of a destitute king. He felt the little bastard fall down his back and bounce off his shoe. Peering down, he saw the little yellow and black striped body.

Yellowjacket, he thought. *Prolly come from under the shed, prolly a whole nest of 'em under them ol' floorboards.*

He probed his neck and damn if there wasn't a goose-egg rising where the little bugger stung him. He stepped on the yellowjacket and twisted his heel for good measure.

He remembered his daddy getting set upon by a whole swarm of the critters in the summer of '09 while cleaning out a woodshed. Hundreds of tiny welts had covered his back like angry red constellations and had swollen up to knots by early evening. His momma had spent half the night rubbing vinegar and cold cream on them, his daddy face-down on their bed, sobbing with the pain. His skin crawled at the memory.

Amos inspected the shed wall. There was a dime-sized knothole in the lowest plank. The humming was coming from there, but much louder now, like an electric socket about to give up the ghost. Sounded like a whole damn *hive* of the things.

Maybe that's what the ol' cuss was warnin' me away from, Amos thought. But he was almost certain the dog hadn't brought him to the ass-end of nowhere to smoke a bunch of yellowjackets out of an old shed. In his gut, he knew it was more. Just looking at that shed, he knew.

His business was with whatever was inside.

He got the timber busted up and hauled it to the porch. The screen door was closed, but the front door was open. The inside was dark, but he could see by the fire's orange glow. He walked up and gently kicked the door jamb.

"Sir? You there? I gotcha wood, here. Where you want it?" Silence, then another awful, retching coughing spell. Then: "Bring…bring it on inside."

Amos hooked the handle with his pinky finger, opened the door and stepped into the house. The screen door slammed, startling him.

The first thing that hit him was the smell. He gagged aloud, uncontrollably, and cringed in disgust. The load of wood clattered to floor.

"Q-quiet, damn you! You gonna…" He coughed violently. "You gonna wake the m-missus and the young'un."

Amos had been in some nasty places—slaughterhouses, boxcars full-up with winos that slept in their own shit and vomit, outhouses that had never seen a drop of lye. He'd once fished a wedding ring out of a compost heap because he needed to eat and had helped pull the bloated, fish-eaten corpse of a chain-gang escapee out of the Mississippi River. He was a man used to the unsavory.

But this was a different animal altogether. To say it was foul was saying water was wet. It went far beyond that; it was an abomination. The stench was a creeping thing, sinful and malicious that threatened to unhinge him mentally, his reason threatening to mutiny along with his stomach. A sickly-sweet smell with a metallic tang. He hadn't smelled it earlier, even on the front porch steps, but now it hit him full-bore.

The smell of a dyin' soul, he thought. *Oh, dear God.*

"S-sorry," Amos said, catching his voice at last. "I'll put it on the hearth, right w-where you can get at it."

He collected the wood from the floor, sweeping his gaze around the room, looking for the source of the stench. It was thick and sharp and seemed to come from all quarters.

The man sat in an easy chair built low to the floor. The shotgun lay on the floor beside the chair, within reach. The man's arms drooped off the chair, his face beyond the edge of the firelight. His breathing was reedy, raspy, and sounded like wax paper being crumpled. His thin chest rose and fell with the effort.

A dim shape moved in the corner, back and forth, back and forth, rhythmically. Amos started, then realized it was a rocking chair, it joints creaking like a casket lid. Patchwork quilts covered a pair of shivering knees.

The lady of the house.

The creaking, coupled with the smell, was about to rob him of his will. As he stacked the wood, he had to fight the urge to run screaming from that death house, from the dark madness of this family's misery.

"Ma'am," said Amos, tipping his hat like his momma taught him.

No reply. Just the infernal creaking as the woman continued to rock, her blank eyes seeing nothing but misery. Her face was drawn and pinched, and her eyes, red-rimmed and sunken, were full of water and edged with what looked like pus. The right shoulder of her moth-eaten gown was pulled low, and she held what Amos took to be a baby under a cloth at her right tit, giving it the milk.

Pulling his eyes away from her misery, Amos grabbed the poker and coaxed flame from the coals, then threw a couple of dead logs on top, which caught immediately. The flames rose up high, brightening up the room, and Amos caught a glimpse of the room before they died down.

The man sat in the chair with his head lolled back, mouth open, breathing in shallow and letting out shallower. Amos had heard a man breathe like that once in the War—it was called a death rattle, what some say is the soul clawing its way out of the mortal coil.

Then the fire died down and Amos backed to the door, quiet as possible.

"I'll be goin' now," he said. "Just gonna sleep right outside, und'neath the porch, case it rain. G-Good night, then."

He closed the front door behind him, let the screen door softly tap shut, and leaned against it breathing deep, glad to be free of the reek of slow death. He fetched the lantern from the chopping stump and crawled under the porch.

The lantern light cast a feeble, ghostly glow along the underside of the house, revealing the brick supports but swallowed by the darkness beyond. The welt on his neck hurt like all hell, and he didn't want to chance anymore yellowjackets. He looked as far as he dared, but didn't see any nests. He spread his suit coat out and made a wallow in the soft dirt under the porch.

He put out the lantern, and in the quiet, he could hear the man's rattling breath through the floorboards overhead. Amos tipped his hat over his eyes and tried to drift off to sleep, knowing it wouldn't come easy, but hoping. His left hand found its way to his guitar case, his very own worry token. Stroking its cracked leather, he let his mind play out. Today had been bad, and if experience was any teacher, tomorrow would be worse.

In the seconds before sleep took him, he realized that the crickets weren't singing.

* * * *

His thirst woke him. He sat up, smacking the night out of his mouth and bumping his head on the floor of the house above him. He cleared the cobwebs from is mind and remembered where he was. His hand went out to his guitar case, unconsciously grasping the handle.

Half-standing, he began to make his way out from under the porch when something slithered out of his pant leg and plopped on the ground. He gave shout and hit his head again as the corn snake wriggled into the dirt. He watched it head for the back of the house and movement there caught his eye.

Backlit by the morning sun, long slender heads and sinuous silhouetted bodies rose and fell. As his eyes adjusted, he could see hundreds, if not thousands of writhing snakes, like a massive, undulating carpet, hissing, snapping at each other in the dim shade under the house.

Crying out, he crab-walked backwards on his hands and feet, desperate to put as much distance between him and the slithering nightmare. He jumped to his feet in the yard, dancing, shaking, and hollering. He pulled and tore at his clothes, frantic to find any others that might have settled in for a warm snooze during the night. Satisfied, he sat down on his guitar case, alternately praying and cursing.

How could so many of the things gotten under the porch, and why? Had they been there all this time? Were they there when he went down to sleep? Did the man know what sort of hell he was living above?

His thirst was almost unbearable now, his throat like cracked desert hardpan. He stood and staggered to the well at the north side of the house, giving the porch a wide berth.

The pulley squeaked and moaned as he worked the rope. The bucket came easily for about five feet, and then hit something hard and wouldn't budge. He tugged some more, feeling it give slightly. He pulled harder, bending at the knees. He strained with the effort, and it wasn't until the bucket was three-quarters to the top that it dawned on him that the bucket shouldn't be that heavy.

And then the smell struck again.

He pulled until he heard the bucket handle hit the pulley.

The little dress she'd worn was gingham, probably made by the mother. She was a little bigger than the bucket, frail legs hanging over the side, a single, scuffed red shoe on one foot. The flesh on her arms and legs was scraped raw, as if she'd tried to claw her way up the well. Her face was sunken in, like her parents, and her eyes were gone, leaving only black periods. He tied off the rope, and just stared, unable to swallow.

Whatever sickness the folks had, the girl had. *Everything* here had it—the crops, the animals, the land itself. The little girl probably come out here to get water, dying of thirst, and ended up falling in.

Did her parents, too weak to help, have to listen to her cries, day in day out, for God knew how long, until at last, they grew weaker and weaker and stopped completely?

He looked at the girl's skin. He lifted the gingham dress and all over the gray-green skin, there were welts, like bites. Like…stings. His hands went slowly to the sting at the base of his neck.

Oh, Lord, no. Lord, Lord, Lord…!

He reeled away from the well, screaming until he thought his throat would crack from the strain. He barreled onto the porch and kicked open the front door. The stench assailed him so that he almost lost his footing. It was the smell of the charnel house.

The man still sat in his easy chair, arms over his eyes like he couldn't bear to watch his world crumble around him. The woman sat motionless in her rocking chair near the hearth, the babe still wrapped in a blanket at the woman's breast.

The woman's mouth was frozen in a rictus of helpless terror. Her face was gaunt, shriveled like a prune underneath her gray hair, which apparently had been falling out in clumps for some time. Strands of it lay like cobwebs on the dusty floor.

Amos gagged, cupping a palm over his nose. He rushed to the

man.

"Mister!" Amos yelled between gags. "Mister! You gotta get up! It's your wife, she's—!"

He shook the man's elbow, trying to rouse him. The man's forearm snapped like a dry twig, a cloud of ashes and dust billowed from the stump.

"Oh, God!" Horrified, Amos stumbled over to the wife, not wanting to see what was next, but knowing he had to, if this was all to be finished. He tenderly, almost reverently, drew back the blanket, then promptly vomited up whatever bile was left in his belly.

The baby lay dead, drained of life as its parents had been, still feeding at a tit that would never again give milk. Amos couldn't tell whether it was a boy or girl. It just hung there like a grape dried in the sun, its mama clutching it even closer in death.

Steadying himself, Amos stumbled back over to the man, hesitated, then rifled through the man's pockets. He found a wallet with a driver's license that told him the shed, the house, and all the misery attached to them belonged to one Everett Earl Clanton.

Amos took the six dollars that were in the wallet. He knew it was bad mojo to be filching a dead man, but it wasn't the first time. The road gave few opportunities and a man traveling had to grab what he could, *when* he could, that was all.

Thin slits of sunlight filtering through the clapboard house caught the man's eyes as they stared into eternity, filling them with an unearthly glimmer that didn't bear thinking about. Amos tried to close the lids and was sickened when they came off in his hands, turning to dust like old parchment.

Amos tripped over his own feet in his hurry to get clear of the house, crawling the rest of the way, desperate to be back out in the fresh air. He collected himself and his guitar, and walked around to the shed.

Somehow, whatever had affected the land and everything in it had taken up residence in the woodshed. He could hear the humming and buzzing again, could *feel* it in his mind, sawing through his consciousness, trying to get in where he lived.

The Presence jangled his spinal cord, rising up with like an electric current to vibrate his teeth, as wave after wave of the Thing's influence crashed against his will. He sensed that if he gave in for even a second, it would enter his mind and begin to hollow him out, like it had done to the Clanton family. It had already started, in fact, with the sting of a single yellowjacket.

But he had to know more, had to find out what it truly was if there was to be any hope of driving it away, or God willing, destroying it altogether. For just the barest of moments, Amos relaxed and let the humming chorus enter his mind.

In that instant, he saw civilizations rise and fall. Here were basalt ziggurats on a vast desert plain, covered with blight, a haunted wasteland under an uncaring sun. Next, a shining crystal city, minarets stretching to the heavens, fell into the sea as the blight claimed its island paradise. Then there were horsemen fleeing over grassy steppes as tribal lands were eaten up behind them, and fire fell from the heavens on a coastal city in answer to the darkness spreading over the land.

Grunting, Amos slammed the door on his mind again, staggering to his knees with the strain. He felt a slow tickle on his jaw and found his ears were bleeding. Looking up, he saw the woodshed had disappeared under a dark cloud of roiling yellowjackets, locusts, cicadas, every manner of insect the good Lord created, and some He *hadn't.*

This here's an old *power,* Amos thought, *ancient when man was young. It was 'round when the blood from Abel's body was still dryin' on the ground. The Hebrews had that smell in they noses as they left for the wilderness, the women of Egypt wailin' behind 'em over the bodies of they young. It washed over Europe in the dark times, bringing the plague and now it's here, come to do the same. It won't never be full. Not ever.*

Amos fretted right then, for he didn't know what chance a broken man had against something that had survived the centuries. This thing had turned the land against itself, had perverted nature to its will before bleeding its very life and everything in it.

He spied the lantern's kerosene can sitting in the weeds. He shook it; there was enough. He could burn it *all*—the shed, the fields, the house. Dry as everything was, the fire would spread for miles in all directions, might be one of the worst wildfires in the history of the South.

But Amos knew that wouldn't be enough. There was work to be done first—*dark* work, like always fell to him.

Amos knew a few things about the Craft, what most called folk magic, and even some darker bits that he daren't use except in greatest danger. For those were knacks of old—powerful things, but black and sinister things, and the price they bore was too much for any man.

He hefted the axe and began by tracing a circle in the dirt around the perimeter of the shed. He made it deep—it had to be, or the hoodoo wouldn't work. It wasn't a perfect circle, but as close as he was likely to get after an hour of drawing.

Amos stood, cracked his back, and tilted the kerosene into the trench he'd made, walking the circle until the can was empty. From a pocket he produced a leather pouch, unlaced it, and emptied it of a grainy white substance into the circle, mumbling under his breath.

The buzzing in his brain was louder now, more insistent, making his mind sluggish. He walked as though he was moving through marsh water.

LIE DOWN AND DIE, CREATURE. LIE DOWN AND LET US IN. WE ARE HUNGRY.

It was a single Voice, but more like a million metallic voices speaking in unison, echoing each other across eternity. The Voice hurt his fillings and shook him badly. His vision blurred momentarily, and he fell to his knees, the world spinning crazily on a completely different axis.

SHRIVEL. DECAY. WITHER ON THE VINE. YOU ALL COME TO SAME PLACE IN THE END.

It knows, Amos thought. *It knows what I come for, what I aim to do, an' it's gonna fight me tooth and nail. Prolly ain't nobody ever stood up to it before. Might be that work to my favor.*

The Voice crashed against his mind once again, harder, louder, threatening to lay him waste, knowing that an end to its existence, after long, strange eons, might be finally at hand. Amos's ears began to bleed again, followed by his nose. He struggled against the onslaught and opened his guitar case.

As soon as his hand touched the old acoustic guitar, the Voice immediately dwindled to a dull hum. Amos wiped his nose with his sleeve and shouldered the strap.

The guitar was one of a kind. It had been hand made by an old

Creole man in Assumption Parish, a man who used to fashion such things for certain people. He had long since been with the Lord and Amos doubted if there was more than three or four of his instruments left in the land.

The strings were special, hand-pulled and tuned during a ritual that lasted a week. There were six of them, one for each day the Lord worked creating, and likewise, the man had also rested on Seventh day of the ritual. The topmost string was iron, for strength; the second, stainless steel, an alloy representing unity; the third was copper, taken straight from the earth and shaped without refining; the fourth, gold, a symbol of purity; the fifth was brass, a protector of souls; and the sixth string was pure silver, and gave a high, fine tune that rang with the harmony of the angels and had gotten him out of tight spots more than once.

Amos sat down on the old cutting stump, shifted around a bit for comfort, and gave a quick strum with a callused thumb. In his mind, he could feel the Presence withdraw, shrinking before the sound of the instrument, and bump into the power circle he's inscribed around the shed. The goofer dust had done its trick and the Presence was trapped but good, until Amos saw fit to break the circle.

He closed his eyes and reached down deep down inside himself, deeper than he ever went for a song. He went to a place where the hurts were never forgotten, and indeed, were very much alive. He pulled from that place of a thousand miseries, of heartache and despair and loneliness, from the place where everyone goes but no one ever truly returns.

He drew it up in him, thinking of the man and his family. Maybe he wasn't a good man, but then what was that? Amos hadn't known many, and he certainly wasn't one himself. The man had died trying to protect his family from something his mind could never *hope* to wrap itself around, and he had died hard.

He thought of the little girl in the well, trying like mad to get a drink, to get *something* in her little belly to quench an ancient thirst that could never be quenched. He thought of the mother, desperately trying to suckle her little one, knowing that her other child was long gone and this one wouldn't be far behind.

Then he thought of the world as it was right then, in his time—death, agony, and poverty to spare, but so little hope—and Amos despaired. The Presence rallied one final assault on his mind, his soul, and the buzz-saw Voice in his head reached a crescendo, blotting out reality, a cyclone of desolation, and him the eye of the storm. He took on all that hurt in himself, all that pain and anguish, and the song poured out of him in a voice that was plaintive, weary, dejected and hopeful all at once:

How I got over,
How I got over, my Lord
And my soul looked back and wondered
How I got over, my Lord.
The tallest tree in Paradise,
Christians call it the tree of life.
And my soul looked back and wondered
How I got over, my Lord.
Lord, I've been 'buked and I've been scorned
And I've been talked 'bout as sure as I's born
And my soul looked back and wondered
How I got over, my Lord.
Oh, Jordan's river is so chilly and cold
Chill your body but not your soul
And my soul looked back and wondered
How I got over, my Lord.

Over and over it came out of him—the Word of the prophet, the Word that felled kings and brought men low, and he had never questioned its power, nor how he came to wield such a thing. But what Amos Harlow—called Black Dog Harlow by some—never knew, even until his dying day, was *why*. In the end, he merely accepted that the power that flowed through him from time to time and allowed him to see what was beneath and behind the world. It drew him onward with a merely a mangy hound for company. He accepted that power as his price for a life wasted. It was a road—*his* road—and he walked it.

Time passed, hours came and went, and all he knew was the song and power that lay within. He played on through the day and into night, losing all sense of time. There was only the music and the world it shaped.

He was only dimly aware of the buzzing Presence in his mind, now diminished to a low hum, and he knew It was in pain. He knew It lay powerless now, after the centuries of hurt that It had caused. He played on, sang on, until his throat was raw with the effort, never faltering, never ceasing, just plodding on, one foot in front of the other, like every other day of his life.

At one point he was aware of a stabbing pain behind his eyes. He slowly opened them to greet the morning sun, rising over the pines in the distance. Amos looked around him, slowly taking in the surroundings, like Rip van Winkle waking from his long nap.

The air was no longer still. A fresh breeze blew in from the south, promising rain. The calluses on his fingertips, built up over many years, had burst and shredded from hours of playing. He'd never even registered the pain during the night, so lost in the song was he, but the evidence was spattered all over the guitar. With the realization, the pain came rushing in, so much so that he cried aloud to God, in a burning, brand new agony.

He rose, tottered, and managed to steady himself on the chopping stump. He would need food and drink, both easy enough to come by for a man who knew how, but that would have to wait. The work wasn't finished. He placed the guitar back in its case, snapping the latches. He wiped his hands on his pants and again withdrew the small box of matches from his coat pocket.

LUCIFER KITCHEN MATCHES, the box read, accompanied by a little red cartoon devil, complete with pointed tail, horns, goatee, and pitchfork. "GUARANTEED TO STRIKE THE FIRST TIME, EVERY TIME!" it assured. In a voice-bubble warning, the devil admonished: "Don't play with fire!"

"Heh," Amos chuckled. "Heh, heh!" This turned into a belly laugh of mass proportions, Amos holding his sides for fear of bursting. The tears rolled down his face, and he removed his spectacles to wipe them away.

"Seems like tha's all I *do*, nowadays!" he roared, and broke out in a fit of laughter all over again. The pain and anguish seemed to leave his body as he laughed, washing away the madness of the last two days. When it subsided, he grew sober again, opened the box, and removed one of three blue-tipped matches. He struck it, cupping it with his left hand to block the wind, and dropped it into the circle around the shed. The kerosene caught immediately, streaking the circumference of the circle in seconds.

The Presence in the shed let out a wail, one last defiant roar that rattled his mind like shutters in a windstorm, promising all manner of revenge. He stepped up to the burning circle, scuffed it with his foot in a straight line, breaking it. The flames immediately roared higher, streaking out to engulf the shed and making a beeline for the house.

The screams rose in pitch as Amos watched the shed and house both catch like fatlighter. They burned with a greenish hue, and as they were consumed, the grayish green cloud of insects appeared again, swelling, and rose above the flames, wailing in torment. The cloud dispersed momentarily, then collapsed in on itself and vanished in the smoke and embers.

Amos watched as the dead grass around the farm began to catch, and then the dried up husks of crops, and the flames slowly crept to the edge of the forest. He knew that nothing would ever grow on this patch of land again. Not a single blade of grass, not even *weeds*, before Gabriel blew his horn,

For many years to come, people would shun this place, almost on instinct. They would simply turn to the right or left on their way over the creek or fields, as if it were the most natural thing in the world to do so. No one would ever question the disappearance of Everett Clanton and his family, would not even *remember* a family by that name.

Most would chalk the burned countryside up to a drought fire, kindled by lightning, and that would be that. Amos figured that was for the best. In his experience, it was good that people not look too closely into the dark, because most times, it looked *back*.

Amos hefted his guitar, shifted his hat on his head, and hiked slowly north, back across the creek, through the woods, and finally to the road. It was late afternoon, and he expected he might thumb a ride—hell, maybe even on the same farmer's truck that had brought him out this far.

He settled down in the grass at the crossroads and thought he'd just listen out for an engine while he rested his eyes, just for a short while. His head still throbbed maliciously from his fall the day before, and he hadn't slept since the night before. But in that eternal instant before sleep, he was roused by a rustling in the bushes to his left.

He looked up, bleary-eyed, and saw the black dog standing at the edge of the road, tongue lolling stupidly, but all certainty in its eyes. It looked at him, then down the road leading west, then back at him again.

He put his face in his hands, sobbing gently. He was tired, soul-weary.

Redemption for Amos always seemed just over the horizon, around the next bend, up the road a piece. He knew he had to keep walking, keep moving, or else, he may never get there.

And that was the worst thing, he knew—to never get there. It was worse than anything he could possibly imagine.

And so, looking left and right at the crossroads, hoping for a ride and finding none, he trudged after the black dog, toward the west, toward Tylertown, toward wherever the road to redemption might take him.

But, oh Lord, he thought, *sometimes that road is so long and so dark, with nary an end in sight.*

HIGH LONESOME MOAN

A Song of the Black Dog

You can hear the whistle,

you can hear the bell

From the halls of Heaven

to the gates of Hell.

And there's room for the forsaken if you're there on time...

—Tom Waits
Down There By The Train

Sometimes the worst pain of one's life comes from being alone. Surely, there is pain in loss, in grief, in a love unrequited, even in death. But those pains are fleeting, temporary, and tend to fade with living. Loneliness, however, eats at the core of a man, gnawing slowly, savoring each morsel, until it's a dull, constant pain that one comes to live with simply because there is nothing else.

Amos Harlow knew such a pain. He had known it for most of his adult life. There was sadness in his eyes, the creases around them the pages of an ancient book, just waiting for someone to care enough to open them and read.

On a cool October evening, he sat with those eyes closed in the darkness of a boxcar, jouncing occasionally when the train hit a rough patch. He pulled deeply on an old cigarette butt from a pocket of many he'd collected over the last week, softly exhaling silvery blue smoke that wound lazily to the roof of the car, and then was swept away in the backdraft of the train. The lonesome moan of the train's whistle drifted through the surrounding forest, echoing the loneliness that sat like a stone in the bottom of Amos's heart, reminding him of all he'd done and all that was yet to be done, and that no one would be there to help him carry the cross.

He crushed out the cigarette butt, careful not to let any stray embers get into the hay on which he sat. Then he reached for his guitar, the one friend he could count on, strummed a muted C, and spoke back to the train:

These rails, they say
Lead straight to Hell,
and Hell is where I'm bound,
'Neath autumn moon,
and starry sky,
blows that high and lonesome sound.
Moan! Moan ! Moan!
That high lonesome moan,
tollin' me where I'm bound!
'Neath autumn moon
and starry sky,
tollin' me where I'm bound!

He finished, the chords trailing off into the night behind the locomotive's smoke. He held his eyes shut a moment longer, savoring the dying melody, then opened them, remembering where he was. The boxcar was locked solid, he knew. He'd managed to slip on board before the line check and hide amidst the hay. He knew it had been too easy; he was expected.

Just like he wanted.

Amos stared at the front of the car, the moonlight casting slivered shadows across the floor through the wall slats. He drifted back through the days, fatigued and fighting sleep, trying to remember just why he had chosen a boxcar smelling of crushed grain and cow shit as his casket.

* * * *

The week before, Amos had crossed the state line into Oklahoma using backwoods game trails to avoid the local constabulary. Though they suffered vagrants, they weren't above tapping heads to brick walls or giving a rap with a billy-club if they didn't like a face.

The trails themselves were well-worn by hunters over the years and used by many a hobo traveling the southern roads. They meandered through some of the wildest country in the south, full of wildcats and brambles, rattlesnakes and hornets' nests. Most folks hereabouts knew the trails, but shied away, leaving them mostly unused, save by the homeless savages they had come to fear. Truth told, most of the tramps passing through the wilds were fairly harmless, just people out of doors looking for work, a meal, a better place. The trails never seemed to lead them there, though -- just on to the next town, and the town after that, until a man was fair to run out of road.

Amos came up on a cedar tree, its bark shaved back at chest-level on a man his size. A mark had been carved on the bare spot—a square with an arrow through it, pointing up.

A town, then—Tulsa, if he wasn't mistaken. The trees ahead began to thin and he could just make out tin rooftops off to the north. A little farther west, he could see tufts of white smoke billowing up through the clear blue sky, and heard voices, many and varied, drifting through the trees—a mad rambling of male and female—and the chuffing of steam-powered pistons. He knew he was near the Tulsa Line station.

He pulled a long gold chain that hung from his pocket and consulted his battered pocketwatch. Three-oh-five, and right on time. The pistons grew louder, faster, more insistent. He heard the goodbyes of a hundred folk and could see arms waving from the platform as the train moved off west, slowly at first, then picking up speed.

Movement caught his eye at the edge of the tracks, and three hobos, dressed in little more than rags, shot out of the undergrowth and jumped up on the ladder of the last boxcar. They moved like steelworkers along the ridge to the door of the car, flipped the latch, and slipped inside, slamming the door with a boom.

"Rank-ass amateurs," Amos muttered, as a man in tattered overalls and engineer's cap stuck his head out the window of the caboose at the sound.

The caboose door flung open and the biggest man Amos had ever seen jumped down on the gravel and sprinted for the door of the car. Amos moved to get a better view. Crouching down behind a large pine, he saw the big man jump up on the step, wrench the boxcar door open, and leap inside, all in one smooth motion.

"Here it comes," he said to no one.

Seconds later, two of the hobos went flying out of the car, arms akimbo, landing hard in the gravel and rolling down the slope of the ditch. A few seconds later (Amos assumed this one must've put up a fight), the third hobo appeared in the doorway—held high above the head of the large railroad bull. With a roar, the bull threw the hobo down onto the gravel. The hobo landed on his head at a perilous angle and Amos heard the neck pop like a pine-knot in a fire, even from where he sat.

The other two hobos ran to their friend who was flopping like a landed fish, and then was suddenly still. The two men looked up at the train disappearing down the line. The big railroad bull was hanging out of the car by one arm, watching them as the train picked up speed and rounded the bend, daring them to try their luck another time.

"Lord God and Saint *Peter*," Amos breathed. He'd heard of some hardass bulls that sometimes got rough and might kill a hobo in the mix, but this one was harder than Alabama granite. He looked like he *enjoyed* his work—took *pride* in it.

Amos stood and picked up his guitar case, his joints popping. On up ahead, he could see the trail split off north and south. He wasn't so sure about north, not with all the law buzzing around the dead hobo like flies on roadkill. Hitching his pants, he turned south to see if there was still any hospitality among brothers.

The southern path, less worn than the trail, landed Amos where he knew it would. The smell of frying bacon and the sound of coarse laughter told him he had made the right choice. He walked until he could hear the rushing water of a river and slowed his gait.

People didn't set out in life to become road ghosts, haunting the backlands of their own country, looking for a place to bed down for the night or maybe a handout. But times were hard, and most did what they could to survive on their own, and when they couldn't, they did what human nature binds them to do: they banded together with others like themselves.

The Brotherhood of the Road—or just the Brotherhood, to people in the know—was, at first glance, a loose-knit bunch of stragglers of the times, forced together by circumstances and the want of another warm body for company. They came from all over, and went just as far, knowing each other by reputation, mostly. They kept in touch with signs carved in places any of their number might travel, like the one Amos had seen earlier on the path, signs that only another hobo could decode. It wasn't an official club and nobody sent off for a decoder ring, but there were dues, God Almighty yes, there were dues, and most of the Brotherhood had paid them in full.

A man didn't have to be in the Brotherhood to enjoy its hospitality, but it helped to know them that were. Amos was a loner by nature, and so had kept to himself in his travels, but again, every man needs another, and with the smell of frying bacon in his nostrils, he eased on down the embankment toward the river.

Shouts, laughter, dirty jokes, and raucous conversation died on lips as Amos strolled into the hobo jungle. Fifteen sets of eyes turned blank stares on him. No one made a sound as he moved through the crowd of outcasts. He stopped amidst the small crowd, dropped his guitar case, and turned around in a circle, surveying the crowd.

Two men, one fat, one skinny, paused by the stream in mid-wash, old tin pots and cups in their hands. Another group of five, dirty faces all, sat around a campfire with plates held in expectation, letting their breakfast burn as they stared. Four more, two whites and two blacks, stared at him from a game of gin rummy, just inside a dilapidated boxcar, cards held in hand, one of them breaking his stare long enough to peek at top card of the deck. The last four men held weapons -- two two-by-fours, a lead pipe, and a chair leg -- and slowly circled Amos with dark, brooding faces.

"Well, well, well," muttered Amos, taking in the scene. "Never thought I'd see the day a brother wasn't welcomed to the table amongst friends."

"You ain't *got* no friends here, Black Dog," said the one with the chair leg, tapping it nervously against his thigh. "Best shuffle on down the trail afore things get itchy."

Amos looked the man up and down. "Tom Ritter," he said. "That Birmingham John Law done crack yo' head in two, so you done forgot who sprung you outta his hoosegow some time back?"

Ritter hung his head a little, then looked up at Amos from under a furrowed brow. He seemed about to speak, but Amos had turned away.

"And you, Grady Terhune," he said to another. "S'pose you done forgot the poison I sucked outta that timber rattler bite last Spring." The man unconsciously scuffed one shoe on the other. "Bet you walkin' with a limp, too, ain't it?" The man said nothing, but lowered the pipe, drawing circles in the dirt.

Amos turned to face the other two. "Boomer? Harry? Y'all gonna start swinging them sticks at the same man that you done broke bread and drank corn liquor from the same jug with?" The men eyed him nervously for a moment, then lowered their gazes as well as their planks.

"It's a damn sight poor for a fellow brother of the road to get a welcome as such," Amos began, "but if y'all's set upon it, I reckon I could take the four of y'all with some spit and sass left over for another."

The four men looked at one another. The rest of the brothers around the camp stayed put, waiting for something to come down the pike. Amos just stood his ground, wheeling every so often to look in each man's eyes. None ever met his.

"Well?" Amos asked. "How 'bout it?"

The four men slowly turned, drifting back into the camp, looking over shoulders and muttering like scorned children. Amos stood, watching them go, and wondered what the hell was going on.

One of the two men at the creek dropped his dishes on the bank and ran double-quick to Amos. "You got to come on, Harlow. Come with me right now and don't speak another word to nobody, hear?"

He pulled Amos by the elbow and Amos let himself be led out of the clearing, keeping eyes on the rest of the men about the camp as they went back to their business. Once amongst the trees, the wiry man turned to face Amos.

He was scared, pure and simple. His face was smudged and cherry-red with exertion. The hair at his temples had salt-and-peppered, and the lines around his round blue eyes had deepened since Amos had last seen him, but Feedbag Jake was the same as he'd left him two years ago.

"Seems like thing's changed since I last been 'round, Jake," he said.

Jake had begun building up a dwindling fire. He didn't speak until it was fairly crackling again. "Some," he said, "but others ain't changed much a'tall." He set a coffee pot down into the coals and sat back on his haunches, eyeing Amos steadily. "Why're you here, Amos?"

Amos sat on a log across from him, sighed with the effort, and eyed him back. "Just amblin', same as always. Man can still do that, far's I know. How 'bout you? Last we seen each other, you was washin' dishes for ol' Codwell up to Tupelo. What happened?"

Jake poked the stick, dropping his gaze. "Job dried up. Town wasn't big enough for an old diner no more. Ol' Man Codwell let us all go and up an' sold the place. Hear tell he's gone to Atlanta to live with kin thereabouts." He absently stirred the fire, which didn't need stirring. Amos leaned over and grabbed his hand, stilling it. Jake flinched like he'd been shot.

"What's goin' on 'round here, Jake? What's got the boys jumpy? I never knowed you to be a-scairt of no man."

Jake dropped the stick into the flames and sat back, eyeing his friend. "I'm awful sorry, Amos. That wasn't no kind of greetin' for a friend, but you got to be careful. Word's been spreadin' 'bout you."

"Mm- *hmm*," Amos said. "What kind o' word?"

Jake shifted on his heels, squinting up at Amos. "Folks say you been involved in some witch-stuff. Word is you chased out some haints, broke bread with a giant, and even treated with Satan hisself. That true, Amos?"

In answer, Amos took his old worn guitar from its case, slid his gnarled fingers across the frets, and called up the whispered hint of an old, forgotten tune.

"Folks on the road are scared of you, Amos," Jake continued. "They say you keep company with a hellhound, and that wherever you show up, ain't nothin' but bad times foller."

"Might be some o' that's true and right," Amos said, not looking at Jake. "Might be some's a haul o' bullshit. What do *you* say, Jake?"

Jake stared at Amos across the fire. He shifted from foot to foot, trying to decide how to move on. "If even a hair of any of that is true, I say might be you come at the right time."

Amos trapped the strings, muting the music, and looked sharply up at his friend. "Whatchu mean?"

"Well," Jake began. "You seen them boys a'tryin to hop the 'car on your way in, right?"

"I did," Amos nodded. "Looked like a bunch o' greenhorns from where I was sittin'. Them sumbitches didn't look to have they first shave yet -- still wearin' they short-britches from the look of 'em."

"Right enough," Jake agreed. "Buncha local-yokels settin' out for California. Heard tell of all the 'grand adventure' and what-not to be had on the road. Amos, they's just farm boys from up north o' town. Wouldn'ta lasted three days nohow, the lot of 'em."

Amos nodded, tuning his strings to his satisfaction, meaning for Jake to go with the tale. Jake mustered up a wad of phlegm, spat, and went on.

"Well, you seen what that railroad bull done to 'em. Broke the one's neck—the *biggest* one, mind—and hauled him right over his head, he did, like a sack of grain. And them other two was lucky to get out with their skins still on."

Amos tuned another string a notch, strummed lightly, and nodded.

"Well, damn, Amos," Jake whined. 'Don't you *see*?"

"Alls *I* see," Amos replied, strumming, "is that three corn-fed white boys got a lesson in life and shoulda stayed down on the farm. Road ain't no place for greenies, Jake. You know that."

"Really?" said Jake. "Well, s'pose I tol' you that bull done kilt *eleven* other 'bos, including Hank Strapper and Boulder Jenkins?"

Amos cut him a hard look. "Bullshit."

"Ain't nary a bit, I swan," Jake vowed.

"You tellin' me that there bull done in for two of the biggest men ever set foot out they mamas' wombs? At the same *time*? Ain't no way."

"It's so," said Jake. "Jenkins had his head twisted right the hell around like a hoot-owl's, and Strapper was folded up *backwards* like half a sandwich, God's own witness."

Amos laid the guitar on his lap, pulled his hip flask from an inside pocket of his coat, and took a hard pull. He held it out to Jake over the fire, who took it and pulled a hard swallow himself, wincing.

"Reckon you ought to fill me in, then," said Amos.

Jake took another pull and handed back the flask, wiping his mouth on his sleeve. "His name's Brick Hansen, a Swede from up Minnesota way. He come down here to work the Santa Fe line about three years gone, when the boss men got tired of 'bos hitchin' free rides out west. Nobody'd ride the rails with all us heathens on board. So Brick was brung down from up north.

"He had a reputation for being a hardass up there; guess the cold can do that to a man, 'specially in his heart. Say he ran a clean line clear out to Portland, not a single tramp on that line, long as Brick was ridin' herd. Prided hisself on it, he did.

"S'funny, though. He busted heads, sure. Ain't a bull worth his salt cain't do that. Word is, though, he never kilt a man 'til he come here. Word is up north he was a good fella to be 'round. Had a boomin' laugh, so they said. Liked a joke as much as the next man, even if it was on him. After a spell in here in Tulsa, heard tell he got moody, then downright mean, so's even his own *bosses* didn't do nothin' to rile him. Also heard that his wife took their three young'uns and cleared out, so a'feared of him, she was.

"Not rightly sure what his Christian name is, but they call him Brick on account of that big ol' cinderblock he carries with him. Got it bolted to a chain, he does, and it's said that he swings it like Ruth goin' for the fences. Drags it under the train, too, trying to knock hobos what's ridin' the frames a'loose."

Amos took a pull from the flask, offering it over again. "Seems easy to me," he said. 'Jes' stay off the Number 14. Ain't always smart to fight; sometimes it's smarter to clear out. Rules of the road, ain't that right?"

"Normally, I'd agree with you," said Jake, accepting the flask again. "But Brick didn't get Strapper and Jenkins on the train. He come for them in their *beds*."

"Hellfire," Amos breathed.

"Them boys was down here a month or so back, just a-talkin' 'bout how they was gonna run that rail all the way out to New Mexico, right to the very end. Downright *braggin'*, now, and none dared doubt 'em, big as they was. Next mornin' Cooter Richards found 'em both mangled up, but nary a sound in the night so that the passel of men around 'em woke."

"Law ain't done nothin'?" Amos asked, knowing the answer. "Eleven men's enough to raise *some* eyebrows, ain't it?"

"Not when they's a buncha dead tramps, and don't you know it. The more the better, far as they's concerned. That's why Ritter and them others was totin' sticks when you come up; we set to puttin' up a guard."

"I tell ya, Hansen ain't *natural*, Amos," said Jake. "All the brothers are afraid to talk about him, for fear he'll... well, *hear*. I know it sounds crazy, but... there it is."

Amos took the flask back, capped it halfway, and stopped. "What's all this got to do with me, Jake? What you think I can do different that all them others couldn't?"

"Well," Jake said, "that's what I ain't tol' you yet. That night he come for Jenkins and Strapper, I was in camp, awake. I was so scared, I couldn't move in my bedroll. I heard his boots crunchin' in the rocks and strained to see from whichaways he was coming.

"He strutted right through all them sleeping tramps toward me. I saw him through the fire, his shadow right beside him on the ground in the firelight. Then, I swear a'fore God himself, Amos: his shadow *moved.* It crawled right up his back and kinda hung around his head. When he walked, it sort of *smeared* against the night out behind him, like it was hangin' on—like it was *ridin'* him.

"Then he was at my side. He hunkered down right beside me. I tell you, Amos, I couldn't move. Pissed my pants I did, and I ain't ashamed to say. He leans in real close, like he was to kiss me on the cheek. He whispered in my ear, and God's witness, Amos, his breath smelt like an open grave.

"' *Are you the black dog?* ' he says. 'No,' says I, barely able to hold a thought in my head. He put a hand the size of a trashcan lid on my head, waited a tick, then said:

"'*You know him. Tell him to come to me. We have business, he and I. Tell him or I'll come back, again and again.*' After that, he up and walked away, and by God, I haven't slept a night since."

Amos sat and stared into the fire. His hand found the stopper on the flask and twisted. He drained the last of it in a single swallow, then tucked it away. "He come back, like he said?"

"Last night and night before," Jake nodded. "Didn't matter to him nobody knew where you was. Kilt Davy Nettles and Brewster Coggins, one a night. Reckon he'll be back tonight for somebody else. Don't matter if we run. He'd catch us, anyhow. Besides, you know the Brotherhood, Amos—we pull together when it gets thick and the fur flies."

"Except for a brother that's the cause of the flyin' fur," Amos said.

"You cain't blame 'em, Amos. They's scared. The road ain't the safest place to begin with, but they all pulled together for safety. Now they ain't even got *that.* Nobody wants to run from a fight, but this here's a fight we just cain't win."

"No," said Amos, sighing, getting up. "Reckon it's on me to settle it."

"You mean it?" Jake asked, rising with him.

"Ain't nothin' else for it, is it?" Amos said. "C'mon." They walked together into the clearing, straight through the camp, toward the rail station. Men rose up as they passed, eager to see what would happen, eager to see the end of their suffering, even if it meant somebody else had to pay the price.

The host of men grew with every step, and soon the crowd looked like a flock of birds heading south with Amos at their lead, guiding them. They made their way up the embankment and across the hunting trail to where the rails lay like iron ribbons, stretching into infinity. They stopped this side of the rails and Amos scanned the crowd.

People from the station, waiting on the next train or having missed the one before, stood gawking at the swarm of road men that had boiled up out of their backwoods hive that everyone knew was there, but none acknowledged. Pretty soon, the crowd was buzzing on both sides of the tracks. Amos searched the sea of faces on the platform, knowing Brick Hansen was there, somewhere, watching and waiting.

Above them, the water tower for the steam engine stood like a sentinel over the station. The names of hobos that had tried the Number 14 to Santa Fe were scrawled all over it in white chalk, some in yellow. That was tradition—a taunt and a dare to the railroad bulls who worked the lines. With all those names, it reminded Amos of a headstone, a monument to the dead.

Amos looked at Jake, who stood nervously at his side, expecting a demon with graveyard breath to come swooping down upon them.

"Help an old man out?" Amos asked, holding out a piece of white chalk he'd fetched from his coat pocket. "It's been a fair piece since I done any climbing."

Jake, hand trembling, took the chalk and scurried like a squirrel up the tower's ladder. He reached out over nothing, found a big blank spot between the names of Strapper and Jenkins, and scribbled in a block letters like a child:

BLACK DOG HARLOW—#14—12:01 TO SANTA FE

Jake scrambled back down the ladder, jumping the last three rungs to the ground, fairly throwing the chalk to Amos, like it was a cursed thing. Amos caught it and pocketed it, looking around at the crowd one last time. Eyes everywhere were upon him—mocking, leering, some disgusted, some smiling.

"Well," he said, "that's that."

He turned and led the way back down the slope to the camp, feeling one set of unseen eyes in particular staring holes in his back, as the day waned and the night waxed ever closer.

* * * *

And so here he sat, waiting on what he knew might be Death waiting on *him*.

He'd managed to slip out of the ditch near the tracks just before midnight, after the engineer and shovel-man had done their rounds checking for the likes of him. They'd all seen his name; anyone with two eyes had seen it. He'd jumped on the last boxcar, and finding it unlocked, crawled in and slammed the door. He wasn't surprised to find the car empty and unlocked, nor was he shaken when the car was locked again from the outside.

After all, he was expected.

None of the 'bos back at camp had met his eye as he left. None could. Either out of shame or knowledge of the death they knew they were surely laying at his feet, the men shuffled back to their bedrolls and their watches and their card games, but none in good humor, and all silent in their guilt.

The Number 14 pulled out, straining against the rails, picking up speed. The whistle blew; it was a death-knell to his ears. He tensed, waiting on the night to come alive, waiting to meet the thing Brick Hansen had become. His palms sweated and he wiped them furiously against his pant legs. His mouth was full of cotton, his spit long gone. The wait was killing him an inch at a time.

Presently, he heard a shuffling gait across the roof of the car. The footsteps came to the middle of the roof and stopped. Amos replaced the guitar, latched the case, and fished another cigarette butt out of his pocket and stuck it between his lips.

A latch was thrown on the roof's trap door and the wind whipped down into the car, stirring the straw into small, vicious eddies. A great cinderblock dropped through and hit the floor with a thud, followed like a snake by the tinkling chain bolted through its middle.

Amos watched as a hulk of a man dropped through the roof and landed stock-still on his feet without a sound, like a cat. The huge figure reached down and coiled the chain around his great fist until only a foot or so was left between it and the cinderblock. The door slammed shut like judgment above them and they took stock of one another in the near-dark, the countryside whipping by outside.

"Took your time," Amos said, striking a match on the sole of his shoe. He lit the butt, inhaled deeply, and shook out the match.

The giant stood silent, unmoving. His great frame was crosshatched with shadow and moonlight from between the slat walls of the boxcar. His breathing was heavy, mimicking the locomotive that pulled them toward New Mexico. The chain chinked softly as it hung in his grip.

"Shee-it," Amos said, blowing smoke. "You's smaller than I heard. Them boys been drinkin' too much shoe polish." He hoped that the train's clacking wheels covered the sound of his hammering heart, which was like to pound right out of his chest at any minute.

Hansen remained silent. His chest rose and fell, his breath a bellows at the furnace. Amos was starting to get itchy. He drew on the butt again, breathing out a plume of blue smoke.

"Hear you been' lookin' for me," Amos said. "Why is it, I wonder, that you couldn't find me and had to go about killin' a bunch of folks got nothin' to do with anything to get at me?"

Brick Hansen—or whatever was using his body—took a deep breath, held it as if searching for the words, and spoke in a rush of air that seemed to have substance, a thickness almost tangible.

"You have a bold tongue for an insect. Why our Master would be bothered with you is beyond our thought. Crushing you will be beneath our station."

"Hm," Amos said. "Funny how you got to have a big strappin' fella like that to crush me. What's wrong? First you cain't find me, now you got to have someone else do your killin'?"

"INSECT! You dare speak thus? Our time is not yet come to pass, but soon, soon we will swarm over this mudball and drive you all like cattle to the slaughter! For now, this form will suffice for your death. The Master commands it."

"Brick? Brick Hansen? You hark me, boy? Come out here and talk at me!"

"He cannot hear you, bug. He is in here with us, now. He is of *us. You'll not drive us out."*

"Why don't you let the boy go? Come out here an' face me yourself? Or you too chicken-shit?"

The demon laughed, a mocking, terrible choking sound. "*A weak ploy. And a useless one. This flesh is ours now, and satisfactory for the task at hand.*"

Amos saw it was true. Hansen's eyes were dead, like a doll's eyes, blank slates for any number of evils to be written upon. There was no hope for Hansen. But that was the way of the devil's minions -- they acted on whatever was in a man's heart to begin with and made it bigger, until it swallowed him whole, like Jonah's great fish.

Had Hansen been weak-minded, or had he made a deal? Either way, it didn't matter, and it made things a whole lot easier for Amos.

"All right, then," Amos said, standing and taking the cigarette from his lips.

"Let's see what you got."

Hansen sprang at Amos, faster than Amos would have believed for a man that size, but the devil riding him made it possible. Amos was ready.

He sidestepped the big man, tripping him into the pile of hay where he'd been sitting. Before he could recover, Amos flicked the cigarette butt into the hay. The dry, brittle hay went up like gasoline, engulfing Hansen in flames and spreading to the pine walls of the boxcar.

The giant rose, a pillar of walking fire, the walls burning like the gates of Hell behind him. Unperturbed, he began to swing the cinderblock on its chain above his head, the flames licking down the chain to the brick, making a whooshing sound with each twirl.

"Oh hell," Amos muttered.

The cinderblock came down at his head in a rush, crashing into the wood floor and catching it alight. Hansen dragged the chain back and began to whirl it again. Amos juked one way, then the other, and the flaming brick crashed into the door of the boxcar, leaving a hole the size of Amos's head. Moonlight and wind spilled through the hole, whipping up the flames into a greater frenzy. His porkpie hat was yanked from his head and sailed out into the night.

Amos backed up, looking frantically for a way out, as the big man gathered the chain up once more. He tripped, falling hard on his back, the breath leaving him in a great gasp. He just barely managed to avoid having his chest crushed as he rolled out of the way of the giant's next swing, but he wasn't quick enough. The cinderblock glanced off his shoulder, tearing a gash and drawing a gout of blood. The fire sealed it almost as soon as it was made, and Amos gave out a cry of pure agony.

"HA!" cried the Hansen-Thing. *"See how the insect squirms!"* It gathered the chain and began to advance on Amos, who was scrabbling back toward the front of the boxcar.

The entire car was burning now, a funeral pyre on wheels, racing through the autumn night like a comet. Amos knew that soon the engineer would notice the fire when the train took a bend in the tracks, but he couldn't wait for help. He had to end this now, or die in the attempt, which was becoming more likely with each second. Slowly, he staggered to one knee before the front wall of the car.

"Come…come on, then. Do it," he panted. "Do it and damn you back to hell," he croaked.

The demon-ridden Hansen, a charred, burning thing without humanity, stalked forward, swinging the brick in a wide arc before loosing it at Amos's head. The split-second before it hit, Amos threw himself to the floor. It passed so close to his head, Amos could feel the hair on the top of his head as it burned away and the blisters that rose up in its place.

The cinderblock broke through the wall of the car, catching on the metal frame outside as Hansen tried to yank it back. The wall began to give, but Amos didn't give it the chance. He planted his feet and threw himself in a tackle at Hansen's flaming body, knocking him through the flaming wall and out over the car couplings.

Wind roared in through the hole where the wall, weakened by flame, had finally given out. Amos could hardly breathe in the smoke and the heat. He leaned out the hole and took a big gulp of night air.

He looked down and saw Brick Hansen, now a physical reflection of the evil inside him, hanging onto the chain of his favored weapon, the tracks below him a blur in the firelight. The Hansen-thing's feet stuttered and popped against the rail timbers as the train picked up even more speed. The brick had become wedged between the iron frame and wood of the car wall and offered purchase for it to climb up, but the iron was beginning to bend with the heat, buckling outward.

As the wind stoked the flames consuming Brick Hansen, he raised his head and looked at Amos, a wicked grin spreading slowly across his burned visage. Amos couldn't be sure—he later thought it a trick of the smoke and his own mind—but he thought he saw a thick, smoky shape rise up above Hansen's head. It seemed vaguely cat-like and serpentine at the same time. It laughed its choked, echoing laugh again that, even in the midst of the burning car, froze Amos's heart.

"YOU CANNOT HIDE, PROPHET! WE KNOW YOU NOW! WE ARE YOUR END! "

"Maybe," Amos shouted above the wind and flames, "but not today." With that, he drew back and kicked the burning wall for all he was worth.

Sparks flew like crazed fireflies and chunks of wood blew outward as the weakened wall gave out and the brick and chain--the hobo-killer of legend--came loose with a vengeance.

The burning man shrieked in surprise and rage. For a half a second, Hansen—the *real* Hansen—emerged, shedding the unholy visage that served as a face. Amos, in the eternal moment that the bull hung in midair, saw the very human look of sorrow and helplessness on Hansen's young face, and then the man and his devil tumbled out of sight beneath the train. The boxcar shuddered once on the rails, and the screams were brief, then mercifully silent.

Amos could feel the train slowing. The engineer must have seen the burning wreck of his last car. Just when he thought he might end up a pile of ash along with it, the train slowed enough for Amos to jump off. He grabbed his guitar case and leaped, rolling as he came up on the train's blindside, and laid quiet in the ditch, his shoulder throbbing like murder.

He could hear the engineer and the coal-man working their way down the train, cursing and yelling fit to bust. He never knew how long he lay there waiting for the car to burn out enough for the men to uncouple the boxcar. He looked up at the stars until the pain in his shoulder was more than he could take, then he knew no more.

* * * *

Amos came to with the familiar chuff-chuffing of the steam engine. He rolled over on his good shoulder, and saw that the crew had managed to maneuver the burned boxcar off onto a side track and were now getting into position to set off again.

He jumped up, grabbed his guitar case, wincing out loud at his complaining shoulder and burned face, and ran alongside the train until he came to a flatcar loaded with bundled drainage pipes big enough for a man to slide into quite nicely. Climbing up, he slid his guitar case into one of the pipes and leaned back against the mouth of it as the train picked up speed.

The train rolled along over a trestle, and Amos found another cigarette butt in his pocket—his last—but he knew there'd be plenty more in Santa Fe. Groping for the matches, he felt something hard and powdery and pulled out the chalk. He fingered it, thinking of all the names on the tower back in Tulsa, all those men that had lost their lives so he could be found. It was all on his account, and he knew it.

He put the chalk away, thinking he'd write his name—*all* their names—on the tower in Santa Fe, even Brick Hansen's. The last look on Hansen's face would haunt Amos for many a sleepless night thereafter.

Amos's hands shook as he pulled a match and lit the butt, drawing deeply and breathing out just as deeply. He thought of the demon's last words.

YOU CANNOT HIDE, PROPHET!

Prophet? He had no notion of what that might mean, but something inside him stirred the barest of recognitions, like seeing a forgotten friend on a crowded street, then watching them disappear into the sea of nameless faces.

WE KNOW YOU, NOW!

Amos was suddenly anxious, as if the entire world were watching him. The night seemed a tad colder, a bit more unfriendly, and the full moon was no longer a source of comfort in the night sky, but a bright, intense eye, spying out the land. He huddled down, pulling his coat collar up against the wind, and hugged his knees, unconsciously trying to make himself smaller.

He smoked as the train rolled away into the night, toward New Mexico, to whatever lay beyond, and never felt more alone in his life.

HIM BELOW

A Song of the Black Dog

Maybe there is *a beast… What I mean is… maybe it's only* us.

--William Golding
Lord of the Flies

It was the whitest town Amos had ever seen in his life.

He'd passed through some real whitebread towns in his time, but that's all it had been -- just passing through. He'd known better than to stay no more than the time it took to get his bearings and press on. Most of those places didn't cotton to hobos, especially not those of his color. It was the same all over; Northerners just hid it better. Illinois was the birthplace of the Great Emancipator, but hiking through Peoria was like a leper strolling into a hospital. The way people looked you, you just knew they were half a jump from bidding on you. They looked you up and down as if sizing you up for a white dinner jacket and wondering if you could be taught the King's English.

That's why when Amos trudged into the small town of New Hope, Alabama, he half-thought he was dreaming.

The road into town gave no sign of any settlements, much less a town of import. It was mostly strewn with crags of granite, jutting from the hillsides like dragon's teeth. Trees were scattered here and there, not much to look at even in the dead of summer, with branches that resembled the straw on a witch's broom and bark like old skin, dried and crusted.

But when he rounded the bend, the land that stretched out before him was as green and fertile as any he'd seen in the Northwest, much less in the Deep South. Rolling hills gave way to a cobblestone street. Houses as bright as fresh laundry lined the main drag, with whitewashed picket fences surrounding each one and multi-colored flowers in rich, freshly-tilled soil. Storefronts sat on corners at right angles so perfect you could steer a ship by them, their bright green awnings snapping in the light breeze. At the far edge of town on a high hill, a church looked down over the town like a shepherd tending its flock, its stained-glass windows sparkling like trapped rainbows in the sun.

That was another thing Amos noticed: the weather. Along the road, there had been a damp chill following an early morning rain. The clouds had gathered over the sun, blocking any warmth he might have gotten. But in New Hope, the weather was just...well, *perfect.* The sun shone down on the town with a benevolent heat that seemed to caress the land and its inhabitants.

The townsfolk seemed to be celebrating. It was like a postcard from 1900. A ragtime band was blaring out tunes from a bandstand gazebo in the town square Picnic tables were lined up and down the main street, red and white checkered tablecloths flapping at the fringes in the breeze. The tables were loaded with every dish a Southern woman could conceive of: fried chicken, green beans, mashed potatoes, boats of rich gravy, pot roast, collard greens, corn on the cob dripping with butter and salt, and on and on for the length of the tables. He swore above it all he could smell the buttery crust of freshly-baked pies, and Lord, wasn't that a thing?

Amos's stomach turned somersaults. He hadn't eaten more than a stick of venison jerky in two days, and if hunger could drive a man insane, then Amos Harlow should have been fitted for a straightjacket.

But wariness gave pause to hunger. How could he just wander up into their midst and set himself down at their table and dig in? That would just be asking for trouble he didn't need. No, it would be better for him to mosey around the edge of town and keep moving. He scanned the crowd. Some were dancing to the band, women in fine cotton skirts that whirled like matadors' capes as they jitterbugged, and men in their Sunday best, string ties coming loose in the frenetic motions of the dance. Red faces from glad exertion, greasy faces born of chicken and mashed potatoes, smiling faces turned up to the sun, but not a one of them black faces.

He stood at the lip of the hill, shuffling from foot to foot, desire arm-wrestling with reason, when he noticed a familiar face in the crowd—or a familiar snout, at least.

The black dog was nosing around one of the picnic tables, slipping in and out of legs, hoping for a loose morsel to make its way into a lap or even better, its gaping maw. The dog trotted to one end of the table and lifted himself up on his hind legs, supporting himself on the table with his front legs. It turned its head sideways and began to pull a drumstick from a towering platter of chicken. It dropped from the table and began to gnaw the chicken leg in earnest, the crunching of bone almost audible from where Amos stood.

Amos couldn't believe it. He was used to people not seeing the dog. He knew from experience that the dog was for him alone. So far as he knew, no one had *ever* seen it but him, but in such a crowd of people, surely *someone* would notice the giant black head of a creature somewhere between a bloodhound and a Kodiak filching supper from their table. But the folks continued eating, not missing a beat, while the mutt snatched biscuits from a wicker basket, knocking it over and spilling the biscuits all over the table. A few rolled off the edge and hit the ground. They lasted no more than two seconds before disappearing into dog's jaws which worked like a machine grinding them to paste in seconds. It dawned on Amos that he'd never seen the dog eat. He never thought the dog *needed* to eat, for that matter.

Then the dog turned to look at him, tongue wagging, and Amos thought the damn thing was actually grinning at him.

Well, it seemed to say, *y'all gonna get in on this, or what?*

"Git from there!" Amos hissed, waving his arms in a come-hither motion before he realized that it didn't matter; the people couldn't see the dog more than they could see the breeze around them.

His motion *did* attract attention, however. A tall man in a straw derby and suspenders turned from the dancers and clapping spectators and began walking toward him.

"Oh, hell," Amos muttered. "Here it comes." He took an involuntary step backwards before he realized it.

Then the man waved his own arm in greeting and picked up his pace. Amos stood his ground. He was in it now, for better or worse.

He raised his own hand and returned a weak wave, trying to make himself as small as possible.

He soon realized that his fear was unwarranted. The man was smiling wide as he approached. The last few steps he lowered his hand and extended it to Amos.

"'Lo, there!" the man said in a high, friendly voice. "What brings you by our little hamlet, friend?"

Amos accepted the hand uncertainly and shook. The man's grip was firm and friendly, with no show of bravado. His daddy had taught him you could tell a man by his handshake and know whether he was worth his salt or not by the grip. He had thought then that it was some fatherly nugget of wisdom that held no more water than a cracked bucket, but now he was glad to be proved wrong. It wasn't the first time and wouldn't be the last. He returned the shake with the matched vigor, his apprehension vanished entirely.

"Don't mean to intrude on your festivities," Amos said, trying to let go of the shake, but the man held firmly. "I was just passin' through. Be on my way directly."

The man let out a belly laugh. "Nonsense, my friend, nonsense! We're just celebratin' our Golden Jubilee here in New Hope! Yessir, fifty years and goin' strong! Have you eaten lunch yet? Come, come! Have some lunch with us. There's plenty to go around, as you can see. Never let it be said that the town of New Hope let a stranger leave with an empty belly!"

"Well, I could stand a meal, that's for sure," Amos said, "but I don't wanna raise no hackles."

The man guffawed again and clapped Amos heartily on the back. "No hackles raised, I can assure you, Mr…?"

"Harlow. Amos Harlow. Amos'll do just fine, though."

"Where in God's green earth are my manners? My name is Horace Taylor. I'm mayor of our little burg. Mostly just a title, though I do get to judge the pig show and the pie–eating contest every autumn."

"A pleasure, Mayor Taylor," Amos said.

"Oh, now come on with that. Just Horace. We're all friends here. No need to stand on ceremony. Why, you just come with me and set yourself down at the table and dig in! We have tons and more on the way. Some good pie down there and truffle, too. Band's in a good place, as well, don't you think?"

"Sure is," Amos smiled.

"Well, lets get at it then. After you, sir?"

Amos was fair to bursting with glee. After so long on the road, to have a town open right up to a total stranger and pay no mind to the color of his skin, why that was as close to a miracle as Amos had seen in a long while. He walked in step with the man, his guitar case bumping on his hip. The man noticed it swinging from its strap.

"You a musician, then, Amos?" he asked.

"I play a bit. Know some old tunes, got a few of my own, too."

The man lit right up at that. "Is that a fact, now?"

"Sure is," Amos said.

"Well, maybe you'll favor us with a song or two later on?"

Amos shrugged. "If you like, I'd be willin'."

Horace Taylor roared laughter again and slapped Amos even harder on the back, almost sending him stumbling forward.

"That will be splendid, Amos! Most splendid!"

Amos smiled and let himself be seated at the first table they came to. A plate was set in front of him by female hands whose face he never saw. He piled it high with roast beef and collards and doused everything in a puddle of brown gravy. He set to right quick, almost forgetting to use his fork.

This here ain't half-bad, Amos thought as he dug in. *No siree.*

It wasn't until much later he realized the black dog was nowhere to be seen.

* * * *

Hours later, the sun was an orange flame on the western skyline, and Amos sat under a fine old poplar, smoking and watching small-town America played out before him.

People lazed in the grass of the town park, patting their stomachs and hiding a belch here and there. Menfolk pulled on their pipes, the sweet-smelling scent of Ol' Mickelberry's rising into the afternoon air. Women bustled and hummed over the tables, cleaning, packing up food, and nagging one another good-naturedly, every now and then bursting into fits of cackling that turned heads.

This here's the way folks ought to live, Amos thought, smiling contentedly. *Workin' together, passin' they lives away in peace, celebratin' the fact that they's just alive.*

Horace Taylor was talking with three men over by the bandstand. He lifted a hand and pointed at Amos across the park. The men nodded and followed Taylor over toward Amos.

"Here he is, gentlemen! Our very own guest of honor. I'd like you all to meet Mr. Amos Harlow, late of New York City," Taylor said, plopping down in the grass next to Amos.

"This here's Buck McCoy, our sheriff, and a fine one, at that. Been reelected three times, now, ain't it?"

McCoy grinned and shook his head. "Four, more like," he said, "but who's countin'? Pleased to meet you, Amos," he said, offering his hand.

Amos took it. McCoy was different from any John Law he'd ever known. Man wasn't even wearing a hog-leg, no badge to boot. Amos never heard of a lawman not going heeled and wouldn't have pegged him for a sheriff anymore than he would've Tallulah Bankhead.

"Big ol' cuss there's Hank Deal. He's the local lumber man. Keeps us in timber year 'round, ain't that right, Hank?"

"Some, I reckon," he said, staring at Amos with deadpan expression. He extended a hand that looked like the business end of a mallet. Amos gripped it and the big man shook it hard once, adding a little grip that like to crushed Amos's knuckles into powder.

"He chop it with his hands, I guess?" Amos said, flapping his wounded hand in jest.

Horace broke out in a gut-busting laugh. Half a second later, the men joined him. Amos noted their laughter was a mite forced, and they hadn't started until Taylor did. Deal, in particular, laughed with his mouth, but not his eyes. Amos figured right then that Hank Deal didn't cotton to strangers like the mayor did—or seemed to, anyway.

"Oh, Amos, I think you'll fit in mighty fine with us old badgers," Taylor said.

He turned to the third man, a thin, waspish fellow that reminded Amos of a scarecrow in an autumn cornfield. "Last but not least, this here's Rollo Moultrie, New Hope's undertaker."

Moultrie's hand was so thin Amos swore he could see the bones reaching right up into his forearm. He was almost afraid to take it, thinking that it might be as cold as some of his customers'.

"*Funerarian*," Moultrie corrected in a whispery drawl. "'Undertaker' has not been in use since we drove out the Redcoats. Pleased to make your acquaintance, good sir." The hand wasn't cold, but moist and clammy. Amos fought the urge to wipe his hand on his pants leg afterwards. He was plenty nerved-up, too, at the way Moultrie's eyes seemed to run the length of his body, as if the man were sizing him up for a casket.

"Well, it's a real nice town y'all got here," Amos said. "Don't know if I've seen nicer anywhere hereabouts."

"We're real proud of it, that's for sure," said Taylor, when none of the others spoke up. "It's our little piece of Heaven before the fact; that's what we like to tell folks."

Amos ground his cigarette out in the dirt. "You know, I musta passed this way a dozen times before, and I ain't run across this place once. Fifty years, you say?" The others exchanged a look, then looked to Taylor.

"Quite so," the mayor said, doffing his hat theatrically, "and thank you for the segue, sir.

"Town fathers settled here back in 1883. Had it hard in them days, that's for sure. Tried to eke out a living in these hills. Weren't no more than scrub bushes and granite, though. Then in ought-five, my own granddaddy got the notion to make lemonade with lemons, so to speak. Started a granite mine that became somewhat of a goldmine. There's so much of the stuff in the ground here that New Hope practically grew right on top of it. Rich folks needed fancy polished dance floors in their manor houses, proper sidewalks in their cities, and sturdy headstones for their departed loved ones. Granddaddy was only too happy to oblige. There was so much of the stuff that he could charge a pittance for it and still make out like a bandit. Undercut bigger, more established mines and all that green stuff come a flowin' in to what you see about you."

"Sounds like a happy ending," Amos said, and he meant it. "Still do any mining?"

"Oh, Lord no," said Sheriff McCoy. "Mine dried up about twenty years back. Ain't nothing left but a big hole in the ground, right outside of town yonder," he said pointing north. "Quarry's pretty much a small lake now, filled up with rainwater. Ain't no telling how deep the thing is."

"Bet y'all got the devil's own time keepin' the young'uns from 'round there," Amos said.

No one said a word, but the men stiffened visibly. The tension in the air seemed to rise like yeast bread. Mayor Taylor stepped in, the consummate politician. .

"Well, that's done, then. We all know each other," said Taylor, mopping his brow with a white handkerchief. "Amos, I was just telling the boys you were a musician. They agreed as how they'd like to hear a song or two, that is, if dinner ain't weighed you down too badly." He chuckled at his own jibe.

Amos looked at the men around him. They all looked like someone just farted in church before cussing the preacher. A question formed in his mind, but it was gone before it could reach his lips.

"Well, I'd be glad to," he said, the unformed question nagging at the edges of his brain. He decided he'd mull it over later, when the town fathers weren't standing over him. Besides, it was turning into a nice evening and he didn't want to waste it, since he didn't know when another just like it would pass his way.

"Let's head on up to the bandstand," said Taylor. "The ladies are just about finished tidying up and I believe I smell coffee a-brewing. You take cream and sugar, Amos? Or maybe something with a bit more *legs*?" He nudged Amos with his elbow and winked, kicking off another spout of forced laughter from his friends.

Taylor helped Amos to his feet and led the way down the hill to the gazebo.

Word had spread of the guitar man and the townsfolk had gathered, patiently waiting to be entertained as the sun sank below the horizon. Japanese lanterns strung across the town square began to wink in the gloom, bathing the park in hues of green, red, and orange. A chair had been set up for him on the bandstand, but Amos sat on the topmost stair. He looked out at the crowd. They smiled politely, expectantly. He removed his guitar and strummed it once, twice, tuning it to his satisfaction until he got a suitable G out of it.

"Hope y'all don't mind," he said, "but I been playin' on doorsteps so long, I couldn't get a decent sound sittin' in a chair."

They all laughed and Amos smiled in return. He strummed the G-chord again, cleared his throat, and began to sing.

Been eatin' possum so long,
Cain't get rid of the taste.

But that's all the old lady like,
So none go to waste.

Possum don't taste like chicken
Possum don't taste like corn,
S'pose I been eatin' possum
Since the day I was born!

Lord, Lord, Lord,
don't that possum go down hard!
Reckon I'll throw the rest
To the dogs in the yard!

Lord, but how the crowd cackled at that tune! Amos smiled and waved. "Most songs I play come from personal experience. I'm here to tell y'all folks that one there ain't no different."

They all howled at that and shouted for another. Amos was already into the first bars and picking up the tempo.

Go to bed with busted rib,
Go to work with a black eye.
To the church-house with bloody nose,
But nobody askin' why.

'Cause they all know my woman,
She got a mean streak a mile wide,
Know they start axin' questions,
She gonna strap they hide.

Livin' with a mean-streak woman,
Ain't really livin' a-tall.
But she the only woman who'll have me,
So I got to take the fall.

Amos got some hoots and hollers from that one, mostly from the women, who nudged their husbands in the ribs. The menfolk just hung their heads all sorry-like and laughed to their neighbors, jerking thumbs back their wives and received playful slaps on the arm for their trouble.

The crowd died down as Amos finished. "Folks," he said, strumming a C-chord gently, "as you can probably tell, I'm a man of means. What I mean to say is, I'm out of doors and ain't lookin' to be behind one of my own for a while yet."

They all clapped and nodded. Some muttered aloud about the Depression and what the government was or wasn't doing to fix things. Some even offered condolences or places to stay. Amos raised his hands to quiet them.

"No, I ain't meant to draw sympathy with that, and you folks seem like the kind who'd take in a wanderin' soul, but that ain't my point, either." He strummed the C-chord again, this time louder. "No, what I'm drivin' at is that there's certain things I don't expect to have at my age and station. Like family," he said, eyeing the crowd.

"Like children."

The crowd seemed to jolt as one, as if they'd all sat down on a live wire at once. The heads that weren't suddenly looking intently at their feet were staring at him as if he'd just cussed them for fools.

Feet shifted. Throats cleared. Some peeled off the back of the crowd and headed into the night. Women wept silently into their husbands' shoulders, and the husbands patted their wives' backs. Amos went on.

"I cain't rightly say as I'd be a good daddy, though I had me a good one, myself. But this here song helps me when I get to thinkin' 'bout what I might be missin' and what I might never have."

He strummed the first bars of an old hymn his granny used to sing while hanging the laundry. He remembered the wet sheets seemed to keep time with the lyrics when she flapped them before pinning them to the clothesline.

Suffer the little ones, O fathers,
Suffer the little ones, O mothers,
Suffer the little ones, O people,
Suffer the little ones to come unto Me.

Harm them not, O fathers,
Harm them not, O mothers,

Harm them not, O, people
Less'n you want the millstone about your necks
An' be cast into the deep blue sea.

Amos opened his eyes as he closed out the tune. The crowd had dispersed, milling about, talking in low whispers amongst themselves. Some walked away across the park, making for houses and slamming oak doors behind them. There was no applause, only pointed looks and furtive glances. Soon, he was left with Mayor Taylor who stood at the base of the bandstand, leaning on the rail.

"I do somethin' wrong?" Amos asked, putting his guitar away.

"Naw, naw," Taylor said, removing his hat and smoothing his hair. "Them women'd cry over a spilt bucket o' paint, I reckon. You did fine, just fine, up there. Thank you, sir, for sharing your gift with us meager folks."

"Well," Amos said, "it was my pleasure, though I feel downright awful. I believe I'd rather send 'em home laughin' or cozyin' up to one another, but I guess there ain't no tellin'."

"Well, I'd say you more than earned your dinner this evenin'. Night in a good bed, too, yessir. Come on up to the house with me. Greta'll make us a pot of coffee and we can sit and dish about the way of the world afore sleep takes us."

Amos slung his guitar case over one shoulder and gladly followed Taylor out of the park and up the street. They reached the mayor's house, a Craftsman number in the center of town. Elm trees shaded the yard just right. Moths flitted and played around the porch light, casting the shadows of huge winged monsters on the lawn.

Taylor opened the door and beckoned Amos in. Amos took one last look around at the dwindling crowd. He heard screen doors creak open and slam shut. Lights winked out in windows. The cherry-red tip of a cigarette glowed in the dark while a dog did its necessary in the front yard for the night.

It was right about then the thought Amos had been trying to catch hold of earlier hit him smack in the forehead.

There were many married couples in New Hope; he'd seen them clapping and dancing and singing that very afternoon. He'd seen them hold each other while he played the hymns and the melancholy tunes he knew so well. He saw them walking home, arm in arm, talking quietly to one another.

So where were all the children?

* * * *

Amos waved off the offer of company with a polite smile and an endearing chuckle.

"Thank you, kindly, but no thank you. I just need to stretch a bit, let some of all that food settle down. 'Sides, I ain't used to sittin' much anymore these days. Too much walkin', I guess. Gets in the bones an' I cain't rightly get sleep 'til I run 'em a bit."

"Nonsense," said Horace Taylor. He was already up and pulling on his boots and hat. "I could use a good walk myself, at that."

Amos tried to hide his annoyance. He'd hoped to get off on his own and think his suspicions through, maybe see the town and try to figure things out. But, he couldn't rightly refuse what seemed like a friendly off from his gracious host, not without raising some eyebrows.

"We'll back be before long," Taylor said, kissing his wife, who gave him a sharp, anxious glance before turning and heading to the kitchen to clean up.

"Let's go, my friend," he said, clapping Amos on the back. They left the house and stepped out into the street. The cicadas were singing their chorus in the trees, months shy of leaving their husks behind clinging to pines. The smell of rain was in the air, but far enough away to likely pass them by without so much as a shower. Street lamps lit Main Street, casting a pale glow in circles on the ground. Moths darted in at the light, making popping sounds that sounded like bream hitting the surface of a pond. It was a fine, pleasant summer evening, and Amos wished he could enjoy it.

"Where we headed?" Taylor asked.

"Oh, I don't know. Thought I'd wander a bit, see what there is to see. I've always found a place really shows its secrets when folks ain't around to muck up the scenery," Amos said, looking sidelong at Taylor.

Taylor gave a nervous laugh, thrust his hands in his pockets, and looked at his shoes. "Heck, if that ain't the truth, now ain't it?" He continued to look at his shoes, his hands fumbling in his pockets.

Amos decided to push the envelope. “Thought I might take a look at that quarry of yours. Sounds like an interestin’ place.”

Taylor laughed uneasily. “Don’t see why it would,” he said. “Ain’t nothin’ but a big hole in the ground full-up with rainwater. Same as it’s been for a long as I can remember.”

“Well, when I pass through a place, I like to see all there is to see, you know? Take in the local flavor. Don’t know when or if I’ll ever be passin’ through again.”

“Oh, sure,” Taylor said, but he sounded downright anxious to Amos now, and his shoes must have been the most important things in the world at that moment. “We’ll stroll out there, if it please you. Only let’s not tarry; Edna’s a worry-wart. Can’t blame her, though. She’s only a woman, right?”

Amos laughed along with the mayor, but his eyes still searched for a sign, a tell that would let him know he was in the right place—as if the dog had ever led him wrong.

They strolled up past the north end of town. About a mile out, the road sloped up into the hills again and broke off to the west, becoming a dirt road that wound down into small hollow. The ground grew progressively rockier and Amos kicked small chunks of granite that filled the road, almost paving it under their feet. At the bottom of the hill, the dirt road opened up into a wide covert, covered in granite. The gibbous moon broke through the clouds and revealed a huge, yawning gap cut into the earth.

The quarry was indeed filled with water, a dark, quiet pool, more resembling oil in color and thickness. No ripples crossed its surface, not even when a gentle summer breeze blew across the quarry and met their faces.

Amos stiffened. The breeze was cold, unnaturally so, but Taylor didn’t seem to notice. He stood, hands in his pockets, and nodded toward the man-made lake.

“There she is,” he said. “Big ol’ hole, like I said. Ain’t no fish, neither, but that never stopped them young’uns from comin’ down here with cane poles.”

That broke Amos from his chill. “That’s somethin’ I been meanin’ to ask you,” he said. “Haven’t seen any children since I been here.”

Taylor winced visibly. “Oh, that,” he said. “Most of our young people done growed up and moved on to bigger and better, I reckon. Kinda quiet in town without ‘em, that’s for sure.”

“All of them?” Amos asked.

“Well, no, not *all* of them,” Taylor said, with that nervous chuckle again. “There’s a scant few, I’ll allow, but their parents keep ‘em close, know what I mean? Better seen and not heard, and all that?”

“Yeah,” said Amos, “But I ain’t even *seen* ‘em.”

“Well, hellfire, son, you ain’t been in town twenty-four hours, yet. Trust me, when them kids get loose, you’ll know. Sound like a band of wild Injuns runnin' on the warpath!”

“Mm-*hmm*,” Amos said, staring out over the ebony lake. The moon was reflected on its obsidian face, and Amos shivered at how it looked like a great, cold white eye staring at him from the depths. No sounds met his ears. No crickets, no junebugs, nothing, save for the gentle sound of water lapping the stony walls.

The feeling came upon him in a rush. He hardly had time to register it before it overtook him completely. An urgent sense, an intense feeling of dread, a fervent desire to just turn on his heels and run as fast as his legs could carry him. He’d heard of a good hex doing that very thing, a mark so perfect, its sides and corners so tight that it made a person want to flee on the spot. This was like that, but ten times, a *thousand* times greater, and more insistent.

“You all right?” Taylor asked, looking into Amos’s face as he stared at the lake.

“Yeah,” Amos whispered. “Yeah, I’m fine, just…fine.” He broke his stare and shook off a chill. “You ready to head back?”

“Reckon so,” said Taylor with a wink. “Edna’ll think I got a girl.”

Amos dredged up another polite laugh, though his mind was practically screaming at him to beat feet. He mastered himself and smiled congenially, though his insides were turning to jelly with fear.

They walked back up the dirt road, scuffing their boots on granite and chalky dust.

“You satisfied?” Taylor asked without looking. "Seen what you needed to, and all that?"

Amos turned and looked over his shoulder. The feeling of dread had diminished, but he knew it would be in the back of his mind, waiting patiently for him to fall asleep.

"Just a big hole, like you said," he said, still looking over his shoulder until they had rounded the bend and the quarry disappeared from sight.

* * * *

The next day, Amos sat on the front stoop of the New Hope General Store munching a green apple. The townsfolk were all about their labors, as fit a weekday. He watched as a lumber truck sidled down Main Street carrying a load of timber, bound for parts unknown. Men and women nodded politely to one another in greeting, but when they passed him on the steps, their faces seemed to tighten and they suddenly found the blue sky overhead or a loose string on their shirts the most interesting sight in the world.

Amos took another bite and scanned the street. He wasn't expecting to see the black dog. It was never around when Amos looked for it; their relationship didn't seem to work like that. It was almost as if the dog was tied to the road somehow, and once it led Amos to a place and he stepped off the road, the dog got scarce. He used to think it might have been the drink, but there the dog would be, licking its ass in the street and Amos sober as a deacon on the Sabbath.

Once he had begun to realize that either the dog was his own hallucination or, in fact, real, he stopped questioning its presence in his life. He figured he owed it that much, since it had literally pulled him from the blood-soaked trenches of a hellish place called the Somme.

And hell, if he was honest, he enjoyed the company.

But whether the dog was product of a shell-shocked mind or the result of too much good-timing after the War, it had a way of steering him from what seemed like random wanderings to places that could use his help, however he could give it. In that way, the dog was his own compass, morally speaking. And he could no more abandon it than he could cut off his own arm.

God knew he'd tried, and more than once.

A tug at his pants leg broke his reverie and looked down between the steps to see a dirty face staring back up at him. It was a boy, maybe ten, twelve years old, but it was hard to tell from the grime caked to his face.

The boy stared mutely at him with wide, dark eyes. Amos had seen these same eyes as his unit had passed through countless French farms and bombed-out villages. They were eyes that had known terror and would know it for life, if only in the dark hours of the morning when sleep wouldn't come.

Amos scrambled down off the steps and hunkered down in the dirt.

"Hey, there," he said. "Whatchu doin' down there in the dirt?"

The boy's eyes widened in panic and he scrabbled backwards like a fiddler crab heading for its hole.

"Hey, wait!" Amos called. "I ain't gonna hurt you none. Just wanna talk, is all!"

The boy skittered around foundation beams with the agility of a cat and peered out at him with those haunted eyes from behind a center support.

Amos looked around the street, then back at the boy. He fished another green apple out of his coat pocket. "You hungry?" he asked, holding out the apple.

The boy continued to stare at him, unmoving. Amos set the apple down on the ground and held his hands up. "Go on," he said gently, "it's yours if'n you want it."

He backed out from under the porch, his hands still raised. He straightened up and returned to his seat on the stoop. He scanned the town nervously, though he wasn't sure why. The boy could be from anywhere, after all. He'd seen more than his share of homeless, parentless children in his wanderings; hard times didn't make exceptions. But he knew different. He knew it because that's what his gut told him, but he knew it more because the dog was nowhere to be seen. Because the places the dog left Amos weren't regular places by most folks' understanding.

They were sometimes places where the world was thin between this one and another place, a place where things were broken, out of step somehow. Places that, if looked upon in the right light, were a shade dimmer than the world. They were places that it seemed he was destined to walk and mayhap do whatever he could to brighten them again. The dog held no answers for him, just direction. And so it was that Amos figured he was once again in that dim place, and that this frightened boy would be the key to understanding his chore in New Hope, Alabama.

He dropped to his knees again by the steps. "You under there, boy?" he asked. He could hear the boy's jaws working the apple. "It's all right. C'mon out and talk to me."

A shadow fell over him. "Lose somethin'?" asked a mocking, deep voice.

He jumped like thief caught and looked up into the sneering face of Hank Deal. The man loomed over Amos, sawdust covering his boots, his thumbs hooked into the straps of his denim overalls. He practically blotted out the sun while he waited for an answer.

"How's that?" Amos asked.

"Wonderin' if maybe you lost somethin' down there," Deal replied, a smile playing at the corners of his mouth. "Ain't every day you see a body pokin' around under the steps of the general store. Looks a might strange, is all."

"Oh, that," Amos said, recovering his wits. "Thought maybe I dropped my pocket knife. I's getting' ready to cut this here apple and reached for it in my pocket and it wasn't there." He shuffled the dirt here and there under the steps and shot a furtive glance under the store. The boy had pushed himself into a corner at the back of the store; Amos could see his eyes wide in terror. He was shaking and holding himself about the shoulders.

"Need some help?" Deal asked with a sneer in his voice. "Maybe another set o' eyes?"

"No, no," Amos said. "If'n I don't find it, I'll get me another directly."

"Nonsense," Deal said smugly, making to squat down beside Amos. "Lemme get under here and see what I can see."

"NO!" Amos shouted, shooting to his feet. Deal was chest to chest with Amos, a good head taller and twice as wide. Amos stared up into his hard face. The big man *was* smiling now, and it wasn't the kind that invited friendship. It was the kind that the cat wore when it found the canary cage open while the family was gone.

"Here's what's gonna happen, blackie," sneered Deal. "I'm a-gonna have me a look under that porch. Who knows? Maybe I'll see your knife, maybe I won't. But I'm a-lookin' all the same."

Amos glared back, but realized he was powerless to stop the big man. Oh, he could take him, he had no doubt of that. But that would only draw the wrong kind of attention and give up the game before Amos had even figured out the rules. So he gritted his teeth and held his breath while Deal hunkered down and looked under the store.

"Well," said Deal after a time, "didn't see nothin' down there." He stood and slapped off the dirt on his overalls, giving Amos a direct stare. "Nothin' at all."

Amos returned the hard look, toe to toe with Deal. "Thanks for lookin'," he said evenly.

"Don't mention it. Guess you won't be needin' to crawl about places in town most folks don't usually give a damn about no more."

"Guess not," Amos said, nostrils flaring.

"Reckon you gotta get you a new knife," Deal said with a hard smirk.

"Reckon so," said Amos through clenched teeth.

Deal smiled wide and backed out into the street. He tipped his straw hat. "Be seein' you."

Amos watched him walk away down the street and snuck a quick look under the store.

The boy was gone. Squinting, he could make out the apple core in the dim, resting in a little depression of dirt.

Sighing in relief, he rose to his feet and looked down the street. He saw Hank Deal speaking to a group of ladies. The ladies suddenly broke out into a fit of laughter, as if Deal had told the world's funniest joke. He doffed his hat and continued on up the street. The whole scene rang false, and Amos's suspicions were confirmed when the ladies shot quick, poorly-hidden glances at him before crossing the street, chatting amongst themselves a little too loudly.

So the shuck and jive was on, and Amos was sure it had something to do with the children, or *lack* of them, in any case. Sometimes it took a while for the big picture to show itself, and sometimes, like now, it fell right in his lap.

At times like these, Amos wished the black dog would do more than point to danger like a setter and act more like an guard dog.

He sure could use someone watching his back for what he was about to try.

* * * *

It was black as pitch at three in the morning as Amos crawled out of the Taylors' guest room window. The window sill boards creaked with his weight and the sound was like gunshot in the stillness of the early morning.

He paused, half in, half out of the window, straddling the sill and listened. Crickets chirped in the flower beds. A whippoorwill sang its lonesome song into the night and far off, another answered. When no alarm came, no lights winked on in the house, he figured it was safe. He whipped his left leg over the sill, his knee joint popping in protest, and dropped to the ground.

He gently slid the window shut and scanned his surroundings. The town was quiet. He searched for signs of life—the furtive shadow of someone on the run, the soft sound of new grass squishing underfoot, the smell of a late-night cigarette -- but was met only with the placid sense of a town at peace with the world, sound asleep in their beds, awaiting another day of the good life.

Amos was a man of the world, which meant that he knew people and was good at sizing them up right quick, to boot. He'd seen enough of small-town America and knew that some of the worst secrets lay behind pristine oaken doors and window flower boxes. It might be jaded to most folks, but in his experience, if a thing was too pretty or too perfect, well, then that something was rotten on the inside. Even the choicest apple on the tree could be brown and mushy at the core.

It was that apprehension that set him off in the dead of night along the outskirts of a town that had welcomed him, a perfect stranger. The business with the boy and Hank Deal had been pointed, there was no denying it, and Amos couldn't let things lie as they were.

He paused at the edge of the park in the center of town and looked south, back where he'd come in not two days ago. He could walk off right now, just grab his gear and stroll right out of town and up the road, put his back to whatever stain was on the soul of New Hope.

But that was a lie. Doing that would be suicide, if not to his life, then to his soul. The guilt that would overtake him would make living a kind of death. And besides, Amos had never backed down from a fight, even if he didn't wholly understand the nature of his life as it was on the road. He knew deep inside, in a place he didn't much care to think about most times, that to leave would be almost sacrilegious, a blot on his spirit that nothing would ever wash away.

So he plunged ahead through the dark, not stopping until he reached the general store.

The place was dark. Business hours were long over, but it seemed the place held another darkness, almost tangible. Gooseflesh sprung up the back of his neck and down his spine. He knew enough by then to recognize the presence of evil when he felt it, and there was no mistaking it. Something was rotten in paradise, after all.

Lord, he thought, *I wish just once a place was what it looked like on the outside.*

There was no fighting it, though, and Amos knew he'd have to push on. He crept around to the back of the store, where he'd seen the boy last. He looked up under the store again, but all was dark. He pulled out a box of matches and struck one. The hiss of the flame was ungodly loud and he quickly looked around to see if he was being watched. Seeing nothing, he cupped the match with his left hand and ducked under the general store.

The going was difficult, as he only had one hand with which to crawl, but he managed to scoot far enough under to where he'd seen the frightened boy. There was a small indentation in the soft dirt, like where a blue tick hound might wallow in the heat of a summer's day. It was big enough to have been made by a child. He raised the match and saw small footprints and handprints leading back toward the north wall of the store. He followed them until he came to a spot where they just vanished. He looked all around, then up, and saw a small square cut into the floorboards above.

The match guttered out, burning his fingertips. He cussed in a whisper and sucked his fingers. He struck another match and examined the square. It looked like a trap door, a storm door, maybe. Tornadoes were common in these parts, especially when they spun off the dozen or so hurricanes that slammed into the Gulf each year. The owners probably made it so they wouldn't get caught without a safe place to ride out the storms, if they came.

He moved the match around the square, looking for any sort of hole or latch that would gain him entrance, but found none. They were probably installed on the other side. If folks were down here, they could always crawl out from under the store real quick and make a run for it.

The ringing of a bell almost stopped his heart. It came from the front, and Amos realized it was the bell over the front door, the one to let the owners know they had customers. But there wasn't any customer that came calling at three in the morning. Amos doused the match in the dirt and sat in the dark, wondering if he'd been found out after all.

Voices filtered down through the floorboards, soft at first, but getting louder as footsteps echoed across the floor, drawing closer to where he sat. He budged not an inch, and sat waiting for the axe to fall.

"...cain't believe we ain't sent that darkie packin' yet!" said a deep voice.

Hank Deal.

"Bigger question was why he was allowed in town to begin with," said another, so softly that Amos could barely make it out. It was clammy-hands, what's-his-name, the scarecrow...Moultrie, the undertaker. Scratch that—*funerarian.*

"You know damn well why," replied another voice, forceful, commanding.

Amos choked back a gasp.

"Hell, Horace," said Deal. "We could kill that spade right here and now, wouldn't nobody bat an eyelash. But here he is sleepin' up to your house—your *very house*, and sharin' your table!"

"Hank," said Taylor, "you got all the sense of a tree stump. That boy ain't had a meal or seen a bed in a coon's age. We're gonna treat him right, feed him, rest him up, and send him on his way. That way, we don't draw no attention to ourselves, save the kind we *want.*"

There was silence. "He's right, Hank. We're down to the last two. What happens when they're, when...well, when they've been *used*? You found a tree that grows 'em up there in the hills?"

"You took him down to the quarry, Horace! The damned *quarry*!" Deal shouted. "What in hell were you *thinkin*'?"

"*You* think for a minute, Hank," said Taylor. "We do right by Harlow, he goes out into the world talkin' about the fine people of New Hope, Alabama, and what a pretty little town they got, and why, it'd be a fine place to raise a family. Why, these days most folks're like to up and move here, put down roots, settle in just on the hearsay. And what've most of them got that we ain't?"

"It's a hell of a longshot. I still don't like it," Deal muttered.

"You ain't *got* to like it. You just got to *do* it. We done took a vote. You know what'll happen if…if *He* don't get what he wants. I don't think anyone here wants *that*, am I right?"

"But Horace," Deal all but shouted, "you didn't see him this afternoon out front! He was snoopin' around under the porch! He knows somethin', I tell you! Maybe not everything, but his ears're pricked!"

"Hank, you know as well as I do them kids is locked in the storeroom." Amos heard the clacking sound of a padlock rattling on the door frame. "See there? Locked up tighter'n Dick's hatband. Grady Tucker's got the only key. There just ain't no way they getting' out 'til we *let* 'em out. Hell, maybe the old coot *did* drop his knife."

"Wasn't no knife," Deal muttered.

"You see them young'uns?"

Deal hesitated. "No."

"Well, that settles it," Taylor said. "Ritual's tomorrow night. That boy'll be gone long before then, I'd wager."

"What if he isn't?" asked Moultrie.

That gave Taylor some pause. "Well," he said, "if he ain't, then I reckon Hank'll get his way."

"Shoulda been that way from the jump," Deal harrumphed, but said no more.

Amos held his breath as the footsteps and voices moved away. He heard the door open again and the bell chime, and the men clattered down the steps into the street. When he was sure they'd gone, he let out his breath and tried to assemble all he'd heard in his mind.

There was some kind of ritual; it involved the children that were most likely right above his head. They wanted him to leave and spread the world about their little slice of heaven so folks'd bring *more* children because they was running out. He had to do something.

Amos peered out from under the store and checked the eastern sky. It was still dark, but he figured he had at least an hour or more to work. He pressed his hands against the door above him.

The door gave about half an inch, and then refused to budge. He quickly checked the street, looking for any approaching legs. Finding none, he gently knocked on the door.

Nothing. He tried again, a little louder.

Scuffling of feet, then harsh whispers, arguing. Then, a latch slammed back and the door creaked open. Amos struck another match and held it aloft.

Two faces loomed at him out of the dark. The boy he'd seen earlier that day, and a girl, her long hair framing a thin face. She was obviously scared, but holding her fear barely in check, probably for the boy's sake.

"Hello," Amos said. "Don't be scared, now. I ain't gonna hurt you."

The girl looked at him with piercing brown eyes. "You with them others?" she asked.

"If I was, reckon I'd be comin' in through the front door," Amos replied.

The girl stared at him for moment. "Guess you would," she said. "But you can't help us. Nobody can."

"Let me in, maybe we can see about that," Amos said.

"It's all right, Anna!" the boy said excitedly. "That's the man that gave me the apple!"

She studied him a moment longer. "I guess it's okay," she said. "We ain't ate near on three days."

Amos clambered up into the door and lifted himself in. The boy gently closed it behind him.

He stood, knees popping, and found himself in the storeroom of the general store, just like Taylor said. Nailed barrels of grain, crates of hardware, and other sundries filled the room. It was small and cramped for what it was, and Amos figured most of the owner's goods were in the store proper. But it was just right for a jail cell for two kids. At the back of the store, no one would hear them yell for help, and the ones who did knew what they were here for.

"My name's Amos. What's yours?"

"I'm Anna McGee, and this is Bailey. Don't know his last name. He don't either."

"I thought you all were brother and sister," Amos said.

"No. My brothers is all dead. They killed 'em when we passed through here a month ago. Bailey was already here. Killed his folks, too."

"My Lord," Amos said. "They killed your *parents*?"

"Took us in the night, they did. My family was farmers in Oklahoma. We were headed for Georgia. My daddy was gonna get work in the onion fields in Valdosta. The mayor put us up for the night in his own house, fed us real good. Then they come in the middle of the night. Killed my parents and my older brothers, and brought me here."

"What in the hell for?" Amos asked.

Anna shrugged in the shadows. Amos wasn't sure, but he could hear her voice tighten, and he knew her eyes must be filling up.

"And nobody in town said nothin'? *Did* nothin'?"

"They knew," she said bitterly. "They *all* knew, everybody in town, especially the man who runs this place. We ain't the first. There was other kids here before, ain't that right Bailey?"

"Sure was," the boy said. "There was three others here when they got me, but they wasn't here long."

"They usually bring us food," Anna said, "but they haven't in a couple of days."

"Probably on account of me," Amos said, thinking of the enormous feast the day before, and feeling guilty about how he'd gorged himself while these two sat here in the dark, hungry and scared.

"But why? Why would they do such a thing?" Amos said, mostly to himself.

"We heard they take them out to the quarry," Bailey whispered.

"The quarry? What for?"

"Don't know," said Anna, "but there was this one girl in here before—Maggie was her name. She never said more than two words when she said *anything*. Then one night, after they came for another child, a little boy, she just started talking, but she wasn't making sense."

"Like how?" Amos asked.

"She... she just kept mumbling about how all her friends were waiting for her at the quarry…with *Him*."

"Him *who*?"

"I'm not sure," Anna said. "She was scared out of her head, just kept rocking back and forth, holding her knees, and repeating it over and over."

"Repeatin' *what*?" Amos asked, frantic.

"'Him Below, Him Below, Him Below', just like that, over and over again. Said her friends were there and she was going to see them all. Said we'd be there before long, too, and we could all play down there at the quarry." Her voice broke and rose into a whine.

She was a strong little girl to hold together for so long, Amos thought, but he heard Bailey slide across the floor to sit by her. He heard clothes rustle and knew the boy must be holding her. They were all each other had left.

"Not if I can help it," Amos said. He scooted across the floor until he felt them near. He put his hands on their shoulders and spoke gently.

"I'm gonna leave for a bit," he said. He felt them tense up at that. "But I'll be back, I promise. I'm gonna get my things and we be gone before first light, okay?" The children said nothing but Anna whimpered softly.

"We gonna get you all someplace safe. Nothin's gonna happen to you, you hear?"

"O-okay," Anna said.

"They know about the trap door?" Amos asked.

"They think it's nailed shut," Bailey said.

"How'd y'all get it open, then?"

"*We* didn't" said Anna through sniffles. "Somebody did before us. We got the last two nails out. But those others…"

Amos scratched his last match on the box. The flame lit the room and the kids, hid their eyes. He held the match over the trapdoor.

Frantic scratches and dried blood from untold numbers of fingernails covered the door. Amos shivered. *Lord God*, he thought.

"Y'all just sit tight. I'll knock again, like I done before, all right?" Amos hesitated a moment, then gathered the children in his arms and hugged them tightly. "It's gonna be all right, now, I promise." They hugged him back and after a minute, he let them go.

He stood and popped the latch on he trapdoor and opened it, and let himself down under the store. The door closed behind him and he heard the latch catch.

Amos retraced his path through the dirt and came out behind the store.

Something heavy came down swift and hard on the back of his skull. Amos knelt, surprised more than dazed from the blow, and looked up, his vision reeling.

A lantern blazed to life, casting the shadows to the edge of the yard and blinding him. He held up a hand to shield his eyes and saw a shadowed form towering over him, a shovel in its right hand.

"Find your knife?" Hank Deal sneered.

The shovel descended again, and Amos's world went dark.

* * * *

"What the hell are we gonna do *now*, Horace?"

Amos heard the words as if they passed through cotton in his ears. His mind rose and fell like a boat in a storm-tossed sea. He only heard some of the conversation, but enough to know that he was in it deep.

"We cain't leave him here and we cain't let him go, neither." The voice was Sheriff McCoy, and he was nervous.

"Tell you what we oughtta do," said Deal, unmistakable in his deep baritone. "What we shoulda done at the start. Lemme and the boys take him up in the hills and bleed him, leave for the cougars."

"We ain't doin' nothin' 'til *I* say we're doin' somethin'," said Mayor Taylor.

Amos dared open his eyes into thin slits. The four elders of the town stood over him, obviously panicked. Moultrie, silent as ever, was peering down at him. Sheriff McCoy was wringing his hands. Amos shut his eyes again before someone noticed he was awake.

"Well, Mr. Mayor, I'd say waitin' on you to do somethin' is what got us into this mess. Time for waitin' is over."

A few grunts of assent followed this, and the heat in the room rose a few degrees.

"Ain't but a couple hours left, now. It's high time we took care of this jig and got on with business," said Deal.

"Hank," said Taylor tiredly, "if we listened to you, the town'd be in worse straits than it is now. We're down to our last two because every time the lumber haul comes in a bit short, you shout about obedience and fealty and what not, and suddenly our kitty is low and we're hijacking folks off the road. We got time is all I'm sayin', time to figure things out."

"You *know* how He is!" shouted Deal. "He's… *hungry* more and more of late. And if you bothered to come from behind that white picket fence more than twice a day, you'd see things is getting' worse. Have you seen the country outside of town? It's fallin' apart! Take a good look at the hydrangeas along Main Street, or the grass outside your own house! One sags and droops and the other has brown patches a mile wide! Look at 'em real good and then tell me we got time, Horace! Then you just tell me we got time!"

Silence met Deal's tirade, a silence that underscored the truth, and they all knew it.

"All right," said Taylor quietly. "Might be we *can* do somethin' after all. Just gimme a minute with him."

A few snorts met this, but Amos heard a door open and footsteps clomping out. The door slammed behind them.

Taylor gave a sigh. "You can open your eyes, now Amos," he said. "I know you heard most of that. Let's us talk. You deserve to know what's about to happen, anyhow."

Amos opened his eyes slowly, letting them adjust to the dim light of a lantern in the dark room. He tried to stand, but he was trussed-up like a Christmas goose.

"Sorry about that," Taylor said. "Couldn't have you runnin' off. You may be the only salvation we got."

Amos gritted his teeth and spat at Taylor's feet. "I'd say you's *all* damned, no matter what happen to me." He looked around the storeroom. "Where's the kids?"

Taylor waved an impatient hand. "They're already down at the quarry, but I think you know that by now." He shook his head. "I told Grady Tucker to seal that damn storm door ages ago. Few nails ain't gonna keep nobody out. Well," he waved another hand. "Don't matter now, anyhow."

Amos stared at the Mayor. "There's somethin' in that pit, ain't it?"

"Oh, yeah," said Taylor, removing his hat and wiping his brow with his handkerchief. "It's somethin', all right. Somethin' none of us counted on, that's for sure." He bent his head and Amos waited for him to continue.

"See, Amos, our picture-perfect little community ain't all it looks."

Amos grunted. "You don't say."

Taylor gave a bleak little laugh, then his face grew hard and tight.

"You see, we come to south Alabama at a time that makes the Dust Bowl look like the land of milk and honey. There were about two-hundred of us, then. Some died on the trip south, some got took by the Injuns, others caught the sickness and wasted away soon after we decided to settle here in the valley.

"Well, the town elders decided we needed a trade, somethin' that would put us on the map and bring in money, maybe attract a doctor and a business or two. We seen how much granite was in these hills and decided we could make a go of it.

"So we dug that thrice-damned hole in the earth. At first, things looked pretty good—hopeful, in fact. More folks moved in, set up home and shop, and our little town was thriving. Then one day word come down from the quarry that we'd hit rock-bottom in more ways than one.

"The quarry run dry, nothin' left but solid rock, limestone, maybe some shale. Folks started getting antsy, thought about pullin' up stakes and heading west. We could see our town dying right before us.

"Then one night, the nightmares started. People wakin' up in their beds, screaming like banshees all over town. No one knew what to make of it, but folks was plenty scared, I can tell you that for free. Then the dreams stopped, and it was quiet for a time, and we found out why.

"One morning, everybody, and I do mean *everybody* in town, woke from a peaceful sleep to find themselves standing on the lip of that quarry. Every single soul in town—man, woman and child—right out there in the early morning in their skivvies. Not a one could remember how they'd come to sleepwalk a mile out of town. All anyone remembered was a voice, no more'n' a whisper, tellin' em to come, come, come. An' like moths to a flame, they came, myself included.

"Lemme guess," Amos smirked. "The devil made y'all do it."

Taylor shook his head. "Not the devil. But, Lord God Almighty, in my deepest soul how I wished it *had* been.

"We dug too deep, Amos. We woke somethin' up down there, somethin' that's been sleepin' for God knows how long, just waitin' for the right ones to come along. Hell, there's some that allow—Rollo

Moultrie, chiefly—that it sent us the very *idea* to start diggin' for granite. Maybe it was down there for a reason, Amos, like it was, I don't know, caged up under all that rock on purpose. After a while, I come to believe that very thing. And we went and set the damned thing free."

"Why didn't you all up and leave when you found out? Seems to me like folks what's scared, first thing they do is run."

"You would think so," nodded Taylor, "and many tried that very thing. Soon as they got to the lip of the valley, though, they found themselves right back in the middle of town. See, whatever's down in that quarry made us all a promise. It told us all in dreams that it would see to it that we all would live forever in splendor, in plenty, and all we had to do was keep our end of the deal."

"The children," Amos breathed. "It wanted your children."

Taylor nodded. "Much to our eternal shame, we committed the worst of all sins. We give up our young so's we could have a life at all. Amos, it—*He* –wouldn't have let us go! It was either do what He said and live in perfection, or die, the lot of us. Ain't much of a choice in that, is there? Surely you can see that?"

"You right," said Amos. "Ain't no choice at all. I'd eat my own *gun* 'fore I let my soul be stained like you done. They was your own *children*, man! And then you go and steal somebody else's and offer *them* up to save your own sorry ass!

"No, there's *always* a choice, so don't go givin' me that line of bullshit. You all *liked* the easy life, or we wouldn't even be *havin'* this conversation."

"Damn right we did!" shouted Taylor, getting down in Amos's face. "You ain't got no right to be judgin' us, you gutter-trash! You got no *idea* the hell we went through to get here—the hardship, the plague, the suicides and starvation! You ain't nothin' but a loafer and rounder what picks a guitar for food and spare change!"

"Maybe," Amos grinned fiercely, "but ain't nobody got a mortgage on my soul. It's mine, free and clear. How 'bout *you*, 'Mayor'?"

Taylor struck Amos a hard backhand across the teeth. Amos rolled with the blow and smiled up at Taylor through bloody lips.

"That's what I thought," he said.

"You filthy beggar," Taylor hissed. "I was nice to you, brought you into our town, showed you respect and kindness when no one would. And here you sit, big as Billy-be-frigged, scornin' what you don't understand!"

"I understand an evil *sumbitch* when I see one," Amos said evenly. "And I understand when you fresh outta kids to feed that thing out yonder, your asses gonna be in a sling, ain't that right?"

Taylor eyed Amos, standing up. "I reckon you're right, Amos. I thought to bring you into our little haven, here. Then I thought maybe we could get more folks to come here if'n I let you go to spread the word. All that's long gone now, but I'm thinkin' maybe we can stretch what we got just bit longer. McCOY!"

The sound of hurried work-boots thudded down the hallway. The door burst open and McCoy stood in the doorway, an enormous .44 revolver in his hand. The barrel wavered in his quivering grip. The sheriff's whole body shook in a nervous palsy, teeth clacking in his mouth.

No wonder he don't carry a piece, Amos thought. *I wouldn't let him hold a sack of bread.*

"Buck, put that damn thing away before you shoot your foot off," Taylor growled.

McCoy holstered the pistol in a leather waist rig on the third try. "Damn, Horace! You scared the shit outta me! What the hell's—"

"Where're the others?" Taylor interrupted.

"Up to the quarry, getting' things ready, like you said."

"Been a change of plans, Buck," said Taylor. "Tell the boys to hold off on them young'uns."

McCoy looked aghast. "What in hell are you *talkin'* about, Horace? We ain't got time for anymore dallying. It's almost time—"

"It's okay, Buck," said Taylor, smiling through shark's teeth. "Mr. Harlow here just give me an idea. Might be we can buy us some time, after all."

"I don't get it, Horace. What—"

"As usual, Buck," said Taylor. "And you ain't *got* to get it. Just fetch the horses and help Mr. Harlow into the saddle."

Both Amos and Sheriff McCoy looked at the mayor in surprise.

"I think it's high-time Amos here got to meet the *real* town father, don't you?"

Realization slowly dawned on McCoy, and a maniacal grin spread across his face.

"You bet, Horace. You bet."

McCoy jerked Amos to his feet, cut his foot bonds, and led him out the door at gunpoint. Amos shot an angry glance over his shoulder. "You comin', or you just gonna sit back while your bootlickers do the deed *for* you?"

"Oh, don't worry about me, Amos. I'll be along directly. Got to prepare. You see, Him Below, why he likes us to do things proper. Don't you fret none. You're gonna help out a lot o' folks, Amos. You're doin' us a good turn, and we thank you."

"Go to hell," Amos spat and was dragged away though the general store.

Taylor heard the bell ring as they exited.

I'm hopin' it won't come to that, he thought.

* * * *

It was a dark congregation there in the moonlight. They all stood expectantly, reverently, holding torches and lanterns as Amos was paraded on horseback through their number. Every man and woman in town stood smiling, some of them crying, as if he were about to be baptized into their flock. He felt hands brush his thighs and pats of genuine gratitude on his back as he passed.

My God, he thought. *My God, this is it, ain't it?*

There was no hope of escape, he knew. The people of New Hope were too far gone. There would be no voice of reason, no outrage at the proceedings. They had bought in whole-hog; they really believed. Their faces told the tale. They were happy for him, grateful that he would be the reason they lived to enjoy another season in the sun.

He hated them all, and found no guilt in the hating. To hate evil, well, wasn't that the highest form of piety?

No, Amos's worry was for that of the children with tear-streaked faces, who stood at the edge of the quarry, tied back to back, between Hank Deal and Rollo Moultrie. Both men held cut-down shotguns. Deal mockingly tipped his hat and smiled as Amos passed. Bailey and Anna, who had tried to be strong, who had held out hope that a broke-down old hobo would be their deliverer. He had never felt lower in his life.

McCoy stopped the horse at the water's edge, grabbed Amos by the belt and dragged him down the stone promontory until they stood nearly at its terminus. Amos peered through the dark from the middle of the lake. The faces of the faithful blurred together as they looked on with feverish expectation.

"Careful, there, Sheriff," called Hank Deal. "Don't wanna bruise the goods. Him Below likes 'em fresh, unblemished. You know that."

McCoy jerked Amos to his feet by the collar and pulled him close. "Looks like you gonna be hangin' around here after all, mud-duck. You'll like it down there. Nice and quiet, so I hear."

"Bring the sacrifice forth," called a forceful voice. "Let it be received with all due respect and submission!"

Amos looked out to the end of the promontory. Horace Taylor stood out starkly against the shadowed mounds of heaped shale dressed in a white baptismal robe, its hem hovering just above his feet.

"That's why ol' Horace gets to do the honors. Ain't none of us got the vocabulary for the job," McCoy chuckled. "Off you go, now, boy." He shoved Amos forward, who stumbled and fell, cutting his knees on the jagged granite shelf. He stood, and McCoy prodded him with his revolver. Amos complied and turned toward Taylor.

The water came right up to the promontory, lapping over the edge and soaking his feet. It was cold -- *damned* cold. Colder than it should have been in the middle of summer. The feeling he'd had the night before out here, that sinuous, snaking sensation of dread was overpowering, and he felt himself turning away. McCoy thumbed the hammer on his .44 and motioned with the barrel.

"Go on, now," he said, shaking. "I'm a-warnin' you. Take another step this way and I'll blow you to hell."

Amos laughed as he watched the .44's barrel trace wide circles in the air. "You couldn't hit water if you fell out of a damn boat."

"G-good enough to plug you, anyhow. An' I got six tries. Now how you wanna play it? One step." For a coward, Buck McCoy knew how to talk shit.

Amos thought about doing just that. Just one step and this would all be over. Then he spied Bailey and Anna up on the shore, and something that Deal just said hit him.

Him Below, he likes 'em fresh, unblemished.

"Buck, goddammit, you pull that trigger and you'll be down here in his place!" Taylor shouted. McCoy lowered the pistol and glowered at Amos. "Don't matter none, anyhow," he said. "You'll be gettin' a bunch worse, directly." He sneered and stalked off to the shore.

"Amos, come on down here," Taylor said. "Ain't no use in fightin' it, now."

Amos glanced up at the children. He made up his mind. It was a calculated risk, but one he couldn't afford not to take. He walked straight to the end of the promontory and stood face to face with Taylor.

"Guess not,' he told Taylor.

Taylor smiled sadly. "Sorry it has to be this way, Amos, I truly am. But we have to have a sacrifice. Him Below demands it."

"Tell me somethin'," Amos said. "You ever look all them children in the face an' tell 'em that? Did you talk smooth to 'em while they was screamin' and cryin' for they mamas and askin' they daddies why they weren't helpin' 'em? Why they sendin' they own blood to be et up by some filthy-ass thing in a dried-up mineshaft? Tell me, you ever do that? TELL ME!"

Taylor smiled again. "Your scorn falls on deaf ears, Amos. It's almost time for Him to come and speak to us, to take what's rightfully His."

"You tellin' me we couldn't just all walk away, that what you sayin'? You sayin' we all prisoners?"

"It's too late for that, Amos. We'd all be dead before the thought entered our minds. Don't you think we haven't tried that? After fifty years, don't you think we haven't even entertained the notion? This is all we have left, and nobody's takin' that away from us, hear? NOBODY!"

"Then you really *are* damned," Amos said.

"Maybe," said Taylor. "but we'll ride first-class into Hell. Now turn your ass around."

Taylor took Amos by the shoulder and spun him around to face the crowd. Amos glimpsed the children, huddling against each other and crying out loud. The crowd murmured in hushed voices and the mayor of New Hope raised his voice to address them:

"BY THE MERCY OF HIM BELOW, OUR BENEFACTOR THROUGH THE LONG YEARS OF HARDSHIP AND WANT, WE BRING A GIFT TO RETURN TO HIS BOSOM!"

The crowd responded with a shout and raised hands.

"ALL PRAISE TO HIM BELOW!"

"THIS MAN, THIS INTERLOPER, SPURNED OUR OFFER OF FRIENDSHIP AND BROTHERHOOD AND BELONGING! HE WOULD TAKE AWAY WHAT IS RIGHTFULLY OUR MASTER'S AND BRING LOW OUR PARADISE AND WAY OF LIFE!"

Again, the crowd yelled, but this time in anger and resentment. Fists were clenched, and some threw chunks of granite into the water, falling short of Amos, but dousing him with splashes of the icy water.

"FRIENDS, FRIENDS! STOP! DO NOT MOCK THIS MAN! RATHER ACCEPT HIM FOR WHAT HE IS -- ANOTHER YEAR, ANOTHER SEASON, ANOTHER BREATH OF LIFE!

The crowd murmured amongst themselves, returning to their previous state of thankfulness. He was their meal-ticket, after all. Rocks fell from open hands all along the shore.

"NOW, MY FRIENDS, LET US GIVE PRAISE IN SONG TO HIM BELOW! LET US SING WITH JOY AND THANKS FOR THE GRACE HE HAS SHOWN US, LO THESE LONG YEARS!

The crowd began to sing, low at first, then rising in pitch. The words were gibberish to Amos, and his heart was chilled to its core as he realized that it wasn't gibberish, but a language—some forgotten tongue, its syllables blasphemous, profaning the souls of those who sang and the minds of those who heard. It was a tongue not meant for humans, but for perverse things that bore no resemblance to anything *remotely* human. Their hard, consonant jangle rose to the stars and the black spaces in between.

The depraved hymn went on and on, and Amos thought he would go mad. It rattled his nerves and gripped his soul so that he cried out. He fell to his knees, head thrashing, trying to shake the perverse music from his mind, and his breath caught in his throat.

Deep below, from unplumbed fathoms, a greasy green light opened in a perfect oval and began rising to the surface.

The ghostly light grew from the size of a quarter to the size of a manhole cover in seconds. It moved at astonishing speed, and Amos could see the water swell and flutter as it rose.

As the light grew ever closer, Amos could see a dark line through its center that grew with the light—larger, wider, almost filling the lake's width. The light slowed and came to a stop twenty feet from the surface.

Then it blinked.

Amos felt his blood congeal.

Dear Lord, he thought. *It's…it's an eye. An* EYE!

"COME! COME, LORD, AND TAKE WHAT IS OFFERED AND BLESS US WITH THE TAKING!" Taylor's arms were outstretched in supplication and ecstasy.

Amos stared in mute horror at the giant eye hovering just beneath the surface of the black water. His mind could not wrap itself around the reality of what it witnessed and was threatening to collapse into fragments of broken sanity.

The crowd was in rapture, wailing like mad men and tearing at clothes—their own and each others'. Their voices were frenzied howls to their dark god, and beneath Amos could hear Bailey and Anna screaming in terror. He added his own voice to the mix as something thick, rubbery, and horribly flexible snaked around his legs and pulled.

At once he was under the water, with barely enough time to take a breath. He was pulled down, down into the murky lake, water rushing into his ears. Down he went, toward that great green eye, until at last he stopped, floating in the dark water, his arms akimbo.

Gathering the courage to look, he opened his eyes. The water blurred his vision, and for that, he was eternally thankful.

He hung above the eye, colossal now, its light driving away the shadows of the deep. In the green glow, he saw what looked like an impossibly large beaked mouth snapping hungrily at his feet, and a tongue with a thousand puckering mouths slid up his thighs and around his body.

He was frantic now, his lungs burning. He struggled to kick upward and rise to the surface, but the long tentacles held him fast, the sickening tongue exploring his body, questing, feeling out its meal.

Just when he could stand it no longer and was about to give in, the tongue paused. It investigated on his face, the tiny mouths making popping sounds that echoed underwater. It felt his beard, his hair... his wrinkled skin.

The next thing Amos knew, he was flying through the air, hurled from the lake like a child's toy to land in a heap on the rocky shore.

For a moment, everything was still. The unholy crowd had stopped debasing itself and was staring out at the water in shock.

Horace Taylor stood in bleak amazement as the water around him roiled and bubbled and frothed.

Fresh. Whole. Unblemished.

The beast was angry. The beast was offended. The offering was unacceptable and now the covenant was broken, the deal off.

An ear-shattering screech rose from the depths. Tentacles, impossibly gargantuan, thrashed from the lake. The green eye blazed with indignation. The water in the lake boiled to a froth as Him Below, at long last, rose to greet his worshippers face to face.

Shrieks erupted from the crowd as a sickly green, crackling energy arced out over the water and consumed them where they stood, burning human flesh to ashes in an instant. Some of the townsfolk tried to run, only to be snatched by the beast's tentacles into the water and fed into its gullet, its monstrous beak working overtime.

"MY LORD, MY LORD!" cried Horace Taylor, his white gown stained red from the blood of his friends and neighbors. "WHAT HAVE WE DONE? HOW CAN WE STAY YOUR WRATH? FORGIVE US, O LORD! FORGIVE—!"

Taylor's pathetic pleas were cut off as two massive, mottled tentacles snaked around his mid-section and constricted, ripping the mayor in half and tossing the separate pieces into the far reaches of the lake.

Hank Deal stood in shock, then somehow found his wits and began firing buckshot into the creature, the children forgotten. He emptied the shotgun and reloaded, firing as he backed away up the quarry trail. He might as well have been throwing spitballs. The green energy shot out from the great eye and lanced up his leg, knocking him to the ground. He watched in horror as the lightning ate his leg, disintegrating it from the foot up. He screamed in agony, frantically clawing at the ground, trying to escape.

Amos shook his head and slapped himself hard in the jaw. His mind cleared momentarily, and he saw his chance in the confusion. He limped his way along the promontory toward the shore, careful not to look back over his shoulder, no matter how much his mind screamed at him to do so. He reached the children, breathing hard, and set about untying their bonds. Anna grabbed him around the neck as soon as she was free, sobbing into his wet shirt.

"All right, now," Amos said, patting her back. "All right. We gettin' outta here, like I said." He eased her down as the chaos raged around them. A severed head smacked the ground nearby just as Amos freed Bailey.

"Don't look," Amos said, clutching their heads to his chest. "Don't look."

But ignoring his own advice, Amos looked, and later wished he hadn't.

The entire population of New Hope, Alabama was being consumed in a hail of pent-up fury, as the town father chastised his children for their disobedience.

The eldritch green fire leapt from the gravel pit and arced out into the night sky like malevolent bottle-rockets. Above the treeline, Amos could see the glow and hear the roar of flames as the town itself was consumed in the old god's wrath.

"Can…can we go, now?" Bailey asked weakly.

Amos shook off his fugue. "Damn *right* we can go," he said, hauling the kids to their feet.

A loud roar cut through the din, and Amos stopped cold as buckshot kicked up the dirt by his feet.

"Where you goin', mud-duck?"

Amos turned, Bailey hanging off one shoulder and Anna clinging to his waist.

Hank Deal racked another shell into the chamber, fighting unconsciousness as he steadied the barrel on the stump of his leg. "This is all your fault," he said through clenched teeth. "I t-told Horace it was a mistake to k-keep you around. You g-gonna pay now."

The children clutched Amos tighter. Amos closed his eyes, waiting for the shot.

The shotgun roared and Amos flinched. A bloodcurdling scream tore from Deal's throat. Amos opened his eyes in time to see Deal flailing from the grasp of a tentacle, high above the water. The shotgun went off one final, futile time, and the beast flung Hank Deal into the air and caught him in its beak. The sound of crunching bones was all it took to get Amos moving.

"Let's go, let's go!" he shouted, and he slung Bailey over his shoulder like a sack of grain, grabbed Anna's hand, and the three of them ran without looking back, leaving the thing in the quarry to its revenge.

Behind them, the quarry shuddered as the beast's massive form thrashed and contorted in rage. Huge slabs of granite, broken off from the quarry walls by flailing tentacles, plunged like falling asteroids into the lake. Him Below shrieked in an unholy fury, bringing down his prison upon himself once more, and entombing himself in an uncaring earth to await the next hand of greed that would release him.

* * * *

Later, the three of them stood on the hillside outside of town, right where Amos had come in just days before the nightmare had started.

Surprise, surprise. The black dog was sitting by the roadside, licking its balls in a most uncouth fashion. For once, Amos was glad no one but him could see the animal.

Anna and Bailey sat arm in arm, watching the fireworks. Green fire licked and crawled all over the ruins of New Hope, the heat washing over them even from afar. A green haze painted the night sky in a flickering, soft glow.

Ten minutes earlier, they would have been caught in that conflagration. They'd paused long enough for Amos to grab his guitar from the Taylor's house. Even so, Amos had managed to get his eyebrows singed and half the hair on his head burned away. Now they watched as the Taylor house and every other building in town were consumed in the green fire, reduced to ashes in minutes. Yet the fire still burned.

"Salt the earth," Amos muttered, watching the town burn.

"What's that, Mr. Amos?" Anna asked. She was stroking Bailey's hair as he slept on her shoulder.

"Hmm? Oh, nothin', child. Just an old man thinkin' out loud."

"Why didn't that…that thing, well, *eat* you?" Anna asked.

"I expect 'cause I wasn't no young'un, like you all and them others," Amos said. "See, somethin' that's pure out and out evil got to have somethin' that's pure good. It craves it, hungers for it."

She thought about that for a minute. "But then, wouldn't it make sense for somethin' evil to want somethin' else evil, too?"

Amos shrugged. "A body'd think so, but I reckon it has to do with jealousy. It wants somethin' that it ain't got, somethin' it won't *never* have. And when it has that good thing, it destroys it, 'cause it reminds the evil thing of what it won't never be."

Anna chewed her lower lip, looking at Bailey's sleeping form, then back out to the emerald fires, which were beginning to die out in places.

"What's going to happen to us?" she asked.

"Well," Amos said. "Been thinkin' on that. Reckon we'll camp here tonight, wait for dawn, then move on. I know a fella up in Tupelo, a lawman. He walks around wit' a stick up his ass, but he a good man. Believe I'll take y'all to him, see if he cain't find relatives that'll take you in, or failin' that, a good home for both of you."

Anna nodded. "I want us to stay together, though. We gotta stay together."

Amos smiled and brushed the tears away that spilled down her cheek. "You will," he said. "Now get some sleep."

She turned over and rested her head on Amos's knee, curled up next to Bailey and was asleep almost instantly. It was a testament to the resilience of youth, Amos thought, to face something that would make most adults claw their eyeballs out and still be able to sleep rock solid. He smiled at the pair and turned, frowning, back to the north, toward the quarry.

In the days and weeks to follow, in the dim, twilit world just before sleep, Amos would see a great, black chasm yawn before his mind's eye.

As he drifted off to sleep, he would hear an insistent *THUMP, THUMP, THUMP,* as if a great heart beat beneath the bedrock, or an immense hand was knocking, knocking, knocking at the door of the world, waiting to be let in.

He would see the green, phantasmal outline of a cyclopean eye wink open in the void and burn with an unfettered hatred.

But nightmares he could handle; he had those to spare. The thing that kept him awake through the long nights, the thing that made him bolt upright in bed, drenched in a cold sweat, was the persistent thought that if Him Below was still down there, waiting to be unleashed on an unsuspecting world—how many *others* like it were there?

The next good sleep Amos Harlow knew was in death.

MY BABY DONE GONE

A Song of the Black Dog

And do not fear those who kill the body but cannot kill the soul. Rather fear him who can destroy both soul and body in hell.

—Matthew 10:28

Terrebonne Parish was more somber than Amos Harlow remembered. The sky draped the earth like cheap gray curtains, coloring the world underneath like a poor man's funeral. Time was the cane fields would be humming with the sound of cicadas in the noon heat, the steady rhythm of honest toil, neighborly conversation and laughter, and the uneven but earnest harmony of hymns to pass the time.

Now, a lonely silence greeted him, and the ghosts of better days lingered on the edge of the Bayou Blue road. Passing through Bourg, he'd encountered the same. He'd felt the suspicious stares as he'd passed, and from the corners of his eyes caught the flurry of curtains quickly drawn. He wondered at his own surprise; the Dust Bowl had affected everyone in strange ways. Even a solitary traveler was suspect in these hard times.

Misty rain began to blow from the southwest in small gusts and the smell of deer-tongue and wild onions rose to meet him on the breeze. He tried to focus on his visit to the Hollis family, the one thing that could downright crush the melancholy that had begun to blossom in his soul.

For a man set on a path of wandering through the world, with nothing but the clothes on his back and an old guitar, real friends were a rare thing—friends closer than family were rarer still. He passed under enormous primeval oaks with elephantine branches that teased the ground. Spanish moss hung from them like wizened beards on ancient faces. He paused and sat on one of the low branches, and the past washed over him like a warm summer rain. He took a pull from his hip flask to help the memory along.

Amos and Luther Hollis had met back during the Great War. They were part of an outfit called the "Harlem Hellfighters," an all-black infantry unit. Support, they were called, but in layman's terms that meant "cannon fodder." Positioned at the front lines more often than not, it came as no surprise when German artillery drew a bead on their trench and wiped out all but Amos and Luther and a few others. Amos left Europe with a crescent scar above his left eye and a milky-white cataract; Luther made it back to Bayou Blue with shrapnel in his knee and a leg bone that had never healed right. Amos recalled him in later years limping and wincing with every step. Whenever Bess asked about those days, Luther would only shake his head. "Just a lot of dyin' and cryin', baby" he'd say. They had all seen a fair piece of hell on that French dirt, and no mistake.

Luther had made Amos promise to come and visit, and Amos had been as good as his word. The Hollis family had taken him in even when his own family had cast him out. They were the nearest thing to real family that Amos was ever like to have again in this life.

Amos smiled at the thought and his pace quickened a little. Surely the Cajun spirit wasn't gone from this place. In a few miles, maybe, he'd hear the clear, tinny whine of the squeezebox, whipping the locals into a dancing frenzy from the back porch of Boudreaux's grocery. The smell of boiling crawfish and boudin from a dozen backyards would set his mouth to watering. A few miles more and he'd be at the front stoop of the Hollis place, making his manners, drinking whatever they put in his hand, and hefting whichever little ones hopped in his lap.

Later, after a fine meal and fit to bust his britches, Amos would sit on the porch with Luther and roll a smoke, not a word spoken between them, and let the early evening seep into his bones. Around twilight, the children would spill out onto the porch, raucously breaking the silence to beg for a song. He'd play a few favorite tunes for the family, and a few new ones he'd collected since he'd seen them last, with Luther following him chord for chord on harmonica. As the sun slipped down past the cypress trees, there might be a game or two of dominoes with little Cherìe and Tobias or a skip-rope with Bernice and Monique. Amos could still skip a rope a sight better than most young people.

On into the night, the fire low in the hearth, Amos would smoke the day's last cigarette and hold with the children about all that he'd seen and done, being out of doors and seeing everything there was to see over the land. Sometimes, he'd tell haint stories, tales his Uncle Don had told Amos and his siblings to set a fright in a pack of rowdy young'uns on a sticky summer's night—the Wang-Doodler, the wandering corpse of a hanged cook who banged on his pots and pans to scare up fresh grub in the form of young children; the wampus kitty, the swamp cat with teeth like steak knives and the tail of a scorpion that screamed like a woman in the night; and old Timbalier Tommy, him with no head, hands, or feet, who brought the dead back to life to revenge himself on a cruel world.

Amos smiled wider, in spite of the bleak day. Better times had a way of coming around again, just when it seemed like the rain in a man's life would never stop. The Hollis family had the way of hospitality, of making a stranger and a drunkard feel like he was never absent from their table or from their hearts. It was a gift that was sorely lacking in the world, except for parts like south Louisiana, where it was all *anybody* knew to do, because it was all they ever *had* done.

But it wasn't always so; Bess didn't cotton to Amos when she first laid eyes on him. She thought he was shiftless, no-account. She kept her tongue because she knew he and Luther were closer than brothers for what they'd shared in the War. After a spell, she came around to Amos, seeing how he was with the children, and how, over the years, the world just got heavier about his shoulders.

Bess knew there was more to Amos than what most folks saw, knew it in the way he'd disappear with Luther after supper for a quiet word out on the porch, or stroll down to the bayou and sit for hours at a time. Every time Bess asked her man about his and Amos's walking spells and nattering, Luther grew cold in the face and asked what was for supper. Soon, Bess learned not to ask anymore; some things could only between two who had faced death together.

The road curved east and the horizon darkened with the coming of early night and thunderclouds pregnant with rain. Amos searched the dirt road before and behind. Dead cane fields lay to either side of the road, miles of fallow farmland burned off and blackened in hopes that the new planting would bring good harvest. He was alone out on the old dirt road, and it made him skittish where she should have felt relief.

He'd gotten used to the black dog's presence, but had seen neither hide nor hair of it since Mississippi. Normally, he'd chalk it up to nerves or too much booze, but the way his life had been these past few years, the dog's absence was almost as much a mystery as its existence.

The old hound kept its own council and went where it would. Sometimes, Amos would wake from a dead sleep to find the dog lying by the fire, tongue lolling. Other times, it would appear in middle of a deserted highway like a mirage or at the mouth of a boxcar, or at the limit of some nameless, forgotten town, scratching its haunches and waiting for him to catch up.

Whether it was instinct, or a something greater, Amos knew to follow it wherever it led. Oh, there were times Amos refused to follow, especially in the beginning of his years on the road. He would shout or throw rocks at the dog, then turn in the opposite direction. But no matter where he wandered, somehow the dog was always there, ready to turn him back to true north.

Soon after, Amos figured out that he really had no choice in the matter, that he and the old mutt were inextricably bound. He had also figured out that the dog's appearance usually meant trouble—trouble of the kind most folks would disown as drunk-talk—and it was on Amos's head to fix that trouble.

Maybe this time, he thought, *there won't* be *no troubles*.

But Amos knew better. There was much he didn't speak of to his friends, but he didn't *need* to. Luther and Bess Hollis were good Christian folk, but they still held to the old ways. There was a horseshoe above the front door on the inside, its prongs up toward Heaven, and goofer dust in a clay urn by the hearth. Bess had a chair in every corner of each room, so nothing could enter uninvited. Rock salt lined the windowsills, and sometimes the smell of eucalyptus was like to knock a man over backwards.

The Hollis family understood that part of Amos's life—the dark part that carried him into still darker places. They knew there were more things under heaven than most folks believed. Amos always suspected that was one reason they'd caught on so fast as friends. He could speak to them about the dark and they would know it for themselves, and it was a balm to Amos's soul. Or he didn't have to say anything at all, which was even better.

Amos felt a guilty tug at his heart as the neighborhood came into view. He'd not darkened the door of his friends' home in nearly six years, partly because of straightening circumstances and everyday life conspiring against his wishes, but mostly because he'd been elsewhere, learning and doing things that brought him no end of trouble, and he wished to keep that trouble from his friends' doorstep.

Lord, but them children must be growed up like Georgia pines, " he thought, trudging down a side alley. *Hell, Luther and Bess mighta made some* more *by now.*

Amos found his heavy heart pounds lighter for the first time in a long time. Some dogs from a nearby house chased him, playfully nipping at his heels as he fairly ran along the road. Rounding the bend, he stopped and turned around in a circle, listening.

The day's tomb-like silence held. No shouting children, no neighbors calling greetings to one another in the streets, no music or laughter.

All was silent as the grave.

Amos trudged over the clapboard bridge, its railroad struts smelling of creosote, as a good-size 'gator peeped up through the muddy bayou water at his passing. He crossed the street and up to the Hollis's porch to knock. It hit him then that he couldn't recall *ever* knocking on this door; they'd always been out there to meet him.

The knock sounded hollow in the house, and before the third rap fell, the door opened up a crack. A pretty young girl with coffee-cream skin stuck her head out.

"Yessir?" she said in a sweet voice.

"Why, Bernice, is that you?" said Amos. "Girl, you done grown into a young lady since I's around last."

Bernice looked Amos up and down a good minute. "Who're you?" she said finally.

"Who is it, Bernice?" a tired female voice called from inside, getting closer. The door opened all the way. "Who's—oh. Amos. We wasn't expecting no company."

Amos could've fallen down then and there. Bess, even though she'd never cottoned to him, had always treated him with courtesy; the brusque manner she'd greeted him with wasn't in her nature.

Bess had aged, and none too well. Her dark curls were splotched with gray, like dirty blackboard erasers, her eyes puffy around the bottoms. Amos took off his battered porkpie hat and held it to his chest.

Somethin's wrong, Amos thought.

"Bessie," he said. "Good to see you again."

Bess looked him over for a second like her daughter had done, then her eyes darted left and right and she stepped back, holding the door.

"Well," she said," 'spect you better come on inside 'fore the neighbors start waggin' they tongues. And knock off all that mud 'fore you do."

Amos dutifully kicked his heels together, scraped the dirt road off of his old shoes, and entered.

The Hollis place felt different to him as he followed Bess through the living room into the kitchen. Everything was as he remembered it on lonely nights in the middle of nowhere, everything in its place. But whatever made a house a home—that intangible something—was gone. All was stark, bare, and cold. What had once been warm and inviting now seemed only empty courtesy.

"Got some chicory. You want a cup?" she said to Amos, not looking at him.

"That'd be fine, Bess," Amos said.

"Go put the kettle on, Bernice, then run on out and fetch that laundry from the line 'fore it rain, hear? Sit on down, Amos."

Amos sat as he watched the girl set about the stove, stealing glances at him when she thought he wasn't looking. She finished up and went outside to do as her mother bid.

Bess sat across from him at the table, folded her arms, and said, "He's dead, Amos."

"What…who…?" Then it hit him. Amos felt his stomach clench.

"Cancer got 'im 'bout three years back. We tried to get word to you, but…" Amos stared for a full minute, then hid his face in his hands, weeping silently for Luther. Disease had done what the Kaiser could not. 'Oh, Lord, Bessie. I'm sorry. I'm so sorry."

Bess hesitated, then reached out across the table to rest a hand on Amos's arm. "Lord took him quick," she said. "Doctor over in Houma said he ain't suffered none."

"You believe him?"

"No," Bess said, staring blankly.

Amos looked up, tears rolling down his weathered cheeks. "The kids?" he asked.

"Cherie took up with a fella from Shreveport, big lawyer man. Nice enough boy, got his manners about him. He asked her hand from Luther 'fore he passed, and Luther gave it. Monique's up to the college in Baton Rouge, doin' fine but missing home. Bernice's stayin' busy with high school, boyfriends, and whatever mischief she can get up."

Amos finally smiled. "She's a growin' just fine. Lookin' like her mama, too, I see."

Bess gave a smile that withered on the vine. "Not so much lately, I hope," she said, fingering her gray hair. Her face grew tight, her chest hitched in a broken sob, and she grasped both of his hands in hers. "He's gone, Amos. My baby's gone." And she began to cry fit to fill a well.

Amos rose and went to her, held her around the shoulders, rocking her as she wept. "I know, lady. I know. Luther was good man, and we all gonna miss him."

Bess pulled back and looked at him, tears rolling. "I'm talkin' about Toby!" she cried. "Toby's gone, and he ain't comin' back!"

"Gone? Gone where, Bessie?" Amos said, kneeling beside her.

"Just gone! Run off in the night, 'bout t'ree days back! Don't know where! Oh, Amos…!"

Amos grabbed a towel from the sink, wetted it, and wiped her face with it, like a child. "Let's you an' me have a cup and you tell me all about it, hear?"

He poured them both some chicory brew in two chipped, mismatched coffee cups. Bess told him, and Lord, was it a tale.

Toby had been courting Esther Haynes since high school and they were engaged. Luther had been set to cut them a parcel of the family land and help Toby build a house down the bayou a ways. Toby had been working at the grocery after school, saving money to get the house started, when Luther had taken ill. After his daddy died, Toby took over Luther's job down at the docks to feed the family and keep his little sister in school. He and Esther were still to be married, but now they were just going to build on to the family house instead.

"Toby started to get strange 'round that time," Bess recalled. "He started stopping by the gin joint out on St. Charles near every night. Esther would come 'round askin' after him and foot it all over town, huntin' him down.

"He'd come home after midnight smellin' like a still, singin' them old songs you used to sing at the top of his lungs. Then he'd go to his room and pass out 'til mornin', risin' late for work or sometimes not at all. It was like Luther was his hold on things, and once he was gone, Toby just started to come undone."

She took a sip of chicory, and the bitter twinge on her face had nothing to do with the coffee. "One night, we sat up with the coffee made, waitin' on Toby to come strolling in with another song and gin on his breath. We got a knock on the door 'round about midnight. It was Sheriff Broussard, askin' after Toby, and did we know where he was."

"I know the sheriff," Amos said. "Knew his daddy, too. We done had our run-ins, but he's good people."

"Well, he said we was gonna have to find Toby, and right quick. Mr. Boudreaux found Esther lyin' in the alley by the grocery after he locked up for the night. Somebody shot her, Amos. They shot that poor girl and left her lyin' in the street!"

Bess started wailing again like never to stop. Amos held her hands and stroked the hair out of her eyes. When she'd recovered, he urged her on.

"Surely they ain't thinkin' Toby done it?" he said.

"No," she said between hitching sobs. "Sheriff said he didn't think Toby had it in him to do a thing like that, 'specially not to Esther, not when they's 'bout to be married. But…"

"Go on, Bessie. But what?"

"But they said it didn't look too good, what with Toby being gone like he was and not showin' for work a week straight. Said they just wanted to talk, to ask him some questions."

"He quit on his job down to the docks?" Amos asked.

"Talked to Mr. Voclan, Luther's old boss, and Toby's. He said Toby didn't show for work one day, then another, then didn't show at all. Never gave no word of leave or nothin', just stopped showin'. Said he had to give his job to another, times bein' as they is."

"Huh," Amos said, sitting back and mulling it all over. He knew that Toby had hit some hard times, and who hadn't? But he knew how that boy doted on his Esther, and knew that ain't nobody'd kill the one bright spot in their lives, not for any reason.

Bess sat in her chair, coffee gone cold, staring at the cup before her, her chest hitching every now and then.

"Look here," Amos said, patting her hands. "Toby's a good boy. He's just hit a rough patch like everybody else. He ain't no more killed that poor girl than you or I. Tell you what I'm gonna do."

Bess flicked her eyes up at Amos, a sudden flash of hope within them.

"First light I'll head out and look for him. I know these parts better than most. I know all Luther's fishin' holes, all the dog trails, and every cypress tree what's got roots in the swamps. If he's still around, I'll find him. Don't you fret none."

Bess got up and came around the table to take Amos's face in her hands. She leaned down and planted a kiss on his wrinkled forehead, a benediction for an old friend.

"I thank you, Amos," she said, smiling through tears. "I know I wasn't good to you always, but you was Luther's friend, and that was always good enough." She began to sob again.

Amos took her hands and kissed them back, and frowned good-naturedly. "Now don't start up with that ol' female cryin' business again. We sit up at this table any longer, we be bawlin' like two babies with nary a teat to suck on."

Bess laughed at that, a warm sound that reminded them both of better times, of who they'd been not so long ago.

"You can have Toby's room, if you like. I'll have Bernice put some fresh sheets on for you."

"Nah," said Amos, rising with a groan. "I believe I'll bed down on that couch of yours, if it please you. I recall it bein' mighty comfortable, and I reckon it knows the curve of my tired old ass better than I do."

She laughed again, and this time he joined her.

* * * *

Amos woke in the night to a police siren screaming by like a banshee out for lost souls. He sat bolt upright on the couch. The sheer curtains billowed out into the room on the evening breeze.

He scrambled to find his glasses, fumbled them on, then buttoned on his old blue chambray work shirt. He opened the front door, and the smell of Confederate jasmine hit him like a gentle fist. He stepped out onto the porch, then down the steps and onto the lawn, the early morning dew cool under his feet. Amos could see the cruiser's brake lights flare up as it crossed the bridge and then disappear as it turned left at the center of town.

Footsteps clumped down the hardwood floors and Bess came into the living room, her robe pulled tight around her, her face worried.

"What in the Lord's name…?" she said, as two more patrol cars whipped by out on the road, their whining sirens fading into the night.

"Don't know, but it looks like trouble," Amos said, staring out the front door after the fading taillights of the police cars. "They headed towards town from the look."

"You think it's Toby?" asked Bess, hopeful and terrified at the same time.

"One way to find out," said Amos. He pulled on his hat and shoes and slipped out into the warm night. The crickets resumed their chirping chorus in the ensuing silence.

Bess watched him go, pulling her robe and shawl tight around her, shivering, but not from the cold. A bad wind was blowing, and she knew they were all at the center of it. Amos was a friend, had been for a good many years, but that same bad wind seemed to bear him along wherever he went. She knew none of this was his doing, but right then, she wished to God he'd passed up Bayou Blue this time around.

Amos walked into town over the bridge and came upon a sea of red. Three Parish cruisers were parked helter-skelter out front of a large antebellum house, their lights washing over the neighborhood. Townsfolk, eager for gossip, leaned out of doorways and open windows, trying for a look. Some had already gathered at the edges of the street, talking in furtive whispers.

The Greek columns lining the front porch were weather-worn, their white paint flaking. Windows on the upper floors had been boarded up with disuse. A single light burned on the porch, casting those gathered into shadow. The place was run down, but still possessed a nice come-on-in feel. Getting closer, he remembered why. Ten years gone, the place had been a cathouse, and that little red lamp could be seen shining through the front window like the mightiest come-on in the world. He'd spent many an hour in that place himself.

Amos could see some of the sheriff's men milling about in the street, placating the lookie-loos that everything was under control and urging them to go back inside their homes. Others were talking amongst themselves and pitching cigarette butts into the bayou. They saw him coming and all wheeled about at once, their hands going to the big pistols at their hips. Amos was about to call out to them, when a booming voice from the house hailed him.

"My, my, my. Look what the wampus kitty done dragged out the bayou."

A large black man stood framed in the doorway to the house, sporting a uniform that was at least two sizes too small for his frame. The sleeves of the shirt were rolled up, revealing enormous muscles that strained against the fabric. His hands rested on his hips, the right one strayed near the butt of a revolver bigger than a cast-iron stove.

Sheriff Leon Broussard of Terrebone Parish both frowned and looked slightly bemused as Amos trudged up to the white picket fence and stood at the gate.

"Ain't seen you in a coon's age, old man," he said, taking in Amos's disheveled appearance. "Seems to me like some things never change, do they?"

Amos stared back Broussard, not flinching. "Leon," he said. "It *has* been a fair piece, ain't it?" Neither man moved for long seconds.

"Well," said Amos, breaking the staredown. "You gonna come down here and talk to an old man, or we gonna holler at each other 'cross the damn yard?"

The deputies snickered loudly at this, but stopped when Broussard cut them an even glare. He trotted down the porch steps, clearing two at a time, the old boards creaking under his burden. His eyes never left the trio of deputies as he opened the gate and strode up next to Amos.

"You three got nothin' better to do than warm the hood o' that car with yo' asses?" Broussard yelled. "Get inside and help with the body, and see if one of you goldbrickers can remember how to dust for prints. Move it, now!"

The deputies jumped like they'd been sitting on a live wire and made for the house. Broussard watched them all the way inside before turning to Amos, frowning. Amos looked the man up and down, which was quite a task, seeing that Broussard was easily a head and chest taller.

"Little big fo' your Daddy's clothes, ain't you?" Amos said, a smile playing around the corners of his mouth. Broussard looked back hard, trying to hold his frown, then threw his head back and laughed loud and deep, breaking the tension.

"You ol' goat!" he laughed, clapping an arm around Amos, squeezing him tight in a python grip. "How'd you make into town without me smellin' you?"

Amos smiled big and clapped him in return. "Maybe you ought to bathe more, *yeself*."

"Stayin' down to the Hollis place, I reckon?"

"That's a fact. Good to be back, even for short spell. Damn shame about Luther, though."

"It was at that," Broussard agreed. "One of the good ones, he was."

"More than you know, son," Amos said.

"Look here, Amos," Broussard said, guiding Amos down the street, away from the house. "Sorry 'bout that welcome, but I got a reputation as sort of a hardass 'round here, now. Gotta keep it up, you know?"

Amos laughed at that. "Mr. Sheriff of the Bayou if-you-please, is it? Signs and wonders, signs and wonders."

Broussard laughed again, but it died down quickly. "Guess you heard about the ruckus here lately. Bess done got to where she don't sleep so good no more."

Amos nodded. "She's totin' a load of care, seems like. No word on Toby, yet? Where he mighta run to?"

"No," Broussard said, a worry creeping into his eyes and creasing his forehead. He looked like his daddy more than ever right then to Amos. "I know Toby better than most, Amos. I know that boy ain't got the sand to do what's been done, but it looks bad, Amos—real bad. And after *tonight*, well…"

"What's goin' on at Selma's old place?" Amos asked, nodding toward the old house.

Broussard, stopped, looked back over his shoulder, and turned to face Amos. "It's bad, Amos. You remember Viola Martin?"

"Selma's granddaughter, ain't she?"

"*Was*," Broussard nodded. "Daddy run Selma out of town after the townfolk started leanin' on him 'bout what she got up to in there. Everybody knew, just no one ever spoke it. You know how it was." Amos nodded.

"Well, Viola was still in school and didn't wanna go to Jackson with her *grandmère*, so she stayed on. Things was pretty quiet on this end of town for awhile. Daddy looked in on her from time to time 'til he retired and even after, 'til he went to the Lord. Viola finished up school and things was pretty good for a time. But then, well, you know how folks' tongues get to waggin'. Pretty soon, Viola wasn't no better than her *grandmère* in the eyes of folks and I started gettin' visits from wives 'bout lipstick on collars, perfume on shirts, and late workin' hours.

"People started to shun her, Amos. They spit in her path when she walked by in the street, if they paid her mind at all. It was heartbreakin' to see it happen, but I knew there must be somethin' to it. I had a talk with her and she swore it off."

"She and Toby?" said Amos.

Broussard took off his wide brimmed hat and wiped the sweat off his brow, nodding. "I guess Luther dyin' got Toby to thinkin' how he might be stuck here, what with his sisters off at school or moved away. He musta figured he'd never leave the bayou. A man gets that kinda down, ain't no *tellin'* what he'd do, even if he *is* a good boy like Toby."

Amos swore deep and low. "And Esther found out, I reckon."

"Poor girl took it hardest of all," said Broussard. "Parents found her in the bathtub, tub-full of bloody water, and her daddy's straight razor in the soapdish."

"Hold on," Amos said. "Bess said somebody'd done shot her in the street!"

Broussard looked around sharp, his head almost coming off. "Keep it down, for God's sake!" he hissed. He eyed Amos directly.

"That was *after* she'd killed herself in the tub," he whispered. "*Two days* after."

Amos let out a long, low whistle. "I take nobody else knows this here piece of information," he said.

"Nobody but ol' Boudreaux down at the grocery, seein' as how he's the man shot her."

"Hell, you say," Amos breathed.

"Two days before he seen her in the alley by the store, her body disappeared from the funeral parlor across town. After ol' Boudreaux shot her, I took the body back to the funeral home and found Tilly McGee drinkin' himself into a stew, half-crazy with scare and worry, screamin' about how he never lost a body before. We put the body back, but Tilly called two in the mornin' sayin' the body was gone again. Then tonight, we get a call from a neighbor 'bout a ruckus over here at Viola's place, and here we are, and Lord what a mess.

"Had the devil's own time tryin' to keep all this hushed-up, but the Haynes' is askin' questions 'bout their daughter's funeral. Ol' Tilly keeps tellin' em he's got a number to do on her body, so's they can have the open casket, but that line's wearin' thin."

"Uh- *huh*," Amos said, starting to see where the big man was leading.

"So, tonight, when I heard you was in town again— "

"You thought you'd look me up and see if I could see what you ain't—or *caint*." Amos finished for him.

"That's about the it of it, Mr. Harlow."

"*Mr. Harlow*, now, is it? Things *must* be changin' in these here parts, you start callin' on me like a gentleman. You was callin' me by name since you sat at my knee with the Hollis kids, listenin' to all my breeze 'bout haints and spooks and what-not."

Broussard looked strained. "Yessir, that's right. I always figured you knew more about them tales than you let on. Most of us did, though we'd never say it aloud. When I saw you comin' down the road a bit ago, it was like the angels saved me the trouble of callin' on you."

"Don't know about *that*," Amos said, looking unconsciously around for his four-legged friend, who was still nowhere to be seen.

"Will you look into it for me? Will you help me find the boy? I know he's figgered into all this, but I can't see *how*." Broussard stared at Amos, fiddling with his hat.

"I wanna see the girl first," Amos said, motioning to the house with his head.

"Amos, I don't think that's a good idea. She's in a bad way and—"

"Look, boy," Amos said sharp and even. "I been in the worst war this world's ever seen. I seen shit that'd curdle your soul, son. I ain't no stranger to death. You let me in that house. I need to see what I need to see 'cause Lord help me, if I'm right, we got to move *fast*, you hear?"

Broussard eyed Amos for a full minute, then nodded, leading the way back to the house. Amos followed, a sour feeling in the pit of his stomach. If what he thought was true, it might already be too late—too late for Toby, for Esther, for damn near everybody in Terrebonne Parish.

The sheriff knocked once on the door, opened it a crack, and called for his men. Amos could see two of the deputies wrapping a woman's body in a sheet and a third peeling some tape with black smudges off a doorjamb.

"Head on back to the jail, boys," the sheriff said. "Take whatever evidence you got and stick it in the safe. And don't go home just yet; wait for me to get there."

The men looked up from their tasks, wide-eyed, and stared at Amos, then back to Broussard. "What?" he said. 'Y'all need a note from y'all's mammas to do like your boss tell you?"

Once again, the men looked whip-smart filing out the door like chastised schoolboys. Broussard rolled his eyes at Amos as they went by, then closed the door. Amos heard their cars start up and pull away a moment later. He didn't look around until the engines had faded into the distance. When he did, his breath caught in his throat.

It was a bloodbath. There was enough red in the room to paint a barn. Broken furniture was scattered about the living room like a roadhouse after hours. What appeared to be claw marks were gouged in the walls and floor, and everywhere, *everywhere*, the color red.

Amos knelt down and gingerly, almost reverently, pulled the sheet back from the body.

Viola Martin lay there, looking the picture of her grandmother, had the old lady been run through a wheat thresher. There were large chunks of flesh dug out of her, more claw marks dug here and there on her body. There were bite marks—*bite marks*—in four different places, one of them had peeled her left cheek to the bone like a grapefruit. Her nightgown was in tatters, and her eyes wide open in shock. A meat cleaver lay near her hand, spattered with blood and bits of flesh, and Amos knew she must've put up one hell of a fight.

Amos looked at the tiny bits of flesh on the wide blade, then carefully leaned down and smelled them, wincing at the smell, understanding dawning in his face.

"Salt," he whispered.

"Salt?" Broussard asked, raising his eyebrows.

"Get me some salt outta the kitchen. Rock salt is best, but table salt'll do, short of that."

Broussard was taken aback. "What the hell you need *salt* for, Amos? C'mon, now. You done seen the body, and I got to—"

"You got to do what I *say*, boy!" Amos exploded. "You want a whole town fulla this shit? You jes' keep what wits you got left and get me some damn salt!"

Broussard felt the words like a hammer between the eyes. Fish-eyed, he walked into the kitchen, rummaged around in the cupboards before finding a bag of rock salt under the kitchen sink. He took a drinking glass, filled it with some of the salt, and walked it back to Amos.

He found the old hobo opening drawers and cabinets, searching for something. Amos pulled back an easy chair and said "Ah!" He came away with a sewing basket and returned to the girl's body. Amos took a length of blue yarn, bit it off, and proceeded to thread it through a big needle taken from a pin cushion in the shape of a tomato.

Amos reached back over his shoulder. Broussard handed him the glass of salt and watched as Amos pried open Viola's mouth and poured its contents down her gullet.

"What the *hell* …?" he began.

"Just stand there and make sure nobody come in," Amos snapped and returned to his grisly work. Broussard looked over his shoulder at the door, wondering what he would say if the deputies walked in on this scene. When he turned back, he started violently.

"Amos, in God's *name*!"

"Lord ain't had nothin' to do with *this*, son," Amos said, threading the girl's lips shut with the needle and yarn. "Now just mind that damned door, hear?"

When he'd finished, he stood, and Broussard could see his handiwork. Viola Martin was a horror, a nightmare rag-doll, bits of rock salt showing white between the bright blue stitches in her lips, her bloodshot eyes wide in death and shock.

Amos gently closed her eyelids, and resting his hand gently on her forehead, he closed his own. "We ain't done yet," he said.

Broussard doffed his hat and wiped his great sweaty brow once again. "My God, Amos. What the hell *else* you gonna to do?"

"*I* ain't doin' jack-shit. *You* are."

"*Me*?" Broussard said. "What—?"

"Pick up that there meat cleaver," Amos said, all business.

Broussard looked aghast. "What do you…? Why should—oh, hell no. No, no *no*, Amos!"

"It's an old charm, a ward against the dead comin' back," Amos explained. "You remember the stories, boy—salt's pure, so it purifies. But you gotta take the head, too, and bury it like past sins."

"Amos," the big man said, quaking. "I ain't never, I mean, I *can't…*!"

"It's gotta be right across the throat," Amos continued, as if not hearing the big man. "And it's gotta have *weight* behind, understand? Case you ain't noticed, you about the biggest mother in the *parish*, let alone this *room*."

"I—oh, *God*, Amos!" Broussard said, staring glassy-eyed at the corpse, knife in hand. "It's…I—I *can't...*"

"It's okay. I understand," Amos said, quietly, soothingly, rising to stand in toe to toe with Broussard, so close that he could smell the chicken stew on his breath and see the gravy stain on the big man's collar. "I understand that the son of Big John Broussard, who was the fear of every dishonest man within a hundred miles, ain't nothin' but a coward wearin' his daddy's badge, 'long with the *rest* of his clothes."

Broussard jerked his head at Amos, away from the body as if he'd been slapped and looked about to hit Amos square in the teeth. Amos was unmoved.

"You go ahead, *coward*," Amos softly growled. "You go on and take your best shot. But I been *shittin'* bigger than you for the last twenty years, and I ain't scared of you *or* your hurt pride."

The sheriff's grip tightened on the cleaver, his dark brown knuckles fading pale.

"That's right, smartass. You go ahead and kill the only sumbitch in the whole *world* that can help you right now. You got any idea what the hell will happen if we don't get that girl's head in the ground? *Do* you?"

Broussard's wide eyes flicked at Viola and her yarn-stitched lips.

"She gonna crawl outta whatever hole she's in two days from now and bite the first poor soul she see! Then *that* one'll get sick, like she is now, and bite someone else, and that'n'll bite another, and another, and so on, 'til you ain't the sheriff of nothin' but one big graveyard!

"But you go on back to your fine office with your certificates and honorariums and what-not and sit there, all safe. Spit-polish that there badge, while you're at it. Make it shine mighty fine, now, got to make yo' daddy proud, yessir!"

Amos's voice rose gradually, and there was murder and disbelief in Broussard's eyes. "Yeah, then you can drive on outta town, knowin' you coulda done somethin' for these folks hereabouts you done swore to protect, knowin' you's nothin' but a *coward* that cain't--"

Broussard gave a shout of anguish and raised the meat cleaver. For a second, Amos thought he was about to die. He stumbled backwards, throwing his hands up in a futile gesture and tripped over the body. He hit the floor, landing in a pool of blood, and looked up just in time to see Broussard sink the cleaver into Viola's neck -- and three inches into the floorboard beneath. The girl's head came away from her shoulders like a ham hock, rolling a few feet away from the stump of her neck, which oozed blood onto the hardwood.

"Well, now," Amos said shakily, slowly getting up. "That'll do all right, I reckon."

Broussard whirled on him with the cleaver.

Amos held up his hands in a placating gesture. "Take it easy, now. Had to be done. She woulda come back and brung the rest of Hell with her." He moved over the easy chair and grabbed a crocheted afghan from its back. He picked up the head with it and twisted the ends, forming a makeshift sack.

"You get on back to the jailhouse and tell them boys of yours whatever you need to tell 'em. Just make sure they don't talk to nobody."

Broussard let the cleaver fall limply to his side, the spit and vinegar sapped out of him at once, replaced by confusion. He hung his head and rubbed it as if trying to purge the memory of the last five minutes.

"Leon," Amos said, putting a gentle hand on his massive shoulder. "There wasn't nothin' else to be done. You made good on that vow to protect. I just need you to hang on a bit more. Let me do the rest, hear?"

Broussard began to weep silently, his big chest hitching at intervals. Amos let him for a minute, then said: "You talk to Tilly over to the funeral home and Boudreaux down to the grocery, make 'em keep they peace 'til I do what I got to do."

The big man looked up, laughing mirthlessly, tears streaking down his face. He wiped them away, still holding the cleaver like a ward against the dark.

"Tilly ain't gonna talk, nohow. Not with that old 'shine still out back o' the funeral parlor. Be a shame if the G-men had to find it; bad for business."

"Well," Amos smiled. "He sounds like an honest man to *me*." They both shared another laugh. "You gonna be all right?" Amos asked when it had died down.

"Someday," Broussard replied. "After all this is over, you and me's gonna sit down to the table with some of Tilly's best and talk about what we done. I'm startin' to think all them stories wasn't stories."

Amos opened the front door, his shoulders stooped. "You don't know the half of it, son," he said, and closed the door behind him.

* * * *

The bayous of south Louisiana are no place for a body to be at night. In the day they're bad enough—mosquitoes bigger than hawks, alligators you'd swear were waiting on you to step on them, snakes big around as a man's thigh. The land itself seems to fight against you, too. Cypress trees grow big as cathedrals right up close together, every one looking like the next, so a man unfamiliar with the land is liable to lose his way forever. God knows it had happened many a time. And the water—shallow in one place, fathoms deep in another, black as the darkest corners of a man's heart, and concealing just as many secrets.

But at night, it was another world, a world that seemed to press in on you the deeper you delved into its realm. The trees were no longer trees; they became giants with leering mouths open in silent screams. Night sounds, a cacophony of a million different animals—frogs and toads, insects and birds, and who knew what else—sang together, on and off-key, a chorus of the damned.

And then there were things—*older* things—in the bayou at night. Things that folks only spoke of in the barest of whispers, things that kept the alligators, panthers, and other predators in their place, afraid to venture out. Here, two small yellow lights flickered and died, only to reappear closer the next time you saw them. They might well be lightning bugs, but who's to say they weren't a pair of eyes, pupils slitted like a cat's, and following a man, drawing ever nearer, waiting for the right time to pounce?

Amos thought on these things as he poled the little pirogue through the night swamp, pushing off trees and submerged stumps when he drifted too close, searching for the signs of a trail. In the dead of night, with no more than a lantern fastened to the prow of the little boat, Amos felt like he was swimming through molasses blindfolded.

He'd told Bess what all he'd learned, as well as his plan, and had asked for the boat. She'd shown him where it was, tied to the back of the porch on two struts. She'd given him a small sack with two ham sandwiches and a thermos of coffee, and then offered Luther's old Navy Colt. "For snakes," she'd explained.

"No, no, girl," Amos had laughed. "What the hell I'm gonna do with a big ol' hogleg like that? I'd be on my ass soon's I pulled the trigger!

"'sides, Luther was never no good at cleanin' his piece, even in the Army. That thing prolly blow right the hell up in my hand. No, you hang on to it." He removed a rusty but sharp machete from a nail above his head, near the boat pegs. "I'll take this instead. Bush gets a might crazy out that way," he said, sliding the machete through his belt.

"You still gonna go out that way tonight? Why not take off early in the mornin'? I'll cook you breakfast," Bess said.

Amos was already shaking his head before she finished. "No, Bessie, no. I done tol' you this thing is about to get outta hand. If that girl—if *Esther*—is what I think she is, then we ain't got time to fool about waitin' for daylight. I got to go *now*, and pray Toby ain't done something stupid like I'm a-thinkin' he has."

Bess lowered her chin to her chest, sobbing. She looked up with red, puffy eyes. "Amos, if something... *happened*, if Toby is...,"

Amos cupped her chin in his hand and pulled it up to face him. "I'll find your boy, one way or another. I'll fix things a-right, Bess."

She began to cry in earnest and turned back toward the house. Amos gathered up his things and set out for the bayou, pulling the pirogue behind him. Once at the water, he shoved it in, climbed inside, and stood there with the pole in his hand, looking back at the house. Bess had disappeared, and as he shoved off from the bank, he heard the screen door slam.

Now, poling through the swamp in the dark, he wondered if he could keep his promise to Bess, wondered if poking his nose into something like this for the millionth time was going to be *last* time. As he pushed off an old fat-lighter stump and headed left, something white in the lantern light caught his eye. He canted the prow of the little pirogue back to the right and dug the pole into the muck to stop.

The thing that had caught his eye was a human skull—not a real one, but the image of one carved into a cypress tree at about chest level. With one hand on the trunk to steady the boat, he looked closely at the image, running the fingers of his free hand over the carved tree. A ten-penny nail was driven into the center of the skull's forehead.

A hex mark.

Amos had heard tell of such things, though he'd never seen one. It was said that a man wishing slow death on another would carve his enemy's image into a tree at midnight and drive a nail into the forehead—just one tap. Every night at midnight, the person would drive the nail in another inch, and every night the hexed person would grow weaker, sicker, wracked with pain, until the nail was all the way in, and then…

He pushed away from the tree and set off to the right, now. The hex mark gave him the gooseflesh, but it also told him he was on the right track. Luther had told him about this place, and he hoped his friend had been wrong. If he was right, then Luther's only son was in a danger most grand.

The trees here seemed to be much older than the ones to the outer edges of the swamp. Larger, with gnarled limbs and knots, they became warped old men by lantern light. The water was still, almost a dead calm, untouched by any sort of breeze. He was deep in the swamp, deeper than he'd ever been. Just when as he wondered if he'd ever get out again, he saw a weak light flickering in the darkness ahead.

It was a house—a shack, really—set at the edge of a natural lagoon formed by the cypress trees, and up on stilts. The ramshackle place looked like a stiff breeze would send it toppling into the dark water. The trees surrounding it had grown into it, probably all that kept it upright and steady, but also making it look like a living thing—a dreadful, nameless monstrosity hunched over the water, ready to devour trespassers. A man would have to be either a fool or desperate to seek out such a place. Amos thought he just might be both.

He steered the boat up to a small dock and tied it off, testing the boards before putting his full weight on them. He hitched his pants up, the machete snug in his belt, and gingerly stepped out onto the dock. Reaching the old staircase, he paused at the bottommost step.

"Toby! Toby, come on out, now, boy! It's ol' Amos! You remember me, don'tcha?"

Silence from within, then, weakly: "Whatchu want?"

"You got yo' mama worried sick, boy. Everybody lookin' for you, thought you might be dead!"

"Might be better if I *was*."

Amos took two careful steps up the stairs. "C'mon now, boy. You don't mean that. Ain't nobody blamin' you for Esther. But it don't look right, you runnin' off like that!"

"Go away," the boy said, crying. "You don't know nothin' 'bout nothin', and it's better that way."

Amos crept up the staircase, careful not to put all his weight on either foot. The old planks creaked and groaned under his weight, but held firm. Amos could feel the influence of the place settle over him like a burial shroud. It seemed to take more willpower to take the next step than the one before. All the menace that lived in the swamp seemed to settle on this old hut, to damn near swirl about the place like a cloud of no-seeums. Finally, he reached the porch and stood before the door, a worn oak number, stripped and discolored by the humidity from what might have been a deep shade of green.

"Tobias, I'm a-comin' in now, and we gonna talk a spell." He turned the doorknob, an old multifaceted glass job that looked like a soot-covered diamond in the grime of the place. The door refused to budge at first—probably warped in the jamb from exposure—but finally gave after a hard shoulder, and Amos entered.

His first thought was that Luther had been right; his second was that *he* had been right, and the thought sickened him.

The shack was a one-room affair, low-ceilinged and close, more a cave than a house. A dying fire flickered in the hearth, which was strung up with strange herbs and unfamiliar weeds tied into bunches. Three chairs sat around a long oak table that was split and water-damaged from the leaky roof above, and was covered with three to four-dozen lit candles, all in various stages of use.

In the center of the table—the *exact* center, Amos noted—sat the remarkably accurate wax sculpture of a young girl, surrounded by a sea of melted candle wax yet untouched by any of it. A knife lay on the table next to the poppet. Dark, rust-colored stains mottled the blade, the table and the figure. A massive tome, complete with leather bindings and brass fasteners sat at the head of the table—due north, if Amos wasn't mistaken. It was open nearly halfway, with pages of what looked like rough vellum but, as Amos found to his disgust as he yanked his hand away, were instead human skin.

The pages, yellowed with age, were covered with a scrawl barely recognizable as handwriting. It was in French, and Amos could make out nearly every other word, enough to get the gist:

Shape the beloved from the leavings of a hundred burning candles.
Give it life from the left hand,
Bid it live, live again,

And come unto you with haste.

A shuffling behind him made Amos whirl, bringing the machete around to rest at the neck of a young man with hollow eyes and trembling hands, the left one wrapped in a bloody bandage. The boy obviously hadn't slept in days and was scared beyond words. Sweat rolled from his forehead and beaded on his upper lip. In the low light of the shack, Amos could tell the boy was strung tight and liable to pop any second.

"Toby! Damn, son, you lookin' to get dead?"

Toby stood, shivering in spite of the heat. "At first I thought…I thought you might b-be…"

"Who, boy?"

"H-her," he said. "Esther."

Amos winced, removing his glasses and massaging the bridge of his nose. He'd suspected it, but hearing it was something altogether different. Viola's headless corpse at the bottom of Bayou Blue was proof enough.

"Toby," he said in a harsh growl, gripping the boy's shoulders, shaking him. "You got any notion what you *done*, boy? Have you lost your damn *mind*?"

Toby began to cry, a sobbing that wrenched soul from body. "I loved her, Amos! I loved her! And I killed her! I *killed* her!"

"Steady on, now," Amos said. "You ain't killed tht girl. Sheriff said she done it in her folks bathtub. Cut her wrists."

"I know," Toby said between hitching sobs, "but I might as well have drew the razor acrosst them myself."

"Foolin' about with the Martin girl and she found you out, that about it?"

"The look on her face, Amos…she walked *in* on us. Wasn't no yellin', no nothin'. Just stood there starin' right into me, like I was a complete stranger. I never seen someone broke, but that's what it was. She was broken glass on the inside. I just tried to put her back together."

"You know better than most not to fool with the likes of this business," Amos said, gesturing at the book and wax figure. "How you come to find this place?"

"*You* told me," he replied. "In them ol' stories you told us when we's kids. The one about Mama TouTou and the corbies. Thought I'd see were she real, and could she do what folks say."

"She's real, Lord yes," Amos nodded. "Or *was*. She was a conjure woman, used to do rootwork for sick folks, mostly, but she do a hoodoo workin' every now and then. Only one I ever knowed to stick a fright in Big John Broussard. No one else ever knew what happened to her, whether she moved on or died, but she left this place and everything in it. Your daddy knew, though. Even been out here."

"He…out *here*?"

"Damn right. Come out here with Broussard and his posse the night he arrested Selma, Viola's granny. They planned to do the same to TouTou, but she put up a helluva fight. Two men went crazy and clawed out they eyeballs, another shot a fourth and turned the gun on hisself, an' that was all before they got to the front door."

Toby looked horrified. "They…they *killed* her, didn't they?"

Amos took off his glasses and wiped them with the edge of his shirt. "Yeah. Matter of fact, your daddy done the deed. Shot her dead while she had Broussard screamin' on the floor, thinkin' he was burnin' alive."

"Daddy…?" Toby said, sinking to the floor down the wall.

"Couldn't be helped, son. Luther knew that. He didn't *wanna* kill her; he just didn't *hesitate*. He remembered what war was like; if you hesitated the least bit in a fight, you kill yourself and them around you. He did what he had to."

Amos sat down in one of the chairs, pulled out a cheroot and lit it with a candle, and continued.

"See, TouTou and Selma was sisters. They used to rule the roost 'round here 'til Big John Broussard got hisself elected sheriff. Selma run the cathouse back in town and TouTou lived out here doin' her thing.

"Business got to dryin' up for Selma after the War. Boys comin' home from 'cross the ocean had they fill of whorin' for the last four years. All they wanted was a warm bed and wife to cook for 'em after the mess they seen, I 'spect. Anyhow, Selma got with TouTou and they made a pact: TouTou would hex the menfolk about town, make 'em fall hard for Selma's girls, like they couldn't get enough of 'em. For a while, that worked just fine. Both women were makin' jack left and right. Selma from the repeat business at the cathouse, TouTou from the men's wives, lookin' for charms that would make their men be true again, or hexes that would cause 'em no end of pain.

"Then things got outta hand. The jinxed men would get jealous of the whores, they'd beat they wives and kids for ruinin' they lives, and beat Selma's girls, too, for seein' other johns. The hex backfired on the women, and Big John Broussard couldn't turn a blind eye to the troubles no more. They shut Selma down, arrested her and sent her off to the farm at St. Roche. She sweated out six years there before she got out, and I'm here to tell you, boy: one day on the farm is like thirty years in hell, 'specially for a woman, even a customer as hard as Selma.

"When Selma got wind of what Luther, Broussard and his posse done to TouTou, she was fit to bust. She swore revenge on Big John and Luther—swore they'd never see it comin'. But I think your daddy saw it comin'. He used to walk with me and tell me all about it. Your mama just thought we's rememberin' old war stories on our long walks down the bayou, but Luther was confessin', and I reckon I was his priest."

"What happened to Mama TouTou, you know… *after*?" Toby asked.

"Well, the way I had it from Luther, he and Big John sunk the old gal in the swamp, right here 'neath this shack, swore never to mention it to another soul. I guess your daddy figured he had to tell a body, and the only person he could think of to tell was a fella didn't live in the bayou, a person he'd shared death with too many times before. S'why I used to come 'round nearly every year, to hear that confession, to ease his pain if I could."

"Selma's still around, then. She getting' her revenge now, that it?" Toby said.

"Naw," Amos said, gently blowing smoke. "Selma been neighbors with the devil these last three years. Killed by a jealous boyfriend, or so I hear tell. Kinda like poetry, ain't it?"

A hoot-owl screeched outside in the cypress trees, and Toby about left his pants, he jumped so high. "So Viola," he began, looking nervously out the window, "what's she got to do with all this?"

Amos shook his head, frowning. "Boy, you so shook up you cain't put two and two together?"

Toby looked around at Amos, and Amos could tell the boy knew what the deal was, but was afraid to admit it.

"Big John Broussard kicked about three years ago, heart attack, face down in his étouffée. Luther had the cancer and died, cheatin' Selma outta her revenge. But lo and behold, both men had sons, and what does the Good Book say about the sins of the father?"

Toby's skin went pale, paler than his mama's Creole skin she gave him at birth. "Oh Lord, Amos. Oh, no. She's…"

"That's right, son. She played you all like a banjo. My only question is, did she hex you, or was you just that big of a dumbass?"

Toby tried to speak, but the words were wedged tighter than a wood screw in his throat.

"I'll spell it for you, then," Amos said. "Viola was one of Selma's girls, Toby. Woman pimps out her own granddaughter need to be shot, anyhow. TouTou taught her niece all she knew 'bout hoodoo, then set her to work on the johns that come 'round at the cathouse.

"After the fracas with TouTou, Selma set Viola on the town. Oh, she went off to medical school, alright. She got the papers, gonna be an animal doctor and, Lord, ain't she a shade better than her granny. But she come back with a plan. She found a poor ol' sumbitch to seduce, made sure his girl knew she was bangin' him. After Esther killed herself, she seen an opportunity. She knew TouTou's shack was still here, and all her workin's. She put a little bug in the boy's ear about savin' his woman from death's door, knowin' the boy would bite. She tol' you 'bout a spell, I bet."

Toby's gaze slid to the open tome on the table, and he nodded. "She said she was tryin' to help, that this was a way for me and Esther to be together again. Things could back like they used to be. She--"

He began to weep uncontrollably after that, and Amos moved to put an arm around his best friend's son. Toby leaned into the crook of his shoulder, burying his face in Amos's chest. "You ain't the first man been done wrong by a woman. Lots more been used before you, and lots more will after you."

"But I'm the reason she dead, Amos! She was all I ever loved, all I ever *will* love! One mistake! It was just one mistake!"

"Sometimes that all it takes, son," Amos said, putting out the cheroot in a puddle of wax. "Take it from a body that knows."

"Look here," Amos said, holding Toby's shoulders. "You done a bad thing, but now you got to be the man you s'posed to be, the man yo' daddy was. You got to make things right."

Amos pulled out a chair and set the boy down in it. He pulled his hip flask from his coat pocket, unscrewed the cap, and held it out to Toby. Hesitating, Toby took it and winced as the liquor burned his throat.

Amos took back the flask, took a pull, and handed it back. "Look here, now," he began. "We got some dark work ahead—dark and bloody, but that's the only thing that comes of foolin' with the dead."

Toby took another pull, coughing a little less this time, and handed it over.

"Power over life and death belong to the Lord God. Always has. When men start to muckin' around with it, the Lord take issue. It's an abomination, you understand. Jesus raised up Lazarus, and that was fine, but when people get to thinkin' they can do the same, they gets to thinkin' *they's* God, too." He took another sip and handed Toby the flask, leaning forward to whisper, scared of what might be listening.

"'Cept they *ain't* God, and these hoodoo men and women, they gets their power from another place altogether, a place laid aside for black hearts and lost souls. It's a place that once a body go there, there ain't no finding they way back. Mama TouTou was such a person. Oh, she helped folks here and there, so most folks let her be, but mostly they was a-scairt of what she could do—of what she *had* done.

"That spell you worked up in here, well that's a working for bringing one back from death, but when they come back, they ain't like they loved ones remember.

"See here, Esther ain't been dead long enough, Toby. Lazarus was raised *four* days after he died, 'cause the Jews' custom was to wait and bury they dead after three days in case a fella wasn't really dead. Happened a lot in them days, buryin' a man alive. So Christ needed to prove to the Jews that Lazarus was *truly* dead, and that none but the Son of Man could bring a man back from his eternal reward.

"But the place between Heaven and Hell is a long, dark road, full of twists and turns, and in some ways, *worse* than Hell. It changes a body, makes 'em less than human, getting' em ready for the journey up or down, you understand. Once they's with the Lord or with

Scratch, there ain't no comin' back, and your spell woulda been a lot of hot air millin' about this old dusty shack.

"But Esther was walkin' the ghost road, Toby. And the miles that spun out beneath her changed her, twisted her. When you yanked her up off that road, she come back a monster inside, and all she knows is to feed on others, to make other people like herself, a sick soul in a rotting body. She's a zombie, boy. She walkin' the ghost road in her mind and this world in her body. As long as she here, she'll spread that disease to everybody she know. Sound to me like she remembers enough to get the ones that done her wrong to start with.

"*That's* what TouTou and Selma wanted, that's they revenge -- turn the whole town of people that did 'em ill into a house of the dead. I think they figured Viola would do the deed and get away, but she ain't run fast enough."

"She— she dead?" Toby said.

Amos nodded. "Twice over. But she set some things in motion that we gotta deal with now. It's down to you and me. Mostly you, though, and it ain't gonna be easy."

"What…what you talkin' about? What am I gonna have to do?"

Amos looked incredulous. "Boy, who you think she comin' after *next*?"

As if in answer, they heard a creak on the stairs. A beat later, another. Then another. A shuffling gait followed before stopping just at the door. Amos hefted the machete and shot a warning glance at Toby.

"Not a word, you hear? Not a one," he whispered. He moved to stand at the left of the door. Gently he placed his ear to the jamb. A throaty, raspy voice called from beyond.

"*TO-BYYYYYY…*"

Toby lunged for the door and Amos caught him by the shoulders, shoving him against the wall.

"No, boy! Now *listen* to me, dammit, and listen *good*!" Amos leaned in so close to Toby, his lips brushed the boy's ear. "We gonna do this *my* way."

"Let me be, Amos!" Toby struggled against the old man, who held him fast. "That's Esther! She come back! Just like Viola said! She come back!"

Amos slammed him harder against the wall, rattling the boy's teeth in his skull. "Ain't you heard a damn word I been screamin'? That ain't your girl no more! She done crossed over! She's lost, boy, and we lost too, we don't deal with her! Us, ya mama, ya sisters, the whole damn town! Straight to Hell, or near enough!"

Slow, steady pounding on the door shook the little cabin to its frame. Dishes rattled in the cupboard. Amos glanced at the door for the merest second, but it was long enough for Toby to push off the wall and shove Amos across the room. Amos stumbled, tripping over his own feet and fell, smacking his head on the corner of the table. He reached up and felt a sticky wetness, and stars burst and swirled in front of his eyes.

Toby rushed to the door, threw it open, and stood with his arms out wide. The cool, uncaring moonlight poured through the door, bathing Toby in a surreal silver glow.

Esther, come home at last, stumbled through the door, reaching out for her lost love, reaching out to embrace him from the ghost road one final time.

She was a horrid sight, the peeling scars on her wrist like thick red bracelets, her hair thick with filth, and the air was filled with the stench of rotting flesh. Moonlight shone through the fist-sized hole in her chest old Boudreaux's .45 had made. But love was blind, and Toby pulled her tight, sobbing into her neck, paying no mind to the maggots wriggling into his hair from her face

"Oh, baby!" Toby cried. "Oh baby, I'm here, I'm here now, and it's all fine, now. All fine. I'm so sorry, *so* sorry, baby. But it's all right now. It's—"

His sobbing broke off into an agonized cry as Esther sank her rotted teeth into his neck. Toby's lifeblood spurted into the air like a geyser. He tried to push her away, but she wasn't having it; they were reunited now -- in love, in death. She bore him to the floor, gnawing at his shoulder, his chest, his face, frantically searching for the river of life within him. Toby's screams died on the air as she tore out his throat and began to feed.

Amos tried to speak, to move, but his head wouldn't let him decide what was up or down. He slumped to the floor. In the last moments before darkness took him, he saw the two lovers as they writhed on the floor of the dead witch's cabin, the light dying in one's eyes, the light long gone from the other.

His vision blurred and then all was night.

* * * *

Amos came to with a start, much to the chagrin of his head. It hurt like a bastard, so Amos knew he must still be alive. He peered out from under half-lidded eyes to see Esther munching on something long, slick, and ropy stretched between her hands, like a perverse Cat's Cradle. It took but seconds to recognize a man's intestines; Amos had seen his fair share in the trenches.

He couldn't have been out for more than a minute or two, thank God. If only God would grant him a steady hand for the next few minutes. It was time to put a stop to all this once and for all, or drift forever in a twilight world, shunned by both God and Satan.

Slowly, gathering his wits about him, Amos rose to his knees. Keeping his eyes on the zombie, he reached across the middle of the table, trying not to draw Esther's attention from her meal, until his trembling fingers found what they sought.

Ever more slowly, he drew the wax figure of Esther back across the table and passed it into his left hand. Once again, he reached across the table, stopping every time Esther made a grunting sound, thinking he'd been discovered, but the girl was only enjoying her meal. He gently drew the burning candle off the table and held the wax figure above the flame. The wax began to run, slowly at first, then pouring over Amos's gnarled old fingers like lava. He failed to stifle a cry as the wax continued to run down his forearm, burning his skin and hardening as it went.

Esther wrenched around at the sound, crying out in the god-awful voice that death had bestowed. Anger and desperation lived in that cry, as she rose to her feet and tottered toward Amos.

Six feet away, Amos watched as the candle's flame melted the right arm off the statue and almost gave a shout of triumph as Esther's right arm fell to the floor, disappearing in a puddle of fluid that ran between the cracks of the old wooden floor and into the swamp beneath. Esther cried out in rage and shock, sensing that her true end was at hand. She took another step, and her left leg disappeared at the knee, then at the thigh, and she fell forward, face first, three feet away from where Amos lay shaking in terror. She bellowed once again and began dragging her mutilated body toward him.

"Come on, come *on*," he breathed, moving the flame to the figure's torso, then looked up to see the right side of Esther's midsection melt away into nothingness. She screamed again, flailing with her right hand and managed to catch Amos's boot. She yanked and pulled him toward her gnashing maw. Amos lashed out with the same foot, connected, and yanked free. He quickly went to work on the head of the figure, but in a flash, she was on him, baring rotted teeth, the breath of the grave and fresh blood washing over him. She snapped like an alligator, trying to gain purchase on his neck.

"Burn, you ugly bitch, burn!" Amos shouted. He kicked again, shoving her away, and in that moment, he thrust the head of the figure into the flame, hollering in pain as the wax scalded his hands. Holding the lumpish wax figure, which once represented a pretty girl not yet known by a man, he watched in horror as both heads—real and wax—melted into formlessness. A short scream, a thud, and then it was over.

Amos threw the wax lump across the room, crying at the pain in his hands as much as the anguish in his heart. He slowly got to his feet and stared across the room, taking in the carnage, and his stomach heaved and rolled. The whiskey burned sour in his throat. He staggered to the door and retched until there was nothing left but remorse.

He looked down at the remains of his best friend's only son and his heart cried out. He sobbed for a time, wondering at how fast true love had come to such a bad end. After minute, he calmed somewhat, knowing that the work wasn't over, knowing what else had to be done. He picked up the machete and placed it on the table beside his hip flask. He fell into a chair, unscrewed the flask's cap, took a long pull, and waited in the dark.

It didn't take long. Toby's corpse twitched, spasmed, and began to rise. Amos waited until Toby was on his knees. The boy bared his teeth at Amos, uttering a low, hungry growl, his eyes gone milky white.

Amos stood, steeling himself, and raised the machete. "I'm sorry, Luther. Sorry I couldn't-a done better. Sorry I wasn't here for you and yours like you always was for me. Rest now, boy. Find your daddy on them golden shores, hear?"

He brought the machete down in two-handed stroke, splitting Toby's skull like an overripe watermelon. Toby's corpse fell to the floor for the last time. Amos dropped the machete, shut his eyes tight, and grabbed the table's edge to keep from swooning. Red flickered at the edges of his vision and his felt his mind coming unhinged.

It wasn't everyday that a man killed his best friend's son.

He finally choked down the sorrow and stood; he'd mourn later. Right then it was time to get out of the damn swamp. After one last look around, Amos took a lit candle from the table and one by one, set the shack's old curtains ablaze. He waited until they caught proper, flames licking the ceiling, and then left the shack, shutting the door behind him.

He poled the pirogue away from the shack, which was fully alight now, a burning torch that drove away the dark and set nearby trees afire just from the heat. He poled past the tree with the hex mark and saw tree sap running down from the tenpenny nail, streaking the skull like blood.

As omens went, it was a pretty bad one.

* * * *

Sheriff Leon Broussard sat behind the wheel of the old police cruiser his daddy had once sat in, brooding. He was watching Amos and Bess Hollis share a long embrace.

Bess held on to Amos like she'd never let go and Amos had to gently pry her away. He watched the older man hold her at arms' length, smooth away the hair from her face, and plant a gentle, slow kiss on her forehead. Amos touched his wrinkled brown forehead to her smooth coffee-colored one, and they both stood that way for a spell, silent, sharing grief in a way that only two close friends could.

Finally, Amos broke away, picked up his bindle and guitar case, and walked toward the car. Bess watched him go for a time, and then turned and walked back into the house, closing the door. Amos opened the passenger's side and climbed in.

"How'd she take it?" Broussard asked.

"How would *you* take it? Only son killed by black magic on the heels of losin' her husband? How the hell you *think* she took it?"

Broussard started the car and peeled out onto the street. He peered over at Amos, who was studying his feet. "I 'spect you ain't told her *everything*, right?"

Amos shook his head. "Only what she need to know. Boy burned hisself up in a fire over his grief. Helluva thing to tell her, but the truth don't seem to do no one no good these days, do it?"

Broussard shifted in the seat, nervously glancing over at Amos, and then quickly back to the road. "No," he said quietly. "No, I guess it don't."

As they approached the county line, Amos was startled to see it lined with cars and the rest of Broussard's deputies. "What the hell we got goin' here? Bon voyage party?"

"Somethin' like that," Broussard said, braking and putting the car into park. "Get out now, Amos." Amos stared at his friend. Broussard couldn't meet his eyes. "Please understand, Amos. There wasn't nothin' I could do. I tried, but…" Broussard opened his door and quickly got out before he had to say more.

Amos got out with his guitar case and stood facing the entourage of men, his stomach tight. All the deputies were there, watching warily as he strolled up to them. There was another man present, a white man, dressed in his Sunday best -- a white suit and hat with a black string tie. He held a folder to his breast, the kind the tax man might keep every jot and tittle of a man's earnings inside. The whole company looked as solemn as a morgue.

"Afternoon, boys," Amos said, trying to break the ice. "Mighty nice of all y'all comin' out to see an old man off like this."

No one spoke. One of Broussard's deputies spat a stream of brown juice from the tobacco in is cheek. The white man stepped forward.

"Daniel Amos Harlow?"

Amos started. "That...that's me."

"Mr. Harlow, I'm Circuit Judge Lawrence Rayford. I have here a warrant for your arrest for the murders of Viola Gray Martin and Tobias Luther Hollis."

Amos went cold. "What the hell… There must be some—"

"Mistake? No, sir, I assure you there's nary a one," Rayford drawled in a thick plantation accent. "We have a witness that places you at both murder scenes and tangible evidence says your hand felled both parties."

"Witness? Who the hell would…" Amos broke off, understanding dawning on his seamed face. He slowly turned to gaze at Broussard, who had a thousand mile stare going past the toes of his shoes. "I see," he said, face turning to stone.

"We have ourselves somewhat of a sticky situation, here, Mr. Harlow. We cannot have the good people of Terrebonne Parish a-feard of ghosts and ghoulies an' telling passer-through all manner of things folks get up to here. We take care of our own down the bayou."

Amos felt a rock in the pit of his stomach. He was drowning on dry land and there was no one to throw him a line.

"Try to see it our way, Mr. Harlow. If any of this ever got out to the rest of the state, we'd all lose our jobs, our positions, hell, some of us might wind up in prison. It wouldn't be good for the *community*, you understand.

"Besides, there isn't a soul hereabouts willin' to testify to the story you've given Sheriff Broussard, here. Leon's a family man. He has to keep in good standing with the parish and the greater state of Louisiana to keep his pension, retirement, and such."

Amos stared daggers at Broussard, and if it weren't for the heat, Amos would have mistaken the salty sweat rolling down his cheeks for tears. "How much is that pension—thirty pieces of silver?"

Broussard flinched as if he'd been struck across the face.

"This file I hold officially records the entire affair, Mr. Harlow," said Rayford, ignoring the exchange. "A drifter, a known rabble-rouser and vagrant, comes into town and visits a known house of ill-repute, only to find it shut down and the granddaughter of the previous tenant unwilling to welcome his advances. Fight ensues, the crazy bastard up and kills her, lops off her head and throws her into the bayou to boot. As far as the boy goes, why, he walks in on your little tussle with Ms. Martin and you chase him out into the swamp, kill him, and burn him up in that old shack to hide the crime."

"Got all that on paper, do you?" Amos asked, eyes still glued to Broussard.

"All right here, all nice and *very* legal, I assure you." Rayford replied, a slimy grin stretching across his face.

"Even though that paper ain't good for nothin' but wipin' yo' ass?"

"Mr. Harlow," said Rayford. "Let me pay you the compliment of being blunt. It wouldn't matter if there were nothing but a child's *chicken-scratch* on this paper. I will make it stick like tar to your forehead and have you in the first noose that can be tied. But I think you know that."

Amos did know it. Rayford's type of justice often got no further than the tree they stood under. Besides, his kind of person wasn't welcome at every table; the world wasn't like the Hollis house. Amos realized he'd been set up from the beginning.

"So, what? We goin' to the jailhouse or you gonna stand here in this heat and run yo' mouth off some more?" Amos said, finally turning to meet Rayford's eyes.

"It *does* get rather sticky around this time of year, doesn't it?" Rayford said, producing a handkerchief and patting his forehead. He replaced the handkerchief in his coat pocket. "No, I would say what comes next depends on you, sir. Don't get me wrong, now, Mr. Harlow. We're all grateful for the service you rendered. As a matter of fact, I'd go as far as to say we couldn't have done it without you."

"Smartest thing come out yo' mouth yet," Amos said.

"Ha! Yes, well, you see that sign over there? That's the Parish line. You start walking, *keep* walking, and never show your itinerant ass in Terrebonne Parish again, and we won't have to open this file up and see what it's got to say. You with me now, son?"

Amos hefted his guitar case, hacked up a wad of phlegm, and spat it on Rayford's shoes. "I'm with you, and I ain't your *son*."

He walked toward the group of men, which parted for him like the Red Sea, almost forming an honor guard to the Parish line. Amos passed Broussard without a glance, then stopped, his back to the sheriff.

"How Daddy's clothes fittin' right about *now*?"

He didn't wait for a reply, just walked on, aware of the eyes on him. He caught movement at the side of the dirt road and heard a familiar rustling in the underbrush.

The black dog trotted out of the woods, tongue lolling, as if he expected Amos to be walking down this very road at this very second. Five years ago, he would have been surprised, maybe even scared. Now, however, it was anticipated, like an afternoon thunderstorm.

"You was here, all right," he said to the hound. "I just didn't see you 'til it was too late."

He removed his hat, wiped the sweat from his brow with his coat sleeve, and ambled along after the dog, like always. As he walked away from the last happy place he would ever know, he pondered on the evil that had set itself into the Hollis family, into the quiet country parish that was once a sanctuary, a haven for a wandering soul.

He wondered if the ghosts of Toby, Esther, and Viola would ever rest and if the evil that had stirred them up would stay buried, right next to the truth. He asked himself and God, if such evil could *ever* stay buried, especially when it was bound up with love.

He never got an answer.

BLOOD ON MY HANDS, HURT IN MY HEART

A Song of the Black Dog

A man is not old until regrets take the place of dreams.
--John Barrymore

The air was redolent with smoke, a fog bank in the low lights of the juke joint. The old man sat in the rear of the place, one hand on a shot glass, the other on a bottle of Kentucky redeye, his head on the table in a puddle of spilled liquor.

A blues quartet blared onstage, a jangle of horns and drums that sounded like a war party bound for Jericho. It made no difference to him, lost in the booze as he was. Best thing that ever happened to him, Prohibition being repealed. He'd never been happier. Ironically, the only thing keeping him in the chair was the drink. He wanted it—*needed* it—if he was to finish his business in the Big Easy.

The front man of the band moved to the mike, a fat, slick-haired bastard that had never known a hard time in his life enough to talk about it, let alone sing it. Yet he bellowed into the crowd, a deep baritone that came from some church choir, not the Mississippi Delta, not Harlem, as sure as *hell* not Dauphine Street, the heart of the *real* French Quarter.

Blood on my hands,
hurt in my heart!
Blood on my hands,
hurt in my heart!
My woman took off with another man,
Leavin' me no place to start.

I been down so long, baby,
I can't remember up.
Said I been down so long,

Can't remember up,
Took a smokin' gun and a bottle of gin
To help me settle up.

The old man raised his head long enough to tip the bottle to the glass, his hand shaking so bad he could hear the clinking over the music—*his* music. He killed the shot, wiped his mouth with the back of his hand, and stared at the scarred tabletop.

I can do this, he thought. *I can do this. I* will *do this. An' then New Orleans can kiss my black ass. I ain't* never *comin' back to this shithole.*

He glanced at the guitar leaning against the wall behind him, and a bitter taste filled his mouth as bile rose in his throat. He grimaced, filling the glass again, shaking a little less this time. He always found it funny the way liquor seemed to clear his head instead of clouding it. Or maybe it made him crazy, granting liquid courage to do things a normal man might find tasteless. Either way, he needed a clear mind, or a crazy one, to do what he'd come to do.

A brunette in a slinky red dress—obviously a working girl—slid into the seat across from him. Unlike most of the hookers in the Quarter, she was striking, almost unbelievably beautiful. Her eyes were pools of the deepest brown, like the Mississippi River, where a man cold drown if he weren't careful. Her lips were full and painted to match her dress, which, he noticed, stopped just shy of her secrets.

"Buy a girl a drink?" she shouted over the music.

He stared at her, bleak and bleary eyed, but hard as a stone. "Bet you made enough money tonight to buy the whole damn street a drink, twice over. Get your own."

"Aww," she cooed, unperturbed. "Don't be like that, dad. Why don't you pour me one and play me somethin' on that old axe back there?"

He poured another shot and downed it, slamming it on the table with a sound like a gunshot.

"For a street-smart whore, you don't *hear* too good. I ain't playin' *shit* for the likes of you."

The woman eyed him warily, frowning, not used to rejection.

"'sides," he said, pouring another, "we both know *this* ain't the kinda drink you had in mind."

He looked up in time to see her face flit from beauty to horror in a split second. Her eyes flashed completely black, no whites at all, and bulged like eight-balls from her eye sockets. Her pouty lips spread in an impossible angle, revealing a set of teeth that would have been a doctoral thesis for any dentistry student—pointed, jagged and crooked around a tongue that belonged in a serpent's mouth. It was just a flash, a brief glimpse of what lay beneath.

He downed the third shot in a row, unimpressed. She stood in a huff.

"Leave me be and go get your boss," he said, staring at the shot glass as if it were a diamond he'd just plucked from a coal bin.

The woman hissed like a cat, and a thin stream of saliva hit the table, sizzling like acid. She turned on one spike heel and headed to the bar. He watched from the corner of his eye as she talked to the bartender, a brick of a man who was wiping a glass. Drowned out by the music, she was plenty mad, and gestured violently toward him. The bartender finished wiping the glass, left the bar, and headed up the nearby staircase.

He pushed back from the table and turned back to the band, as they finished out the set with his song:

Why you made me do this,
I'll never know.
I say why you made me do this,
I'll never know.
Gotta run from John Law, now,
All the way to Mexico, lawd.

It was an insult to true blues, not just him personally, the front man bopping and preening up there like a rooster in a henhouse. The man didn't know what he was singing about, beyond what the lyrics told him. The song was a lament worthy of Old Testament prophets and told of pain and loss beyond measure. What he was hearing was a commercial jingle for dish soap.

Shaking his head, he wondered if this was the future -- fame and fortune built on the sorrows of unknown men. If it was, then the future had nothing to offer but more of the past.

"Well, well, well!" came a jovial voice from behind him. "You got real nerve showin' up back here, old man!"

And Amos Harlow turned to face the man he'd come to kill.

* * * *

The voice, high-pitched and reedy, belonged to a man, tall and lanky, in a white suit and fedora. His skin was black against all that white, like a tire in a snowdrift. His smile was wide and dazzling, perfect teeth arranged around a silver tongue that had lifted him to the lofty perch on which he now sat. It was the smile of a satisfied jungle cat, predatory in the extreme.

Two men the size of office buildings in dark pinstripe suits flanked him. Both wore black sunglasses, though the sun had long sunk below the horizon, and each grasped his left wrist in his right hand, a casual position that could easily turn into a deadly one were they to twist the bottom buttons of their double-breasted coats. The bulge under their left arms told Amos they were packing heat, promising that the hot July night could get hotter if the need arose.

The black man in the white suit began to sit, even before the goon on the right pulled the chair out for him. Once seated, he turned slightly.

"James, why don't y'all wait at the bar, hear? Ain't no trouble here," he said, turning back to face Amos, that toothy smile again. "Just a couple of old friends playin' some catch-up."

James and his twin sauntered off to the bar, eyeing Amos as they leaned on the bar. The hooker in the red dress sashayed over and clung to James's arm, staring hungrily at Amos.

"Well, now," said the man. "It must be…what? Five years? Seven?"

"Ten," said Amos, peering at him over the shot glass with bloodshot eyes. "And a damn sight not long enough."

"Naw, ten?" said the man laughing. "Lord, how time do fly, Amos Harlow. Yessir, it do, sure enough. What brings you back to New Orleans?" It came out in one syllable, 'Nawlins.'

Amos downed another shot, slow and steady. "You know damn well what," he said evenly. "I want some peace, Delbert. I come to ask you for some peace."

Delbert Gill threw his head back and let loose a barking laugh. "Now what you playin' at, ol' buddy?"

"Don't throw that shit my way," Amos growled. 'You gonna sit here an' tell me them weren't your boys in Kansas City? Or Memphis? Atlanta, neither, huh? That what you gonna say, you Judas-goat bastard?"

The wide smile faltered for the quickest of seconds, only to come back wider, brighter. He looked around and leaned in close. "Yet here you sit, none the worse."

It was Amos's turn to smile now. "Atlanta was a near thing, I grant you, but maybe your boys oughtta start carryin' watches. Daylight come *early* back east."

Delbert's face went cold, his eyes black, stony pits. "We had a deal, old man."

"*Ain't* no deal," Amos snarled, death in his voice. "We never agreed to *nothin'* like you got for us. We never wanted no *part* of that!"

Delbert slammed his palms down on the table, the sound so like a gunshot that James and his partner snatched at their coats for their pieces.

"Ain't *nothin'* in this life ever like we want, Black Dog!" he roared. "You'd do good to 'member that."

The music stopped, every eye in the place on the two men. James and his buddy had their hands inside their coats, fingers scratching triggers. Then just as quickly, the storm passed, and Delbert smiled at the room.

"What the hell y'all doin'? Ain't nobody said stop playin'! This a bar or a convent? C'mon now, drink up! Round on the house!" This brought raucous cheers as the entire room seemed to slink toward the bar at once to the music of the house band.

Delbert turned back to Amos, his one-time partner, drinking buddy, and fellow carouser. His eyes were stilettos, sharp and pointed.

"You an' me, we got business, an' it's high time we settled. You want your peace of mind, there ain't but one way of getting' it. Now you think hard on that, Amos. Think hard on how you want this to play out."

But Amos *had* thought about it, had thought about it for quite a while now. He thought back to how it all started, how this two-bit hood stole his music, his future, and almost his soul.

Ten years. Lord, *had* it been ten years? Had he run that long?

The two men stared at each other over the table, over the whiskey and the blood and the years that lay between them. Amos searched his old friend's eyes for something of the past, something of the good times, and found nothing but death.

****

The place had been jumping, roaring. Shoulder to shoulder, ass to ass, they'd crammed into Delbert's swill hole on Dauphine for music and a good time, and they got what they came for.

The Broke-Down Boys had just finished a set fit to rile the dead from the grave and make them dance, and the only thing that flowed more than the illegal hooch was the sweat from Amos's face, back, and nethers.

He set his old guitar down and mopped his brow with the evening's third dry towel. Hefty Creech was hollering something in his ear, but he couldn't make it out, so he just nodded and smiled in all the right places. It must have worked, because Hefty just clapped him on the back, laughing as he tucked his harp back in his shirt pocket.

The crowd thinned out a bit and Amos made his way to the bar. James saw him coming and set a bottle and two glasses on the bar with a nod and made his way down to the paying customers.

Halfway through the pour, Lowdown Sam Elvin slid into the empty stool in front of the second glass. He took the full one, and Amos shook his head, grinning.

"Lawd, yes, they's some hormones in here *tonight*," Lowdown said, scratching his beard.

Amos smiled wide, lifting his own glass. They made to drink when a couple of lookers swished by, eyeing them and smiling sideways. The men watched them head off to the ladies' room, dresses clinging to their ample frames with the evening sweat. The men leaned to keep them in view.

"Indeed there is," Amos replied. "Indeed there is." They clinked glasses without looking away and drained them, wincing in absolute pleasure, and slammed the empties on the bar.

"Damn, Amos you was really swingin' that axe last set. What got up your ass tonight, son? You plannin' on taking the act solo, that it?"

Amos laughed, pouring two more. "Hell no, boy! The Broke-Down Boys is a *group* venture, you know that! And what 'bout you?

Up there slappin' that upright like you holdin' a grudge!"

Lowdown howled, draining the second shot. "Shoo, ain't nothin' but rhythm, son! I got that in spades. But a man cain't bass hisself into a contract, nossir! Speakin' of which, where's ol' Delbert? That ol' fox done talk one o' these here ladies outta they skirts?"

"Naw," said Amos, throwing back his shot. "He went to fetch Crawley for the last set."

Lowdown smiled. "This is it, ain't it? Our shot."

"Now don't go jinxin' the damn thing," Amos said. "Delbert said he'd get us a listen, that's all. Couldn't promise no more than that."

"Yeah-bob," Lowdown went on, "but that's more than we ever got before, right? That's *somethin'*, ain't it?"

"Yessir," Amos replied, pouring a third time. 'It is *that*, alright."

Lowdown raised his glass. Amos followed suit. "To the Broke-Down Boys. Long may they play," Lowdown said.

The two women strolled back in from the restroom at that moment, still sweaty, still smiling, and one of them traced a finger sensually along Amos's leg as they passed.

"And long may they *lay*," Amos added.

That set the two to laughing fit to bust and they drained their shots, which Amos dutifully replenished.

They hit the last set and they hit it hard. Hefty blew that harmonica like a freight train whistle and they treated the crowd to some of their best numbers—"Back Alley Blues," "Hard Rain Fallin'," "Root Workin' Woman." They'd saved them for last, knowing that Delbert would be back directly with Crawley, and they wanted to shine.

About halfway through the set, Amos spied Delbert slip in the side door with a tall, slick dude in a white suit and hat. The man was flanked with six low men -- hired muscle from the look -- but Amos could tell right away they weren't needed. The man had a presence, a will that almost sapped the life from the room.

When the man's hard, searching eyes met his, Amos felt cold, and the music, loud as the Second Coming, fell away to a distant murmur. The only people in the world were Amos and the man.

Jackson Crawley.

His white face was drawn and tight, large black circles under his eyes, his mouth invisible under his drooping salt-and-pepper mustaches. He removed his white fedora, his eyes never leaving Amos's.

Those eyes… hard-bitten, determined, *hungry*. They followed Amos as the man strolled unhurried behind Delbert, who smiled and glad-handed his way to the back room, and held the door for Crawley.

Crawley paused ever so briefly, holding Amos's eyes rapt for a heartbeat more, then disappeared through the door, trailed by his toughs. Delbert caught Amos's stare, winked, and slipped in behind them shutting the door.

Amos was dimly aware that the boys had downshifted into the slow, muddy tempo of "Blood on My Hands, Hurt in My Heart," and the dance floor was a gyrating throng of intertwined bodies, swaying like a teeming mass of cobras in a giant basket. Gradually, as if slowly rising from underwater, Amos came back to himself just in time to make the chord change.

Amos was the guitar man for the band, sure, but he was also the songwriter. He'd written all but three of their songs, mostly from past experience. The blues were more than just some rhyming words hung on some sweet chords and dressed with a little flair. No one knew that better than Black Dog Harlow.

A good many of his tunes were upbeat, good-timing numbers, but there were others, dark elegies that spoke right to the heart of every man and called him to account for old sins. "Blood on My Hands, Hurt in My Heart" was such a one, and though it reminded Amos of past wrongs, of events best left in the dark, it was one of his favorites, and it bled his conscience with a sweet, almost divine pain and left him wanting more.

So lost in the song, in the reverie and outpouring of loss was Amos that he barely checked himself in time to polish off the last riff with a downturn that brought catcalls and whoops from the dance floor. As the applause rattled, Hefty gave their thanks and bade the crowd hit the bar for last call, as it was on past three in the morning.

Amos was wiping his axe and putting it back in the case when he was clapped hard on the back. He stumbled and turned to see Delbert Gill smiling wide, teeth impossibly white in the haze of the barroom.

"Mm, mm, *mm*! Y'all damn near tore the *roof* off tonight! Gonna have to take it outta y'all's cut of the door, you know!" That set him to laughing right hard; laughing at his own jokes was but one skill among many for Delbert.

"Well," said Amos, "what'd he think?"

"Ha, ha! Why don't y'all come on back and see for yourselves? I'll get James to bring us some drinks. C'mon, now! Man don't like to be kept waitin'."

The Broke-Down Boys filed past the patrons of the speakeasy who were leaving by the alley door. Pats on the back, propositions, and knowing looks were exchanged for promises to come back and play for them all again soon.

Normally, the Boys would hang around past three, jamming amongst themselves and a few select regulars who were brave enough to sit in, but tonight they had business. If that business was good, the promises to return would be as empty as the shot glasses that lined the bar.

The narrow hallway they walked through opened onto a low-lit room with several poker and blackjack tables, a pool table, and a roulette wheel that had seen better days. Few people with lots of dollars got into this room, and lots of people with fewer dollars left it.

At the far end of the room, set back into a booth with a banker's light casting a green glow on the scarred table, sat Jackson Crawley, he of the white suit and hard eyes. A bottle of dark wine and an empty glass sat at his right hand, and Amos noticed the man's pallor was better, the dark circles gone, his mustaches now black as the Ace of Spades. His face fairly shone, his cheeks rosy, no longer wan.

This man, Amos knew, might be the Boys' ticket out of the juke-joints and roadhouses and into Radio City or Chicago, the easy life. For Hefty and Lowdown, it was a chance at the Big Time; for Amos, it was salvation itself. He didn't plan on leaving this room without it.

"C'mon in, boys, c'mon in!" drawled Crawley, his Southern-gentility oozing like molasses. "Set yourselves down and let's us hold palaver between us, what say?"

The boys made to sit down and were stopped by two pairs of ham-sized hands, as Crawley's men began to pat them down. Satisfied, they turned to Crawley, nodded wordlessly, and took positions to either side of three empty chairs at the table. The boys looked at each other in turn, hesitating.

"Come now, boys, sit on down. Forgive me, but one can never be too careful; a man in my position makes a lot of enemies. But you boys ain't no such animal, am I right? That's right. We all friends here, now, all friends, indeed."

James the bartender pushed through a hidden door to the kitchen made to look like the brown paneling of the back room wall. He set a tray with a jug of clear corn liquor and three Mason jars on the table, then faded back through the door like a ghost.

"Now, let us share a drink," Crawley said, filling the jars halfway, "and toast what I hope will be a fortuitous endeavor for all involved."

He poured himself more wine, and Amos couldn't help noticing the stuff flowed out slow like syrup. Lifting the glass and twirling it, he closed his eyes and sniffed the dark liquid. Amos watched the wine swirl around the glass, clinging a bit more than it should to the inside.

The boys lifted their jars in return, and everyone drank. Crawley rolled the wine around his palette and licked a drop off his lower lip, making a low, satisfied sound at the back of his throat.

"Delbert here has informed me what an investment you all might be, and from what I heard in there tonight, he might be right for a change."

Delbert perked right up, like a puppy that had brought the master his slippers. "Yessir, Mr. Crawley, I tol' you, ain't I? Tol' you them boys could wail! Ain't they everything I said? Ain't they just --"

Crawley shot Delbert a glance, brief, but hard enough to carry the message. Delbert Gill was speechless, something that Amos had never heard tell of, let alone seen.

"Well," said Crawley, smiling again at them. "They certainly are the best I've heard in and around these parts. Now, before we get to talkin' scratch, boys, I'd like to hear a might more about you, where you from, how you met, an' such." He twirled his hand in an impatient gesture, indicating that someone should get the ball rolling.

"Well, sir," Amos began, clearing his throat, "Hefty's from out Yazoo City way, an' he been knowin' Lowdown from way back, playin' up and down the Delta."

"Tha's right," said Lowdown. "We all met up in Jackson few years gone. But ol' Amos here, he the only Yankee in the bunch -- a New York man, if you please."

"Well, now, that so?" said Crawley, smiling wide. "You sure stroke that guitar like you ain't never *heard* of New York City."

Amos chuckled. "Hail from up 'round Mt. Vernon. Learned my pickin' in Harlem."

"I see, I see. And what brings you down South? Cain't be the *humidity*."

"Nossir. It's… it's a long story, sure enough. Mostly needed a change is all. Lookin' for what's down the road a piece."

"Ah," said Crawley, pouring them all another. "Wanderlust. The ol' travellin' itch. I know what you mean, boy. In fact, it's what brought *me* here, many moons ago. Come down with General Jackson to fight the Brits and take back the pearl of the Mississippi. Been here ever since. There's no place on earth quite like it."

Hefty frowned, doing the math. "But, that was…what? Eighty, ninety years gone? How—?"

"Ninety-three, to be precise, Mr. Creech. As to 'how,' well, the Crescent City has been a crossroads of the world for longer than the combined years of every man in this room," said Crawley, languidly swishing the dark wine in its glass.

"Folks from all over passed through these streets at one time or another—England, France, Germany, Eastern Europe. It's this last that concerns us here. A man, royal blood from Romania, once offered me a deal, similar to the deal I'm about to proffer you all. I took it and never looked back. As you can see, I have indeed prospered by it, and I mean to share that good fortune with you tonight."

Amos was dumbstruck, not sure where this was all going, but the short hairs on his neck were beginning to stand to attention. There was something wrong with this whole deal.

Until three days ago, he'd never heard of Jackson Crawley. He'd figured Delbert knew everybody he didn't know. That's how it'd always been. Delbert was the mover, the shaker, the one to glad-hand and palm-off a twenty with a Cheshire cat grin. Amos and the boys had always been along for the ride. Now it seemed the ride was coming to an end.

"Now, then, to business," Crawley said, leaning forward, lacing his fingers at his sharp chin.

"You would play five nights a week here at Delbert's, and at the occasional soirée at my plantation. Drinks, of course, would be *gratis*, as well as all the women you could bed. And, of course, shall we say… ten percent of the house take, including the gambling. You'd be pulling in, oh, I'd say about two hundred a week, give or take a slow night. That sound amenable to you boys?"

Hefty whistled long and low. "Hell you say! Two- *hundred*? For that kinda scratch we could cut our *own* records!"

Lowdown half-rose, fit to bust. "Now hold on! What the hell we *talkin'* 'bout, here? This ain't what we was tol—ow!"

Amos moved his foot from Lowdown's shin. "I believe," he said, "what my friend is tryin' to say, sir, is that we had an understandin' of a recording deal. Delbert here said you was well-connected, could get us some high-profile gigs, maybe some studio time, and the like."

"A-*ha*!" said Crawley. "I see now, Mr. Harlow, that you are the spokesman of the group. Forthright, yet respectful! I like that, sir! I like it, indeed! We shall make good company of one another, I can tell!" He swirled the wine and threw it back with an audible gulp.

"What you say is true, Mr. Harlow," Crawley said, wiping his lower lip with a thumb. "It is certainly within my power to do all you say…and *more*."

"More?" Amos asked, seeing Hefty and Lowdown lean forward out of the corner of his eye at the prospect of 'more.'

"Oh, almost assuredly more—more than you ever dreamed possible." He paused, looking down at the table, fingers steepled at his lips, considering his next words before looking up again.

"What would you say if I told you that you could be more than you are, that whatever ails you in the moment—mind, body, and soul—would vanish for all time? That you would never grow old and never die?"

The question hung in the air for a long moment. Then Amos burst out in cackling laughter, followed by Hefty and Lowdown. Crawley joined in, and not to be left out, so did Delbert.

"Well, sir," Amos said, drying his eyes, "I'd say either you been into a bad batch of ol' James's shine or you pullin' our legs somethin' fierce."

Crawley smiled thinly. "I assure you I have not and I *am* not."

The laughter died immediately.

Crawley continued, unperturbed, "After our… *transaction* is complete, you would be in my employ. Nay, *service* is a better word. Strict obedience and deference is what I require in exchange for immortality."

"Sounds like slavery to me," Lowdown said. "An' Mr. Lincoln threw that out with the garbage in my Granpappy's day."

"Yeah," Hefty chimed in. "I'm with Lowdown. We ain't much for being dogs on leashes, don't matter how much money on the table."

Crawley smiled wider than he had all night. "And what say *you*, Mr. Harlow? Is it unanimous, then?"

Amos twisted in his chair, suddenly aware of the presence of Crawley's goons. They seemed agitated, like hounds on a scent, straining against the leash. He rose slowly, and the boys followed suit.

"I think," he said, doffing is hat, "that our business is finished here, Mr. Crawley. There's obviously been some misunderstandin', and we sure sorry we took up your valuable time this evenin'. We just be goin' now, sir."

Crawley's smile never faltered, his eyes never left Amos. "Oh, there's definitely been a misunderstanding, Mr. Harlow. *You* seem to misunderstand; this was a non-negotiable deal. I want you, and I will simply *have* you. Curtis? Monroe?"

The two goons moved like shadows, slipping up behind Hefty and Lowdown, each circling an arm around each man's middle and grabbing their throats with the other hand.

Amos moved quick, grabbed up a pool cue from the table, and brought it down on Curtis's neck. The big man didn't flinch or break his hold on Lowdown as the cue snapped like an old pencil, leaving Amos holding a foot of splintered wood. He had barley registered a curse in his mind when the world fell in on him.

Amos hit the floor, his head reeling, and rolled over to see Delbert standing over him with a broken chair. But it wasn't Delbert, not the one he knew. The thing that stood before him had rows of jagged, warped teeth in such profusion that they extended out over his bottom lip. Delbert smiled the same 'jes'- folks' smile, even through all those teeth and a long, pink sinuous tongue slithered out from between them.

"Tried to tell you, son," the Delbert-thing said, tossing aside the mangled chair. "We coulda' had it good, alright. We coulda' run this town *forever*, but you had to go and queer the deal. I shoulda known, I guess. You never *did* know a good thing when it was starin' you in the face."

Delbert walked back over to Lowdown, grabbed the man's bearded chin, and jerked his head to the right. "But you 'bout to find out."

Delbert drew a long-clawed finger across Lowdown's neck in a quick stroke, as if he were flicking a bead of sweat. Blood welled up in a long crimson streak as Delbert pushed his head further back.

"A-Amos…" Lowdown gurgled through his severed throat, straining under Curtis's grip. His eyes pleaded for help that Amos was unable to give.

"Don'—don't…" Amos croaked, trying to crawl backwards, not wanting to see.

"Well, boys," said Crawley. "I suppose it *is* getting' on about suppertime. Eat up, now. Mr. Harlow, we'll speak again once you've, ah… come *around*, hear?" He got up and left the way James had come in, through the hidden door in the paneling.

All at once, Crawley's goons shed their skins or so it seemed to Amos in his haze. Their clothes fell away in tatters, revealing rough, scabby skin underneath. Jaws unhinged and rows of serrated teeth sprung forth. Guns were dropped in favor of six-inch talons. Eyes shone orange, jack-o-lanterns in the dim light of the room.

Delbert was laughing wildly, now, as he'd done many a drunken night on the town with Amos. He stared at Amos, pinning him down with laughter in his eyes, and sank his jaws into Lowdown's throat, tearing at it like a lion on a gazelle. Blood fountained across the ceiling, the wall, pattering to the floor like crimson rain. Lowdown thrashed, gave a half-strangled cry, and went still, his eyes staring into eternity.

Then Curtis and Monroe, each holding an end of Hefty, began to feed on the big man, one mangling his throat, the other steadily drinking the lifeblood from his thigh. Hefty drowned in his own blood before he could cry out.

Amos, too terrified to breathe a minute gone, now found new strength in terror and heaved himself off the floor, backing away toward the window. He grabbed a chair and swung it, breaking the glass, the cool night air giving him the clear head he needed.

"Where you goin', old man? Nobody 'scused you from the table!" Delbert taunted. He was on Amos between blinks, razor claws clutching his throat. Amos went dizzy, purple spots exploded at the edges of his vision.

"Just hang on, brother," Delbert cooed. "Few minutes, you gonna be thankin' me, I promise you."

Delbert's jaws unhinged impossibly far back, like a python's, the coppery scent of Lowdown's blood mixed with the smell of rotting corpses assailed his nostrils.

Near to passing out again, Amos reached in his pocket, flicked his wrist down, and brought the straight razor in an arc across Delbert's neck.

His old friend let out a screech that no animal on earth could ever match, clutching at his neck. Delbert reeled in shock, black-gray smoke curling out between his fingers. He pulled his hand away, looking in amazement at the black ichor that covered it, and began cackling madly again.

"That…" he gasped between laughs. "That… *hurt*!"

Amos stared for half a second at the blade, which was as clean and shiny as the last time he shaved. The junk shop man he'd bought it from said it was a fine blade… for the right man. Amos had wondered what the man had meant, but now was not the time for retrospective. He pocketed the razor and jumped, tumbling ass over elbows out the broken window.

He landed hard on his back, his fall broken only by bags full of trash and glass empties, which shattered under his weight and cut him mercilessly about the shoulders and arms. Breathing like a bellows, he ignored the pain and hobbled up the alley.

"Go ahead, Amos!" screeched Delbert, hanging out the window. 'Go on and run, son! We ain't finished, you hear? Not by miles, Amos! Not by *miles*!"

Amos *did* run.

He'd thought his days of running were long past when he met Hefty and Lowdown. Lord, how they'd talked of days to come, of the horn of plenty that awaited them when they hit it big. But even when they just sat around making music, picking up on each others' jams and carrying them on out into a song—those were the times Amos loved best. Just them and the music. No more running.

And now here he was, running again, down a different alley, from a different past.

He cried at last, the night's horror finally hitting him. Three blocks later, he noticed he still clung to the broken pool cue like a talisman against the dark. He ran on into the night, east, toward what he hoped would be daybreak.

Delbert's cawing laughter echoed throughout the city streets, following him.

****

"I'm tired of runnin'," he said.

"Ah- *hah*," Delbert said. "An' you just 'spect me to believe that?"

"Don't give a damn *what* you believe. I just want muh peace, 's all."

Delbert leaned back in his chair and searched Amos's face for any sign of bullshit. He unbuttoned his collar, spreading it wide, and lifted his chin.

"Still hurts when it rains," he said. The scar was ugly, a broken and yellowed thing that hadn't faded with age. "Never could figure out why the damn thing never healed proper."

Amos ignored him and drained another glass, studying its bottom as carefully as he'd studied the last dozen or so. "I suppose Crawley just up and retired, that it?" he asked, gesturing to the white suit Delbert now wore.

"Let's us just say he lived a might *too* long. Old man got lazy, sloppy. Didn't take no genius to see that somebody'd make a move against him. Why not me?

"It was right easy enough to take over," Delbert bragged. "He done all the heavy liftin' way before I got here. Didn't take no more than a minute's work one night after he got drunk-up on some nice school girls I got fo' 'im. Slipped in while he laid up in that four-poster bed like a fat ol' leech, took care of business all nice and tidy."

"Drugged them girls when you stole 'em, did you?" Amos said impassively, pouring another round for himself. "You could always count on ol' Delbert to think 'round them corners, ain't it?"

"Yessir, boy," Delbert grinned. "You know me." He leaned in over the table. "But now we got to figure out what we gonna do to settle up, Amos. See, I let you walk out, my boys get to thinkin' I ain't leading type, get it? An' I done worked too long and hard for that."

"Cain't have that, can we?" Amos muttered into his empty glass.

"That's right, old man. We cain't. The offer's still on the table, jes' like before."

Amos thought about it and for a second, he wondered what it would be like to be free of pain, free of the weariness that threatened to drag him down, mile after long mile. He could stop running. It could all end here, now, with a word and a moment's pain.

Then he thought of the monster he would necessarily become -- a thing of the night, shunning the daylight, feeding on the lifeblood of others. Then he wondered if that would be any different than the monster he was at present.

"I'll take it," he said.

Delbert laughed loud and long, clapping Amos on the back hard enough to rattle his teeth. "*That's* my boy! I knew you'd come 'round!"

Amos grabbed Delbert's wrist, snake-quick. Delbert's laughter died fast. James and his twin were at the table flanking their boss, hands inside jackets. Amos never even saw them move.

"Not here," Amos almost begged. "Not here in front of everybody. Not after… not after that *night…*" he said, eyes welling up with tears.

Delbert glanced up at James, dismissing him with a nod of the head. James gave a questioning look. "It's all right, man. He right. This is somethin' between friends. It's cool. Keep an eye on things, hear?"

Delbert stood, holding out a hand to Amos, who heaved a giant sigh, his chest hitching in quiet sobs. After a long minute, Amos took the hand and let himself be led around the table and across the dance floor, his legs unsteady, shaking.

Faceless dancers glanced up at them as they passed, orange eyes flickering like candles, gyrating with abandon to the slow sound of Amos's stolen song, a cotillion of the damned swaying to the eternal rhythm of hell.

Delbert reached the door and held it open for Amos, who trudged through, every step a chore. The night's humidity nearly drowned him, but he was sweating from more than the heavy air, more than the whiskey. He heard the door shut and turned around.

His old friend stood framed in the alley door's light, a shadow with eyes of fire.

"Guess we both knew it would come to this," Delbert said. "Cain't say I'm sorry, neither. But don't you worry, ol' buddy. Ol' Delbert ain't gonna leave you in the cold, nossir. There's… *precautions* you gotta take to livin' like this, but there's glories, too, Amos. Oh, the *glories*…!"

Amos shifted foot to foot, wondering when the bastard would shut his face.

"Yessir, there's a whole *world* waitin', Amos! You always was the smart one out the bunch, and you gonna be right there with me! Ain't gonna be like ol' Crawley wanted, nossir! We gonna be big time, Amos! Chicago, St, Louis, hell, maybe even Los Angeles! Whatchu think about that, now?"

"That… that sounds… mighty fine, I reckon. But…" Amos said.

"But *what*? You backin' out now? Time for second thoughts done long passed, old man."

"Naw, it's just…" Amos began, "could -- could you do something for me, Del? 'Fo' we see them glories?" He reached into his coat pocket.

Delbert tensed like a bunched spring. He'd expected the old fool to try some nonsense, some last ditch business. He still remembered the damned razor, that curious, wicked little bitch from some forgotten corner of hell that had almost stolen his life -- his *new* life. He was ready.

Amos pulled out a sterling silver flask, unscrewed the cap, and took a drink. He winced as the fluid burned his throat. "Drink with me? Old times' sake an' all that?"

Delbert relaxed, crowing in laughter that made the windows shake in their frames. "Damn, Amos! I'm liable to get plastered on the first drop of your blood, son! You always *could* hold your liquor!"

"Yeah, I reckon," Amos chuckled, "but you know, just for good times gone, better times ahead, right?" He held out the flask.

Delbert cocked his head, peering at Amos through heavy lids. Then, grinning wide, he took the flask, shaking his head. "Doors closing, new ones openin', like that?" he asked.

"Somethin' very like that," Amos said with a weak smile.

"Well," said Delbert toasting Amos with the flask. "Old times, future glories," and he tipped the flask to his lips and took a good long pull.

Delbert grimaced. "Amos, all that drinkin' musta killed yo' taste. That there hooch is watered dow -- *acgkk*!!"

"Yeah, I know," Amos sighed, looking at his shoes. "With holy water."

Delbert's face was contorted in a rictus of terror and white hot pain, pain that would never stop, never end. His neck swelled up like an inner tube, bubbling and distorting, threatening to explode. He clawed at it, black talons digging furrows in his neck from which black ichor spilled, painting the ground darker shades of night.

"Yeah," said Amos, biting the tip off a cheroot, spitting it out. "Got it from over to St. Anthony's on Bourbon. *You* remember St. Anthony's, right?" He lit the cigar with his last match and tossed the empty book to the street. He leaned against the alley wall, blowing smoke. At his feet, Delbert gagged and clawed at the ground, dying by inches.

"You 'member— heh, heh!—you 'member the time ol' Father Feeny run us off after he caught us pissin' on the manger scene that Christmas, drunk as two coots? When was that—'24? '25? Lord, but that ol' man could holla, yes he could!" Amos shook his head, laughing to himself at the memory.

Delbert had managed to get to his knees. His face was that of a thousand bee-stings, his eyes bulged in and out of their sockets like pistons. He wheezed, clinging to unholy life, trying to stand. Anger and equal parts surprise coursed through his dying body.

Who's sloppy now, *Del,* Amos thought. *Who's sloppy* now*?*

Amos glanced down casually, as if he'd forgotten Delbert was there, the nightmare that was his former friend, bleeding black in the Big Easy back-alley where it had all started. He hooked a hand under Delbert's armpit and helped him to his feet.

Delbert clawed spastically at him, trying to hook even one claw in Amos's neck, frothing at the mouth. Amos swatted the hand away and slapped him hard across the teeth.

"Listen to me, you dumb shit," Amos growled, low and even. "You took my music, you took my friends, you almost took my life. But you ain't gettin' my *soul.*"

He reached under his coat again and pulled something long and skinny from his belt.

"You remember this? Huh? You remember it?" Amos yelled, gripping the scruff of Delbert's swollen neck. "Look at it! Look hard!"

Delbert's eyes rolled in agony; one came loose with a loud pop and rolled into the gutter like a child's marble. He was breathing like a spastic locomotive, and his remaining eye widened at the sight of what Amos held.

The jagged end of a pool cue.

"Tha's right," Amos growled, grinning fiercely. "I kep' it all these years, hung on to it with my hate. I touched it every night I bedded down, thinkin' of the day I'd bring it back to you."

Delbert's eye watered with a sudden, terrible knowledge. It rolled up and met Amos's, pleading.

"Hefty and Lowdown say hello," Amos said, and rammed the cue through Delbert's chest, piercing his heart.

The impact threw Delbert's convulsing frame five feet, where he fell twitching, clutching at the pool cue. Smoke began to pour from every hole in his body. Amos shielded his eyes as bright, green-orange flame erupted from Delbert's eye-sockets and mouth, as if he'd swallowed a dozen Roman candles. The strange fire burned so hot that it singed the hairs on Amos's forearm from six paces.

Delbert burned for what seemed to Amos an eternity, and then the flames suddenly whooshed out, and silence reigned in the dark street. Amos looked around, waiting for James and the rest of the gin joint to come spilling out into the alley, hungry for his blood, his life.

But no doors burst open, no shouts of indignation were given, no unearthly shrieks to wake the dead, no slavering maws mottled with the blood of boon companions—nothing like that horrible night ten years gone. The only sound came as a cool night breeze swept down through the eaves like a gift from God, rattling tin cans and chilling the sweat on his brow.

All that remained of Delbert Gill was a mound of ash, vaguely in the shape of a man. Then the breeze picked up the ash, swirled it around in a little eddy, and scattered it into the night. Amos heard the wooden rattle as the pool cue, now free, rolled down the cobblestones after it.

He picked up the flask, wiped it on his shirttail, and dropped it into his coat pocket. No one would put up a fuss over all that had happened—Delbert had been living proof of that. Some other lowlife in his entourage would step in and fill the vacuum, Amos was sure, and the whole sorry business would start over again.

But not for him. That would be someone else's burden. New Orleans was dead to him now. He was out. He'd done his piece.

A low fog bank had crept into the city in the witching hour, swirling around him like lost memories, and Amos beat feet into its heart, putting the past—or at least a part of it—behind him for good.

WAITIN' FOR JASPER

A Song of the Black Dog

Eating, and hospitality in general, is a communion, and any meal worth attending by yourself is improved by the multiples of those with whom it is shared.

—Jesse Browner

Amos "Black Dog" Harlow had never seen so many damned mosquitoes in his life. Not even down on Grand Isle, where they roiled like storm clouds in the Mississippi River Basin, or in South Georgia, where they competed with sand gnats for the blood of the innocent.

He pulled off his tattered porkpie hat and swatted the air in front of him, swirling the miserable bastards into a swarm that would not abate; in fact, it seemed to stoke their bloodlust. Grumbling, he gave up and let them eat.

"Them critters get right hungry, ain't it?" The red-faced, balding man sat in a rocking chair, see-sawing back and forth on the little general store's porch. He grinned, revealing rotted teeth and the gaping vacancies of previous tenants. He was sweeping his own aging flop hat casually in front of him, apparently used to the bugs.

Next to him in another rocker sat a large man, snoring the sweltering afternoon away, a plate with gnawed spare-ribs smeared with barbecue sauce on the small table to his right. His mouth was drawn open in an oval and he breathed heavy and rough. A string of drool hung from his mouth and pooled on a sauce-stained work shirt whose buttons strained at the eyeholes, revealing a pale, hairy belly beneath. Rolls of fat hung bare above his britches and mosquitoes covered them like black stars of strange constellations, but the man continued to sleep. If not for the steady rise and fall of his chest, Amos would have pegged him for a corpse.

"Reckon they do, at that," Amos said, taking another pull off his sarsaparilla. It was cold and pungent on his throat, and he lamented that it was almost gone.

"Gitcha another 'un?" the man asked, gesturing to the bottle.

"Nah," Amos said. "That was my last nickel."

"'s'alright," the man said, reaching into the rusted electric ice chest behind him. "Owner's a friend," he said. "He won't mind; he's off huntin' the swamps. Be back 'round sundown. I'm watchin' the place, see?" He wrenched the top and handed the sweating bottle to Amos, who took it gladly. "Yeah, ol' Jasper, he ain't gonna mind," he said.

"My thanks, Mister…?"

"Dale," the man said. "Ain't no mister to it, just Dale."

"Well, my thanks, Dale." Amos replied. "I'm Amos."

"This ol' can o' lard here is Earl." He smacked Earl in the face with the old flop hat. The big man barely moved. "Wake up and make yer manners, Earl."

Earl stirred briefly after three more swats from the flop hat, shifted his head to the right, and dropped off again, snoring even louder.

Dale shook his head in disgust, peering at the other man through heavy-lidded eyes. "Dammit, if that don't beat the band. Sumbitch would sleep through a *herricane* if I let 'im." He turned to Amos. "Now, you said somethin' about bein' broke?"

Amos shifted a bit. "I'm sort of between things right now," he said. "Thought I'd head up to Carolina, see if I cain't pull me some tobacco for a spell."

"Ol' Tobacco Road," Dale said. "Yeah, I reckon they's always gonna be work up thataway, lessen this drought kills everything like out in the plains. Tell you what," he said. "Why don't you hang about a while? When Jasper gets back, we'll have us some supper 'fore you leave."

"Well, that's mighty kind of you, Dale."

"That's settled, then," Dale said. "Yessir, Jasper always brings home the good eats. Where y'all from, anyhow?"

"New York, originally," Amos said. "Mount Vernon."

"Hell you say! You a Yankee?"

"Born and raised," Amos said, "but I ain't been back in a long while. Prolly never will."

"How's that? You disown the place?"

"Other way around, more like," Amos said, staring into his bottle.

"Well, hell," Dale said, breaking the awkward silence. "I 'spect you all right for a Yankee. Nobody got a claim on home no more anyways, not with this here Depression on."

"Ain't *that* the truth," Amos muttered.

They dropped into silence again, Dale fanning himself against the mosquitoes and Amos pulling hard on the bottle. In the window, a radio played low and Amos could hear the final strains of "Be Thou My Vision" sung in tinny, off-key tones by a congregation.

Then a man's voice, clear as a church bell, rang out above the din:

"That's fine! That's mighty fine!" the voice said. *"God cherishes the sound of praise from His children, does He not?"*

A cacophony of "Amen!" and "Praise Jesus!" sounded through the gathering.

"And we have every right to praise His name, even in the midst of trials and tribulations, do we not, beloved?"

Again, the chorus agreed in scattered response.

"And why shouldn't we? Is it not our sacred duty to the One who gave us life? The One who loves us more than the angels? The One who has set us high in His kingdom?"

More shouting. That preacher-man was hooking them from the jump, Amos thought.

"Who are we but the meek, the downtrodden, the salt and light of the earth? We sit in squalor, sifting through the dust of drought for our next meal. We leave our homes and move to terra incognita *searching for that better life, that land of milk and honey, where we can live out our lives in the peace and glory of the Almighty!"*

"Fella's layin' it on a might thick, you ask me," Dale muttered. Amos nodded, but kept listening, drawn in by the man's sermon despite himself.

"I have seen it all, friends. Arlen Guidry has been to the mountain. I have looked into the valley of the Jordan. I have seen the wickedness that dwells there—men cavorting with men, wanton lust in the eyes of the womenfolk, drunkards, fornicators, warmongers—all of them sitting in their fine clothes and manor houses while the faithful suffer needlessly in the streets, on the back roads of this great nation, in the fields that no longer bear fruit. And I ask you—is that right*?"*

This time the clamor was so loud that the microphones got feedback. Guidry didn't wait for the crowd to quiet.

"NO! No! It isn't *right! But you know something, friends? God doesn't mean for it to be that way, no sir! God wants His children to be cared for, to be*

fed, to be safe.

But that can't happen while we wander in the wilderness like the children of Israel, scraping the dead earth for manna and praying for deliverance! Not by a mile, beloved!

God works His will through His people , *don't you know? That has* always *been God's way! And that's why, friends, we have to step up to the plate, get angry, get busy, and kick Satan and those in his service back to Hell where they* belong !"

Again the microphones screamed in protest. If he didn't know better, Amos would have figured the gathering for a riot, not a tent-meeting. The crowd died down again, but only just, and now Guidry was bellowing so as to be heard above the din.

"BUT BEHOLD, CHILDREN—BEHOLD THE DAY OF THE LORD! IT HAS *COME AS A THIEF IN THE NIGHT, CATCHING US ALL UNAWARES! THE DAY OF REPENTENCE HAS LONG SINCE COME, AND THE DAY OF JUDGMENT IS NIGH!"*

The crowd was beside itself, the clamor so great that Earl snorted and woke with a start, blinking the sleep from his eyes and rubbing his ample belly.

"So what do we do now, *friends?"* Guidry had assumed a hushed voice, full of sincerity woven with just a hint of fear, letting the congregation know that they were all in it together, all adrift in the same boat, looking for the same lighthouse.

"What recourse for the children of the Lord in these dark days? I'll tell you what -- the gospel must reach the four corners of the earth before the Devil can claim it all!

"And how does that happen? It starts right here, right in this tent, in your very hometown. It starts by giving back to the Lord what is His! The gentlemen in the suits will come down the aisles. Won't you give freely, won't you give— "

"I swan," Dale said, switching off the radio, "that's right where them Bible-thumpers always lose me, when they start passin' the hat."

"Whut time is it getting' to be?" Earl asked, swimming up from out of his nap. His voice was syrupy, deep and basso. "I'm gettin' a might peckish," he said, staring forlornly at the plate of bones.

"Hell, you *always* peckish, son. I reckon you'd eat ever' durn thing in the icebox, if I'd let you," said Dale.

Earl raised one cheek off the chair and farted with gusto. "Ain't true," he said, smacking his lips.

"Hell it *ain't*," said Dale. "And anyways you gonna have to wait, just like the rest of us. Jasper ain't back yet. You know how he gets if we start without 'im. 'Sides, he's bringin' supper, so just tighten that belt and keep your peace, fat-ass."

Amos shook his head and chuckled, wondering at these two. He hadn't seen another place for miles around, if one didn't count abandoned farms whose families had moved west looking for work in the citrus fields of California, or the skeletons of tobacco barns standing empty and dark, like forgotten watchtowers at the edge of a dead empire.

He'd figured on trying to snag a catfish or two in the Ogeechee River, not three miles distant. He would string them up on his shoelace while he made a fire on the bank. Then he'd cook them up right with a little cornmeal from his sack, have his meal, and stretch out beneath the cypress trees and weeping willows that hung out over the black water, always mindful of cottonmouths sleeping in the limbs.

But then he'd turned a bend and happened upon the old store, right smack in the middle of Nowhere, Georgia, and these fellows had been kind enough to offer a man—a *black* man, no less—a seat at their table. Luck like that didn't come along often, especially not for him, and the desire to rest had been too strong to deny. It hadn't helped that the sarsaparilla was so damned good, either.

"Yeah, boy," said Dale, fanning himself with his flop hat. "Ol' Jasper sure knows how to find the game, an' that's the truth. Earl, you remember that time Jasper went out to fetch breakfast and come back near-on dark with damn-near twenty head of fox?"

"Oh, yeah," said Earl. "That was a right harvest that day. Musta et off them varmints for least a month."

"Jasper said he found 'em up to the ol' Harper place," said Dale. "Folks had done up and left, and the henhouse was damn-near painted red with chicken blood. Weren't nothin' left but shit and feathers. So he hunted and kilt ever' one o' them bastids an brung 'em to the house, bellies swole up with chicken. Then Jasper says, he says 'Fellas, looks like we's havin' fox *and* chicken for supper.' Now how you like that, Amos? Ain't that a thing?"

"Sure is," Amos agreed, smiling.

"And how about that time Jasper come back from fishin' the river, totin' two dead boars, one on each shoulder, just as neat as you please?" said Earl. "Wasn't nothin' to that ol' hoss. Had them hogs hefted up like sacks of grain, musta been 'bout three-hunnerd pounds of pig, all told. Tossed 'em on the stump out back like doll babies, he did, and set to cuttin'. Had so much pork in the icebox, got to where we was sick of bacon."

"He once-t set a pecan tree ablaze to smoke out a passel of coons hiding in the branches. Sumbitches was already cooked and pecan-smoked to boot, time we got 'em down." said Dale. "Now that was some *fine* eatin', Lord yes!"

"Yessir," Earl drawled, "it's feast over famine 'round here, thanks to Jasper. Hell, I bet he'd even get us one them elly-fants, if one was to be found these parts."

"Your're a damn fool," Dale said, shooting a disdainful look at the fat man. "Ever'body knows them things is in Australia; all them Aussies eat purt-good, use the entire animal, don't you know. Even make furniture outta the teeth, so I'm told."

"Who's the fool?" Earl whined. "Aussies is in *England*, stupid."

"Anyhow," said Dale, unperturbed, "ol' Jasper done kilt nigh-on ever'thing that walks or crawls, but that there's the rub, ain't it?"

"Whatchu mean?" Amos asked.

"Well, now, it's done got so's that the woods 'round these parts got scarce with game. The drought's part of it, but Jasper's had a hand in it as well. Done hunted out the whole county, near as not. Now he's havin' to go farther, look longer, and we havin' to take what we can get, so to speak."

"Ain't had to eat no dog yet, thank Christ," said Earl.

"Hell but if you ain't gonna bring us to just that, you keep eatin' like you do," said Dale, glaring sourly at his friend.

Amos took a final pull on his sarsaparilla and wiped the foam from his beard. Night was coming on, and the sky was a pink and orange blaze far in the west. The moon, full and bright, had come out over the woods behind the store, and silver bands of light filtered through the boughs of the pecans and the oaks surrounding them.

"Y'all want another?" said Dale.

"Lord, no," Amos said. "Bladder's about bust as it is. Reckon I better shake it off."

"Outhouse is 'round back," said Earl. "Watch for them copperheads. Sumbitches look just like the ground; cain't hardly see 'em in the daytime, even."

Behind the store all was black as pitch. Ancient oaks and dogwoods created a canopy that barely allowed the moonlight through their branches. Amos could barely make out the stumps two feet in front of him. His toe caught one and he tripped, catching himself on the stump before he crashed to the ground. He groped on the stump for support as he rose.

The stump's wide surface was grooved with thin hatchet marks. He assumed it was a wood-chopping stump until his hand came away with tufts of what felt like fur or animal hair. It was coarse and dry in his hands. He blew it off and rubbed his hands on his pant legs.

Must be where the ol' boy cleans his kills, Amos thought.

He fetched around in the dark until his eyes adjusted, then saw the looming shape of the outhouse ahead. It was tall and leaning, a little big for a place to shit in. He eased his way forward in the dark, careful to shuffle in case there were anymore stumps.

He opened the door and was hit full-on by the stench. It was the raw, fecund odor of rich earth and slaughterhouses, of decaying foliage and corpses—an undertaker's smell. Underneath that, the almost-pleasant smell of wood smoke, a smell that always brought back memories of red and gold leaves, crisp days and cool nights, the tangy bite of apple cider, and shirt-sleeves before the harvest.

He pawed around in the dark before him, the nauseous odor thick in his nostrils. His left shoulder brushed up against something heavy, causing it to sway away from him and return with a harder bump. He reached out and felt the object and recoiled in disgust, then touched it again, laughing at his nerves.

It was dry to the touch, but Amos had skinned enough animals in his days to know their flesh when he felt it. He reached out around him and felt other hanks of meat, setting them to sway gently in the dark. A dry chuckle escaped his throat.

"What now, Amos?" he asked himself. "You gonna take a piss in the damn smokehouse?"

Shaking his head and grinning, he turned to leave and a string brushed his cheek; he heard the chain tied to it clink on the light bulb above. He gave it a sharp tug and light spilled into the room. He gasped, recoiling in terror.

Faces of the dead stared at him through drawn and agonized eyes atop human torsos that were field-dressed and black with soot, dangling from heavy chains and hooks like sides of beef in a cool-house.

Ol' Jasper done kilt near ever'thing that walks or crawls.

He gave a strangled cry and stumbled blindly backwards, the human carcasses swinging pell-mell into him like punching bags. He tripped and fell into a pile of bones—rib cages and femurs in various states of decay.

We havin' to take what we can get, so to speak.

He cried out again, reaching up to a two-by-four in the wall's frame to pull himself up. It gave under his weight and a row of grinning, human skulls toppled on top of him.

Yessir, we eat purty good 'round here, thanks to Jasper.

He panicked in the middle of that small Golgotha, his mind racing, screaming for him to run. He practically flew to the door, yanked it open, and ran straight into Dale and Earl.

"Whoa there, podner!" said Dale. "We thought you's lost back here! See you found the smokehouse!"

"Outhouse's over yonder," said Earl, lazily nodding to the south. "Prolly should've toldja that."

The two men stood looking at him, as if the nightmare in which they stood was no more than standing in their grandmother's kitchen. Earl was gnawing on a bone from his plate. He tossed it into the yard and picked at his teeth, trying to remove some gristle.

Amos tried to speak, but found speech had left him and sheer terror had filled the vacancy.

"C'mon up the store," said Dale. "Japser's back, and he got us some fine eatin' this evenin', I tell you what."

Dale turned and cupped his hands. "Hey, Jasper! C'mon out here and meet Amos! We havin' him for supper!"

Amos's body acted when his mind refused to. He elbowed Dale in the gut and shoved past Earl, heading straight into the dark woods, caring little for any danger ahead, only to flee that which was most assuredly at his back.

He turned to look back only briefly. In the light from the smokehouse, he saw a lumbering figure in overalls dragging a gunny sack.

And Jasper turned to watch him flee into the night.

He couldn't be sure, even after he was far over the South Carolina line, but in his mind's eye he saw a face like melted wax, with two bulging, close-set eyes that looked out on the world differently from the rest of mankind. Tufts of hair grew like ragweed out of a misshapen head and hands at the end of ape-like arms clutched an axe wet with blood.

Amos ran full-tilt through the woods, his lungs burning like acid, and disappeared into the Georgia night.

The three men watched him go until the crashing of his feet through the forest receded and finally died out.

"Well, what the *hell…?*" said Earl.

Dale shook his head in disgust.

"*Yankees.*"

CAUGHT UP IN THE SPIRIT

A Song of the Black Dog

"Oh what's that in the hollow, so pale I quake to follow?"
"Oh that's a thin dead body which waits the eternal term."

—Christina Rossetti,
Amor Mundi

He watched, detached and remote, as his shadow swung listlessly back and forth in the waning light. Agony had lost all meaning and pain was just a word dimly remembered.

His hands and feet bore no sensation, as if they had never existed, though he could see them dangling uselessly, like a marionette with its strings cut.

Above, he could hear the slow creaking of the rope against the branch as his body pendulumed back and forth in the gentle breeze. His neck was afire, the only sensation remaining, and he could feel every fiber of the thin braid slicing into his skin like a million knives in a million steady hands.

He had long since stopped fighting; thrashing only served to speed death along. What little feeling remained in his tired, broken limbs was reserved for bruises the color of angry evening skies, of apocalyptic sunsets on alien worlds. He was done praying for release from even these minor torments. No worse could be done him.

At first, he'd held onto some measure of faith after the rope didn't break his neck; the white boys had just thrown the noose about his neck and hauled him up. His windpipe, miraculously uncrushed, had closed to the size of a dime and his breathing came in a thin, reedy whistle.

Now, not quite dead, but well on his way, he gazed through swollen eyes out on a wilderness devoid of any hope of escape from his present darkness.

This was good, though. He could watch the sun set for a final time across this patchwork landscape, this carpet of reds, oranges, of greens and yellows that would give Joseph's coat a run for its money. Soon, a final darkness would draw the blanket of sleep over his eyes as nightfall swathed the earth in shadow, leaving diamonds in the sky. He would drink that last dusk as deeply and as thoroughly as he'd ever swilled anything from a bottle.

Realization brought certain serenity, and he was surprised to find he could manage a weak smile as he watched a family of rabbits scamper through the clover, munching and nudging the young along on an evening picnic. They seemed to be in no hurry, casually nibbling here, sniffing there, all the time in the world. He envied them, but only briefly. The daddy rabbit sat back on its haunches, chewing thoughtfully at some milkweed and eyed the stranger in the tree.

Eat up, now, he thought. *Eat up and run along, or ya'll be somebody* else's *supper!*

But the rabbit merely turned its head toward him, as if hearing his ragged thoughts, and stared. It was so lifelike, its movements so *human*, that Amos Harlow was almost nonplussed when it spoke.

"This is your own fault, you know," the rabbit said, scratching its long ear.

Amos thought he must be delirious. After all, the blood in his head was pounding like a hammer, squeezed up into his skull as it was, so he didn't see any harm in answering.

"What..." Lord, it hurt to force words through that tiny hole. "What... y-you *m-mean*?" he croaked.

"Well," the rabbit continued, chewing thoughtfully on some thistle, "*look* at you. This is where all saints end *up*, ain't it? Burning on a pile of wood, nailed to a damn tree, or," the rabbit gestured with a front paw at Amos, "swinging by the neck from a rope. I mean, it's all pretty elemental, right?"

"*I— I...ain't done nothin'—*"

"You 'ain't done nothin' to deserve this,' right? Oh, Amos, *everybody's* done *somethin'* to deserve this—this and *worse.* Don't you *know* that? What—you think you're different 'cause you been *chosen*? Because you been all over, fixin' things for people, helpin' your fellow man and all that Golden Rule bullshit?"

Amos stared at the rabbit as it hiked a leg and dropped six or seven steaming pellets on the ground. The rest of the family was scuttling over the edge of the rise before him, content with the evening feast and apparently heading home.

"Nobody can earn a new life, Amos. Nobody gets to wipe away their own sins. You ought to know that better than most, I'd reckon."

The rabbit turned and headed along behind its family. It paused, glancing over one shoulder. "You just swing there for awhile and think on that. Ain't like you're goin' anywhere, right?" It gave what Amos supposed was a chuckle, but sounded more like a rusty hinge creaking on an old door, and disappeared over the rise and down into the valley.

Amos did think on it, at least until the sun, still just above the horizon, grew dim, and he realized with a certain satisfaction that it was his own eyes, his own personal sundown.

And then all was night.

* * * *

He came around to someone whistling—a hymn, one he recognized. He searched his dwindling memory: "Nearer My God to Thee." He then recalled that the song was played by the four-man orchestra on the Titanic as it went down, and he remembered his own hopeless situation.

He had no idea how long he'd been out—a few minutes, an hour—it was all relative in the midst of his misery. The horizon was haloed in orange fire and the first stars were beginning to twinkle in the darkening sky. So it hadn't been but a few minutes, after all. The air was beginning to take a chill that soon would be unbearable. He wondered idly which would kill him first—asphyxiation or exposure? Or maybe the rednecks would come back in their loud truck to check on him, maybe take some potshots with a squirrel rifle. Three hits gets the kewpie doll.

The whistling grew louder and he heard feet crunching on the dry ground. He peered through swollen eyes and saw the silhouette of a tall white man in a parson's hat, the kind with the wide brim and rounded crown. The man went right on whistling, as if it were an everyday event to come upon a hanged man in the wilderness. The man clasped his hands behind his back, whistling the chorus to its finish:

Still all my song will be
Nearer, my God, to Thee,
Nearer my God to Thee,
Nearer to Thee.

The man stood in the dying of the light, appraising Amos silently, watching him swing in the evening breeze. It was maddening, and Amos yearned for the breath to curse the man just once for standing there, nonchalant, while another man went slowly and painfully to his grave. It struck Amos that the man might think him already dead, but Amos wasn't in the mood for benefit of the doubt.

The man continued to stare, and the blood collecting in Amos's head began to roar in his ears, like the sound of the ocean in a seashell. Just before he blacked out again, for what he knew would be the final time, Amos, through slitted eyes, saw the man shaking his head.

"No. This won't do," the man said. "This won't do at all." He walked toward Amos, his hands outstretched as if to embrace him—Death come at last to take him in his bony arms and bear him North or South, according to his sins.

****

Amos came to with the most brilliant pain he'd known in his entire life. The knives at his throat before were now spears, wielded by Spartans with a grudge, and they pierced him through the throat and chest, pinning him to the ground.

For he *was* on the ground, lying on his back, looking up through the branches of the tree he hung from scant hours ago, at a noonday sun that was both warming and merciless. It burned through his swollen eyelids, carving a kaleidoscope of patterns of the branches above on his retinas. He had slept most of the morning, it seemed. The air was cool and crisp, but the ground was pleasantly warm under him, and he wished he could go on forever just laying there, the sounds of the birds overhead and the wind in the pines soothing him.

He had to take another breath and he dreaded the act. He

carefully inhaled and the pain was worse than when he couldn't breathe at all. His lungs, long-starved, couldn't quite remember their job, and Amos ended up hacking what felt like needles in his chest.

Wiping his mouth, he noticed the noose on the ground next to him, the rope cut a foot above the knot. He looked up and saw the rope swaying in the breeze, frayed and weightless.

The man, the whistler, had cut him down. Amos scanned the landscape, but the man was nowhere to be found. He was alone as he'd ever been.

He tried to stand and fell, the blood not all returned to its proper place, but he had to get vertical for that to happen. He had to get out of these woods and back to a road, back to the familiar, even if it meant risking running into the white boys again. But no, he didn't think that likely; they'd been drunker than hell and were probably sleeping it off in some shotgun shack up in Mountain Rest.

He'd had some trouble once before coming through Appalachia, up around Franklin, North Carolina, but no more than the bum's rush he usually got from being a black man in a white town -- a stern warning from a sheriff that never actually met his eyes.

This time he'd made the mistake of hitching from Seneca instead of footing it up the mountain on his own. The will was there, but his body had vetoed. Amos wasn't yet sixty, but there were days when he felt eighty or better. The road had done its worst.

His plan had been to lay low in the old Stumphouse Tunnel, an unfinished Confederate railroad tunnel, forgotten and unused since the end of the Civil War. It was a known flop for most of the hobos that passed through the Blue Ridge on their way north or south.

He'd seen the three hicks watching him with utter contempt as he rode away on the truck bed from the five-and-dime in the center of town, their slack jaws hovering above brown bottles in paper bags. When the old man had dropped him near Stumphouse Tunnel Road, he'd merely pointed to a handmade, weatherworn sign nailed to a dogwood. The red letters were peeling and faded, but the message was loud and clear. It was a message Amos knew well:

"Don't let tha sun go down on yor black ass in this here town."

Amos turned to thank the man anyway, but the truck had already pulled away, straining in second for its climb up the mountain. The boys had set on him soon after. There were three of them, and while

Amos could pull his own, three-on-one were shit odds for any man, drunk or sober. They'd thrown a gunny sack over his head and tossed him into the bed of a truck, two of the assholes climbing in alongside. They drove for awhile, whooping and laughing, every now and again kicking him in the head, the stomach, wherever they could land a boot.

Next thing he knew he was hauled off his feet, grabbing at his neck, the rope biting deep. They stayed for awhile, yelling obscenities, cursing him with every name for a black man they could find, even throwing rocks, though most of those missed, besotted as they were. Eventually, they left, kids having squeezed all the fun out of a game, and he was left alone in the wilderness to die.

Now here he was, throat raw and bleeding, head the size of a pumpkin, holding forth with talking rabbits and wondering where his good Samaritan had gone. As if in answer to his thoughts, he heard a voice from over the ridge.

"Amos! Amos Harlow! Come on down, now, and let's us talk a spell!"

The voice was of drawn-out sugared Southern gentility, the kind you'd find in a Charleston blueblood, or maybe a plantation colonel down in Valdosta. It was mellifluous, charming, and had the air of gentle ease and grace. He could not help but follow.

Struggling to one knee, he waited until the nausea passed and his head was more or less on straight before pushing up to both feet. He wavered, bobbing like a cork in the water, then steadied himself and peered over the edge of the ridge.

Below him stretched a vast hollow full of briars, tall grass, and underbrush so thick daylight couldn't reach the ground. The small valley was peppered with pines, oaks, and the occasional dogwood, but apart from that, there was no sign of civilization. God's country, indeed.

"Over here, sir. Right over here, now." The voice came from the slope of the hollow to the west, where the briars were the worst.

Carefully, Amos made his way around the lip of the ridge, taking footholds as he found them. One misstep and he'd tumble ass over elbows down into the dark valley.

When he reached the spot where he thought the voice had come from, he squinted into the hollow, searching for the man.

"Down here, Amos."

Amos almost fell, and if he had, he would have fallen right on top of the preacher-man. The man was nestled in the midst of the worst of the briars, as if he were comfortably ensconced in a hammock on a porch. He was upside down, staring into the clear blue sky with a wistful look. His smile was radiant, his eyes a piercing blue like uncut diamonds. He might have been forty or seventy; he had an ageless quality about him that was unsettling. The whole scene was unsettling to Amos, and he said so.

"What—" he winced, the effort of talking too much. "What… are you doin' d-down there?"

"Oh, just lying back and admiring God's creation. A man should really take the time to do that now and then, Amos. Care to join me?"

Amos was leery; the man had saved his life, but he wasn't ready to climb down into a briar patch to thank him.

"I suppose not. Well, enough cloud-watching for me, then. I'll come on up."

Amos felt a rush as the blood returned to his extremities and stumbled toward the edge of the ridge. A hand with a vice grip caught him under the arm and righted him.

"Got to be careful, there, hoss. God's creation has many a pitfall, as well."

Amos thought he must have passed out again. It should have taken the man at least ten minutes to get out of that briar patch without cutting himself to pieces, another five to get up the steep slope. The man seemed to have been instantly at his side in time to grab him.

"There, now," the man said, tightening his grip on Amos's shoulder. All at once, a hot flush went through Amos, a warm sensation that swept him from the tips of his toes right to the crown of his brow. He almost stumbled again and the man steadied him, slapped him amiably on the shoulder. "All better, then, yes? Why don't we walk awhile, hmm? See the rest of what God has to offer, that is, if you're up to it, sir? Surely you feel better now."

It wasn't a question, and the truth was, Amos *did* feel better. He could feel his extremities again, and he flexed his fingers -- no numbness. His throat hurt less, too, and he thought he might be able to speak.

"Thank... " he cleared his throat. "Thank you, mister. What... what did you do?"

"Do? Why, I didn't do a thing, Mr. Harlow. The human body is a remarkable thing, yes it is. You all are hardy things, God's witness. His most *wondrous* creation, no doubt." He said this last with a hint of sarcasm, it seemed to Amos.

"Well, thanks again for helpin' out with...well, you know..."

"With those hooligans? Shame I wasn't here earlier, Mr. Harlow. Wondrous as you all are, it remains a mystery how like the lower beasts you have proven yourselves."

"I don't understand..." Amos began, shaking his head. He must still be shaky from the noose. "This is all so strange."

"Stranger than holding conversations with rabbits?" the old man smiled.

"What did you say your name was, again?" asked Amos, trying to sort his cloudy mind. "And how you know *mine*?"

"Oh, Amos. What's in a name? My name is... *unpronounceable*, in your tongue, at least. You may call me Morningstar. As to your name, surely anyone in these parts knows 'Black Dog' Harlow, the famous—or in some places, *infamous*—blues musician extraordinaire. Oh, my, yes. I have followed your, ah... *career* from afar for quite some time, sir. *Quite* some time, yes."

"Oh," Amos said, a tad relieved, but still on edge, though he knew not why. "Wellsir, not that I'm ungrateful, but what you doin' way out *here*?"

"Ha! Well," Morningstar chuckled as they followed a hunting trail along the ridge. "Let's us just say that I am a man of many appetites, many passions, Amos. And one of those passions is walking abroad on the earth, to and fro, you might say, seeing what I might see. Surely that's a passion a man like *you* can understand?"

Amos admitted that it was, though the only place he'd ever been outside of America was France in the Great War. The man nodded sagely, solemnly. "Yes, Lord Almighty, that was a terrible time, a terrible time. So many sons of Adam lost in that wretched conflagration."

They came to a lookout, a point where the ridge ended and opened up into a vista that took Amos's breath away. The sun, dipping lower in the west, shone through a gathering thunderhead, stippling the rolling hills with thin golden rays. The hills themselves were more of the red, green, and gold—a giant's quilt that rolled away into the horizon.

"Beautiful, is it not?" Morningstar sighed. "So many places like it in Creation; so many more beautiful, still." He fixed his hands behind his back and spoke, his voice wistful, his eyes far away, and Amos felt transported there along with him.

"Imagine, if you can Mr. Harlow, a place so beautiful, so marvelous, that the sight of it by human eyes would render a mortal man to a blithering idiot, crying every ounce of water out of his body in mere seconds, leaving him a desiccated husk.

"Can you conceive, as a man of song, harmonious music so perfect and so sweet, that it would puncture your eardrums, drowning you in absolute bliss as it bled your sanity?" He turned and faced Amos, but it seemed more to Amos that he never moved—he just was suddenly *facing* him, a rapturous, glowing upturned face. In that moment, he was the most beautiful thing Amos had ever seen.

"And is there room, I wonder, in your deepest longings, for a place where the light never dims, where wonder never ceases, and where the answers to every question you ever had are disclosed, only to open the door to an infinity of others?"

Amos was taken aback by the man's fervor, unsure of how to answer. "I… I suppose. I expec' everybody has a dream like that."

"Oh, it's no dream, I assure you, Amos. It *exists*."

"And you been there, I reckon?"

Morningstar turned to look longingly at the sunlight piercing the dark clouds. As he did, the clouds covered the sun completely, darkening the valley below.

"Not for a long time," he whispered.

* * * *

They trudged on down the trail. Amos was getting winded so soon after his ordeal, but Morningstar seemed invigorated, striding along on his long legs, hands clasped behind his back, admiring the scenery as if they were on a country lane. The sun was lingering just above the mountaintops as they reached another outlook point.

Morningstar strode out to the lip of the cliff and stood silently for a time.

Amos looked around the little clearing and was astonished to see the makings of a woodlands camp. There was a small lean-to built from pine branches at the forest edge and a ring of stones for a fire pit. He heard a faint gurgling and spied a small alcove in the mountainside. Water was trickling steadily out of a crack in its face. He walked over to a tall pine tree near the lean-to and saw what he hoped to see.

There was a bald spot on the trunk near the exposed roots where someone had shaved off the bark. There were marks carved in the bare place—some jagged lines over an "x," and beside that, a series of initials.

Amos knew what the marks were, what this place was—a hobo camp, the symbol was a campfire, the initials were the men who had been here before him. Rooting around under the exposed roots, he found a small lockbox under a pile of pine straw. Inside was a fresh box of matches, some beef jerky wrapped in wax paper, and a leather pouch half-filled with coffee. He also found an aluminum pot and a small hatchet. He couldn't believe the luck. Of all the places in this God-forsaken wilderness to find a camp, and right when they needed it. The sun was receding beyond the hills in the west, and soon it would be dark. He turned to report their good fortune to Morningstar, and gave a start, almost knocking the man down, as he was standing right behind him.

"Well, now," Morningstar said. "The Lord does provide, doesn't He?"

The box rattled in Amos's hands as he stood nose-to-nose with the old man. Morningstar's smile was radiant. "Why don't you make us a fire, Amos? I could do with a bite to eat and maybe some of that coffee, eh?"

"All we got to eat is this here beef jerky, but it's better than nothin', I guess."

Morningstar turned and pointed at a spot near a small, shadowed boulder at the edge of the clearing. There was a barely-audible hum, and Morningstar turned to face him, grinning. "I believe you'll find our supper right over yonder," he said.

Amos moved to the boulder, looking over his shoulder at

Morningstar, his anxiety about the man increasing by the minute. Leaning over the big rock, his breath caught in his throat, making him wince with pain.

Lying in the shadow of the rock's overhang, in the midst of a bed of clover, lay the rabbit he'd spoken with scant hours past.

"Not so chatty *now*, is he?" Morningstar said, followed by a laugh that rustled like autumn leaves across the forest floor. "Come. Set our camp and let's talk of things to come… and things that may yet never be."

Amos, as in a dream, gathered up the rabbit and set about the fire and soon had it blazing, orange light dancing like imps across the face of the forest. He spit the rabbit, fetched water from the mountain spring, and set the coffee in the midst of the coals. Done with the chores, he sat down with a groan, knees and ankles popping, and stared across the fire at the man, this strange man with whom he was now entirely uncomfortable. Morningstar simply stared at him with those piercing eyes.

"Who are you, really?" Amos asked.

"There are two worlds," Morningstar replied, ignoring the question. "I think we both can agree on that. One is the world we know, that most folks know. That world labors and breathes and turns. People are born and people die, love and are loved in return or shunned, and the world turns on, uncaring, unknowing, even when the creatures upon it are returned to its dark embrace. Like them, it simply exists, and like them, it too will eventually pass.

"Then there is the other world, the world *behind* the world. Some might say the *true* world. This is the place of wonder and terror, of light and dark, of things glorious and things profane. This is a world only few walk while they live—people like you, Amos, with a foot in each, belonging to neither.

"Every now and then, the worlds touch, ever so slightly, and the mystery of one opens up to the commonplace of the other. When that happens, those very few people can perceive the change. The prophets were such men. They were privy to secrets of God and how those secrets worked in the world of men. And oh, how they cried out to a mundane world that neither knew nor cared for secrets! Some brought warnings, others knowledge, still others revelation. And let me tell you something, Amos—revelation means *nothing* to folks who think they know it all."

Amos took all this in and his unease grew. But he sensed he was at a crossroads, a place he'd been a thousand times before, literally and figuratively, and a crossroads always signaled change. He would play along, though every nerve ending in his body screamed at him to run, to hide. And suddenly he knew in his tired old bones that there was nowhere on earth he could run and hide from *this* man.

In a way, he'd been running from him his whole life.

"So," he hesitated, "you sayin' I'm a prophet, that it?"

"Ha!" Morningstar cackled in his crusty laugh, putting Amos in mind of the rustling of old clothes on bones of the unquiet dead. "No, sir! Let's not put the cart before the horse, my friend. Not by a mile, sir! But," he said, quieting, "you are as near to that office as anyone has been in your lifetime. God is not in the habit of new revelation these days, not for some time, now. But He sometimes sees fit to… *nudge* those He chooses—gives them the wherewithal to perceive the things of that other world."

"What on earth *for*?" Amos asked.

"*Precisely*, my good man! For those on earth! For the wretched crust of reality that He has chosen to be higher than His angels, His firstborn sons! He—!" Morningstar seemed to catch himself, his demeanor falling once again into steadiness. "He chooses certain folks to cry at the edge of the cliff, to scream at the walls of the city. And He uses them not only to forewarn, but to *forestall*—to hold back that black curtain long enough for all the other sheep to wake up and realize that they are in the wolf's maw. That, Amos, is what you are—a shepherd. And the lambs couldn't give a damn less."

The old man was silent for a time, stirring up the coals with a long stick. "Coffee's about ready, I'd wager" he said. Amos reached in with a handkerchief, plucked up the coffeepot, and poured them a cup each. He settled the pot back into the coals at the edge of the fire, took up his cup and stared at it.

"So what is it I'm supposed to do? For that matter, what is it *you* supposed to do? Ain't you an' God, sorta... at *odds*?"

Morningstar laughed. "I suppose you could put it like that, yes. Though some would agree that in *these* days, one of us clearly has the upper hand, or you and I wouldn't even be having this delightful conversation, would we?"

Amos sipped his coffee, waiting.

"To answer your first question, *you* will have to decide how to proceed after our discussion. None but you can do that. You were given the oh-so-touted gift of free will, Amos, just like the rest of the mud-men He made. I cannot help you there, and why ever would I *want* to?"

"Alright," Amos said. "I get it; the Devil don't hand out no favors. So why even help me at *all*?"

"Ah," Morningstar said, "your second question. Let's just say there is a sort of cosmic balance that must be maintained. I am allowed to try to sway you, but that is all. I once had this little tete-a-tete with a man named Job. Perhaps you've heard of him? There was also a young man in Massachusetts named Brown not so long ago. Both were too goody-two-shoes for my liking, but there it is: cosmic balance. *You*, my friend, are just the wheel coming 'round again."

Amos shifted in his seat. "Reckon you gonna have to spell it out for me."

"'Two roads diverged in a yellow wood,' Amos. You stand at the fork. The future is open before you. You have no ties, no responsibility to anyone or anything other than your own whims. 'Go where ye will,' Amos. Ain't that what the Good Book says? Down one road, there is the world and all it offers; it lies at your feet. You may have it and so much more.

"But with the other path lies blood and darkness. Death and much, much worse await you and those around you. Once either road is chosen, you may never walk the other. You will be changed, so to speak, and the other road will disappear like mist in the sunshine."

"I still ain't follerin'," Amos said, scratching his head. "What kinda stakes *you* got in all this?"

Morningstar pursed his lips and bent his head before answering.

"Do you realize just how full my house is, Amos? Of course you don't; you can't *begin* to imagine what my world is like. The damned are shoulder to shoulder down there. Your world has been one continuous off-ramp since the dawn of time. My vassals barely manage to keep them in check. Soon their untold numbers will be unmanageable. Familiarity breeds discontent, you see. Then there is the matter of the *other* tenants of my realm.

"Why is it, do you think, that the horrors that fill your campfire stories and ancient legends continue to walk the earth? They simply have nowhere else to *go*. They roam this world as dispossessed itinerants, very much like yourself. The dam is full to bursting, and a king that cannot control his kingdom… well, leave us say that I will *not* be evicted from *another* throne, Amos.

"Simply put: I need more real estate. And this world is prime beachfront property, as it were."

Amos stared slack-jawed.

"Think on it as annexation; this world is the Alsace to my Lorraine."

"But… why don't you just take it on your own? You got the army, to hear you tell it," Amos said.

"Ah, and there's the rub! You see, Amos, what you say is true. However, such an act would be considered a declaration of war, and I am not ready for a war. Not *yet*. But if *another* were to do the work *for* me…"

Amos straightened. "You mean the Doorway Man."

"Is *that* what you call him? I hear the papers are calling him Herod. I much prefer that one—familiar connotations and all that. You've met him, then?"

"Dreamed him. He just a shadow, ain't got no face. Like a paper doll cut from sackcloth. I seen the world disappearin' right inside him like water goin' down a drain. Things… *dark* things are behind him, pushin' on him, trying to get out."

Morningstar laughed. "Yes, I suppose that's as good a description as any. He's a mixed-up lad, to be sure, and a nasty one. My Father has His emissary, Amos, and I have *mine*."

"Tell me who he is."

"HA! No, Amos, I don't think I will." Morningstar grinned.

"Cosmic balance?"

"You *are* a good listener. Yes, that's it precisely. I cannot *commence* the End, Amos, but I can take advantage of the *results*. That's the beauty of you mud-men—you can always be counted on to do the worst things at the worst times. But enough of this."

Morningstar stood, a movement so quick and vulpine that Amos barely registered it. "Come. It's time to see what you're missing." He held out his hand.

Amos rose and dropped his empty cup. He peered sidelong at the proffered hand, knowing what usually came of taking it.

"You needn't worry," Morningstar laughed. "As I said, cosmic balance. Free will. This is just a Powerpoint presentation."

"A what?"

"Never mind. I forget just *when* I am sometimes. Come," he beckoned. "Come and *see*."

Amos took his hand and they vanished, the fire crackling in their absence an ill omen.

* * * *

"Behold," Morningstar said, one arm clutching Amos, the other spread wide to take in their surroundings.

The pair floated in midair, high above the peak of Mount Mitchell, the tallest peak in the Blue Ridge Mountains, and hundreds of miles from where they'd been seconds before.

Amos gasped and clutched at Morningstar's arm, fighting vertigo and his own mind, which screamed at him that he was about to fall to his death. Morningstar gripped him tighter and shook.

"Take it easy, now. I realize that it's quite a shock, but I figured we needed a little… *perspective* if you are to understand the nature of my visit."

Amos stopped struggling and looked out at the world in a way he'd never even dreamed. The crescent moon lit the world in a ghostly shade of pale, and below them thousands of tiny lights flickered on and off like fireflies as the human race of four states either rose or slept, depending on their daily routines. A nighthawk circled in the sky beneath them, looking for a meal in the mountain's summit. Its feathers resembled armored scales in the silvery light of the moon. Amos watched it with envy and thought that if men could fly they wouldn't do anything else.

"Wondrous, isn't it?" Morningstar said. "It could all be yours, as far as you can see, as far as East is from West. Every inch of soil, every person, every animal, all yours to do with as you please. Think of it: no more stepping and fetching for handouts, no more taking only what you're given, no more 'yassir' or 'nossir.' All the world will bend the knee to you and all you have to do is cry off your path right now."

Amos snorted. "An' I'm s'posed to believe you can do all that wit' a snap of the fingers?"

Morningstar's eyes blazed. "All that and *so* much more, Amos. There is a reason this world was given to me. It is my playground, my game board, and I can move the pieces around as I please. Do *not* doubt me on this."

For a fleeting moment, Amos wondered what it would be like to be king of the world. Riches, food a-plenty, a different woman every night if he wanted. Men would flock to his banner and kings would bend the knee to him. So much power… so much responsibility.

"Nah," he said. "Seems I got enough on my plate without havin' to run a whole damn world. You go on an' keep it. Besides, if I… if I *lose*, you gonna have it anyway. And I figger if you *really* got the world in your pocket, you'd've already moved in. No thanks."

Morningstar smiled. "I *like* you, Amos. I can see why *He* likes you. Very well. Let's have another look… let me see…."

And Amos felt himself being pulled, stretched like saltwater taffy. The world around him elongated into streaks of color. Millions of unknown voices filled his ears, bells rang, a roar filled his mind until he thought it would burst, and suddenly he was snapped forward, shooting through the kaleidoscope sky until he felt pavement under his feet.

A car horn blared—at least Amos *thought* it was a car; it looked like something from the cover of a pulp magazine: yellow, sleek, and long. He jumped out of its way just before its bumper clipped him and sent him flying. The driver leaned out and cursed a blue streak through the window. Amos felt someone steady him by the elbow.

Morningstar smiled down at him. "No need to worry. He wasn't yelling at you; they can't see us." He gestured at their surroundings. Amos drew in a sharp breath.

They stood in the middle of a busy intersection. Concrete and steel rose in Babylon-sized columns into an intensely blue sky, the sun reflecting off thousands of glass windows like tiny ponds. The barest wisps of clouds fringed unseen roofs.

Down every street, thousands of strange vehicles vanished into the distance and giant electrical signs sold everything from Coca-Cola to blue jeans from some place called The Gap. One in particular had a giant-sized moving picture of a half-naked woman—right there on display for the world to see—who was named Victoria and threatened to tell her Secrets.

The strangest thing of all was the people—so *many* of them—bustling and shoving on the sidewalks in business suits and checking wristwatches, waving for yellow cabs. A young woman dressed in tight black leather with hair the color of cotton candy walked right *through* them to the other side of the street and dropped a handful of change in the guitar case of a white boy in nothing but his under-drawers and a cowboy hat. The cowboy nodded and kept right on playing and singing in an awful voice.

"Where the hell *are* we?"

"Nothing looks *familiar*?" Morningstar tittered.

Amos scanned the cityscape again and stopped short. "Hang on—that's the Paramount!" He twirled in place. "And there's St. Mary's!" He looked around at Morningstar.

"Are… are we in Times *Square*?"

"Got it in one," Morningstar laughed. "Give the man a cee-gar."

"But…"

"We are in the year 2011. Quite something, isn't it?"

"Two-thousand--"

"Seventy-five years into your future, to be precise. The marvels of the future surround you, Amos. Of course, you'll be long dead by this time."

Amos was astonished at the sights and realization of the world beyond his own time. A thousand smells assaulted him—pizza, car fumes, hot asphalt, the murk of the Hudson and the heady aroma of sizzling spiced meat from a nearby Greek restaurant. A deep, painful longing for home overcame him and his eyes blurred at the memories behind them.

"Why… why you brung me here?"

"To *tempt* you, of course. I thought I was perfectly clear on that score," Morningstar said, examining his fingernails.

"You will almost certainly never see this wonder before you, not unless I intervene. How would like to live *forever*, Amos? No sickness, no death, just endless years to sample every ounce of a life you will miss. If you think this is something, you should see the *rest* of the world in this time. Wonders and glories, Amos, and you could see them all—dig your toes in the sand of the French Riviera, explore darkest Africa, walk the Outback of Australia, the snowy tundra of Siberia, the list is endless, as you yourself would be. And once again, all you have to do is give the word: leave this foolish task to someone else.

"What has the world ever done for *you*, anyway? You live in the wilderness. You are forbidden even a public bathroom simply because your skin is darker than others'. You owe them all nothing but what they have coming to them. Why not take the money and run, Amos? It's the second-best offer you've gotten today and in a very long time, I think."

What *would* it be like to live forever? He would stay the same age, unafraid to take chances, unafraid to face the world on *his* terms. The world would be his oyster, and without all the hassles of being its landlord.

"What happens when you take over? What kinda world would I be travellin' in *then*? Good as the brochure soundin' right *now*?"

Morningstar shrugged. "It will be a blasted husk of a world, with little to no beauty to speak of and the trace of humanity that is left after I've had my way with them will all be in pens like livestock for the whims of my servants. And for *food*, of course."

"Thank God for cosmic balance. You just talked me out of it."

Morningstar grinned and nodded. "There's just no putting one by you, is there, Amos Harlow?"

"Last one that did is an old man by now."

"Well, then, let's be off," Morningstar said, raising his arms.

"Hold on," Amos said and walked across the street. He stopped in front of a vintage record store, then walked right through the plate glass window. Inside, he walked to the Blues section and looked through the 'H' section. His spirits fell, and he returned to Morningstar, who looked at him with questioning eyebrows.

"Nothin'," said Amos. "Just dreamin', I guess."

They vanished, leaving the future behind.

* * * *

The sea below was calm, almost like polished glass. It was a sea painted by a child, azure water stretching to a cloudless sky, broken only by small dots of land maybe two miles away. They hovered in the air fifty feet above the ocean, staring at the deep blue that seemed to have swallowed the earth. Beneath them, a pod of dolphins broke the water, frolicking and racing each other to the horizon, their silvery bodies undulating and rippling with smooth muscles. Amos watched them until they disappeared from sight, a sadness settling over him at their passing. In all his years of traveling, he'd never seen them other than in books.

"They are marvelous creatures, are they not?"

Amos peered into the sinking sun, trying to spot the churning water from their blowholes. "Never pegged you for a nature lover," he said.

"Amos, just because I want to destroy this world doesn't mean I can't admire it. After all, I used to run the show."

"Then why?" Amos asked, looking askance at Morningstar. "Why you want to kill all this?"

"I was once the greatest of all my brothers, the most beautiful, the most powerful. I was elevated, Amos, *elevated* to that position. I was given the honor of making sure the sun rose and set. It was mine to change the seasons and ensure the harvests. Mine and mine alone was the task of seeing every one of you secure and happy. I had my *place*, Amos. We *all* did.

"And then, it was decided that all of you, the unworthy toys of my Father, would one day be higher than me—*me*, the Son of the Morning, the Bright Star of Heaven!—and I would have to take a back seat to mere creations of mud and dust! I would play servant to those who were unworthy to even speak my *name*!"

"Sounds like to me we all in the same boat. From what I learned, we *all* second-fiddle to *Him*."

Morningstar guffawed. "Can you imagine for one moment, being the most important person in your father's life? Being the favorite, the most cherished son? Can you even *begin* to know what it feels like to have the world at your feet only to have it snatched away from you, to be driven out like a dog from your home, never to return?"

Amos stared into the distance. "Reckon I can," he said softly.

Morningstar peered at him, nodded, and looked back out to sea. "Maybe you can, at that," he said.

"But I ain't tried to take my daddy's place, either," Amos said. "I ain't tried to be more than who I was. I just made some dumbass mistakes, but I owned 'em all. Not you. You just a snot-nosed brat pitching a cosmic tantrum 'cause his daddy told him 'no' and whipped him. You ain't even *tried* to make amends, let alone admit what you done. I'd say you lucky to be where you *at.* Shows your Daddy still love you."

Morningstar was in front of him in an instant, his face changed. His eyes were sunken hollows that burned with pinpricks of orange light, his teeth jagged crags jutting from his lips. His face crawled with the evil of ages, rippling and distorting his features.

"I have bled the souls of greater men for lesser insults, mud-man."

Amos spat and watched it fall to the sea. "You ain't gonna *do* shit, 'cause you *ain't* shit. I know that now. For all the evil you are, you cain't do a damn thing to me. All that power and you still got your hands tied."

Morningstar roared in fury, which turned into an eerie laugh, which somehow scared Amos more.

"You *are* a one, aren't you Amos? I haven't seen your kind since, well," he gestured an arm to the sea, "let's just say there was more water than *this.*"

Morningstar returned to his human form. "True. My hands are tied. But let us see if you're so bold after this little object lesson."

"What the hell are you talkin' ab—"

A rumble in the distance grew until it was the roar of a million waterfalls. Amos covered his ears, but the thunder made it through and rattled his teeth and eardrums. He cried out, thinking they would burst.

The sky suddenly darkened as if the sun had been doused with a bucket of water. Then just as suddenly, it brightened again, a million times brighter, and Amos threw his arm up to shield his eyes. A wave of intense heat washed over the pair, and Amos felt the air in his lungs ignite and rush out through his nose and mouth.

"Behold," Morningstar said. "The fate of man."

A grayish-white cloud, the shape of a giant mushroom blossomed over the little islands in the distance, blotting out the sun and causing the water beneath them to boil. Myriad species of fish and other marine life bobbed like driftwood on the waves, cooked inside their own scales and shells. The body of a humpback whale exploded from the deeps like a submarine blowing ballast, its blubber sizzling in the heat from the boiling ocean.

Amos felt the light from the blast pass through him. Had he been corporeal, he would have been cremated and buried at sea all in the same instant. He watched in awe as the mammoth explosion rolled on, blanketing the tranquil seas and everything between it and Heaven in darkness, ash, and death—a burial shroud for the entire earth.

But strong southerly winds buffeted the mushroom cloud, dissipating it into gray ribbons that trailed like kite tails into the northern sky. Soon, the sun was visible in the west, an angry red eye.

"You know," said Morningstar, "the sunsets in this hemisphere will be of the most ethereal beauty for months to come."

Amos lowered his gaze and slowly turned to Morningstar. "What… what was *that*?"

"*That* was the results of your quest, Amos. If you stay your course and somehow manage to thwart me, this is one of the results."

"*You* did this?"

"Oh, believe me, Amos, I would *love* to take credit for *this* one. I may give a nudge here and there from time to time, but you mud-men never had any difficulty finding new and inventive ways to take one another off the board. I believe this one is called *science*."

In an instant, they stood on the rocky shores of the small island. The sand was smooth glass, fused by unimaginable heat. The red sunlight gleamed off of it like a bloody window pane.

"This is a place called Bikini Atoll. We are deep in the South Pacific. The weapon you just saw tested by your own government has reduced this place to radioactive ash."

They walked further into the remains of the island. "Nothing will grow here for half a century, and when it does, it will be stunted and deformed," said Morningstar, as if he were a tour guide in an abattoir. They rounded a bend and came upon the remains of a small village—burned, black ovals the only remnant of grass huts and outbuildings that an unknown people once called home.

"There… there were *people* here?" Amos said.

"Now don't go getting in a lather, Amos. The indigenous peoples were relocated to another chain the in Marshalls, far from the blast site."

As they passed through the village, Amos gasped in horror.

"Well, *most* of them were," Morningstar amended.

Amos and Morningstar faced a natural rock wall twelve feet high that bordered the outer edge of the atoll. The shadows of several men and women had been burned into the rock, fused into its very surface by the supernova flash from the bomb. The people that made them were long gone, their ashes probably sailing over Australia at that moment.

Amos stared, shocked beyond all belief. How could such a thing even *exist*? Who would build it and when would they *use* it? And on *whom*?

"Oh, everyone will have the weapon," Morningstar said, reading his mind. "Everyone from the dirtiest backwater slum countries to the empires built of steel and blood. And no one will ever know when the other will use theirs."

"*Damn*," Amos whispered.

"So you see, Amos, I have to do very little at *all*."

Amos knew it was true. He tried to weigh the options. Cry off now and the destruction he'd just witnessed would never happen, or keep going, maybe win through, and the world would never know true hell on earth, but would live with the threat of its mirror image every day.

He shook his head. "Either way, I lose, you win," he said. "We *all* lose."

"Surely seems that way," Morningstar said through a sly smile.

"Well," said Amos, "I cain't control this here. You ain't layin' the blame for this on me. This happens, it happens 'cause some other folks make it happen. I got to deal with what's mine to deal with. No deal."

Morningstar hung his head, smiling. "I guess we both knew it would end this way. I have to say, Amos, you are the either the bravest of your kind I've ever met or the most foolish. Others faced with similar choices have wavered, and this world has come oh so *very* close to ending a thousand times before you were ever born. I would congratulate you and wish you well, but… I have a horse in this race, too."

Amos heaved a great sigh. "Well, what now?"

"Now? Now you go back to your life, such as it is. You have

answered the challenges true and our time together is at an end."

"'Bout time," Amos muttered.

"But know this: the roads offered here today are now closed. Only one road is available to you now. We will not meet again—not for some time, at any rate—and you will not remember anything I have shown you. These past few hours will be a dream that will slip your grasp like fog."

Amos wasn't sure if that was good or bad.

"Also, know that I will do everything in my power to see you fail. You will face adversity in the coming days that will make the Black Plague pale in comparison. I will bring every ounce of my influence to bear to see you dead before the end of the road, Amos Harlow. You believe you have known trial and tribulation? You will *beg* for death before the end."

Amos sniffed. "Alright, you made your speech. We goin' now or we waitin' for the wind to carry us someplace?"

Morningstar laughed. "Very well, adversary. Where can I drop you off?"

* * * *

Amos once again stood on a mountaintop in South Carolina, a frayed hemp rope broken and swinging in the early morning breeze above his head. The sun was peeking over the horizon, making the distant peak of Table Rock a dark blue contusion against a blood-red firmament. The broad-winged hawks and bald eagles would be circling the skies there, seeking an early meal for them and their young.

His throat still hurt, though no more than a severe cold he might have caught in any given autumn. He fingered the rope burns around his neck, the ridges of the coils etched in his skin. He would bear the mark for some time and it would fade, but the memory would live on.

He shook his head as if waking from a year-long dream. Try as he might, the contents of the dream refused to be seized, like the freshwater eels he and his father had caught as a youth. There was something important, something desperately important that he knew he had to remember. But as the sun ascended higher in the heavens, the eel slipped the net and was forever gone in the river of his memory.

Across the small glen, his guitar case leaned against the base of a spruce pine, waiting on him like an old friend. He walked over and bent to retrieve it when something bumped his shoulder. He jumped and spun in one nervous motion and cried out in horror.

Above him, in the same tree, hung the three white boys that had strung him up, their faces contorted in strangulation, their bellies slit from belt buckle to breastbone, their entrails dangling in the breeze like dead snakes.

A note to him personally was carved on the chest of the center corpse in jagged handwriting:

FOR A BRAVE FOOL

Amos shut his eyes tight against the display, rubbing at his eyes. When he opened them, the swaying corpses were gone, but the ropes remained, their ends still tied in nooses.

His mind reeled and he felt himself falling to the forest floor. He tried to recall even the remote feeling he'd had that something important had happened, but even that was now lost to him.

But he knew deep-down that he had purpose now, even though he wasn't sure just what it was. He thought of the faceless man of his dreams, the Doorway Man, with all the horror that clawed and gnashed to be free within him. He somehow sensed his fleeting memory and the Doorway Man were tied up in the same bloody business, and he knew it was *his* business to finish.

He got the sudden urge to be far away from that place, to be somewhere where people lived and loved; where there was music and laughter, all the things that drove back the darkness and held it at bay for just one more day.

He hefted his guitar, slung it over his back and picked his way down the mountain, like Moses re-entering the world with revelation no one wanted.

DEAD MAN'S BURDEN

A Song of the Black Dog

To sin by silence when they should protest makes cowards of men.

—Abraham Lincoln

The folks gathered around the grave weren't in much of a hurry; after all, the dead man wasn't going anywhere.

They were all properly humbled and grief-stricken. The women sobbed into handkerchiefs provided by the menfolk, who patted their women on the shoulder, hats in hands.

The minister presided over the scene with delicate grace, mentioning the deceased's many honors, his fine qualities, and the suddenness with which he was taken from their midst. He was sure to mention that the man was free of sin now, gone on to a reward that the rest of them could only imagine, and that their weeping and gnashing of teeth was but a selfish gesture that did no good for anyone present and certainly not for the deceased.

This spectacle went on for an hour or more, each man present moving to the fore to speak for their friend, to offer some remembrance past and send him on his way to eternity.

"Who the hell was he?" Amos whispered a bit too loudly to the man next to him.

The man, a grizzled old elf with a mutton-chop beard and no mustache, glared at him. "Have you no respect for the dead, brother?"

"No disrespect intended," Amos said, failing to whisper again. "I just wondered why so many people's got the waterworks flowin'. Musta been some kinda fella, all this cryin'."

People looked up, shooting disapproving glances Amos's way, and the minister paused briefly, then resumed his litany. The man glared at Amos again, but said nothing. He clutched his wife around the shoulders and eased her away from the rude newcomer, the outsider that had no place at the graveside of one of their own.

The service at last came to a close. Each person in attendance scooped up a handful of grave dirt and tossed it onto the lid of the pine casket in the six-foot hole before making their way to their homes down in the valley, looking back over shoulders, afraid the outsider might follow, looking for a handout.

They all filed away, until at last Amos and the minister stood alone at the grave, while two men with shovels filled in the hole.

"Didn't mean to disturb the service," Amos said sheepishly. "I was just passin' through and couldn't find nobody in town. Heard all the weepin' and made my way up here."

The minister was as stern as any who'd come out of the Amish tradition of Bucks County, Pennsylvania. He eyed Amos with the stone-cold stare of a statue that's tired of being shat on by birds.

"What is your business here, pray-tell, sir?"

Amos cleared is throat. "Well, thing is, I'm sort of out of doors, you see. Ain't wantin' no charity, though. Thought I might work for a meal or two, maybe some change if you all could spare it. Makin' my way out to California. Heard there was some work in the vineyards out that way."

The minister studied him with a discerning gaze. "You will not find work here, sir. We do our own work here, as the Bible commands. Besides, we cannot spare the extra. The drought has hit us as hard as it has you outsiders."

Amos thought about that. He didn't like the minister's talk much; there was a hint of sass that no collar, Roman or otherwise, could staunch.

"I ain't wantin' to be trouble to nobody," he said, "but I heard you all were Christian folk. I thought that included at least a meal. An' I aim to work for it, as I said."

"There will be no work for you here, sir. I regret we cannot accommodate you," the minister said, tucking the small Bible into a coat pocket.

Amos spat, turning his back. "You an' me both," he muttered, walking back up the slope.

The minister fidgeted, his hands working nervously in front of him.

"Sir?" he called. "A moment?"

Amos turned. "Yeah? Gotta be quick. Need to hoof it on down

the road, find some shelter 'fore nightfall."

"There *is* one… *alternative* left you, but… "

"But what?"

The minister wrung his hands, distraught. "Vigor Standish. Lives up on the hill at the edge of town. Maybe he can help you. I can do no more. I have spoken too much already." With that, he turned abruptly and strode back toward the church.

Amos watched him go and figured his options, which weren't many. He could leave, but there was no guarantee he'd find food or even a dry pile of hay before dark. He'd already left a bad impression with the folks in the village. Going door to door would just bring more of the same. He looked to the western end of town.

"Looks like it ain't much of a choice. Let's go," he said to the dog, who had been watching all the hoopla of the last hour with all the interest of a foot sore, and whose presence the minister had not acknowledged.

The massive hound rose, shook his flanks, and headed off through the woods with Amos close in tow, like always.

* * * *

Vigor Standish's place was set back in a copse of woods, almost invisible like the dirt path that wound up to its front door. Amos passed it three times, in fact, and had to double back and hike into the trees.

The place was dreadfully quiet. No birds sang in the trees, no wind blew through the stands of dogwood, elm, and maple that grew like weeds on the property. Amos picked his way along the path until he stood before the front door.

In contrast to the houses in the village, which were all postage stamps on the landscape with whitewashed picket fences and flower boxes in the windows, Vigor Standish's house was, in a word, unkempt.

The pine planking, once white, was now green-gray with mold. Moss and creeper vine clawed at its foundations, winding through shutters that hadn't been opened in more than a decade. The tin roof was rusted through in places and stained reddish brown by rainwater, like seeping wounds on a leper. There was no welcome mat at the front doorstep. A tarnished brass knocker hung from the center of its cracked oak door.

Above the door, in stark contrast to the grim state of the house, a five-pointed star enclosed with a circle was painted in bright white paint. It looked like a fresh coat, the only thing new about the place.

Amos rapped the knocker three times, the sound booming through the house like a gunshot in a tomb.

After a moment, a young girl opened the door. Her long blonde hair hung in braids from above her ears. Her eyes were of the bluest hue, sparkling like lapis-lapzuli in the light. She wore a powder-blue dress with a spotless white apron over top. She was the brightest thing about the place, but her eyes were downcast, as if she carried a sorrow beyond imagining.

"Yes?"

"Sorry to disturb you, ma'am," Amos said, taking off his hat, "but the minister in town said I should come see Mr. Standish."

Her face grew thin, her eyes narrowed. "He did, did he? Well, Father no seeing anyone at moment. Is too weak. Come back tomorrow." She had a thick accent that Amos couldn't place. German, maybe, but he couldn't guess at it.

"I don't aim to be a bother, ma'am. I was told he might be able to help me out, 's all."

"Is too *weak*!" she snapped. "Is too soon! Gracious Palmer die only yesterday. You must wait." She began to close the door.

"Let him in, Hilda," croaked a weak voice from within the house.

The girl named Hilda glanced over her shoulder, then back at Amos disapprovingly, then above their heads at the symbol painted over the door. She looked at Amos again, nodded curtly, and stepped back, holding the door wide.

Amos looked up at the symbol, then stepped over the threshold. Hilda held her breath, watching Amos for any reaction. When none came, she relaxed visibly and closed the door.

The interior of the house was dim, lit only by several candles set at places of work—a desk, over the kitchen sink, and the kitchen table. A feeble glow from a doorway at the rear of the living room told of more beyond.

It was stifling, almost unbearably warm in the house. An overpowering, rank odor filled the air, a heady miasma of old sweat, musty sheets, and drying vomit. Amos covered his nose, but gagged involuntarily anyway.

"Is all right," Hilda said. "One gets used to smell." She walked into the kitchen area and grabbed two oven mitts. She opened the oven door and a smell completely opposite to the stench filled the immediate area. Amos walked over and stooped over the open oven, breathing deeply.

"Lord, that smells fine," he said. "Them biscuits?"

Hilda removed a baking pan full of small sweet breads fashioned into the shape of little men. She placed the pan on the oven top and poked each bread man with a fork.

"Gingerbread men?" Amos asked. "It ain't nowhere near Christmas, last I looked."

"No, though these are where your gingerbread men come from. They are *döed-köeks.* "

"Dead-what?"

"Please, sit. I bring cider."

Amos sat at the small kitchen table. "Y'all havin' 'em with supper?" Amos asked, eyeing the bread men hungrily.

"You no want to eat these," Hilda said,

"Like hell I *wouldn't*," Amos said. "I ain't had but near-on nothin' to eat for two days straight. I'd just as soon eat the pan they in, for good measure."

"No," said Hilda, the smile disappearing. "Pan would be *better* for you to eat."

She continued to poke the cakes until she was satisfied they were done, then shuffled them off the pan into a basket and covered them with a dish towel.

"Did Minister Marsh tell you why come here?" she asked.

"No, he just say come here and a Mr. Standish could help me out, maybe give me a meal, at least," Amos said, still eyeing the cake-men, spit swelling in his cheeks. "Be willin' to work for it, though. Don't want no hand-outs."

Hilda stiffened, her back to him. "Is that so?" she asked thoughtfully.

"Don't even think it, girl," the weak voice called out from the bedroom. "He is guest in our home."

Amos turned and looked back the bedroom door. He couldn't see beyond the threshold, the room dim, but for a low-burning candle somewhere within.

"Who's that?"

"That is my father, the man you seek," Hilda said, ladling stew from a pot on the stove into a bowl. She stuck a spoon in it and sat it in front of Amos.

"He ain't eatin' with us?"

"Is too weak. Especially difficult day for him." Hilda said.

Amos hungrily wolfed the stew. "He sick or somethin'?"

"Something, yes," Hilda said. She rested her head in her hand and watched Amos eat. "Is dying."

Amos ate in silence, every now and again glancing at the bedroom door. A strained wheezing emanated from the room. The only other sound was the ticking of a grandfather clock somewhere in the dim recesses of the house. Between Hilda watching him eat, the reedy breathing and the clock, Amos was getting right antsy, and began to wonder if coming to this place was a good idea at all.

The whole place had held a sense of foreboding, of interminable waiting. The horrible smell returned as the bread men had cooled, and it was like to drive him mad if he had to sit there much longer. He decided right then and there to make his thanks and leave. Sleeping in the open was preferable to spending a night in that house.

He finished his stew and patted his stomach. "That was mighty fine," he said. "Thank you ever so much. I best be on my way. Y'all want me to chop some wood for the meal or maybe—"

"Why are you here?" Hilda eyes locked with his. "Why, really?"

Amos was taken aback. "Well, I told you, I just needed a meal, and I—"

"The minister—he truly not send you, then?"

"Well, no. He told me I could find some help here, maybe a get something to eat, but that's all." He looked questioningly at her.

"You… you weren't here to see Father? To… to pass on your sins?"

Amos dropped the spoon in the bowl with a loud clink. "To pass on my… my *what*?"

"Your sins. That is only reason people come to see Father. No one comes here. No one. Not ever."

"Look here, now I don't wanna be a bother, I just want—"

"Hilda!" The voice from the bedroom was hard now, full of spirit. The man began to shout in German, a string of what could only be reprimands. The girl took it all in stride, but began to weep and shouted back. Amos had no idea what she said, but it sounded to him like a desperate plea, almost begging, as she continued to shout through her tears.

After one last shout from her father, Hilda composed herself, wiping her face on her apron. She collected Amos's bowl and spoon and put them in the sink. Then she came and stood by Amos's chair.

"Come," she said. "Father will see you now."

Amos rose, wondering how the rules of hospitality would suffer if he just bolted right then. He surely had no desire to enter that room. He knew what the smell was now, what the feeling was he'd had when he stepped into the place.

It was a death house, a place where one waited to die with nothing but the ticking of one's remaining hours for company. He should have known that right at first. He had been in enough of those to know them for what they were.

"Miss, I don't think I should—"

"Is okay," Hilda said. "Is what he wishes. He says he waited for you long time."

Amos walked to the front window and peered out. The black dog was waiting patiently by the path.

So. He *was* supposed to be here, then.

He turned back to Hilda and nodded. She led the way into the bedroom, holding the door for Amos. Amos removed his hat and entered the room.

The room was simple, spare. A large four-poster bed took up almost the entire room. A chair sat on either side of the bed, their backs practically scraping the wall. The candlelight fell over the bed, and Amos gasped in horror before he could check himself.

Sprawled on the bed was the most hideous man—if he could be called that any longer—that Amos had ever seen. He was naked, save for a pair of short underwear. His skin was the mottled gray of a desiccated corpse, and here and there bedsores breached the outer layers, giant ulcers laid bare. The man's legs were shriveled, withered twigs, long past use. His arms were not much better, just two bony sticks poking from his torso like a snowman's. His belly, though, bulged to an almost impossible width, like the hump of a camel, completely out of proportion with the rest of him.

Revolted yet fascinated, Amos peered closely. The man's enormous girth seemed to bulge and writhe, as if he were a huge python that had just consumed a live animal that was trying to get out. Rounded shapes, sickeningly like the tops of human heads swelled in places, then fell into the giant mass that was his midsection. It was all Amos could do to stand his ground. His mouth hung agape, jaw working but nothing coming out.

"Is not pretty to look at, no?" Vigor Standish asked, with a weak smile.

"No, I mean… what's the matter? What's he *got*?"

"Nothing catching, I assure you. Merely the evil that men do and then hide within blemished souls."

"What in God's name… ?" Amos could only watch as the hideous lumps rose and fell in the man's bloated upper body.

"Sit. Please, Mr… ?"

"Harlow. Amos Harlow."

"Sit, Mr. Amos Harlow," Standish wheezed, "and I will tell you tale not uttered to outsiders in over a century. I am not long for this earth, and I need to tell it. I have been waiting for one to come who would hear it, one who understand pain. You seem to be such a one. After, you may do as you wish."

Amos sat in the chair nearest the door, not meaning to run, but not wanting to be trapped on the other side of the bed either, if it *came* to running. He wiped the sweat from his forehead and leaned forward on his knees.

"You know of practice of sin-eating?"

"Not at all," Amos owned.

"Is very old custom, very ancient. Is still done in some parts of old country, but very little. Much religion and science has seeped into the far corners where it once thrived.

"In Netherlands, when one was about to pass on, there was a certain man to whom villagers would turn before last rites could be given. He was sin-eater—an outcast, no better than leper. He was shunned, not even spoken of, yet vital part of life in village.

"Sin-eater would come to bed of the dying. Beseechings would be performed over body and then *doed-koecks*—'dead-cakes'—little bread men my daughter bake would be laid upon breast of dying man. Sometimes, initials of dying man were carved in them, sometimes not.

"Beseechings would draw sins of man into dead-cakes, and sin-eater would eat the cakes, taking sins of dying man into himself, so that dying man could pass on safely to Heaven, free of sin. Also, sin-eating made sure dying person no return from death to plague the living. Very important, this practice, but as I said, very rare now."

Amos was aghast. He prided himself on knowing a thing or two about hexes and knacks, but this was something alien to him, something that seemed a good thing, but also held a sense of dread, like a snake ready to strike. If the man before him was any indication, Amos thought that too much of a good thing was definitely bad.

"But… but what happened to you? How did you…I mean, how did you *get* like this? Did somethin' go wrong or somethin'?"

Standish smiled weakly. "Is good money in sin-eating, Amos. No one in right mind want to do it. Alas, my wife died in childbirth with my Hilda, here. She was good woman and took good care of family. When she die, we have no means of living. The world around us has dried up, as you know well. No crops, no work in towns, no work for Amish man, anyhow. This village took us in, gave us place when no one else would."

Standish began to cough, and soon his whole body shook and spasmed. Hilda rushed to her father's side, bathing his head with a damp rag from a bowl at his nightstand. She made little shushing sounds, and soon she had soothed Standish enough for him regain his breath, though he wheezed with the effort.

"She is good daughter, yes?" he said between coughs. "She take good care of father. Like her mother in that."

Amos could feel the heat radiating off the man like fire from a furnace. His fever had to be beyond what a normal man could take. Not that this was a normal man, Amos thought. The rag must be like a drop of water to a man dying of thirst.

"So," Standish continued, "we had place at last, but there was price to be paid. Those who live among the Amish must work. That is what God's Word says, no? If a man eat, he must work?

"But there were no places for to work. Everyone have own farm, own livestock. Everyone work for good of community. So, I offer my services in only other way I know. The folk were troubled at first, but

Reverend March tell them is good thing, tell them village could use man like Vigor Standish.

"Back then, I was younger man, robust, and at first, the few sins I eat no bother me. Money was good, enough for me and my daughter to live at ease. Some die here and there, and money keep coming.

"Then, one of village elders is dying, and they call Vigor Standish. Man is old, long-lived. One of first settlers in this part of country. Prayers are said, beseechings done, and I eat his sins.

"I remember falling over man in bed, the pain worse than anything I had ever felt. It claw at my belly like animal. I weep at the pain. Man's family pull me off of him, throw me into street with money. I see these people in passing later, they turn their backs to me, act as if I not there. That was beginning of things.

"Over time, others die, first people of village, like elder. I am called, I eat their sins as well. Same thing, over and again. The pain is beyond imagining. Then, the dreams come."

"Dreams?" Amos asked.

"Dreams while awake," Standish nodded. "Terrible visions, sins terrible to think on. But they soon gone, like smoke, poof! But the memories… the memories linger," he said, tapping his forehead with a frail finger.

"I know the money's good an' all," Amos said, "but…well, *look* at you. Was it worth it?"

Standish coughed again, spittle flying from his lips like confetti. Hilda came over and wiped his chin. It was only then Amos realized the pathetic man was laughing.

"You… you would not think so," Standish wheezed, "but my daughter grow into fine woman and is safe. No, I do right thing."

"Papa," said Hilda. "You should stop now, get rest. Time for more talk tomorrow, yes?"

Standish nodded weakly. Amos rose and walked to the door. "You stay the night with us," said Standish. Amos winced. He knew the offer would come, but he'd hoped to avoid it.

"Sure," he said. "And my thanks." He started back to the door.

"And Mr. Harlow?"

Amos turned. "Yes?"

"To share another's burden, if only for moment, is great honor. To carry *for* him is sacred. Is why God give us *life*."

Amos nodded and left the room.

As Standish began another coughing fit, Amos walked out into the living room and sat on the couch. Hilda entered a few moments later with a crocheted blanket and a feather pillow.

"Is not much, but will be warm."

Amos took the bedclothes and stretched out on the couch, removing his hat and laying his guitar case on the floor.

"He is dying," Hilda said again, sitting in a chair opposite. "The townspeople, they use him too much. So much sin in village. The man they bury today, Gracious Palmer, he was evil man. Wicked."

"Didn't sound like it to me," Amos said. "Seem like most folks around here thought well of him."

Hilda snorted. "They *would.* They are like him. They no wish to admit the evil in their *own* hearts, so they talk of one another like they are saints."

"Been my experience, ain't *nobody* saints. Not in *this* world."

Hilda nodded. "Is true. And Papa know this. Still he take sins, try to help. I only wonder, when he die, who will take *his* sins?" With that, she doused the candle and drifted away to her room for the night.

Amos lay awake for hours; he knew this because of the ticking of the clock somewhere in the house. But there was more to it than mere insomnia. His mind wandered in a thousand different directions. He thought of what kind of man would take on the mortal sins of others, and not just for the money itself, but for the sake of helping a fellow man.

He wasn't sure he even believed such a thing could be done. But the proof seemed to be in the next room, hacking its guts up every five minutes. He entertained a notion he wouldn't have thought possible before talking to Vigor Standish, before seeing his pathetic form lying in his sickbed waiting to die. Throughout the night he would ponder it, rolling it over in his mind.

Sleep finally came for him in the wee hours, but it was troubled sleep, filled with the nightmarish image of a bloated man, screaming as he was pulled into the Pit by groping hands of sinners long dead, for sins he himself had never committed.

* * * *

"I'll do it," Amos said.

Hilda's grip on the coffeepot slipped and she spilled the hot beverage onto the counter. "What?" she said, not understanding.

"I'll help your daddy. I'll take his sins for him."

Hilda set the pot down gently and wiped her hands on her apron. "You cannot begin to understand what you say," she said, not looking at Amos. "You have seen him, yes?"

"You might be right," Amos nodded. "I may not. But for all I know, he's sick and dyin' with some disease or somethin'. Least I can do is set his mind at ease 'fore he go."

Hilda came to the table, turned a chair, and sat facing Amos. She took his hands in hers. "What you say will bring you no end of pain, of grief. It will haunt your days and plague your nights. Is *worse* than death."

Amos shrugged. "You don't know me from Adam, girl, but believe me when I say I got enough of all that already. Little bit more won't weigh me down none."

Hilda stared down at her hands. "I will not lie, Mr. Harlow. He has always looked for you, or someone like you, to take his burden from him. I would be lying myself if I said it would not make me happy beyond measure. But is something I can no ask."

"Ain't nobody askin' me," Amos said. "I'm the one offerin'. Look here, you folks the only ones showed me any kindness, a total stranger in your midst. I ain't sayin' I believe all this sin-eatin' business. But I'm willin' to do what I can to help, just like y'all done for me. Just like your daddy done for them others and for you, in the only way he *could.*"

She stared up at him, her face awash with tears. "Go to him," she said. "I will prepare."

Amos got up and put his shoes on and shuffled into the bedroom, pausing to knock on the door.

"Mr. Standish? You up?"

"I am awake, yes," came the weak voice from the dark, followed by another coughing fit. "Come."

Amos walked over and sat in the chair by the bed. Standish reached out with his shriveled hand and took Amos's. The man's hand was cold, deathly cold, and the skin was like crushing sandpaper in his fist.

"I know why you come," Standish said. "I know moment I saw you."

"I don't understand," Amos said.

"Men who carry burdens know one another better than brothers, better even than lovers. It was shadow on your back when you crossed my threshold. But you must know what it is you mean to do."

"Got me a pretty good idea," Amos said.

"No, my friend. You don't believe, yet you see what sins of others have done to me, what they will do to you. Your unbelief will protect you for a time, but in end, you will carry world on your shoulders like Atlas, and it will break you."

Amos didn't know what to say to that. He just smiled and said, "To repay a kindness is no burden. If more folks did it, there wouldn't *be* no burdens."

Standish smiled warmly, a triumph in his deteriorated state. "I think I like this one," he said. Amos turned and saw Hilda standing behind him holding a small basket. The smell of freshly baked bread drove out the stench of the grave.

"This will take a moment," she said, removing one of the *doed-koecks* from the basket and placing it on her father's heaving breast. Amos noted the initials carved into it:

V. S.

The little man seemed to dance across Standish's chest with every roil and wiggle of the sins long ago ingested. Amos's own stomach began to dance, but for far different reasons.

Hilda began to recite what sounded like a prayer in her native tongue. Vigor Standish began to moan, which soon turned into a howl as his daughter's voice rose in pitch, higher and higher with every word. Amos looked on, helpless to look away. He knew he was witness to a rite that was ancient when the world was young.

Standish began to writhe, his bloated, distorted body twisting on the bed, the frame smacking against the wall. The springs creaked and screeched like a chorus of damned cats. Still the young woman prayed on, until at last, Standish stopped moving, save for the gentle rise and fall of his chest. Amos thought he might be asleep, or might have even passed out from the torment of the ritual.

Hilda stepped away from the bed and motioned Amos forward.

"Is time," she said, beads of sweat rolling down her fair cheeks and dripping onto her collar.

Amos gingerly reached out for the cake, as if it were a wounded snake. He snatched it up and quickly took a bite.

It was plain, a simple confection, no taste, save for the wheat it had been made from and a touch of sugar. He chewed carefully, as though he had a mouth full of broken glass.

"You must eat all of it," Hilda said solemnly from behind him.

Amos put the rest of the dead-cake in his mouth and chewed quickly, swallowing it in a single moist lump.

Nothing.

Amos wasn't sure what he was supposed to feel, if anything. He didn't reckon he'd plump-up like Standish. After all, the man had been doing it for a long time. Even so, if this was all real, he had just ingested not only Standish's sins, but the sins of every man, woman, and child he'd taken on.

He turned, smiling at Hilda. "Think maybe I could get a glass of milk to wash it down? No offense, but it was kinda dry—"

The pain slammed into his guts like a sledgehammer. He doubled over in the chair and fell forward onto the bed.

The sensation was like that of an open door in the dead of winter, gusts of icy wind blowing in and chilling everything it touched. Once open, no power on earth could shut it again. He clawed at the bedcovers and flipped over on his back, tearing at his clothes like an Old Testament prophet pleading for the sins of Israel. He reached out to Hilda, begging for help, but she just stood mutely and watched. She had seen it before and knew her place in the affair.

Amos slid off the bed and hit the floor with a thud. The visions started then, and Amos's soul was laid bare to years of torment and secret sin.

****

A caravan of wagons bearing settlers came into the great valley from the east. Women sat beside husbands in the carriage seats while children ran along beside, playing and laughing. Fathers admonished the young ones for teasing the horses, promising the strap when they reached their new homes.

As the wagon train crested the rise, a strange sight greeted them. Down below, tribal wigwams stood by the score and small cookfires dotted the landscape, their smoke rising lazily into the summer air.

Men began to dismount the wagons and gather at the head of the train. They seemed to be angry, confused. A man in a black frock and wide-brimmed hat climbed out of the back of one wagon and strode up to them, waving his hands in a placating manner.

"You said this valley was empty, Josiah. You said we would start anew here. Warn't nary a word about no Reds."

The other men nodded and harrumphed in agreement.

"Not to worry, John Calder. The elders and I have a plan in place. We were told we might face some… itinerants in these parts. But don't you worry. Your cabins will be built and our church gloriously erected on this very spot. This I promise. God has shown me the way."

The men walked back to their wagons in a huff, glancing over their shoulders at the right reverend Josiah March, the man who had promised them a new life, a new home, a paradise in which to raise their children, far from the rampant sin of the big cities.

Reverend March strode solemnly over to a smaller group of likewise pinch-faced men and spoke in a hush.

"These savages are known for their penchant for trading. This we know. If you men would be so kind as to gather your foodstuffs and follow me, we'll set it all t'rights. You all know the plan."

One of the men shuffled his feet, scuffing the earth.

"Is there a problem Gracious Palmer?"

"There is," said Palmer. "I am not certain this is the right course. It doesn't seem…well, Christian. *I mean, hellfire, Josiah! We're talkin' about cold-blooded* murder *here! Don't even think to* try *to dress it up different!"*

"Damn your time, Palmer, we all agreed to this afore we even set out!" cried another. "We all knew what measures this called for and now is not the time to be delicate! Or shall we go and tell our families, who've suffered much hardship of their own in coming here that we must move on to parts unknown?"

"Goodman Wager, hold your tongue before I'm to forget myself and hold it for *you!" growled Palmer.*

"Shush, shush, now," March said. We don't want to frighten the womenfolk, as they are delicate and cannot comprehend the ways of men. Let us keep our own council as always and be about it, then."

The men slowly retreated to their wagons, some shaking heads, Palmer kicking a rock that tumbled down the hill.

Moments later, they were down amongst the savages, dispensing gifts of welcome, making friendships that would last no more than mere hours. The Reds, unaware of the viper they had welcomed to their breast, waved a farewell as they sat down with their hot meals, dividing them equally among men, women, and children -- even infants.

Later that evening, as the newcomers huddled in their wagons, sleeping peacefully, dreams of a new life playing out behind their eyelids, the descendants of an ancient people that had traveled from the deepest reaches of Central America to find a new life of their own *, freedom from their barbaric past as members of the Aztec Empire, choked and gagged and died, writhing in pain too terrible to contemplate as the poison coursed though their veins.*

Gracious Palmer lay clutching the sweat-soaked sheets of his pallet, crying out to merciful God for deliverance, from the awful penance he knew must await him on some future day. His wife slept fitfully next to him, never hearing the pitiful mewling cries of the infants down in the Red village.

But Goodman Palmer heard them until the day he died.

* * * *

Amos woke screaming on the floor in a puddle of his own sick. His stomach churned with acid. The pain was so great, he felt it might eat its way out of him, chewing flesh and gnawing bone until it was free.

But it was his now. His to own until death, if that's what it took.

He sat up slowly but the pain made him retch again. This time there was nothing but bile left, and tears ran freely down his face as he wished he could vomit out the pain, the agony, the secret knowledge of sins long buried.

He felt thin, strong arms lift him from the floor and set him in the chair. Hilda kept a hold on his shoulders, lest he fall again. She handed him a cup of steaming tea. "Sip it slowly, now. The worst has passed, but you will need to rest yet."

Amos sipped the heady, murky brew and found his strength returning almost immediately. "What… what is this?" he asked.

"An old recipe: St. John's Wart, wormwood, and chamomile, mostly. It helps, yes?"

"Yes," he said, taking another small sip. "Oh, *Lord*, yes."

Hilda went to her father. Standish's chest was rising and falling gently, which meant he was probably enjoying the first peaceful sleep he'd had in untold years. Her face creased in sorrow.

"He is moving on," Hilda said. "Not much longer."

Amos moved over to the bed and rested a hand on Standish's shoulder. No more fever. It had broken and left behind a sheen of tacky perspiration more akin to saliva covering the man's body.

His torso had shrunk to a grotesque state. Once full and writhing with mortal evil, the skin now hung in flabby folds to either side of him and covered his crotch completely. Amos shuddered, but not at the sight of the poor soul.

"All them years," he whispered. "He kep' all that bottled right up inside him an' never told a soul."

"Except for one," Hilda said, smoothing her father's brow. "Who more than a sin-eater needs to confess?"

Amos nodded angrily. "Them folks, the ones from back east, they killed them Injuns, killed 'em in cold blood with one hand and shook hands with t' other. I ain't never… "

"Yes," Hilda said, pulling the sheet up to her father's neck. "They let us stay here, but make us keep secret. We are prisoners, a place to keep their darkest secret. *That* is why we never leave."

Amos grieved for this man, a father trying to provide for his child in the only way he knew. That's what fathers did, after all. But Vigor Standish would not live to reap the rewards.

And as they watched, the man's chest rose and fell a final time, gently, softly, and an unhurried breath escaped his lips, bearing his soul to heaven, stainless. Vigor Standish, father, husband, and taker of sins, died peacefully, something he had never dreamed possible since coming to this verdant country.

Hilda wept, the sobs wracking her slight frame, and Amos slid an arm around her shoulders and guided her to the couch. He returned and draped the bed sheet over Standish's face.

"Rest easy, old son," Amos whispered.

Suddenly, a hard rap came at the front door and they both jumped. Hilda rose and went to the door, Amos on her heels. She began to lift the bar, but Amos grabbed her arm. "Hold on, now," he whispered, and moved to a side window. A flickering orange glow lit the night outside the house.

"Who is it?" Hilda barked.

"It's Reverend March, child. We've come for the sin-eater."

"Is too late!" Hilda screamed. "He is dead!"

Amos peered out from under the curtains. Almost every man in the village stood in the yard, carrying torches. Some held pitchforks, shovels, and axes—and angry mob if there ever had been one—and all of them looked hard at the house that held their secret.

"Not your father, child. The other—the Negro. We know what he's done. Send him out. We've business with him, now."

"An' what business is that?" Amos yelled.

"Why, an offer, Mr.... Harlow, was it?"

"This oughtta be good, Amos thought. "Didn't seem you was too keen on helpin' me out before."

"Things have changed, Mr. Harlow. You share our burden, now. We cannot have you walking into the world and spreading it about."

"Who you foolin' March? Ain't nobody gonna care 'bout buncha Injuns what got killed seventy years gone."

"True enough," March said. "But most outsiders already think us a threat. What would stop us from rising up against neighbors, they think. We have a peaceful life here now, despite past... *hindrances*. No reason you can't be a part of that."

"You wanna get the cornbread out your mouth?" Amos said.

"You stay here with us, be our sin-eater. You will be handsomely compensated. You will have a home, a place to call your own. You will *belong*, Mr. Harlow. It is a better offer than you are like to have in your life. What say you?"

For a fleeting, guilty second, Amos thought on that. He'd never even *hoped* to settle someplace nice. He had wandered so long and so far, the road had become his home without him knowing it. That's what those bastards that had started all this way back must have thought.

Then he thought of all the grief such thinking had wrought, of the man in the next room who had been the repository of all that grief, and the young woman beside him, scared and angry, who would bear the memory of it still.

"I say you can stick your offer up your lily-white ass," Amos said.

A pause, then: "I thought such would be your stance. I am truly sorry. You force our hand, sir."

Amos peeked out the window again. The men had split up and were placing bundles of twigs around the house. They touched the torches to the wood and it went up in a blaze, sending sparks soaring heavenward like fireflies.

"Oh, shit," Amos breathed.

Hilda was wild-eyed with fear. "What is—*Mijn Gott*!" she cried. The smoke curling under the front door was her answer.

Amos snatched her up by the arm, choking on smoke. "Where's the back door?" They fled to the rear of the house. Smoke greeted them in the kitchen and flames licked the back door. "Is there another way out?" Amos cried. Hilda just stared at the flames, unable to move or speak. Amos shook her hard. "Answer me, girl!"

She snapped to attention, focusing on his eyes. "Y-yes," she said, pointing to the living room. "Root cellar, under table. Opens into woods."

They rushed to the table and Amos flipped it over and tore back the rug underneath, revealing a trap door with an iron ring in the center. Amos tugged twice and it wouldn't budge. The smoke filled the room, now. On the third try, the door gave with a great creaking sigh into darkness below.

"C'mon, let's git," Amos said. "Wait!"

She looked at him askance. He pointed to the kitchen. "Grab the rest of them cakes. I got me an idea."

* * * *

The Right-Reverend March looked around at his charges, nodding.

They would follow him. They knew it was all they could do. They had all known a day like this would come. They had all known that the sins of their fathers would come home to roost on their shoulders, and they all knew that on that day, they would have to pay the price.

The price would be equal parts blood and shares of their own souls.

Oh, what a burden the sins of the past could be, he thought. Hadn't they tried to do the Lord's will all these years, and their fathers before them? Hadn't they walked the straight and narrow as best they could? Weren't God's chosen, after all, due some measure of peace in which to live out their lives?

As much as he wished otherwise, he knew the cup would not pass from their lips. This was their cross, their crown of thorns, and the only way to end it was to face it head on. They could plead mercy and forgiveness from the Father after all was laid to rest.

It was such a shame that the young girl would have to die, as well, though. She was a pretty thing, if the sharp tongue in her mouth *did* cut indiscriminately. That was something that could have been rectified—with the right husband, of course—but, there it was.

The faces of the faithful stared back at him with an eagerness to implement the articles of their own private faith. Torchlight danced across each face, casting shadows into the dark woods and giving metaphor to the bloody work that must needs be done if God's work was to flourish here in their small corner of Heaven on earth.

The smoke rose all about the house now, covering the roof and yard in a blanket of gray. Flames licked out of the cracks between the clapboard walls and curled in unfettered ribbons from the window shutters. The tin roof ticked and popped in the heat like an overworked radiator.

He cleared his throat. "Listen to me, all of you," he began. "We all know what our business here commands of us. We all know that for too long, sin has lain dormant at our very doorsteps. God, in His infinite wisdom, has seen fit to keep that sin caged away from us, away from our families, who lie sleeping only a stone's throw away."

There were nods and grunts of agreement from the men assembled. They shifted stances, gripped torches and pitchforks in fervent hands. All eyes were on their leader, the Reverend March, who had helped them keep their forebears' secret all these years, who had taken on a Dutchman to harbor their own sins, and in doing so, laid their own souls bare to their greatest sin: the sin of silence.

"But now… now, good friends, we have an outsider among us. An outsider who has taken on the sins of Vigor Standish, and therefore, the sins of us all. You know what this means." He let that sink in.

"This," he said, "we cannot allow. Not if it means the sanctity of our home be thrown open wide to the scorn and degradation of others. Others that, when they hear of the past transgressions of our people, will seek to run us out, to send us east of the Eden we have so long called home.

"They already revile us and if this man Harlow leaves, they will have proof to add to their misperception of us. We will be torn down, separated from our women and children, scattered to the four winds.

This land, which is ours by rights, purchased freely in the days of my great-great grandfather with every cent of our forefathers when they came to these shores, will be plowed under and the earth salted, never to bring forth life again. This, my children, is what we face. This, good people of Manchester Township, is what we can *prevent* here tonight."

They all fixed him with wonderment, with pride in their eyes. March felt magnanimous, much like the apostle Paul after his walk on the Damascus road, his face shining with the glory of the Living God.

"The screams you will hear are the screams of sin being purged once and for all from our midst, and never again will we practice the heathen arts! Instead, we will rely on God Almighty to cleanse us of sin, as is only right! So do not be dismayed by them, rather stand fast and make a joyful noise to the Lord, and *know* that we are in the right!"

March began belting out "It Is Well With My Soul," his favorite of the hymns in troubling times. As he sang, the others joined in, and the song rang out above the crackle of the flames.

In the midst of the fire, March could see the future that this one last act of iniquity would bring. He could see families living, growing, loving, and dying, a new unity born from the ashes of the past.

He began the second verse, and the tears rolled down his face, not so much from the heat that curled his eyebrows, but from the second chance, the grace that had been shown them by the Lord. Expurgate the sin, live as He meant them to live, and be accepted by Him on Judgment Day. It was enough to make *any* man cry. He opened his mouth, taking a great breath to sing the third verse even louder than the second.

That was when wiry arms, the tensile strength of steel cables wrapped around his middle, pinning his arms to his sides, and the taste of sweet, freshly-baked bread filled his mouth.

* * * *

Amos could barely hear March shouting over the roar of the flames. Then the singing started, and he got his bearings again. The smoke was everywhere now, and the house a lost cause. It would be ashes in a matter of hours.

Led by the torchlight and the sound of singing, Amos and Hilda made their way through the smoke, water-soaked handkerchiefs tied around their noses and mouths to battle the smoke. Still, Amos had to fight down a cough every second and Hilda fared little better. Amos knew this had to go just right, or they would be dead before the ashes cooled.

They reached what Amos figured was the front corner of the house and squatted in the smoke. The singing had reached a crescendo now, and Amos pulled Hilda close and handed her the dead-cake.

"Okay," he said. "Do your thing."

Hilda coughed lightly and wiped the sweat from her brow. She ran her thumb over the hastily carved initials on the bread-man:

A.H.

She began to murmur in Dutch and rubbed over every inch of the bread-man until she was satisfied. The beseeching done, she held it firmly in place over Amos's heart.

Amos felt a squirming inside him, like a worm too close to the flame. He was nauseous for a moment, and then it passed. Hilda handed him the dead-cake and covered it with his other hand, pressing tightly.

Amos nodded. "Where will you go?" he asked.

Hilda looked to the road out of town. "Back east, I think. Perhaps Connecticut. We meet some nice people there, friends. Maybe they take me in, not knowing… " she trailed off. "They are good people," she said finally.

Amos nodded again. "Now you get goin' while I got their attention," he said, "and don't be lookin' back. Ain't no good ever come o' that."

Hilda smiled sweetly through the handkerchief; Amos could tell by the way her eyes turned up at the corners. "You give my father rest," she said. "Is more than I ever to hope. Godspeed, my friend. I hope our roads are to meet again."

"So do I," Amos smiled in return. "Now go on," he said. "I ain't got no idea if this'll even work. If it don't, well… "

"Will work," Hilda said, and embraced him. Then she thrust him out at arms' length, looked at him fiercely, as if burning him into her memory, then turned and trotted away through the woods toward the east road.

Amos watched her go for a long moment. Then, as the second verse of the hymn died out, he made his move.

* * * *

Reverend March choked as the dry bread was forced down his gullet, spitting crumbs and sucking air in through his nostrils.

The singing abruptly stopped. The only sound was the violent hissing of old pine sizzling as the sap was burned out through its pores. No one moved. No one *dared* move.

“Eat it all, you sumbitch!” Amos shouted. “Chew it up, dammit, or choke on it! Don’t make no nevermind to me!”

His palm covered the minister’s mouth so he couldn’t spit out the dead-cake, the symbol of all the transgressions of his ancestors. Amos pinched March’s nostrils and held his jaw shut, making sure the dead-cake had nowhere to go but down, down into the dark where sin flourishes and thrives like fungus around a man’s heart. He felt March swallow to get air into his lungs, and satisfied, let go.

The others stood aghast, not sure what to do, but veery man among them knew what he'd just seen.

After all, they’d seen it performed all their lives.

Reverend March drew a ragged breath and staggered forward. The men in the front row, ones that had sung the loudest, stepped back, unconsciously brandishing their torches before them.

“Help… help me… ” March begged. He doubled over, retching and gagging, and fell to his knees in the dirt. “Help me… oh, Lord, the pain…!”

“Come on!” Amos shouted. “Help him out! Help out the man what brung all this down on your heads! Help the man who’d let another take all y’all’s sins to Hell wit’ him when he die!”

No one moved, except to take another few steps back.

“What’s the matter?” Amos yelled. “Ain’t he one o’ y’all? Ain’t he a brother in need? Pick him up! Take him home and give ‘im aid! Ain’t that what y’all pride yourselves on? C’mon, damn you!”

One by one, the men peeled off from the crowd and headed back toward town. Several crossed themselves, others forked the sign of the evil eye in March’s direction, but each one carried an expression of disgust on his face. March was anathema now, a social leper, the embodiment of all they disdained in themselves. To even breathe the same air as him was unthinkable.

"N-no!" cried March. "Don't… don't go! Help me! I'm one of you! I'm one of *you*, damn your eyes!"

But his cries fell on deaf ears. They could not—*would* not—hear him, not until one of them was on his deathbed and needed the services of the sin-eater.

March fell flat and sobbed into the dirt, coughing and retching not from the smoke, but from the evil that was already growing in him and eating away at his soul from the inside out.

Amos stood over him. He knew he should hate this creature, but all he could feel was pity. After all, who was *he* to judge another by his sins? Hadn't he enough of his own to go around for three lifetimes?

"We all got to carry a load," he said. "Some just got more than others, that's all."

March looked up at Amos with an unbridled fury. "You… you vile abomination," he croaked. "Viper! Usurper! You will be brought low! The Lord will repay! He will *repay*!"

Amos grimaced. "Of that," he said, "I have no doubt."

He wandered over into the woods and picked up his guitar case and bindle. The black dog was waiting on him, scratching its flank with its hind foot, looking up as Amos approached. Amos watched the dog for a moment, his brow furrowed.

"No doubt at all," he said.

He trudged up the trail and out to the road headed west, leaving his sins behind him, but knowing they would follow him as soon as they were able, no matter how far he walked.

GIANTS IN THE EARTH

A Song of the Black Dog

There were giants in the earth in those days; and also after that, when the sons of God came in unto the daughters of men, and they bare children to them, the same became mighty men which were of old, men of renown.

—Genesis 6:4

The rumble of thunder in the west like a barrel of rocks tumbling down a mountainside, and a cool, stiff breeze at his neck let Amos Harlow know he'd just beat the boomer into the mountains. He could smell the acrid tang of ozone in the air and knew the sky would soon be dancing with lightning bolts from Zeus's own hand.

It was a blessing, he knew, that the two weeks worth of road dust he'd accumulated in his lungs would soon be dampened and the road before him would be wet. The Dust Bowl hadn't been kind, and the downpour likely to follow would be hardly more than a Band-Aid on a shotgun wound, but Amos took his mercies where he found them.

The wind whipped the surrounding pines into a frenzy, their tops dancing and swaying to the encroaching storm's orchestral rhythm. He moved as fast as his old frame allowed, occasionally stumbling over jutting granite or exposed roots, desperate to get to shelter before he drowned.

He cursed himself for not taking the old hunting trails through the Springfield Plateau; the ground there was gently sloped, rolling across Northwest Arkansas like carpet over well-worn steps. Instead, he'd chosen to head southeast into the Boston Mountain range, giving Tulsa a wide berth, as he'd left too many bad feelings there the last time through. Ultimately, he was headed for Memphis to make good on an old promise. It was something he should have done long ago; the boy he'd made it to was most likely a young man, now. Amos hoped he was still around.

His plan had been to skirt the edge of the Ozarks and make for Jonesboro, but that was before the storm forced him into the sanctuary of the mountains. He knew the area was peppered with limestone and dolemite caves—the perfect place to weather Heaven's rage.

The old guitar case was strapped across his back by a makeshift leather strap he'd bartered from a tanner back in Muleshoe, a week before hitting the Oklahoma state line. It bumped and jounced off his ass with every step, but it was good to have his hands free in such treacherous terrain. He'd thought about stopping a spell, taking the old guitar out and working on a new song, using lines from a hoodoo book he'd lifted from a *bruja* woman in Laredo, but that was before the sky turned ugly and yellow, and threatened to grind him into the ground of Tornado Alley.

After what seemed like ages, he crested the rise and stared out into the expanse below. He stopped, hands on his knees, panting like a fox run to ground. The valley was low and deep, stretching at least fifteen miles in either direction; a single dirt track splitting it from end to end, running out of the valley at either side. The valley was so stacked with pines, oaks, hickory and Eastern Juniper, that it hardly seemed able to accommodate the little town nestled in its heart. But there it was, practically invisible in the darkening sky, save for the warm, orange light in windowpanes behind which lay all manner of comforts.

He had not expected to find shelter, except for the aforementioned caves, and the appearance of the town at the height of the impending storm was a either the best luck a broke-shoe hobo ever had, or a gift directly from the bosom of God. Amos had stopped believing in luck long ago. He'd seen enough and done enough to know such notions as childish fantasy; reality was a far grimmer animal with bigger teeth.

Amos debated whether or not to chance the town. Warm and inviting from a hundred yards away could be cold, uncaring—even hostile—up close. Amos was a loner by nature, but it hadn't always been that way. Oh, he liked a crowd, as long as he was on stage, and knew he could play to them. That was the key with folks. You had to match their rhythm, find that one place you connected to them in the thousand you didn't, and then you had them, whole-hog.

But this town felt different. Amos knew without knowing why that he could go down there and turn on all the works and them folks wouldn't so much as crease a forehead. He was running out of options, and he knew it. He trudged to the edge of the road and saw a sign post:

BLEDSOE, ARK.
POP. 113

He looked into the gathering gloom, the evening mist beginning to gather at the bases of the trees. He heard a pattering; slow and soft at first, then picking up tempo. The first raindrops, fat and heavy, smacked the base of his neck like artillery from a cannonade.

"Well," he said. "Whatchu think, boss?"

The black dog, as usual, didn't reply, but had moved about thirty feet away toward the little hidden town in the middle of nowhere. He looked around expectantly at Amos, as if to ask: *You comin'?*

Amos shifted the guitar case on his back, brow furrowed. "That's what I figured," he said, shaking his head. And the two of them set off into the storm, loose shale and pinecones crunching beneath their feet.

* * * *

The little rural community of Bledsoe was unlike any Amos had ever visited. It wasn't really a town at all, more like one of those Bavarian villages or hamlets of which the Brothers' Grimm were so fond, separated from the rest of the world by mystic geography and paths that never really went anywhere.

There were no obvious businesses, save for a small mercantile that was no more than an open-air trading post, and a tall, gray, severe building that was either a church or a school, and probably both. It was perched on a wide ledge above and behind the town, looming over it like a predatory cat, ready to pounce.

The houses along the main street were cozy and inviting, the sort where shoes were kept in a neat line by the front door, where every father read his paper after supper and smoked a pipe, and every mother worked crochet, listening alternately to the radio playing low in the background and her husband's snores. The houses were huddled up together like dwarves in deep conversation, a sight that spoke of kinship, community, and a closeness that bordered on the incestuous. It took hardy, honest folks, ready to lend a hand to their neighbors, to settle such a place and *keep* it settled.

Amos wended his way along the main street, looking for signs of people and finding none. Every now and then, he caught the twitch of curtains being drawn out of the corner of his eye, but no one called out to him or cried a warning of a stranger in their midst. Just when he'd decided to knock on one of the doors, he heard a low murmuring of voices, like a rushing creek after a heavy rain. He turned toward them.

Orange flame licked through the dense foliage toward the center of town. As he neared, the light resolved into the flickering of at least two dozen torches. It was a little town square, complete with bandstand, and it was full of men carrying everything from shotguns to squirrel rifles, and even two or three with axes. One tall man with long mustaches and wearing an Australian bush hat was in front of the crowd, yelling for all he was worth. Every time he paused, the crowd yelled back in answer.

Amos knew an angry mob when he saw one. He pushed his way through the edges of the crowd. The people paid no mind to him, rapt as they were in the spectacle before them.

"Make no mistake, my friends!" the man shouted. "This is no mere man we're after! He's a creature spawned of darkness, an evil in the midst of the fair Eden you all have toiled so long and hard to build!" The crowd roared in the affirmative.

"We must be cautious, but we must also be courageous, for the Lord God is on our side! And with Him, we cannot *help* but prevail!" Again, the crowd responded in kind.

Amos shoved a bit farther, until he was standing at the bandstand's edge. The man in the Aussie hat flicked his gaze down to Amos, jabbing a finger at him. "Who are you?" he shouted.

All at once, Amos heard the sound of two dozen guns cocking, rounds being chambered, and the collective gasp of the townsfolk, their spell broken. He raised his hands slowly above his shoulders.

"Name's Harlow. I was just passin' through, thought I'd see if I might shelter the storm overnight in your town. I ain't meanin' no trouble, nor lookin' for any. Just a roof-- a dry barn or a front porch will do."

No one spoke. The rain was beginning to fall harder now, fat drops hissing off torches. "Didn't see no one, but I heard the commotion over here, thought I'd come see what it was all about. Looks to me like y'all about to hunt down Frankenstein."

A few in the crowd laughed. "You ain't far off, mister," one man said.

The man on the bandstand frowned. "The business of Bledsoe township is no one else's, especially not that of a road bum," the man sneered. "You'd do well to keep moving, sir."

"Beggin' your pardon, sir," Amos said, matching the man's mock civility, "but I ain't no bum. I *work* for my keep an' I pay my debts, so I'll thank you not make presumptions an' I'll try not to do the same. An' in case you ain't noticed," he added, nodding upward, "the bottom's damn near 'bout to fall out. Don't seem like the best time to go huntin', you ask me."

The two men eyed each other. Amos had never been a man to back down from anything, especially not a jumped-up blowhard in a funny hat. The staring contest went on eternal seconds before the man broke eye contact. "We should get started right away. The beast's lair can't be far, and—"

"C'mon, Tolliver, the old boy's right," one man said. "Cain't even find our own peckers in this rain. An' I ain't wantin' to meet ol' Goliath after the sun goes down, nohow."

The man called Tolliver searched the eyes of the crowd, fuming. None met his gaze. He'd had them 'til the old coon had walked up. He saw the drifter's presence as a challenge, the way self-important men are want to do, but just the same, he knew he'd lose the crowd if he pressed them. They were simple people, after all—easy to sway, but just as easy to anger. Simple folks didn't like to be reminded that they *were* simple. It was time to back down, Tolliver thought.

"Alright then, people. Let's pack it up," he said. "The rain lets up tomorry, we'll be back in business. But I promise you all this: that boy *will* be found. He *will* be returned to his father, and the evil that's plagued you in this peaceful valley for so long will be dealt with!" He met Amos's eyes. "By *me*."

There were a few whoops and hollers, but noticeably less than before. The townsfolk began to file away into the oncoming night, muttering and conversing amongst themselves, occasional laughter breaking out here and there. Tolliver continued to stare at Amos, tapping his rifle unconsciously against his right thigh. Amos stared back, rain running in rivulets down his careworn face.

"As I said," Tolliver began, "you'd best be movin' along. I have things well in hand here."

"Maybe you do, at that," Amos said. "But I ain't one to be takin' orders from a stranger, even one totin' a cannon like that one. Matter-fact, I think you a stranger here, too. Where you from? Sure as hell ain't Arkansas."

"Where I'm from or why I'm here ain't no concern of yours, boy. Now you got exactly five seconds to start walkin' back down that road or—"

"Or *what*, Tolliver? You gonna shoot a man askin' sanctuary from strangers? Might check that Good Book you're always waggin' in front of the others."

The voice belonged to a slight man with graying hair. He carried no torch, no firearm like the others. His beard was scruffy and unkempt, his eyes sunken and hollow, and his complexion so pallid that he resembled an apparition as he stepped from the shadows.

"Now Brady, I know you're suffering right now, but—"

"But nothin', Tolliver. This man has come among us and asked for something in our power to give. To turn him out would be worse than sin." Tolliver shifted from one foot to the other, unable to meet the other man's stare.

"We don't know a thing about this man! Hell, for all we know, he's mixed up in all of this. You mean to tell me you're inviting this… *person* into your *home*?"

"That's *exactly* what I'm tellin' you," the man said, stepping up to place a hand on Amos's shoulder. "He is a guest in my home and will be treated as such for the remainder of his stay." He looked at Amos, then back at Tolliver. "However long that is."

Tolliver looked ready to chew iron and spit nails, but what could he do? He pulled the brim of his hat down low and set off into the evening rain, thunder clapping overhead. "Just be ready to move at first light," he growled as he passed them. Amos watched him disappear into the gloom.

"Sorry about that," the man said, turning and walking with Amos back into town. "You had that man pegged right. He ain't from around here. His manners say that much."

"No harm," Amos said. "I been knowin' the likes of him way too long. They all the same." He paused. "I ain't ungrateful, but why you stick up for me back there? You don't know me from Adam."

"No," replied the man, "but I heard what you said, you know, about working for your keep. I think you mean it, and that's a rare commodity these days. 'sides," he grinned, "I been waitin' for someone to put a boot up that one's ass for days, now."

Amos laughed. "Glad I could oblige," he said.

The man stuck out his hand, not breaking stride. "Name's Carver. Brady Carver."

"Amos Harlow," Amos said, taking the proffered hand, gripping it. "How'd that fella come to be amongst you, anyway? I heard him mention a missing boy."

Carver shoved his hands in his pockets, bending into the oncoming rain. "The boy's mine. He's been missing for three days. Tolliver claims he can get 'im back."

"Back?"

"From the giant who stole 'im."

* * * *

The inside of Carver's house was exactly as Amos pictured. The place had a slight feminine touch to it—red gingham curtains, fresh flowers placed in eye-catching locales, clean-swept hardwood floors and baseboards that damn near shined. A fire crackled in the hearth near the easy chair in which Amos now sat, his feet propped up on an ottoman upholstered with the print of wild roses. His road-worn boots and socks sat drying on a hearth fashioned from great flagstones drug up from some nearby river. Soft light from a dozen candles painted the room a warm orange, and two kerosene lanterns hissed, driving shadows into the deepest corners of the house.

Outside, the storm raged. A fierce howler was blowing from the northwest, bending the tops of the pines. The sky was stitched with crooked trails of lightning, and the rain fell with no end in sight, like God had reneged on His promise never again to flood the earth. But inside the Carver place, there was a silent comfort like Amos had never known. It was as if the house and the people who had made it a home existed as a bulwark against the elements, against all outside harm, like the town of Bledsoe itself, writ small.

Carver hung the coffee percolator from a cast-iron arm and swung it over the fire. He reached up and plucked a gilded-framed picture off the mantel and handed it to Amos.

In it, Amos recognized a younger Carver sitting with a woman and an infant on what he realized was the bandstand gazebo where he'd had his standoff with Tolliver. The woman was pretty in a way that didn't directly call attention to her beauty. Hers was a pleasant face, serene as clouds, and her eyes were wide and dark and smiled right along with her mouth.

"That's my Cora, God rest her. Been with the Lord eight years, now. That was took right after Seth was born. We was so proud…" He bowed his head, his voice breaking.

"Tell me 'bout your boy," Amos said, handing back the picture.

"What's to tell?" Carver said. "He's like every other nine-year old boy—adventurous, curious, *spools* of energy *I'll* never have—you know what I'm talkin'about."

Amos did. "An' you say he was taken by…?"

"A giant," said Carver, staring at his hands. "Least that's what Tolliver and some of the others say."

"A giant. 'Fraid you lost me, friend," Amos said.

Carver absently pulled his long, knobby fingers as he spoke, the knuckles popping like the logs in the hearth. "I work a sawmill over in Candide, just north of here. My wife used to look after the boy, and when she passed, well, times bein' what they were, and still are, I couldn't find work nowhere closer. Seth's too young to stay by himself, but what could I do? We gotta eat, right? So, I asked Mrs. Clayton, our schoolteacher, to look in on Seth from time to time.

"Four days ago, I was walking home from work, and Clete Davis met me at the fork just outside the valley, yelling at the top of his lungs about what, I couldn't tell. After I calmed him, he told me he'd been out huntin' in the north hills and heard a child cryin'. He followed the voice 'til he came over a ridge and saw a man, big as the one King David killed with a rock, totin' Seth up Canebreak Mountain. He yelled at the man to stop. He said the man turned and looked at him with these big ol' eyes. Clete said they held him, somehow, and he couldn't move for love nor money. Then the big man started up the mountain again, toward the old Hagan silver mine. Said the brute hadn't a lick of hair on his head, nor the rest of his body. Clete fired a double burst from that old .410 he carries, but it weren't loaded with no more than birdshot, and Clete said the giant just sorta brushed at his back and head like he'd run into a cloud of pecker gnats and kept on movin'. Clete tried to follow him a piece, but the sucker took one stride where any other man would take three. Shot up that mountain like a comet, he did. That's when Clete ran back to town for help and found me at the fork."

Amos chewed that for a minute. A giant. He'd heard of, even *faced*, many an strange thing in his years of wandering the backside of a nation most folks would never even *hear* of, much less travel themselves. But a *giant*? That was a new one on him.

"So how does this man Tolliver fit the picture?" Amos asked.

Carver got up and fetched the coffee pot, and poured two tin cups of a heady brew that was fine as liquid gold to Amos's palate. Carver settled down on the hearth, shifting his cup in circles in his hands.

"We rounded up a search party, a few of the folks you saw tonight included. Most of the people here's fine folks, good Christians, but Mr. Harlow, you don't rightly see what's on the other side of people's skin until they's afraid."

Amos knew this, and only too well. Seemed like the world was full of such in those days. "It's just Amos, Mr. Carver."

"Well then, Amos, it's Brady to you," Carver said, a weak smile escaping his grim countenance. "Anyway, when the search turned up squat, as nobody wanted to dare the mountain at night—especially not the old mine—we turned back, people promising we'd get him back. But I could see it in their eyes, Amos. Nary a one believed Seth was still breathin'."

"But you do."

"I do," Carver nodded. "That boy is a piece of my own heart, the last piece, if truth be told. His ma took the rest to Heaven with her. I'd know if he were dead, 'cause *I'd* be, too."

They sat in quiet, listening to the rain hammer the tin roof of the cottage before Carver spoke again.

"Two days later, this Tolliver showed up, claiming to be a big game hunter. Been all over the world, he said. Africa, Canada, even Australia. Claimed he'd killed everything from boar to rogue elephants, and even some things most people hadn't heard of, much less seen. Gathered the town together and told us he'd been hired by a Mr. Ricketts, fella who runs a traveling carnival out of a little town in Florida on the Gulf. He said the man had one of his freaks run out on him about six months ago, a dangerous fella by the name of Nimrod—a giant and a strongman. Ricketts hired Tolliver to bring him back, but I think Tolliver just wants another trophy for the wall."

"Tolliver say this Nimrod ever hurt anybody?" Amos asked.

"He said Ricketts told him Nimrod had gone stark crazy one night—knocked down a tent, flipped a truck over on its side, and beat three men to death before he run off into the night, just outside of Merriweather where they was camped for a county fair."

Carver shifted uncomfortably. "To tell the truth, Amos, I'm more afraid of Tolliver than the giant."

"How that?" Amos asked.

"My boy's still alive, I know it, but I prepared myself for the worst, just the same. But if he *is* alive, I'd like to keep him that way. This man Tolliver, he don't care about nothin' but killin', and I think he means to kill the giant no matter what, and that means my boy is in the crosshairs."

Amos had come to the same conclusion, but he hadn't voiced his thoughts. He set his coffee down on the hearth and held Carver's eyes with his own.

"We gonna get your boy back. I'll set off in the mornin', rain or no."

"But… why? You don't even know me, Amos."

Amos shrugged. "No more than you knew me."

Carver shook his head. "This'll be dangerous, Amos. I cain't ask you to do what I got to do myself."

"You ain't asked; I tol' you what was happenin'. It's the least I can do."

Carver stood, clapping Amos on the back. "Amos, that's…I'll come with you! We'll take the hunting trails -- "

"No," Amos said, already shaking his head. "I'll go on my lonesome. You need to be here to keep that fool from runnin' a mob up that hill behind me. 'Sides, if this giant's crazy like they say, better you stay alive in case Seth come home on his own."

Carver looked like he wanted to cry, to scream in frustration, to strike Amos, but he couldn't shake the logic. He remained taciturn, but Amos could see the maelstrom of emotion roiling inside him, warring with his better judgment. "All right," he said quietly. "I'll do what I can to stall 'em, but I'm just one man."

Amos smiled and gripped Carver's shoulder in return. "Take it from a body who knows," he said. "Sometimes, that's all it takes."

* * * *

Morning came, but the only way Amos knew it was the smell of coffee and frying eggs. The sky outside was almost pitch, and still the rain fell. Amos wondered, as he gradually climbed out of sleep, how much rain it would take before the entire valley was filled, and the sleepy town of Bledsoe became an underwater relic, like the lost city of Atlantis, the sun never reaching the once-bat-infested belfry of the church.

"Hope you like eggs," Carver said from the stove. "Been a coon's age since I got to the market. There's toast and marmalade, too."

"We all on speakin' terms," Amos said, his belly growling.

Amos rose from the sofa where he'd made his bed, the scent of the poor man's feast pulling him like a bull by the nose-ring. He fetched his boots and socks from the hearth and slipped them on, sighing at their warmth. He stretched and popped his back, groaning in pleasure.

Few moments in his troubled life were worth remembering, but Amos would hold these precious hours at the Carver household within his mind like a robin's eggs, taking them out to admire them and remember their warmth in the cold days ahead, careful not to crush them.

Carver set the plates on the table, and after a mindful grace, the two men tucked in. "I been thinkin'," Carver said through a mouthful of eggs. "If Tolliver is the Great White Hunter he wants everybody to think he is, then why rouse a mob to follow him?"

Amos shrugged. "Could be he just need the help," he said, egg yolk dripping onto his shirt, "seein' as how that boy crushed three grown men to a pulp and tumped a truck over."

Carver shook his head. "That dog don't hunt," he said. "Man like that don't want a bunch amateur yokels underfoot, scarin' the prey, an' all. Folks that go huntin' 'round these parts go alone, maybe one more in case one gets hurt in the woods, or snake-bit."

"You think he wants to put on a show, that it?" Amos asked.

"Yep. I think he's a blowhard that ain't never killed no more than a skeeter what bit 'im on the neck," said Carver, mopping up the last of his yolk with a piece of toast. "I think he's tryin' to make a name for himself, an' I think that's why he's dangerous."

Amos nodded, pushing back from the table. "Way I figure it, he's gonna wait 'til the rain slacks off. He ain't gonna get nobody to trudge up that hill in a storm, an' that means he won't have nobody to tell him what a brave soul he is when he parks one in that big boy's melon." He brushed some crumbs off his chest and looked out the window.

The rain had not stopped while they broke their fast, and showed no signs of doing so in the near future. Tolliver might be a blowhard, but he wasn't stupid. He wasn't chancing the mountain until he could be sure of safely showing off his skills for the locals, if that was his aim.

But Seth Carver's life hung in the balance, and when it came to children, Amos had a soft, white underbelly underneath the crusty scales a life on the road had armored him with. When a child was endangered from the evil that men do, Amos went to a special place inside him, a red and black place where all thought ceased and anger seethed and frothed like the cauldron of a volcano.

When Amos returned from the War, scarred, beaten, and nursing a serious drunk, his father had given him a job as foreman in the family lumber mill at Mt. Vernon. He'd shown up for work an hour late one day. He'd been drinking heavily the night before down at the club where he'd make the girls holler on stage, where they'd make *him* holler *behind* it. Two fingers of whiskey and a beer back was his poison.

Clarence, his only nephew and all of sixteen, was being groomed for the business when he came of age, and that day it was Amos's job to see it done properly. The future of the business depended on it, his father had said. Clarence had high marks, after all, and a head for business. He could be the first black millionaire in New York history, hell, in American history, his daddy'd said. Yessir, many hopes were being pinned that fine young man.

Whether it was the fact that Amos was still lit from his debauchery the night before, or the grating thought in the back of his mind that he would soon be answering to an eighteen year-old, he couldn't remember.

In fact, he couldn't remember much of *anything* about that day, except for the black dog trotting through the mill as if he belonged there. He remembered running after it, yelling insensibly at what no one else but him could see. He had vague impressions of men yelling at him, their voices sounding as if they were underwater.

And he remembered the nightmarish, anguished screams of Clarence, who was being sawn neatly from shoulder to hip by the giant plywood table saw Amos had knocked him into in his furious pursuit of the dog.

Amos hadn't waited around to be disowned by his family. He'd taken his guitar, thumbed a ride out of town, and hit the drift, soaking his memories in copious measures of booze, and burying the pain in every roadhouse whore he could bed. He had never lived it down and likely never would. He wouldn't *let* himself live it down.

Now, here was another child—a stranger's child—with no hope but a broken old man with a past and a jacket in three states. He could not wager the Fates with the life of another child, but he would stack his *own* chips in the middle of the table and tell those bitches to roll them bones.

"I best be getting' on," he said. "I go now, I can be up the mountain by sundown, I reckon."

Carver rose and followed Amos to the door, where Amos picked up his guitar case. "Head on up the north face, then take the switchback through the pass and around the east side. The mine is right at the summit; you cain't miss it."

"My thanks for the eggs," Amos said. "Be seein' you."

With that, he walked out into the storm, the wind-blown rain lashing at his tattered clothes like a cat-o'-nine-tails. Carver watched him go until he disappeared into the storm.

"I surely hope so," he said.

* * * *

Amos Harlow had traveled through some of the worst country America had to offer. He had been in places that sane men shied away from, if not downright shunned—dimly-lit recesses of humanity where horror was just a word, and where nameless fears lay in wait, cursing the daylight.

There were countless times he'd wished his path had taken him on a more mundane, circuitous route, where his only worry was finding a diner that would let him wash dishes for a meal, or a dry barn filled with sweet-smelling hay in which to bed down.

Footing it up the pitch-black, rain-swept slopes of Canebreak Mountain in the middle of what was possibly the worst storm in the history of the state of Arkansas now ranked highly among them.

The wind didn't so much push him as grow hands and threaten to toss him over the side like a sack of grain, that, upon hitting bottom, would split at the seams, spilling out its insides, a feast for wild animals.

The rain came in sheets at that altitude, and Amos reckoned he might as well be walking under a waterfall. Every foot he gained, he lost another two just trying to stay upright. The forest floor, normally blanketed with a soft, aromatic down of pine straw, was now a quagmire tugging at his shoes, filled with broken limbs, crushed limestone and other mountain detritus, and quite possibly some of the rattlesnakes from which the mountain took its name.

Yes, Amos had known brighter times and better circumstances and it was to these his mind wandered as he made his way up the mountain like a prophet in the wilderness.

He thought of a raft, constructed from oak logs and railroad timber, gently drifting down the mighty Mississip, the morning sun bright on his face, the only sounds the crickets in the grassy banks, the lonely staccato rhythm of a red-headed woodpecker looking for breakfast in a dead pine, and the slow swish of the oar in the great dark waters as the rudder man propelled them toward the Delta.

He thought of a cave high in the Sierra Nevada, where he had once taken refuge from the night. He recalled the crackle of the fire, its light playing shadows on the walls. He remembered the warmth of his bedroll, the small ecstasy of settling in for the night, and the soul-comforting balm of safety of his little hideaway. He remembered staring out at a violet sky, its gibbous moon hung like a giant onion, before passing into the sleep of babes.

He thought of his friends, Luther and Bess Hollis and their passel of young'uns, down in the sleepy little town of Bourg, Louisiana. He remembered a long, drowsy summer afternoon, him and Luther sipping fine Kentucky redeye, their lines in the bayou behind the house, bream popping the surface of the water like firecrackers in the dying light.

And he dreamt of a beautiful woman in a white cotton dress, with skin the color of café au lait, walking toward him down the long hallway of a shotgun shack. She was barefoot and wore a smile meant for him only, lips full and dark, eyes shining with desire. Her hair hung in dark ringlets, and when she passed an open door on either side of the hallway, the afternoon sun caught them, highlighting the streaks of natural blonde that were her mother's gift. And, as always, when she was near enough to see his own reflection in her chestnut eyes, she reached up and put her arms around his neck, only to vanish, the scent of lilacs on the air.

And as always, he would fold that memory as tiny as he could manage, and put it back in its little box in the back of his mind before his grief could overtake him.

Swimming up out of reverie, Amos realized that he had reached the summit. He began to squint through the darkness, searching for the mine entrance. But he didn't have to search long.

Orange light bloomed out of the black before him, and Amos could make out the flicker of torches and the steady beam of a lantern.

A shadow passed in front of the light, but the wind and driving rain blurred Amos's vision. He removed his glasses and wiped his eyes on soggy shirtsleeves. As he replaced his glasses, thunder tore a hole in the sky and bolt of lightning lit the mountaintop in a bas-relief negative. His breath caught in his throat.

Standing before the mine entrance was a man, a giant, ten feet tall if he was an inch. In the brief flash, Amos saw arms the length of truck beds, knotted with great corded muscles like mooring rope. He saw legs the size of cypress trunks and a great, bald head with a low brow that hooded eyes with ill intent.

And me without a sling, Amos thought.

* * * *

The two men stood for an eternal moment, staring at each other across a space Amos knew the giant could cross in a matter of three steps. His mouth was full of cotton as he realized he had no plan, no idea beyond getting up here and finding Seth Carver. He'd made no plans concerning the giant. Maybe he'd figured he'd slip in like ol' Jack in the fairy tale and make out with boy while the giant slept.

He had no weapon, not after that John Law in 'Frisco had shaken him down. His .38 was still riding piggy-back in that fat bastard's waistband, for all he knew.

"Who are you?"

The voice was deep and sonorous, like Amos had expected, but with an accent that Amos couldn't quite place. It was vaguely musical, elegant, the words rolling off his tongue like spooled silk, and in direct contrast to the body it came from.

"I asked who you are," the giant called again. There was no malice in his voice, only a surety, a guarantee of unwanted trouble if not answered, and that right quick.

"My name's Harlow, Amos Harlow. I've come for the boy." No sense in stalling.

The giant stood another moment, staring, then turned to the mine's mouth and retrieved what at first Amos took to be a walking stick, and headed out into the storm toward him.

Amos tensed and almost bolted when he saw that the stick was no mere shaved sapling, but a *four by four*, the kind used to shore up finished mine shafts before further digging. The stick was at least five feet long and had to weigh more than seventy pounds, but that old hoss was toting it in one hand like it was a lady's umbrella.

The moment of decision passed, and Amos held his ground, which did wonders for his honor, but was third-degree murder on his nerves. The giant covered the distance in seconds and Amos suddenly found himself in the shadow of what seemed like a massive oak that had instantly sprouted to full growth right before him.

The giant gazed down at him though heavily-lidded eyes. He wore the skin of a great animal, most likely a black or brown bear, about his groin. Amos could hear the man's great lungs heaving like a bellows inside his massive chest. Everything about the man before him spoke of power restrained, and so Amos, at navel-level on the great man, craned his neck until he was looking into the giant's face, in what he hoped was a staredown.

"Are you dangerous?" the giant asked.

Amos was stunned. "Am *I* dangerous?"

The giant nodded.

Amos thought about it for a moment. "I guess I'm as dangerous as any other man, but I intend no harm, if that's your meanin'."

Spears of lightning fell to earth with a thunderclap, splitting a nearby tree in half, blinding Amos, and making the hairs on his arms stand tall. The wind had picked up and was bending the pines surrounding the clearing almost to the ground.

The giant held Amos's stare a moment longer, then looked up into the sky, his great smooth brow furrowed, then back at Amos. "Come." He turned and began to walk back to the mine entrance, tossing aside the four-by-four like a toothpick.

Amos followed at a trot, unable to keep pace with him. The giant reached the mine entrance, bending almost in half to clear the entryway, and pulled a torch from a sconce. He waited for Amos, who came trudging up, out of breath, exhausted from the climb and the terror of his encounter with the behemoth before him.

Carver's friend had been right. The giant was smooth as a baby's bottom, head to foot. His skin held a pale, pinkish cast in the torchlight, and the muscles in his arms and legs writhed like vipers under a bedsheet.

His eyes were unnaturally large, like fried eggs with amethyst yolks. He held Amos's own eyes, not with malice, but childlike curiosity, as if *Amos* were the oddity that had wandered into his midst of *his* life.

The giant didn't speak, but the worry was evident on his considerable brow. He stood tensed, as if waiting to run at the slightest provocation from Amos.

Amos found himself at a loss. He had expected a fierce, menacing presence, and had found himself confronted with what appeared to be a small, scared child trapped in the body of a colossus.

"I've just come to take the boy home. His daddy's real worried," Amos said, staring up at the man-child.

The giant said nothing, but looked toward the back of the main mine tunnel, which stretched around a corner into darkness. The giant turned to face him again.

"You aren't dangerous?" he asked, in hushed tones.

"No, sir," Amos said. "Not to you, I ain't, and not to the boy."

The giant took a torch from another sconce and handed it to Amos, motioning toward the tunnel with his own. Amos walked forward, full of trepidation, examining his surroundings.

The mine was an old one, a mid-to-late 19th century model, constructed with old timbers that shored up the ceilings at intervals. The walls were scored with cylindrical tracks, old holes that were once chiseled into the bare rock for the insertion of dynamite. It was an old technique, once used by coolies for blasting railroad tunnels through mountainsides during Westward expansion.

Mine car tracks ran the length of the tunnel floor, scarlet with rust from years of exposure to moisture, and spiked off here and there into side tunnels that opened like dark mouths to either side of the main. Every now and then, Amos could hear the earth shifting in its bedrock, dirt and pebbles sifting down in little showers from the pressure of the millions of tons of rock above.

A sudden gust of wind whipped through the passages and their torches guttered out, leaving them in Stygian darkness. Amos froze; a fear of dark, tight places gripped his heart in a meaty fist. All around him, that steady trickle of dirt, pebbles, and debris grated his mind like Chinese water torture. He could almost *feel* the pressure exuded on the mountain above him, could almost *hear* the brittle snapping of splinters within the ancient timber that kept it at bay. His panicked mind told him to run, to get out of the near-tangible black that threatened to suffocate him, mind, body and soul. This, in turn, conjured the vision of him running off helter-skelter and falling into a forgotten shaft, his body broken and dying at its bottom, an easy meal for things that may or may not thrive in the hidden cracks of the earth.

At the moment he decided to throw caution to the wind, a vise-like hand clamped down on his shoulder, nearly driving him into the earth like a fence post.

"Don't," the giant said behind him. He felt a hand the size of a Christmas ham reach down and gently take his. "Stay close," he said.

The giant led Amos down the main tunnel, as if he were a child being brought to Sunday school. The tunnel floor began to slope gently, then turn; Amos shuffled along behind, still in the grip of bowel-wrenching fear. He had never known fear like it before, a crippling terror that he would experience but once more in his life. He looked up at his companion and jumped, nearly stumbling in surprise.

The giant's eyes floated near the ceiling of the tunnel as if disembodied, giving off a faint glow, just enough for Amos to make out the pupils and irises. The eyes turned down, regarding him, and looked ahead once more.

"I can see okay in the dark," he said, his basso still childlike to Amos's ears. "It's not far now."

Sure enough, Amos could make out the faint, flickering orange glow of a campfire up ahead. His eyes began to adjust to the new light and he saw the glow in the giant's fade slowly as the firelight grew brighter, until he could make out the low dip of his brow above them.

They rounded the final bend into a high-ceilinged cavern. The roof supports were minimal, and Amos supposed this was a natural cave formation in the limestone mountain. It made sense that the giant would make this his home, as he didn't need to bend over in the yawning space it allowed.

The campfire burned low, its smoke drawn steadily up through a natural vent in the ceiling, and a cook-pot was bubbling with something that smelled so divine that Amos was sure men had killed to get it at one time or another. The giant set about the pot, stirring the contents and motioning for Amos to sit down.

A small figure lay huddled beneath a bearskin blanket near the fire, one foot bound in a makeshift splint, and shaking visibly, though near the fire. Seth Carver moaned in his sleep, shifted his injured leg slightly, then jerked upright, screaming in pain, sweat pouring from him in rivers.

When the pain subsided, the boy blinked slowly, waking fully from troubled slumber. His face was drawn and haggard, his cheeks rosy with fever, and he looked up at the giant, who was handing him a bowl of stew, and gave a weak smile.

"Thought you'd never get back," he said through a mouthful of stew. His gaze turned to Amos, and took on a puzzled expression.

"Who are you?" he asked.

* * * *

When they had eaten, Amos watched the giant gather the dishes and rub sand in them, scouring them clean. Seth Carver watched him, too, not merely in fascination, but with something like admiration.

"He saved my life," the boy said, his color returning somewhat.

"Oh, yeah?" said Amos. "How'd he manage that?"

"I was out walking the woods, exploring and all. I ain't supposed to, not while Pa's at work, leastways. Wait—you won't tell my Pa, will you?"

"I ain't no tattler," said Amos with a grin.

"Well, I was out explorin' like I said, and I slipped on a boulder covered with a buncha green moss and fell 'twixt that boulder and another 'un. Twisted muh leg up real good. Hurt like almighty hellfire—um—you won't tell my Pa I said them words, willya? He don't like that kinda talk."

"I busted my leg up like you done, I wager I'd say a heap worse," Amos allowed. "I spoke with your Pa, you know. It was him sent me up here after you."

"Why-come he ain't here, 'stead of you?" Seth asked.

Amos looked at the giant, who was busying himself with the fire. "I reckon that's somethin' I need to talk with your friend about, here."

"Daddy shoulda come," Seth said glumly. He don't care 'bout nothin' but work anymore. That's why I *really* why I run off."

"Look here, son. You're daddy's worried sick. He workin' to feed you, put clothes on your back. You oughtta show more respect than that." Amos stared into the fire, his mind years and miles away. "Ain't everybody got a daddy like that," he murmured.

Seth stared at Amos, then down at his hands. "I just wanted him to notice me again. He ain't been the same since Mama died." His chest hitched and he hid his face in the crook of his elbow. Amos got up and put his arm around the boy, patting his shoulder.

"Y'all gonna be all right," Amos said. "We gonna get you off this mountain come tomorrow, if this rain let up. You go on an' get some sleep. You see your daddy real soon, hear?"

"Aw, Lord, I cain't sleep, no-ways," Seth said, wiping his face, "'specially not with company about. Pa says it ain't polite," The boy gave a craterous yawn.

The giant crouch-walked over to Seth with a steaming cup of something that smelled of burning tires in a compost pile, and with one great arm, shifted the boy into a sitting position and tilted the cup to his lips with the other.

"Aw not again, Nimrod! This stuff'd take the hide offa boar!"

"Drink," Nimrod said. "It'll help with the swellin' and the pain."

The boy crinkled his freckled nose at the mixture, glanced at the giant, and frowning, took the entire measure in one gulp. He coughed, a thin line of the stuff trickling down his chin. He recovered, smacking his lips distastefully, and turned over on his side, careful not to jostle his bum leg. "Guess I *will* try to sleep," he said, already dozing, "though I'm bound to have dreams 'bout this muck. Yeeech!"

In minutes, the boy was snoring softly, his brow smooth and easy, as if he was back in the pleasant little world that his parents had made for him. Amos stared over the fire at the giant, who was lost in his own thoughts, gazing into the fire as though trying to discern a glimpse of the future in its flames and embers.

"See you know some rootwork," Amos said, by way of breaking the ice.

The giant shifted on his haunches, stirring the fire with a broken sapling branch, and shrugged. "Just some herbs my mama taught me. I get real bad headaches from time to time, have since I was a boy. They help with the pain."

"Boy said your name is Nimrod. My name's Amos."

The giant stirred the embers and added another small log to the fire. "I know. I heard you out there. I got pretty good hearing, too. Another gift from my mama.

"My name ain't Nimrod, either. That's just a name Mr. Ricketts give me when I started at the carny."

"What's your real name, then?"

Nimrod smiled faintly. "Ain't pronounceable in English. You couldn't say it right if we sat here a month of Sundays. Nimrod's fine. 'Sides," he said, "nobody ever cared enough to try, 'cept my mother, an' she's gone, now."

A great sadness seemed to settle over the big man like a wet blanket, and Amos could sympathize. He knew what it was like to be ousted from what people called "normal" folks. Hell, every hobo on the road could claim the same. But this man's sorrow came from a deep well and flowed into the world without surcease. If he weren't so tall, Amos thought, he might drown in it.

"Tell me about it," Amos prompted.

"About what?"

"About everything. Maybe I can help."

Nimrod locked eyes with Amos, and the sadness was nearly palpable in those great purple pools. "I doubt it, mister, but I ain't had nobody to talk with in so long…" He looked up at the cavernous ceiling, the rain at a steady, dull roar on the mountainside. Nimrod heaved a great, weary sigh and spoke.

"I wasn't always this big," he began. "Hit my first spurt when I was thirteen, but even then I was only this side of six foot. Nothin' for folks to point at, just another big ol', well-fed Tennessee mountain hick.

"Got a little bigger in high school, 'bout seven foot, and lost most of my hair. That's when people started to point and snicker. I didn't have many friends to speak of because of it, 'cept for this one fella named Ronnie. He was quiet and shy-like, and had these glasses that were real thick, like the bottoms of Coke bottles. He was picked on real good-fashion by a lot of kids. I felt sorry for him and we became friends. Walked home from school every day, went fishin' together. We was pretty close, almost like brothers.

"One day, I left the schoolhouse and seen a buncha toughs, real mean boys, crowded around Ronnie shovin' on him and laughing when he fell crying in the dirt.

"Well, that set me afire. I grabbed the biggest boy—the one who did the shovin'—and grabbed him in a bear hug 'til I heard somethin' pop like logs in fire. He cried out somethin' fierce and I dropped him. He flopped on the ground like a fish on a riverbank.

"The others scattered, yelling for their parents. Ronnie just sat on the ground, staring up at me like I was a leper. 'Don't hurt me,' he says. The look on his face and them three words cut me to the quick. I turned tail and ran for home.

"Mama was waitin' on me as usual, sittin' up in her great featherbed my daddy had built for her 'fore he died. It was built thick and sturdy, and we had to put it in the living room of the cabin, 'cause it was so big, big as King Og's bed in the Old Testament. You know that story?"

Amos shook his head.

"Well, it was big, and had to be. See, Mama was as big as I am now, maybe a mite bigger. Anyways, I told her what happened, an' that's when she sat me down next to the bed. She stroked my head and told me the story of the Anakim again."

"The Anakim?" Amos asked. The fire had begun to die down and a chill was creeping in through the vented ceiling. He threw some more logs on and stirred the coals. The flames caught, and Nimrod continued.

"The Anakim were descendants of the Nephilim, the first giants on the earth, or so the Bible says in Genesis. Mama used to tell me stories about them. They were the sons and daughters of angels and humans, the ones that got cast out with Lucifer and fell to earth. Mama said they was heroes in the old days, and stories and legends grew up around 'em and all the things they did in the times before the Great Flood. They were tall, oh, so very tall, and their shadows stretched before them like summer oaks. They were strong, fierce warriors, and word of their deeds spread throughout the early earth like a prairie fire.

"But they grew wicked, and folks got to worshipping them instead of God, and pretty soon, the whole *world* was wicked, so God destroyed everything on the face of the earth, 'cept for Noah and his kin. But Mama used to say that when the rains began to fall and the waters started to rise, that some of the Nephilim and their followers escaped deep into the bowels of the earth and hid for many centuries from God's wrath.

"After a time, they returned to the world of man, determined to carry on in their great deeds. But they found the world changed—civilization in the form of great cities and all manner of strange customs abounded. They found that they no longer fit in anywhere, that they were hated and feared, so they took themselves back to the mountains they'd crawled out from and there they carved out their *own* civilization. They raided nearby cities and took them easily, for what army could stand against those that were each an army unto their own? The Nephilim took wives and husbands of the pagan cities they conquered and so began the line of the Anakim, the 'long-necked ones.'"

"A race of giants?" Amos asked. "*Real* giants? Like Jack and the Beanstalk?"

Nimrod was nodding. "Just so," he said. "Mama used to say that's where all them stories come from. When folks would fun me 'bout my size or I was having one of them skull-buster headaches, she'd take my head in her lap and rub it, and tell me stories 'bout our ancestors, and how they's always bein' hunted 'cause folks thought they was abominations. 'You're in a mighty company,' she'd say. 'Nimrod the Hunter, King Og, he of the thirteen-foot bed, Goliath and the Sons of Gath. You got nothin' to be ashamed of.'"

"Hold up, now," Amos said. "You sayin' you's one of these giants from the *Bible*?"

"Well, why not? It always made sense, and Mama didn't never lie, no sir. And hell, *look* at me! Last time I measured up at the carny, I was right at ten foot, though Mr. Ricketts put twelve on the show posters to milk the rubes."

"What about your daddy?"

Nimrod shook his great head. "Never knew my daddy. He died when I was a baby, and Mama never spoke of him. It's funny, though."

"What's funny?"

"Well, I ain't never met no others like me. In all my travels, you' think there'd be at least one or two. But hell, Amos—I think I might be the last."

Amos digested that and found the notion profoundly sad. The last of one's kind is *truly* alone in the world. Shaking off the thought, Amos changed the subject.

"How'd you get mixed up with this carnival?" Amos asked.

Nimrod grew quiet at this, brooding under that massive forehead. It was some time before he spoke.

"Mama died one night. She'd get the headaches same as me, only worse. The herbs helped, but only so long. She said it was the curse we bore for them angels not keepin' their proper place. One night the headache hit her hard in her sleep. She woke screamin' somethin' awful. I tried to help, but all I could do was watch her scream, and scream myself. After she stopped, I knowed she was gone, and I buried her outside the old homeplace. You ever get up to Round Knob in Irwin, Tennessee, you can see the mound out back, big as a hilltop, it is. I hear younguns play on it now, dare each other to climb it at night.

"After she died, I just couldn't go back to school. No one would take me, I knew that. So I wandered a bit, but I never found a place I could rightly call home. Fella down in Carolina tol' me 'bout a town down in Florida on the Gulf -- Gibsonton, it's called, Gibtown to folks in the trade. It's where all the carnies shack up after the circuit's over for the year. So I made my way down there, and I have to tell you, it *was* like comin' home.

"It wasn't just a place for carnies to bed down for the winter, it was a whole *town*, just for them. There were elephants and circus trailers in nearly every front yard. There were Monkey Girls, Lobster Boys, Siamese Twins, and even a counter for dwarves at the Post Office. I strolled into town and spoke to a gent that was covered head to foot in scales, just like a 'gator straight outta the Everglades. He didn't bat an eyelash at my size. He just tol' me where to find Ricketts. I guess Ricketts knew a money-maker when he saw one. Had me a job in two shakes and little place right near the beach all my own. For the next five years, I had it pretty good, I guess, for a man that started with nothin'. I had respect, friendship—*a place to be.*"

"What happened?" Amos asked.

"I couldn't take it no more. Couldn't take bein' looked at through velvet curtains, sittin' up on that damned pine stump for folks to point at, laugh at. One night, some college boys was drunk and had their girls with 'em. They all stood there, laughing, pointing, some of the boys shoutin' mean, dirty things, like them boys shouted at poor Ronnie.

"Ricketts could see things was getting' outta hand, and I was working' up a head of steam. Mama always told me that I had to hogtie my temper, but it was so hard sometimes, especially that night, 'cause I was getting one of my headaches, the worst one ever. I was trembling all over, damn near tears, clutching my head like a watermelon that was about to explode. Ricketts come in then, and started showin' 'em the way out, yellin' that their money was up, and if they wanted to see more, they'd have to cough up another two-bits. One of the boys threw a handful of coins into Ricketts' face, which he bent down and picked up out the dirt, one by one. Then his eyes met mine, and I knew he wouldn't help me. I was just property to him. He looked away, and passed out through the tent flap. I stared to cry, right there in front of them assholes.

"Then one of boys said somethin' 'bout my mama, and what a whale of gal she musta been, and how my daddy's, well… how his bait and tackle must have been whoppers to turn out a hoss like me. I went crazy, started screamin', just like Mama did the night she died, and after that, I don't rightly remember much.

"I remember Mr. Ricketts yelling like Satan for these four rousties to hold me. I remember swinging my arms and something wet and warm hittin' me in sheets. I remember screams of women mixed up with my own, and runnin' into the night, 'til I came to a stream. I washed myself and sat and cried 'til I fell asleep. I woke in the night to the sound of dogs barking, and I knew they was on my scent. I ran into the hills, then the mountains, 'til I found this place. Been here ever since, and I ain't got no intention of leavin'. I don't belong in the world of men, Amos. Just like my ancestors, just like my Mama. I just want folks to leave me be, that's all. But that's all changed again, I reckon. That's why *you're* here, ain't it?"

"I told you, I'm just here to take the boy back to his daddy. I ain't from the town. I was just passin' through and thought I might could help. It's like the boy said, ain't it? You ain't stole him, did you?"

"I found him out in the woods, about halfway down the mountain. His leg was broke in two places, near as I could judge. He'd a-died out there in the night, be it from the weather or the critters hereabouts. I was all set to carry him into town when that sodbuster yelled out and cranked off two rounds from that scattergun. I tried to talk at him, but he reloaded and shot again. What was I supposed to do? He coulda hit the boy. I ran, like I always done, and got him back here before nightfall. I splinted the leg best I knew and, well, you know the rest."

It seemed to Amos that folks always had that same shoot-first policy anywhere a man went. Lord knew *he'd* ducked many a wad of buckshot in his day.

"You ain't never went down to try to hold with them folks in town?" Amos asked.

Nimrod was already shaking his head before the question was out. "Always figured I'd get much the same reception as the one I got. Folks in a little backwater like Bledsoe ain't ready for the likes o' me. I was all set to live and let live, keep to myself and let them keep to their own. Guess that ain't likely now, though, is it?"

"Guess it ain't," Amos said. "They got a man by the name of Tolliver after you. Name ring a bell?"

Nimrod started, eyes narrowed. "I know him. He's a freak-hunter. Used to find geeks for the carnival circuit. Mr. Ricketts done business with him often. I seen him once in Gibtown, about a month before we hit the road again. Ricketts introduced us, and he looked me up and down like he'd just as soon see my pelt on his livin' room floor. Story was, he hated freaks. Some said his mama was a midget, said he was ashamed of her and threw her off a bridge one night 'cause he'd been picked on. Anyway you cut it, that man's a bad seed. I guess Ricketts hired him to bring me back -- one way or the other."

"I think it's the 'other' he got his mind set on," Amos said. "Best let me take the boy at first light. And you better light out of here, too."

"I'm done runnin', Amos. I just want to be left alone. I intend to live right down here in the earth, just like my ancestors."

"Tolliver ain't gonna lay down easy," Amos said.

The giant shrugged. "Don't matter none," he said, "nothin' matters anymore." He stretched out to his full length on the floor and rested his head on his arms. He looked deep into the fire, a thousand-yard stare.

"Whatchu mean?"

"Ain't you noticed, Amos?"

"Noticed what?"

"The way the world is, the way the times are. Like it's all... *winding down.*"

Amos shifted his weight and stretched out as well, leaning on one arm. "Sorry," he said. "You lost me."

"Look around. You're a man of the road, right? You got two eyes. Surely you noticed by now. Famine, dust coverin' everything. Economy's in the toilet, people cain't afford what food there is to fill their babies' stomachs. Death is everywhere, behind every tree, around every corner. Hear tell of war at every fillin' station and the church pews are full every Sunday. Folks always talkin' about the end of things, the end of the world. Well, who's to say they's *wrong*, Amos?"

Amos frowned. "I know times is hard, but they always been hard. Seein' things from the bottom-up is real different than seein' 'em from the top-down. *Always* been that way."

"What if...," Nimrod began, "what if the end came 'round *more* than once-t? What if it happened often, like a… *cycle*, or somethin'? What if every time the world goes to hell all over, it really *is* the end of the world?"

"Well," Amos chuckled nervously, "that'd mean we *always* livin' in the End Times."

"I know," Nimrod nodded slowly. "An' that's what *scares* me."

An intense silence hung between the two men, and Amos suddenly found himself very cold, despite the fire's warmth.

"The Lord promised Noah that He'd never destroy the earth again with water," said Nimrod, his large eyes wide in the low light of the embers. "But there's *four* horsemen, Amos. And they been real busy of late."

Amos stared across the dying fire at the gentle giant who saved the life of a stranger's only child, who wanted nothing more than to be alone and free, and who was nowhere near the monster that he'd been branded. He watched Nimrod's great eyes slowly drowse, then slip closed as sleep took him.

The offspring of Biblical giants. Flood waters rising. Famine. Pestilence. Starvation. War and rumors of wars.

Death, a constant companion.

It was long hours before Amos fell asleep and dreamt of a tall, long-lived race of ancients, huddled in the deep places of the earth, waiting for the rain to stop.

* * * *

It wasn't the 10-gauge report of an elephant gun that woke Amos in the wee hours before the dawn. It wasn't the fevered shouts of little Seth Carver next to him, begging him to wake up. It wasn't even the voices of two men, one whom he recognized immediately as Seth's father, Brady, pitched in a heated argument.

It was the absence of the continual drone of the rain that had subconsciously been the backdrop for the events of the last twenty-four hours. It had just stopped, not even a gradual cessation, and it took Amos a moment to realize the fact, like a tooth long ago pulled and the fruitless search of one's tongue to find it.

He sat bolt upright, instantly aware of his surroundings and his place in them. This was a trick honed from years of sleeping in boxcars where the railroad bulls were built like fireplugs and simmered in piss and vinegar, and from sheltering overnight in barns whose owners carried cut-down shotguns that flung double-ought buck like angry swarms of hornets. Yessir, a man learned a few tricks being out-of-doors, and every now and then, one paid off and let him live to see the sunrise.

Nimrod was gone.

Amos was up and running to the mouth of the mine, aware that any minute he might step into a sinkhole and disappear into the bowels of the mountain forever. Seth went right on screaming at his back, but he didn't slow.

"Stay there, hear? Don't try to foller me!" he shouted. He had no idea if the boy heard him or not, and he could only pray that the giant hadn't gone where he thought he'd gone.

Up ahead, the shouting grew louder, and as he rounded the last bend, he had to duck as another thunderclap from the big gun broke the night and a fat slug caromed off the stone wall to the left of his head, trailing the sharp smell of cordite.

"I think I got him!" cried a voice, and Amos knew Tolliver thought he'd claimed first blood.

"Stop that damned shootin'!" Amos cried. "The boy's in here!"

"Amos…" came the weak voice from near his feet. He looked down and saw Nimrod, a gaping wound in his right breast pumping dark, viscous fluid onto the dirt floor.

"Oh, Jesus," Amos breathed. "Oh, Jesus Lord. Hold still, now. Don't try to move." He knelt and began ripping his shirt into strips and plugging up the hole through which he could see light; he didn't have the sack to look at the exit wound.

"Amos," Nimrod said again, trying to get his feet under him, and failing. "Amos…you…you gotta t-take the boy and git."

"We *all* getting' outta here," Amos said, more confidently than he felt. "Just don't try to move. Gotta get some help— "

"*Ain't* no help for me, Amos. I knowed that when I busted them fellas up that night. If… if it weren't Tolliver, it'd b-be somebody else. Ricketts ain't the f-forgivin' kind." A gurgling sound arose in his throat, and he spat out a baseball-sized wad of phlegm and blood that made a sickening wet sound as it slapped against the far wall of the tunnel.

Nimrod was a dead man; they both knew it. There was nothing for it but to get the boy and get out. Amos felt his heart sink right down through the basement and keep going. He'd run out on people his entire life: his family, his steel-pot brothers at the Somme, and every friend he'd ever had was either dead or wishing *he* was. He couldn't run again; such an action would surely damn his soul.

Amos felt as though the entire world had collapsed into this one moment and put him into another situation where the decision had already been made for him.

"Now you listen here, dammit. I ain't leavin' you here to die. Way I see it, we's friends, and that's somethin' I'm a might short on these days. We goin' out the front door, hear? You, me, and the boy. You gonna live, hear me? An' then we gonna head down to the bayou, down Houma way, see some folks I know, catch some of the fattest-ass bass you ever seen, drink 'til we can't see straight, and *damn* the end of the world, you hear me, son? You *hear*?"

"He cain't hear you no more," said a voice behind him. Amos whirled and saw Seth limping on his splinted leg.

Amos looked down at the giant, who was motionless, the faint orange glow of his night-eyes fading with each passing second.

* * * *

Outside, the crowd stood watching Tolliver practically dance with glee.

"Y'all see that? I blew that hulking shit right back to hell, yes I did! One shot! *One shot!*"

He paced the clearing, reloading the elephant gun, his favored weapon for dealing with monsters. In his mind's eye he saw himself before a great hearth back at the ranch, cleaning the weapon and etching another notch in the barrel, next to the fifteen others, a balloon glass of thirty-year-old brandy at his right hand, his feet propped up on the giant's head as it stared into fire in the hearth for eternity.

Or hell, maybe he'd stuff the freak, taxidermy the hell out of him. And God, what would the bill be on *that*, he wondered.

And then he heard the nasal whine of his diminutive mother, calling to him from the bottom of some deep ravine in the pitted recesses of his diseased mind. She was chastising him, cursing him like always, driving him to do what she'd made him do the first time.

Always the same, Clayton, always the same. You got a devil in you, boy. One day somebody's going to put you down like a mad dog.

"Yell all you want, you freak! You don't scare me, see? I don't have to be scared of you anymore!" Tolliver yelled at the night air.

The crowd that had come up the mountain behind him looked at one another, unconsciously stepping back from the lunatic.

"Who's he talkin' to?" one asked. "What the hell's he going on about?"

Oh, but you are , *my child. You* are. *And won't that be nice, once someone does you like you done me and all those others? Then we can be together again, down here in the dark. Just a mama and her little boy, like it's supposed to be.*

"Shut up, shut up, shut *up*!" Tolliver screamed, clutching at his head, the elephant gun forgotten in the dirt.

Down, down, down in the dark, black earth… just me and my little boy, forever and all time…

Tolliver sank to his knees, still clutching his head with both hands. Then he stood, ramrod straight, and a kind of epiphany lit his face. This caused the small crowd to step back even further than his fits and ramblings. It was the look of the truly mad.

"I know," he said. "I *know*… ha, ha! *Oh*, yes! I know how to shut you up once and for *all*!" He ran to a man with a huge rucksack on his back, one that he'd pack-muled up the slopes for Tolliver. He ripped open the flap and pulled out two sticks of dynamite.

"I'll shut you up in the dark forever, you and the giant—two freaks to keep each other company for eternity, by God! Then you won't talk me to death every damned night, oh, yes!" He struck a match and lit the two fuses. Sparks leapt and crawled the length of the fuses, and Tolliver began to frolic around the clearing, twirling the two lit sticks of dynamite like sparklers as he whooped and yelled in victory.

"WHOO-EE! Gonna shut your freak mouth, now, ain't I? You *deserved* to die, like *all* the freaks! You'll by God be quiet now, you devil-bitch! You'll be quiet *now*!" He reared back to throw.

"DON'T!" The shout came from behind the crowd. "My boy's in there, you sonuvabitch! He's *in* there!"

But Tolliver was beyond reason, and the first stick of dynamite twirled end over end through the night air, leaving a trail of sparks like fireflies in its wake.

* * * *

Amos and Seth heard Brady Carver scream just before the world fell in on top of them.

The explosion rattled his brain like a kettle drum inside his skull, and he had enough presence of mind to fall on top of Seth. He expected to feel the momentary impact of untold tons of rock before he left the world. When it didn't happen, he slowly opened his eyes in wonder, and his mouth in disbelief.

Nimrod was standing bent over them holding back the mountain like Atlas holding up the ceiling of the world. His arms were spread-eagled against his burden, and his great back muscles were knotted with the effort. A crossbeam had pierced his abdomen, and great ropes of intestine hung from the wound like halyards from a mainsail. Blood flowed from the great man in rivers, and Amos knew that any other man would be long dead, but the giant had blood and will to spare, enough to give them one last reprieve.

"G-go," he said, the strain apparent in his voice. "I c-cain't hold it much longer."

"Come with us," Amos pleaded. "Just drop it and come with us."

"You k-know I cain't. S-second I let go, we *all* dead. J-just… just remember me."

Amos hesitated, then looked down at Seth, who was weeping, tears cutting streaks through the dust on his face. He made up his mind. He gathered up the boy in his arms and began to trudge toward the mine entrance.

"Always," he nodded.

"And Amos…" Nimrod called. Amos turned, tears streaking his own face, now.

Nimrod turned his head to look at him, smiling viciously, his great eyes burning with a fierce, hard light.

"Send that bastard in here."

* * * *

It turned out that Amos didn't need to pass on the message.

As they came out into the cool night, Tolliver was running at them full-tilt, screaming like a banshee, a wild, manic look plastered to his face. His nose was smashed sideways, blood running freely.

"You're dead! Dead, dead, dead! You hear me, mama? You can't hurt me anymore!" Tolliver streaked past Amos and Seth without so much as a look and disappeared into the mine.

Brady Carver, his knuckles bloody, dropped a stick of dynamite, its fuse pulled, and ran toward them, crying his son's name. Amos handed over Seth, mindful of his leg, and Carver cradled the boy like an infant to his breast, whispering thanks to God over and over.

A sudden crash, louder than the thunder of the previous storm, louder than the dynamite's explosion, shook the ground all around them, causing some of the townsfolk to fall to their knees, scrabbling for handholds on their neighbors. A huge cloud of dust and debris billowed forth from the mine. When it cleared, a solid wall of rock appeared in the entrance. Just before the collapse, Amos thought he heard the screams of a man condemned by his past, and another man's laugh echoing through the halls of that dark tomb.

In years to come, the townsfolk of Bledsoe would tell their children and grandchildren not to wander the slopes of Canebreak Mountain unless they wanted to hear the mad laughter of the giant in the earth as he pulled them down to a stony grave.

Amos sat down on the sodden ground, finally able to catch his breath. It would be some time before he could look at another cave, much less bed down in one. He looked over at the Carvers, reunited and happy. Seth planted kisses on his only child's forehead and neck, rocking him gently in his arms.

The townsfolk meandered about the clearing, as if slowly waking from a dream that they had all shared. Some dropped their torches and their weapons—a hayfork here, a squirrel rifle there—and made their way back down the mountain path, wondering exactly what had brought them up there in the first place. Still others came to Amos with eager, shining faces, peppering him with questions that he was not of a mind to answer.

"What did he look like? A monster, sure enough?" asked one.

"How'd y'all escape?" asked another.

"Was he big? Really big?" asked still another.

Amos staggered to is feet at this last question to look the man, to look them all, in the eyes. Rage welled within him—rage at the sheep that followed such a dark shepherd into the night with murder in their eyes. He thought back to the people at the carnival that had tortured Nimrod until he couldn't take anymore and had to escape in the only way he could. And he thought of a man, a giant, now returned to the earth where his ancestors once hid from the end of the world—a man who had given his life to save two strangers and asked only for his memory to live on. He looked at them all, each in turn, and one by one their fervent gazes fell away in shame.

"Bigger than any man here," he said, and walked toward the path that led down the mountain.

LET ME BE

A Song of the Black Dog

Love is a temporary madness. It erupts like an earthquake and then subsides. And when it subsides you have to make a decision. You have to work out whether your roots have become so entwined together that it is inconceivable that you should ever part.

--Louis de Bernieres
Captain Corelli's Mandolin

The old roadhouse stood canted to one side at the crossroads like a drunken sailor clinging to a ship's rails. A dusky pink hue caressed the treetops as night slipped easily into the world. There was nothing for miles around -- no houses, stores, no sign of life, save for the old railroad lanterns hanging to either side of the screen door, their feeble flames hissing low in the dim. No one sane built houses out this way.

He trudged across the dirt road, his feet crunching on small stones and kicking up dust. His pants were covered with it—some of it native Missouri dust, the rest from four other states. It was out of his way, this little side trip—hell, it was out of *anyone's* way—but here he was just the same.

A promise kept is a crown in Heaven, or so he'd heard.

He trod on the crooked steps, the old timber creaking under his weight, giving a little, but holding firm. He could feel the pull out here, had even felt it as far as Kansas City—a dim tickling in his belly that grew to a not-unpleasant vibrating hum. Now here at the source, his guts felt like a kicked hornet's nest and he wondered, not for the first time, if he'd been right about coming back. Somebody had to, and he had given his word. That might not mean much to a lot of folks, but when it was all a man had, it meant everything.

He stood at the screen door, listening. Bottles thumped on hardwood tables. Chairs screeched across rotting plank floors. Soft, suggestive laughter and leering conversations drifted through the screen. But nothing more—no music, no raucous revelry, nothing but the still, sinister air of the oncoming night.

He opened the screen door, its rusty spring creaking like a dying cat. Several bleary faces at the bar turned to look at him and then returned to their drinks, eyeing him in the mirror behind the bar and muttering racial slurs.

The inside was somehow worse than the outside. It leaned, of course, to the left, and a two-plank bar held up by whiskey barrels ran alongside the left wall. He remembered when he was here before a man had dropped a half-dollar during a card game. It had rolled, quietly, easily, following the floor before hitting the wall and stopping cold. The bartender had picked it up, pocketed it, and shot the man a daring look when he stood to protest.

Now the barroom was dim, lit by more low-burning lanterns, and the few tables were empty, save one, where a man that looked sixty but was probably thirty sat sobbing into a half-empty glass. Across the floor, a burly giant of a man sat in a chair, kicked back and resting on the wall behind him. He sat with arms crossed, eyeing the room with heavily-lidded brows. The man scowled at him as he made his way to the bar.

The bartender was wiping the counter with a dirty rag. He never looked up.

"Whiskey," Amos said.

The bartender continued wiping. "This ain't no charity house," he muttered.

"Ain't askin' for none," Amos said, laying two bits on the bar.

The bartender kept wiping, raising his eyes to the money briefly, and shook his head. "That'll get you a look at the bottle," he said gruffly.

Amos picked up his guitar case and set it on the bar.

"Used to be music in here, as I recall. Seems like you could do with some. Play a song for the drink?"

The bartender stopped wiping and looked at Amos. "Ain't no music hall, neither, spook. Now, you payin' or walkin'?"

He shot a glance to the big man by the rear door. The man thumped his chair legs down and sat waiting for the word, staring Amos down.

"C'mon," Amos said. Just one song for one drink, and I'll be about my business."

The big man got up with a groan and strode to stand beside Amos, a little close for all the room in the joint.

"You heard him, nigger," he growled. "Pay or get the hell out."

Amos looked at the man's chest, and followed it up to his face. The man was sweating profusely, a dank, sour smell pouring off him in waves. He was sickly pale, almost ashen, and his eyes had huge dark circles underneath.

"Don't reckon we met," Amos said. "Name's Harlow."

"I don't give a shit if you're name's Jesus H. Christ, mud-duck. Pay for your drink or get out, less'n you want the shit kicked outta you."

Amos looked the man over from head to toe. "Pardon my sayin' so, but you don't look like you could scratch your ass without help, much less rough up one old man."

The big man bellowed and took a swing, a real haymaker. Amos ducked it easily and lashed out with his right foot, putting all his weight behind it, and landed a blow on the outside of the big man's knee. There was sick, wet crunching sound like a sapling branch snapping, and the big man sagged to his knees, a mewling whine escaping his mouth. Amos followed it up with a sharp jab to the man's throat and he went down hard, gagging on his own blood.

"Goddammit, Charlie," complained the bartender, coming around to help him up. "I pay *you* to do that to *them*." The two hobbled over to an empty table, and Charlie collapsed, holding his knee and coughing bloody phlegm onto the floor.

The bartender turned to Amos, not with anger, but tired resignation. "You want the money in the box, take it. I cain't stop you."

Amos shrugged. "Don't want your money. Just a drink. I tried to pay for it two ways and your boy got froggy. I just jumped higher. Now how 'bout that drink?"

The bartender sighed heavily and walked behind the bar. He pulled up a half-full bottle of amber liquid and poured a shot into a dirty glass, glowering at Amos the whole time.

Amos knocked back the shot, wincing as the burn rolled down his throat and warmed his stomach. The hornet's nest in him dimmed slightly.

The bartender was still looking at him, holding the bottle. He reached down and slid Amos's money off the bar and held up the bottle. Amos looked at him. "That's all the money I got."

The bartender poured another shot.

"You said your name was Harlow. That be Black Dog Harlow?"

Amos paused, drink halfway to his lips. "That's right," he said.

"I remember you," the bartender said. "You played here once before, 'bout three years gone, I reckon. A song about movin' on, time's a wastin', or some such thing. 'Bout a gal lost her man and couldn't live."

Amos threw back the shot and nodded.

The bartender poured another shot. "Thought so," he said. "I liked that one real fine. So did other folks used to come in here, even the hard-asses. Talked about you for months."

Amos nodded again. "Used to be a woman in here knew how to treat a man. Merilee's her name. She still 'round?"

The bartender's face tightened. "Why the hell you askin' after her?"

"SHE'S OURS! YOU CAIN'T HAVE HER!" Charlie screamed, holding on to his ruined knee.

"Shut up, Charlie," the bartender growled, glancing disgustedly at the big man, and back at Amos. "I asked you a question, mister." He corked the bottle and braced himself against the bar.

"Somebody who cares about her wants her to come home," Amos said, tossing back the shot.

"Like Charlie said, she ours now," he answered, tensing.

Amos looked up at the bartender, smacking his lips, sucking up the remnants of whiskey caught in his beard. The bartender's face was white with fear and tight with apprehension. His eyes were hollow, sunken, and his hands shook, though steadied on the bar as they were.

"I think you got that backwards," Amos said calmly, looking into those haunted eyes.

The bartender reached down under the bar and came up with a cut-down shotgun and leveled it at Amos's eyes.

"I was tryin' to be neighborly," he panted, "but you had to come in here itchin' for a fight, askin' after what ain't yours to ask after." His grip tightened on the shotgun.

"Now, you play that tune, just once, and we're square on the drinks. And forget about the woman. She ain't no concern o' yours or anyone's anymore, savvy?"

It was hard to argue staring down the twin trash can-sized bores of a shotgun. Amos lifted his hands in placation and backed away from the bar. He picked up his guitar case and broke it open. "Reckon it's what I come here for, anyway," he said.

He walked over to an empty table by the front door and sat down. He settled in and picked out a chord, then began to play and sing.

Oh, let me be, let me be,
I know I hurt you so bad,
But you got to let me be.
There's too much in this world
For a man to go and see.
So I'm beggin you my darlin,'
Let me be.

I can't let go of the pain
That's forever kept me down.
You can't keep on believin'
That I'll always be around.
So move on while you can,
You're just too good of a man.
Just kiss me one more time,
Then let me be.

Amos picked out the last, slow measure of the song, a song he'd written not a day before he'd entered that very roadhouse the first time. It was a strange coincidence, considering the way things had played out that day, but Amos had stopped believing in coincidence long ago. The bartender began to sob, his chest silently hitching. Even Charlie, through the haze of pain, was crying in earnest. Amos waited.

Then, as if on cue, the rear door opened up and she walked out. The humming in his abdomen grew to a dull roar and his loins stirred like a great beast awakening from a long slumber.

She was as pretty as Amos had remembered. She was as pretty as *anyone* remembered. She drifted through the door, her camisole shifting languidly over her full hips as she moved. Her gauzy white skirt floated above the hardwood floor as if made of the air itself. She searched the room and her eyes locked with Amos's. She smiled languidly, lustfully, and he felt the beast in his loins rouse further.

"Thought I heard some music out here," she purred. "Been so long since we had some decent playing, ain't that right Howard?" She eased her gaze over to the bartender.

Howard's knees shook, his breath coming in ragged gasps. "Ohhh…oh, yes, Merilee, ohhh, yesss…yes, it has…!"

The woman named Merilee returned her stare to Amos and he unconsciously crossed his legs. She glided forward, past the injured Charlie, absently brushing a slender white hand across his shoulder. The big man shuddered, then stiffened, and even though his leg bone had torn through the skin, the look of beatific gratification stifled any pain he surely must have felt.

Merilee stopped inches from Amos, bit her lower lip, and looked him up and down. A crooked smile spread slowly across her face, and she regarded him with wicked yearning.

"So," she said, "you came back for more." It wasn't a question.

Amos fought a titanic struggle to stifle his *own* desire. She was perfect, an alabaster beauty, the very image of wanton lust and abandon. He opened his mouth to tell her so, and quickly bit down hard on his tongue. He groaned inwardly at the pain as the coppery taste of blood filled his mouth. But his head was clear, at least for the moment.

"N-not r-really…," he stammered.

Her smile widened. She crossed the last gap between them and straddled his lap, clasping her hands behind his neck.

"C'mon, sugar," she cooed, "you can't tell me you don't remember this at all." She began to slowly roll her hips, first one, then the other, across Amos's crotch, squeezing her thighs in time with each movement.

The buzzing in his torso became an electric hum, and he could feel himself involuntarily returning her thrusts with increasing vigor.

She laughed a throaty laugh, removing his hat and tossing it on the table. "Ooo…you *do* remember," she purred. She sped up the tempo, rocking a little faster. Amos felt himself reach out and grab her hipbones, tucking his thumbs in hard and matching her, movement for movement.

And suddenly, he felt as though he'd not slept in ages. Nausea crept into the pit of his stomach, and he was clammy and weak, as if he was fighting a bad fever. His face began to tighten over his skull and the very bones in his body flared with intense, white-hot pain.

But he couldn't stop, even if he wanted to.

He arched his back and thrust his mouth upon hers, biting and gnashing. She met him with equal measure and dug her nails deep into Amos's neck.

The pain cleared his mind for half a second, and it was all he needed. He shoved with all his strength and Merilee flew backwards across the tables, spilling drinks and scattering glasses, and landed on her ass with a thud.

Amos rose unsteadily, and gaining his balance, walked toward her, using the bar for support.

"Now you look here, you sonuvabitch!" Howard screamed, clutching the shotgun in meaty hands, the barrels shaking violently. "You lay offa her! She's mine, now, you hear? She mine, dammit!" He raised the shotgun and tightened on the trigger. Amos winced, waiting for the blast.

It never came.

He opened his eyes to Merilee standing in front of him, one hand on the shotgun's barrels. Howard just stood holding the other end, lust and expectation on his face, along with something else -- *need.* Amos knew the look all too well. The opium dens of San Francisco were full of it, as were the trench hospitals during the war, the need for morphine practically chiseled on the faces of the injured.

Merilee smiled and stroked the shotgun barrels, up and down, slowly, rhythmically. "Now Howard, dear one, you know I don't belong to *anyone.* Isn't that right?"

Howard closed his eyes, lost in her voice, her presence. "Yesss…yes, I know…but I—"

"That's right," she said, stroking the shotgun harder, longer, as she spoke. "But if you're a good boy—and I know that you *are*—why, we'll have to find *somethin'* to do with ourselves later on. Can you think of something like that, Howard?"

She seized the shotgun around the middle, and Howard stiffened suddenly, as if an electric current ran from her to him through the shotgun. He hit the floor and lay behind the bar with a blissful smile, his eyes rolling back in his head, and a string of drool running down his cheeks.

"There, now," she said, smiling at Amos. "He won't bother us for a time. Where were we? Oh, yes—playin' *rough.* That how you want it this time?" She reached down and grabbed Amos's chin, jerking it up toward her face.

Amos stood before her, barely managing to control himself, and stared deep into her eyes.

Lord, but a man could lose his way in there, Amos thought, *an' a bunch of 'em* have.

Merilee leaned in for another kiss, and Amos pulled back at the last second.

"Walter wants you to come home," he said.

Merilee's eyes, deep pools of brown, suddenly churned and chopped like a storm-blown sea. Her face twisted in a mask of rage. "That name… don't you *dare* mention him to me… EVER!"

She grabbed a handful of Amos's shirt and suddenly he found himself hurtling through the air. He slammed into the wall beside the rear door. Pain flared through his lower back, and as he reoriented himself, he gasped. He was hanging flush against the wall, three feet above the floor, as if suspended from an invisible hook.

Merilee strode purposefully for the rear door, snatching him down as she walked past, and throwing him into the rear room of the roadhouse. Amos flew through the air, bracing for the impact of another wall, but instead met a soft, springy landing.

He opened his eyes, taking in his surroundings—an old room, walls covered in ratty, water-stained wallpaper, and velvet drapes that hung like funeral shrouds over long-dead windows. The bed was old, well-worn, and the springs protested his violent arrival.

Amos saw all of this in the half-second before Merilee was on him like a mountain cat, snapping, biting, tearing at his clothes with fingers and teeth alike. Amos fought back, but there was no heart in it. The vibration in his belly swelled to a deafening roar. It was maddening, driving out reason and blocking out everything in the world except her, and in that moment, all he wanted was her, her, and nothing else ever again.

He returned her passion, yanking at her camisole as she tore his pants off and flung them on the floor next to the bed. She dipped hungrily into his mouth with her own, drawing blood with her teeth and cackling like a madwoman. She pounded his head against the mattress with delighted fury, thrashing wildly atop him. Then, suddenly, the storm abated, and she smiled lustfully at Amos. She reached back and yanked off her camisole.

Underneath, her alabaster skin was smooth as porcelain, and Amos tried to remember something… something important, something that mattered, something he had to do. It was right there, dancing around the corners of his rational mind, but the woman astride him was occupying the rest.

She started to move as before, rolling her hips and swaying rhythmically, side to side, front to back. Amos was in ecstasy. What other woman in the world was there to compare to one such as her? She was a goddess, the moon and sun, the world, and he would die for her, yes die, and—

The humming had grown to a steady drone, louder than ever. The nauseating sensation returned full-force and Amos could feel his skin stretch tight once more, threatening to peel right back off of his skull. He could feel his eyeballs sink into their sockets, and his hands, planted firmly on Merilee's hips, began to wither and shrink. Age spots, barely discernable before, began to spread like leprosy over the back of his hands. Amos's breath grew short in his chest. He could feel himself… *diminishing.*

Above him, Merilee held on fast, rocking faster and swaying harder. She moaned and cried out in ecstasy, and to Amos's horror, she began to *fill in*, become more real, somehow. Her face grew shiny and vibrant, her skin a rosy peach color, her hair lustrous, and her lips a scintillating red.

Amos could feel his heartbeat growing weaker by the second. His feet began to curl in at the toes, his entire body desiccating and shriveling by the second, the flesh shrinking until it barely covered the bone. If he could only remember…

Then something drew his eye. He glanced down at Merilee's hands, firmly planted on his chest. A small, white circular indentation on her left ring finger, the mark of many years of faithfulness.

He remembered, and with a sudden burst of desperation, he tore himself from under her and lunged for his pants. He scrambled in his pockets as the life-force flowed out of him and into the thing Merilee had become.

Amos's eyes were growing dark, and just as his lungs began to wither in his chest, his feeble fingers closed around something small and cold and hard in his pocket. He grabbed it and with his last ounce of strength, shoved into Merilee's forehead.

Her bloodcurdling scream shattered what remained of the windows. She pitched back off the bed and lay writhing on the floor, her forehead billowing white smoke like a locomotive from where the small object lay embedded. She clawed at her head, frantically trying to remove the source of her pain, and then she began to dissolve, evaporating into a white, sinuous cloud, her fingers trailing away into nothingness, followed by hands, arms, and feet.

Before she disappeared, she screamed one final time and looked at Amos full in the face. Her eyes were a blaze of red and her teeth, once white and straight, were jagged, pointed needles, a forked pink tongue slithering out from between them. The scream seemed to last for eons, echoing down the halls of memory, following Amos into the past.

* * * *

The place was jumping for a one-room shack in the middle of nowhere. Seemed like all of western Missouri had turned out, just to hear a broke-down old man play a guitar.

Amos knew better, though. The liquor was cheap and flowed freely, and there were enough hormones in the joint to light a bonfire. They weren't here for him; he just happened to be in the right place at the right time, which was all right with him.

He played through a few more tunes, then played another round of "Jolie Blon" after enough hollering. He was drinking for free and had his guitar case open at his feet with near-on ten dollars in paper and change scattered across its bottom. It was a good night, and he'd not had many of those in a long while. People slapped his back good-naturedly and begged him for another song.

As with most things in his life, it had been too good to last.

A wiry, sad-eyed man walked through the screen door. He took off his floppy farmer's hat and scanned the room. Amos watched as his eyes lit on a black-haired beauty at the back of the room, perched on some loud honkey's knee. Amos saw the man's face sag and knew the whole story.

The woman had been working the room the whole night, looking for the biggest wallet she could find. Amos had seen plenty of whores in his day, but this was something else. He wondered how long the two had been married and guilt washed over him like a rising tide. He'd already had her once that night for free.

The farmer walked over to the table where his wife sat bouncing on the big man's knee and tousling his curly hair. He stared at his hands, lacking the courage to face them eye to eye. The room got quiet, as all the patrons turned to watch the unfolding scene with something approaching glee. Apparently, not much happened out this far, and this was something they'd been waiting to see for a long time.

"Merilee," the farmer said softly. The raucous nature of the room had died down, but the big man and Merilee hadn't noticed. She was too busy trying to get in the man's wallet, and he was too busy trying to get in her pants.

"Merilee," he said again, more insistently.

They both stopped laughing and turned to him. The mix of shock and recognition on her face had been proof enough for Amos.

"Wait yer turn, partner," the big man laughed. "C'mon back in couple of hours and try again. She might *not be too tired, ain't that right, baby?" He slapped her hard on the rump.*

She looked at the big man, annoyed. "Shut up, Charlie," she said, and turned back to the farmer.

"Walter, what the hell are you doin' *here?" she asked with an exasperated sigh.*

"You need to come on back home, Merilee. This ain't no place for a woman to be, 'specially not a married one."

"I told you I ain't married to you no more!"

Walter shifted his hat in his hands, looking sheepishly at his feet. "That ain't what the law says," he mumbled.

"That's what I *say!" she yelled. "An' I don't got to wait for no judge or anybody else to tell me different!"*

Walter glanced down at her left hand which rested on Charlie's massive shoulder. She followed his glance and held up her hand.

"Is this what you're after? Is that all?" she yelled. "Then take it!" She wriggled the gold wedding band off her finger and flung it at him. The ring bounced off Walter's chest and hit the floor, rolling to a stop two feet from Amos.

Walter looked down at her with that hang-dog look, the look of a defeated man. "You don't mean that," he said, his voice breaking slightly, and Amos was afraid the man might actually break down and start crying right then and there.

"I DO mean it, you sonuvabitch! How many times do I have to tell you before you get it through that shitkicker skull of yours? I ain't gonna be trapped on that damn farm for the rest of my life! We was too young and we made a mistake! Why can't you just accept it and move on?"

Amos saw anger flare in the young man's eyes, probably for the first time, as he looked at his wife in the arms of another man. His voice became low and gravelly.

"Only mistake I ever made was not doin' this sooner," he said, and grabbed her roughly by the arm, yanking her out of Charlie's lap. She struggled and fought, slapping him about the head and shoulders, but her husband held on tightly and made for the door.

Walter got three feet before he was spun around in a circle and Merilee went flying into a table. Charlie drove a ham-sized fist into Walter's breadbasket, following with a vicious uppercut to the chin. Walter staggered, blinked a few times, and tried to retaliate, throwing a half-hearted swing at Charlie's chin. Charlie ducked it easily and delivered two quick jabs to Walter's right cheek, followed by a left cross. Walter spun and hit the bar, trying to keep his feet. Charlie waded in and proceeded to pummel the smaller man senseless, Walter's face becoming a wrecked mass of blood and saliva.

"STOP!" screamed Merilee, unable to make herself heard over the din of the bar full of drunks, shouting and cheering the fight on. "STOP IT, CHARLIE! YOU'RE KILLING HIM!"

But Charlie continued his assault, right then left, over and over.

Amos had been about to intervene when Merilee jumped between the men, pushing back at Charlie, then slapping his face, her nails leaving claw marks across his cheeks and nose. He wiped a hand across his face, and it came away bloody.

"You bitch… *" he seethed, and raised his hand to punch Merilee as well. Walter rose to his feet, and with a grunt, grabbed his wife and made to swing at Charlie, when a loud roar silenced the room and the smell of cordite filled the air.*

"Oh…oh, Lord," the bartender said, holding the shotgun, smoke curling out of the barrels. "Oh…! I didn't mean to... Oh, my Lord, what did I…?"

Walter and Merilee stood face to face in each other's arms, their torsos painted a deep crimson, which began spreading swiftly outward.

Charlie, like the rest of the room, stood in shock, watching the couple collapse to the floor, drawing their last breaths.

"Jesus, Howard!" he breathed. "Jesus !"

"I-I was just tryin' to stop the fight! I-I wasn't…it j-just went off!"

The shock lasted another second, then the bar cleared as people ran home or into the woods, already forming alibis in their minds in case the law came around. Amos sat, oblivious to their passing, his eyes on the wedding band on the floor at his feet. He reached down through the frantic foot traffic and plucked it up off the floor. Blood stained its perfect surface, marring everything that it stood for. He looked at it for a time and then pocketed it. He didn't remember leaving, but suddenly found himself on the dirt road, putting one hurried foot in front of the other.

An hour later, he came to a crossroads. As he approached, he saw the man standing at the corner directly opposite. He had hoped to be further away before the inevitable happened, but no such luck.

The man stood motionless, regarding Amos with a humorless, wan face.

"Tell her to come home," the man said.

"You know I can't," Amos said. "Nobody can make ya'll move on. There's free will, even in death.

"Tell her to come home," he said again.

"I'm sorry," Amos said, and turned to walk north. Walter's ghost began to cry behind him, weeping loudly, a sound that would haunt Amos for the next three years.

* * * *

Amos had kept the wedding band, though he'd tried to sell it a number of times. No one would buy an obviously personal piece of jewelry from a hobo. Amos stopped after the last dealer had given him the eye after handing it back. The last thing he needed was the law asking questions he couldn't answer.

He'd tried to outrun Walter, but the dead man's lament greeted him each time he came to a crossroads, junction, or any kind of intersection. Amos would look across to the southeast corner and there he'd be, holding his hat and crying.

Amos finally gave in one spring day on a North Carolina back road, as the man's shade appeared underneath a funeral shroud of Spanish moss hanging from an ancient oak. He promised the dead man that he would do his best to return his wife, though at the time he hadn't known how he would manage it.

The ring had been the secret. When confronted with the symbol of her eternal promise to Walter, Merilee had been forced to face her own evil, as well as the fact she was dead.

Now, as Amos groggily got to his feet, pondering the scorch mark on the floor that marked Merilee's passing, he wondered if he'd fulfilled his promise.

He pulled on his pants, stumbling from vertigo, finally righting himself enough to finish dressing. He situated his porkpie hat and opened the door to the barroom.

The room was a disaster: every chair and table in the pace was overturned. Bottles and glasses had smashed against the walls; even the floorboards were peeled up in places. The force of Merilee's passing had tossed the place more thoroughly than any tornado or raucous Saturday night.

Amos strode carefully into the debris, picking his way over splintered chairs, gingerly stepping on broken glass as if he were barefoot. Pushing aside one table, he heard a groan.

Charlie lay underneath, holding his hands over his head, blood trickling from two burst eardrums. He looked up at Amos with pleading eyes and held out a hand for help.

Amos kicked him hard in his injured knee.

The howl Charlie gave was almost as loud as that of the departing spirit.

Amos frowned down at the big man as he writhed in pain, studying him like he would an unfamiliar insect.

"Better get some ice on that," he said, picking up his guitar case and walking toward the door.

The sound of clicking twin-hammers stopped him short. Amos didn't turn around.

"You uppity nigger," grated a harsh, shaky voice. "You stole her from us! You stole her and now you're gonna die!"

Amos stood at the door, staring out at the night, and sighed. Cicadas whined in the trees and Confederate jasmine was fragrant on the evening breeze.

"She was bleedin' you dry, Howard," he said, "all of you. She kep' y'all around like feedbags—little taste here, little taste there. Had y'all hooked like a bunch of dope fiends."

"You don't think we *knew* that?" Howard cried. "It didn't matter. She was all I had, all I wanted! And you *took* her."

Amos shook his head. "That was just her juju. You wasn't nothin' but food to her. She'd'a sucked the life outta you and left you like a raisin in the sun, 'fore long."

"I DON'T *CARE!!*" Howard bellowed.

Amos opened the door with trepidation. "I'm goin' now. You either gonna shoot me in the back or you ain't, but I ain't listenin' to your whinin' bullshit no more. Way I figure it, you got off light. Double murder ain't an easy thing to cover up, even way out here in the sticks. So pull the damn trigger or piss *off*."

He took a quick breath and opened the door.

No shots. He could hear Howard sobbing uncontrollably, "You took her, you took her, you took her away…"

He quickly jogged down the steps. As his foot hit the last step, the screen door slammed against its frame, and the shotgun went off with a thunderclap. Amos flinched, expecting to feel the buckshot tearing through his body.

"NOOOO!" Charlie screamed himself hoarse from inside the roadhouse, his grief following Amos down the road.

Amos kept walking until he reached the crossroads. He looked across the intersection. The full moon broke from behind a cloudbank, bathing the old dirt road in a silver luminescence, revealing two figures standing at the edge of the woods.

Walter tipped his farmer's hat at Amos, who nodded in return. Merilee stepped forward and glared at Amos. He could see the trees blowing in the wind through the ghost of her camisole. Her hate-filled, hopeless expression said he'd damned her to an unimaginable hell.

Walter stepped forward and put his arm around her, steering her away, and together they stepped off the road and vanished into the night.

Amos stared after them, thinking, not for the first time, that there wasn't always a happily ever after.

Sometimes there was only "after."

BEASTS OF THE FIELD

A Song of the Black Dog

Nobody's perfect. We're all just one step up from the beasts and one step down from the angels.

—Jeannette Walls
Half Broke Horses

The howl split the evening asunder, and Amos Harlow almost missed the fencepost. Instead, he brought the sledge down on its edge, shanking it, and flinging splinters into the face of his partner.

The man holding the post in place, Bill Gettinger by name, armed robber and all-around hardass by trade, let go of the post and casually wiped the flecks of wood and dirt from his face. Tiny drops of blood welled up where the splinters got him, and Amos's bunghole tightened up like a snare drum.

"No problem," Gettinger said. "Just keep your eye on the ball."

Amos held the hammer limply, looking at Gettinger, and his bowels relaxed. "You got it, podner," he said. "Them howls got me jumpy. Sounds like they gettin' closer." He lifted the sledge and brought it down squarely on the four-by-four, the 'thwock' echoing across the range.

"Prolly," Gettinger shrugged. "All this fresh meat sittin' out here on the flat, just beggin' to be et."

Bill Gettinger was a tall, rangy man with a skin of mixed hues of Indian and Negro heritage, what people in south Louisiana referred to as a "redbone." His eyes were muddy pools the color of bayous, and seemed to peer into places others could not see. A pale scar ran from the corner of his right eye, across his face and lips, disappearing under his chin. It stretched and coiled like a serpent when he smiled, which wasn't often. Gettinger carried himself seemingly without concern for his own safety, and Amos wondered whether that was because of the screws with their cut-down shotguns and long-barreled Winchesters strolling in and around them, or because Gettinger possessed certain knowledge that others did not.

Either way, the screws could have picked a worse man to chain him to, like the child molester with the face that never seemed to fade from deep scarlet, or the wife-killer that always looked like he would slit the throat of the first creature with a heartbeat he could get his hands on, or any number of the refuse on two legs he had been spending his time with for the past two weeks, courtesy of the Llano County Penitentiary system.

A shadow fell over the two men as Amos wiped the sweat from his brow. "Fence ain't gonna get put up with y'all cluckin' like a flock of hens." It was Morris, not the meanest bull in the pen, but his mouth ran on automatic when it came to hassling the cons. He was eating a ham sandwich and grinning like a fool.

"You know it, boss," Amos said, hefting the sledge for another whack. The sweat on his brow ran down into his eyes right when he cut loose, and the hammer thudded into the soft earth like a lead coffin.

"Whoo-ee, boy! You ain't gonna win the Kewpie doll for yer girl there, you keep swingin' like 'at!" Bits of bread and cheese flew from his mouth as he laughed.

Amos looked up at Morris. "'s alright," he said. "I got this, boss."

In a blur, Gettinger rose and took the sledge from Amos, so fast that neither Amos nor Morris registered the fact. "Whoa!" Morris shouted as he stumbled back, dropping his sandwich, his hand flying to his revolver trying to clear leather.

"I'll take over a spell," Gettinger said, a slight grin playing at the corner of his mouth. He positioned himself, and Amos knelt and took up the post. Morris, hand still on his gun butt, seemed to deflate with relief. Amos could hear the other screws laughing. This was probably but one of a thousand comical moments in the life and career of Officer Fletcher Morris that his coworkers would never let him forget.

"Well, then…all right. You go on an' get them posts in the ground and no more jawin', hear? I got a mind to sap the both of you ass-cracks right now!" With that, he strode off across the work camp to salve his bruised honor on some other poor soul.

"Damn if that wasn't a sight," Amos said, grinning as he steadied the post.

"Can't let the bulls have *all* the fun," said Gettinger, and brought the hammer down in a fury, driving the post into the earth with a single blow.

Amos fell back, catching himself on his hands. "What the hell…?"

"It's a trifle," Gettinger said, bending to uncoil a length of barbed wire from a wooden spool. "Can't let 'em see me do it, or I'd be the only fish out here workin' these fences."

In an act of "greater charity for the common good," the District Attorney of Llano County, in conjunction with City Hall and the Sheriff's Department, effected a new work-release program for "undesirables, wretches and curs that seek to defame the citizenry and cause public unrest," which in English meant the cheapest labor imaginable for running fence along sixty acres of prime real estate to mark off the Mayor's newly purchased ranch land. In return, all but the hardest cons would be released on their own recognizance with a stern admonishment never to set foot in the greater Llano area for the rest of their natural lives. Amos, along with a few others, would be on the road again—less whatever money they'd had in their pockets upon arrest, of course—in a matter of weeks.

It just didn't pay to get busted on a vagrancy beef in the state of Texas.

But stacking time on the county farm wasn't foremost in Amos's mind; there were worse lock-ups, like Huntsville or Angola. It was the howls—those low, mournful bays, rising to a pitch almost feminine, that kept his hackles up and seemed to get closer every night.

At first, the bulls had chalked it up to wild dogs. They weren't unheard of out this far into the Hill Country, but they were mostly scavengers, vultures of the plains, and rarely attacked humans unless they were sure of weak prey. Now, the guards had split up the night watch, three for the cons and two for whatever was stalking them in the vast expanse of scrub prairie and low rolling hills that surrounded them.

Stalking. That sounded right to Amos, and he couldn't be sure, but in the dying light of the previous three nights, when the sky was an angry orange glow deep on the western horizon, Amos could've sworn he saw that light reflected in pairs of low, creeping eyes just beyond the perimeter of the camp. When he told the screws about this, they shook him down for weed, jibed him for a fraidy-cat, and went back to their corn-mash liquor and talk of hedonistic bravado.

Amos knew he wasn't seeing spiders, and at least one of the bulls believed him.

Ross Tanner was the one who set the extra guard; as head honcho, it was his call. Some of the older guards detested Tanner, as he'd broken up their jailhouse "fun" one time too many, and had a respect for the badge that they lacked. He was the governor's nephew, and his daddy had been a Ranger, and his grandfather before him, and the law meant something to such men. Word had it that Tanner had once broken the teeth of a guard on a cell toilet, right in front of every screw and felon in Cell Block D, after he'd learned the man was trading smokes for sexual favors. After that, the cons respected Tanner, and grudgingly, so did his men, but that didn't mean they had to like him.

Amos was thinking he might try to have another word with Tanner when the chow call came, and the cons were herded back into camp, where role was called. Supper was a plate of beans the toughness of .45 rounds and bread that could used as steel wool. Complaints were heard, but stomachs were filled, and soon sleep began to close about them like velvet curtains.

Most of the cons used their down time before lights-out to smoke, or blow a harmonica at the night sky, or maybe to play a few hands of blackjack using cards with naked ladies on the backs. But some just sacked out entirely, or stared into the fire, morose and sullen, thinking the same sort of thoughts that landed them where they were in the first place.

Amos could not sleep, but stretched out anyway on the ground next to Gettinger and laced his fingers behind his head. Gettinger's eyes were closed, but Amos knew he wasn't asleep. He watched as Morris walked up with a hammer and an iron spike and drove it through the link on their foot chains, pinning them to the ground. "Cain't have y'all ladies runnin' off in the night. Got another mile of fence tomorry," he chided, but Amos could tell his heart wasn't in it. Morris glanced sidelong at Gettinger, as if the man would jump at him, and then slunk off into the camp to fasten the others' chains. Amos watched him go, and then turned to the vast expanse above him.

The steel-colored clouds broke open briefly, and the cosmos was revealed in stark relief. The night sky in the wide open was a wonder to behold. Stars were scattered pell-mell across the black, burning with a luminosity that bordered on the ethereal. The Milky Way stretched out before them, its cluster of distant suns pointing the way to better worlds.

Amos tried to concentrate on all that heavenly glory, to shut himself inside sleep that wouldn't come. Then the clouds rolled in again and suddenly he was tired. He began to drift into slumber. He was just in that twilight place between waking and sleeping when the first howls came. They were close, and Amos sat bolt upright, searching for demonic eyes in the dark.

Tanner barked out orders for the men to check the perimeter. The other bulls were getting antsy, shifting from one foot to the other, and tapping rifle stocks in free hands. Amos knew from experience that jittery men toting guns did not bode well for those about them. He saw Tanner moving about the camp, kneeling to speak to each pair of cons in turn, most likely assuring them that everything was in hand, and reminding them that should they think of running, the guards wouldn't hesitate to scatter their grits all over the countryside.

Beside him, Gettinger lay unperturbed, snoring softly beneath his wide-brimmed hat, one dusty boot crossed over the shackled one in apparent comfort, as if he were in a hammock on a wide second-story veranda in the Keys. His long body was the picture of ease, but after the way the man moved earlier, Amos knew Gettinger's spring was wound tight; he could come awake instantly, if need be.

Suddenly shouts rose to the north, followed by two quick cracks of a rifle and a man's scream that sounded like it belonged instead to a young boy. Every head in the camp swiveled to the north. Most of the cons were on their feet, peering into the distance, some looking as though they were waiting for a chance to bolt. These began frantically pulling at the iron stake that pinned them to a certain death and were rewarded by rifle butts to the breadbasket as Tanner strode among them, shouting for quiet, never taking his eyes from the north side of camp and the impenetrable darkness that that clung to its edges.

Then, suddenly, all was quiet. The only sound for long moments was the grain around them, rustling like whispered names in the western breeze.

Then the howls rose again, louder, in what sounded like victory, only now they were all around them at the edge of the firelight. Two cons—one of them the child molester—were on their feet, straining against their chains, cursing the guards and their mothers for all they were worth. Morris nonchalantly blackjacked the molester across the back of his skull, and the fat man dropped like an anvil. The other con cringed, arms up, sobbing, begging to be freed.

Amos wet his lips, his eyes going from his own iron spike to Tanner. Surely the man would cut them all loose. Surely his decency wouldn't allow them all to be slaughtered. If he could just get the stake loose and go talk to Tanner… He looked at the stake again, judging how far into the ground Morris had pounded it.

"Don't do it, podner," Gettinger said. He hadn't moved, his hands still clasped behind his head, his eyes hidden beneath his hat. "Them bulls'll cut you down before you take two steps, an' you know it."

"What the hell you talkin'?" Amos yelled. "Them wolves is gonna eat us alive, chained up here like lambs! We got to get movin'! Tanner will—"

"Coyotes," Gettinger said.

"What?"

"Coyotes. You said they were wolves. They ain't. They're coyotes. You can tell by the pitch of the howls."

Amos was stunned. "I don't give a shit if they's giant *rabbits*—they got teeth and claws, an' that's all I *need* to know! Now you gonna help me pull up this here stake or do I gotta gnaw yo' leg off at the knee?"

Gettinger pushed the brim of his hat up with a finger. He stared at Amos for a long second, as if deciding. Then he pushed the brim back down and relaxed again.

"Damn," Amos muttered. He began pulling on the stake like a madman, straining with the effort.

Just then another report broke through the howling, followed by five more. Apparently Morris had emptied his revolver. This time, there was a yelp. Amos silently cheered the guard and cursed Gettinger at the same time.

But his joy was short-lived. Two more howls broke through the shouts of the cons and guards, and three sets of red eyes loped out of the night and into the firelight.

The melee that followed was horrific.

Amos was entranced by the ballet of violence he witnessed that night under the stars of central Texas. Gunshots and the screams of the dying intermingled with growling and tearing of flesh to produce a canvas of terror worthy of Hieronymus Bosch.

Lithe, hairy shadows with pointed, high-set ears leapt at the throats of the guards, who fought back with fists and teeth when magazines ran dry. The chained-up cons were just meat on the hoof to the creatures, and their strangled screams echoed across the hills before being cut short.

More gunshots rang out, though they had begun to peter out, and Amos saw Tanner in stark relief against the fire, big as life—a Navy Colt in one hand, a burning log in the other—shouting a challenge to the creatures. They circled him warily, blood-soaked snouts curled back exposing wicked-sharp teeth, looking for an opening.

Amos pulled at the stake and chain until his body began to tremble. How deep had that mother driven the sumbitch in? All around him, he heard the sobs of the dead and dying, the wet sucking of air through shredded lungs, and the squelching of what could only be entrails exposed to air for the first time.

He pulled until he felt something in his back *give* with sudden release, and white-hot pain lanced up his spine. He cried out in agony, as well as frustration.

"Here," said a voice. "Move over."

Gettinger was on his feet, their chain wrapped twice around his fists, which were gripping the stake. He heaved once, and the stake came out of the hardpack like Excalibur from the stone. They were still shackled together, but at least they could move.

"G-good," Amos breathed. He glanced over his shoulder and his breath caught in his throat. The coyotes—if coyotes they were—were all now standing on hind legs, hunched over like cavemen, paws now elongated clawed fingers. They circled Tanner, who was cursing them all for cowards and abominations. One of the beast-men lunged for him, and Tanner caught it in the midsection with the flaming log. It yelped like a coyote, yet cried out like a man as its pelt caught like dry twigs. It burned, screaming that beast/man cry as it fell to the ground, rolling to put out the flames. The other two coyote-men circled, baring rows of stained, jagged teeth that glowed in the firelight.

"Reckon we ought to hoof it, now," Gettinger said, as if ordering a drink. Amos didn't have to be told twice.

Amos lost track of time as they ran through the summer night. It was rough going at first, but the two men quickly learned to time their steps and form a third leg to make the most of their flight.

It was a flight into the unknown. There were few settlements this far out of town, so the starlight had to be enough to light their way. After what seemed like ages, with the only sound the crunch of their feet in the scrub grass and their locomotive breathing, a small, abandoned homestead rose out of the night landscape like a phantom. They could make out the main house, which had burned long ago in a prairie fire, and a barn that crouched at the edge of the property. They made for the barn.

Inside, the smell of old hay and mildew was heady, but they filled their lungs anyway, Amos holding a stitch in his side. A charley horse had reared on its hind legs in his thigh as well, and he knew he couldn't make it three more steps. Gettinger slammed the door, and both men collapsed on the dirt floor. The walls were filled with rusted and forgotten farm implements -- rakes, shovels, hayforks, and the like. The walls were barely standing, and Amos thought that if those things meant to kill them, they'd have no trouble getting in to do the job. No trouble at all.

After a time, Gettinger rose and went to the wall, peering between the slats at the plain across which they'd fled. In the distance, they heard three more gunshots, and then the prairie went as silent as the grave.

"Didn't… didn't think we was gonna make it, podner," Amos gasped, holding his side. "Maybe we ought to find something to get these chains off'n us 'fore them things get here."

Gettinger said nothing, still staring into the distance.

Amos looked around and spied an old tractor under a burlap tarp. A tire iron was leaning against it. "Hey, how 'bout that crowbar, there? That might do the trick," he said. He made to slide over to it, but Gettinger didn't move, and the chain brought Amos up short.

"C'mon, man. Let's get that iron and split. Bet them damn things got our scent by now."

Gettinger remained stock-still.

"Full moon tonight, must be," Gettinger said. "Them clouds covered it up, but it's there, alright."

Amos's hackles rose like Braille on his neck, and bile began to travel the length of his throat.

"Didn't think they'd move on the first night," Gettinger said, almost ruefully. "They musta been gettin' antsy."

"Whatchu mean?" Amos breathed.

"We used to be the big ticket once, Harlow," Gettinger said. "Everybody knew our names. They either loved or hated us, but the respect was there, by God. It was there on every face in every one-horse town west of the Brazos. We helped folks, you know. Gave 'em money we stole, supplies, even medicine when we could get it. Yessir, real Robin Hoods, that was us.

"You couldn't walk into general store or a saloon for miles without seeing a wanted poster with our faces on it. They couldn't catch us, boy, and we give 'em hell when they tried. Oh, we were low-key, all right, but it took money to give money. Times was hard back then—harder than now, even. Rich seemed to get richer off the backs of pioneers and settlers that came out here with nothin' tryin' to tame this cursed country. Seemed only right to help 'em out. We did all right for a lotta years, too, 'til we run afoul of that Comanche medicine man."

Amos was in a dream place. Nothing seemed real, especially not the man before him. Gettinger had begun to *change*, subtly at first, his back hunched, his fingers gripping the slats lengthening.

"We didn't see the young 'uns. We'd just took down the bank in Blackwater Draw—big haul, it was. Rangers had been ridin' our asses since Abilene, and we were gonna pull one last job before hittin' the border near El Paso. We hit the horses at a hard gallop, tear-assin' through town like the devil's own posse."

Gettinger's voice began to shift into a different pitch—higher, reedy, with a slight echo, like there were two people using the same vocal cords.

"Them damned Injuns…they *had* to pick just then to come to town and trade with the whites. We couldn't slow the horses; they was already in a lather. And them kids…they was so tiny, so *tiny*…!" Gettinger's voice began to break.

"The old man just watched us as we rode past, follerin' me with his damned devil eyes right out of town. The womenfolk around him were screaming for their children. Their words were lost on me, but their grief I understood." His garbled voice broke with the memory.

"I ain't slept a night since. I hear 'em, see? Their little screams as they broke like twigs under my hooves… It was folks like them we was tryin' to *help*!" he yelled, and the slats of the door came away in his hands like brittle kindling. He dropped the wood, hanging his head.

"Later that night, we made camp a good twenty miles from town in a box canyon, amidst the hills and mesas out that way. Drunk ourselves stupid and hit the hay. I woke to the sound of my *compadres* screaming. A rout of coyotes were rippin' into them like rice paper. We was outnumbered two-to-one. Them ain't good odds at *any* table. I went for my gun, but two of 'em were on me in an instant, pinnin' my arms in their jaws.

"Then, one of them, the pack leader I guessed, padded over to me and just stared into my eyes. I couldn't look away. He began to change, sittin' back on his haunches, then standing on his hind legs. The fur fell away from him, and the old Comanche man looked at me with the same stark eyes as the beast inside him. He said something hateful, somethin' in his own tongue, and give me this scar with one long claw on his pointy finger." He rubbed the scar absently, as if touching the memory itself.

Hair was shooting at unnatural speed from Gettinger's forearms. His blue chambray workshirt was ripping at the seams, parting down his back like the Red Sea.

"They left us then," said Gettinger, his voice almost unrecognizable as human. "Just left us, no explanations. Turns out we didn't need none. They ain't killed us; they cursed us to walk to the end of our days as beasts of the field, just like ol' King Nebuchadnezzar... just like *them*."

Amos edged closer to the crowbar, his mouth dry as new cotton. Gettinger whirled to face him. Fear nailed Amos to the spot.

The man was completely gone, replaced by the Great Beast of St. John's revelation. Gettinger looked on him with blazing orange eyes, like jack-o'-lanterns in the night, gleaming with a preternatural intelligence and a shining malevolence. His bestial frame was outlined against the early dawn haze through the slats of the barn. Claws like steak knives protruded from his fingers and through the toes of his beat-up workboots. His ears, swept up like the tips of kites from his forehead, twitched in anticipation of the kill.

Power of a feral and primeval nature radiated from the beast, and Amos, all thought long fled, felt his bowels loosen and give way. Panicking, he scrambled away, forgetting the chain that bound him to Gettinger, until he was suddenly yanked backwards and lifted by his shackled leg to face the creature.

Upside down, Amos beat frantically against Gettinger's chest, but might as well have been pounding rocks back in the yard with his bare fists. Gettinger hefted him until Amos's face was level with his elongated snout. He opened his great maw to speak, and the stench of rotten meat washed over Amos, making him gag.

"Don't worry," Gettinger snarled. "I ain't gonna kill you. I didn't wanna kill *anybody*; that was never our way. It was just supposed to be a jailbreak, see? Get in and get out across the plains. But that's before that damned screw set up the extra watch, before they killed my crew! Blood cries out for blood, and I'll have it—one way or another."

"Wh-what you mean?"

"It gets lonely, Amos—hiding from the law for half a century, having to kill cattle, dogs, and... *worse* to survive. My pack are dead and I need the company. Just one bite, one good scratch. It ain't the best life, but it's a helluva sight better than *this* one."

"Th-thanks j-just the s-same," Amos said, "but I done got used to *this'n*."

Gettinger smiled, rows of crooked yellow teeth filling Amos's world.

"That's too bad, podner," he said. "You're fresh outta choices." The wall of teeth opened like a castle's portcullis and Amos braced himself, crying out in the agony sure to follow.

Then thunder rolled, and Amos was thrown backwards across the barn floor, skidding to a painful stop against the old tractor, his injured back screaming upon impact.

He looked up to see Gettinger clutching his chest, early morning sunlight filtering through his fingers. Thunder boomed again, spilling more sunlight into the barn through Gettinger's chest.

Gettinger staggered to his knees, staring unbelievably at the lifeblood of ages gushing onto the dirt floor. He looked up at Amos, and something like peace crept over his face before he fell to the floor and moved no more.

Amos raised a palsied hand, shielding his eyes from the rising sun. As he watched, the fur began to recede from Gettinger's hands and face. The snout shrank into a hawk-like nose, and the claws retracted into bloody fingertips. In seconds, death had granted Bill Gettinger the humanity he'd lost decades before on the Texas plains.

A hard cough broke the silence. Ross Tanner stood in the doorway, a cut-down shotgun broken open over his arm. He was covered in gashes and bleeding profusely from several deep wounds with unmistakable teeth marks. He'd fashioned a tourniquet out of a red bandanna around the worst of these on his right thigh. Four parallel slash marks ran like red ribbons across his face, his damaged right eye bulged from its socket like an egg in a nest. He popped two shells in the barrels and snatched the chambers shut, balancing the shotgun on his hip, and eyed Amos hard.

"You bit?" he asked, almost casually.

"N-nossir," Amos said, shaking all over.

Tanner eyed him a minute longer, then lowered the shotgun and entered the barn. "That's good," he said. "That's good." He slid against the wall and sat down hard.

"My great-granddaddy was one of the men sent after the Gettinger gang back in 1856. 'Fore he died, he used to tell me stories of the wildest sort -- men changin' to animals by the full moon, howls like women's screams out on the mesas. When we busted Gettinger on an armed robbery charge, my ears perked up. I wasn't completely sure he was the same man until I come up on you all talkin' in here. Sorry I wasn't sooner, but I had to be sure."

Talking seemed to drain the man. He sighed loudly, and Amos thought him dead until he unhitched a ring of keys from his belt and threw them at Amos's feet.

"Get them shackles off and get the hell out of here," he said, choking on some of his own blood.

"Sir…?" Amos said, unsure.

"Vagrancy bust was bullshit anyhow," Tanner said, wiping the blood from his mouth. "Get going, and don't come back," he said. "No matter what."

Amos took the keys, his eyes going from the lock to Tanner. After a few unsteady tries the anklet fell off, and Amos rubbed the raw skin beneath. It was chump change compared to the fire in his back.

"You ain't got to worry. Them others is dead," Tanner said. "Changed into people when they died, just like him." He nodded toward Gettinger's corpse. "Three men and a woman -- naked the lot of 'em. Bet we was to check state records far enough back, we'd see 'em all on yellowed wanted posters. Now, go on. Git."

Amos got to his feet. "Lemme help you. I can go back into town—"

Tanner leveled the shotgun at Amos. "Ain't you heard a word I said? *Ain't* no help for me. Not no more. Now get the hell out! GO, goddammit!"

Tanner rested the shotgun on his lap, his breathing shallow. Amos shuffled toward the door, pausing to look back once, then walked out into the prairie, limping toward the brightening horizon.

A hundred yards behind him, the shotgun roared, then all was silent, save for the birds in the tall grass greeting the new day and the forlorn cry of a coyote in the distant hills, waiting for a reply that would never come.

WHERE IS THY STING?

A Song of the Black Dog

Let us go in; the fog is rising.

—Emily Dickinson,
her last words

The streets of Bakersfield, California were unnaturally quiet, which was surprising in light of the thousands of people that occupied them. In the days following the Dust Bowl, untold numbers of Okies had driven, walked, hitched, and ridden the rails in an effort to escape the harsh, blighted landscapes their homes had become and start anew in the Promised Land of the Great American West.

Outside the city limits, the land was peppered with the anthill structures of lean-tos, cardboard shacks, tent camps and hobo jungles that housed all the migrant workers that the Weedpatch Camp, established by the Farm Security Administration, could not. Scores of families lived, worked, slept, and died in ramshackle buildings and gutter hovels not fit for livestock.

The Kern County jails were all full, mostly of drunkards and thieves, but even these were eventually forced to share cells with murderers and child-drowners as the Depression began to take hold and drive men to such extremes. The town council had drawn an imaginary moat around the small city and instituted a no-tolerance policy against vagrants and undesirables that was habitually enforced at the end of a gun or axe-handle. But with times as they were, most citizens were forced to take such matters into their own hands, which was the equivalent of throwing kerosene on a brushfire.

Summer brought temperatures well above the one-hundred mark in the shade. Disease from close-quarters living was rampant. Work was drying up faster than a poorly-irrigated field. Crying babies were merely background noise and roaming packs of coyotes wailed like mourning women in the desert landscape surrounding the town.

Bakersfield of 1936 was worthy one of Dante's circles.

But at the edge of town, beyond the garbage-strewn alleys of the migrant camps and improvised saloons that served rotgut alcohol of strained shoe-polish through slices of bread, a beacon of hope sat like a medieval castle made of canvas at the eastern tip of the Sierra Nevada.

Brother Guidry's Church of Hope and Restoration for All People had come to the San Joaquin Valley with a message for the lost, the dispossessed, the hungry.

But no one in the city of Bakersfield, or in the vast tracts of hobo jungle and the sea of destitute humanity that occupied them, was ready for that message, or what it presaged for the days to come.

* * * *

The flaps of the great revival tent snapped and popped in the desert breeze. Inside the air was stagnant, reeking of sweat and despair, and held no promise of an end to torment. No human stirred in the hellish atmosphere of high noon. This was the time of rest, of escape from the world around oneself, where dry-rotted, daytime nightmares wrestled and roiled in the breasts of men like snakes in a wood-burning stove.

The only motion came from inside one tent, set apart from the main, one in which stood a tall, rectangular cage covered with a burlap tarp. Mutterings in a language unheard by human ears and unknown to human tongues emanated from the behind the tarp and went unanswered by beings above and beyond mortal ken.

The desert wind picked up suddenly, blowing the flap of the tent and rustling the tarp, revealing cold-iron bars etched with strange sigils, and the dusty, work-stained leather of a pair of boots that had ridden trails unimaginable and untrodden.

The wind died as suddenly as it had risen. The tarp settled, the tent grew still, and all was quiet once again, save for the soul-rending moan of a mother whose baby had not woken from his nap, and never would.

* * * *

The soup sizzled and popped inside its can and Amos leaned over it, relishing both the smell of the soup and the heat from the fire. He rubbed his hands together in anticipation and to stave off the oncoming cold of the desert night.

"Lord, don't that smell good," he said aloud. The black dog, who sat at the edge of the fire's light, lifted its massive head from its paws and looked at him without expression then returned to its vigil to the north.

Amos followed its gaze and saw the shantytown around Bakersfield coming to life in the dying light. People rose from restless mid-afternoon slumber and stumbled from their abodes in waking dreams. Mothers brushed dust and sand from their children's dresses and church clothes and fathers in natty suits lit cigarettes, their tips winking on and off here and there like fireflies in the gloom.

Though he couldn't make out their words, Amos could sense a growing excitement in their conversations which were interspersed with occasional laughter and hearty back-clapping, things incongruous with the bleak atmosphere in which they appeared.

Amos could only credit the impending tent meeting for such behavior. Like them, he was here for the same event, though for far different reasons. As such, he couldn't share in their joy; instead, he hung on to a foreboding that clung to the night like cobwebs in a pretty girl's hair.

Pastor Arlen Guidry was unknown to him, save through the occasional newspaper item he found in trash bins all across the country, or the radio broadcasts which had drawn millions of down-and-outers flocking to Guidry's banner. But it was an undeniable hold that he claimed on so many lost souls roaming the desperate landscape that America had become in recent years.

Guidry was an anomaly among his kind, something that was not lost on his followers or the media. His beginnings had been humble, even sinful, to hear him tell it, which in and of itself wasn't much different from all the other revivalists of the age. But that was where they and Guidry parted company.

What made Guidry special, as far as Amos could tell, was that where the other evangelists promised hope and an end to suffering, Guidry actually delivered, and on a regular basis, it would seem. What else but such surety could bring whole families of dispossessed itinerants with nothing but lint in their pockets and the patchwork clothes on their backs over a thousand miles just to get a glimpse of the great man? To see in the flesh what could only be a messianic deliverer from their current agonies?

But to Amos, Guidry was a part of an entirely different skein of cloth. Such men were commonplace in the great underbelly of America, a separate world rarely experienced by people whose chief concern was washing behind their kids' ears or getting up in time for church on Sunday. In Amos's experience, the Arlen Guidrys of the world hid swords behind smiles and drew upon the cult of personality for sustenance like a succubus, caring for little else than the sound of coin on an empty brass plate.

There was more to Guidry, however, and unlike the man's critics (which were many, mostly political in nature), Amos knew it for a fact. Where the Okies, drifters, burnouts and true-believers saw hope, Amos saw an end -- an end to anything and everything good and true, a coming night everlasting that prowled and lurked like a mountain lion at the edges of his vision, only to pounce when sure of the kill.

Normally, Amos would chalk it all up to his innate distrust of authority, of people in power whose grand houses lined the coast of Chicago's North Shore and the Finger Lakes, of people who started wars and never fought in them, of people who looked at a black man like he was something to be scraped off the sole of their shoe.

But looking at the black dog, he knew better. The dog was a supernatural compass, always pointing true north, and always it led him to places and faces and things that were better left in whatever special corner of Hell destined them. He could no more turn away and write off Guidry as another huckster snake-oil hawker than he could cut off his right leg and expect to keep walking. The dog was the messenger and he was its agent, for good or ill. Always, even to the end. At some point in his tragic existence, he had accepted that like he accepted that grass was green.

More laughter drifted on the breeze, followed by a hymn started by a few women and taken up by the men folk and children as they all made their pilgrimage to the main tent, which crouched like a great beast at the far edge of town. "Be Thou My Vision" in a discordant jangle brought Amos to better times and bittersweet memories of Sunday potlucks, Christmas caroling in the sludge that passed for snow in east Harlem, funerals of bygone friends and relatives, and sunrise services on Easter morning.

Yet through the quiet nostalgia of the song ran a black vein of unease and ill portent like a streak of impurity in a coal seam, and suddenly, Amos knew that he would face death, maybe for the last time.

He shivered, more from his thoughts than the chill in the desert night. He pulled a dirty handkerchief from his coat pocket and used it to remove the blistering soup can from the fire. He held it beneath his nose and drank in the aroma, then stirred it with a battered spoon.

"Y'all want some?" he asked the dog. "Ain't gonna find better eats than this in all of California, nossir."

"Don't mind if I do," said a cheery voice.

Amos whirled, spilling droplets of soup that hissed on the burning logs.

A grizzled, pale man sat to his left on a log which had been empty only moments before. His dark suit was in tatters, his button-up shirt that once may have been white showing through various gaping holes. He wore a moth-eaten top hat slightly askew on his prodigious forehead and grinned at Amos through blackened teeth. His eyes were of a silver hue and bright with an intelligence that belied his shabby exterior.

Stunned at the man's sudden appearance, Amos could only stare as the man took the soup can from him and began to ladle copious spoonfuls into his mouth. Rivulets of tomato soup ran through the man's beard and dripped onto his lapels, but he shoveled two more spoonfuls before he realized Amos was staring.

"Sorry, ol' chap," he said in a distinct British accent. "Forgot meself. Robert Edward Wainwright the Third's the name, but most everyone calls me Gentleman Bob." He held out a hand expectantly, then drew it back when Amos didn't take it. "But Bob'll do, right enough, I suppose." He tried handing the can back to Amos, who was still staring open-mouthed, then withdrew it and resumed eating.

"Where—?" Amos began.

"Right," Bob said. "Sorry about popping in on you like that; should've called out. I was coming across the plain and saw your fire, smelled your soup. Sorry about that, as well; I'm afraid I've eaten all your dinner." He smiled guiltily.

"That's… that's all right," Amos said, replacing the spoon in his pocket. "You look like you need it more than me, anyhow."

"Well, that's sporting of you, mate. And I do appreciate the victuals, no doubt," Bob said, blotting the corners of his mouth with his shirttail.

"Say," he said hopefully, looking sideways at Amos. "You wouldn't have such a thing as a cigarette on your person, would you?"

"Matter of fact," Amos said, pulling the last two bent buds from a pack of Luckies, "it so happens that I do."

The Englishman's face lit up like a bonfire, his elation harder to hide than an elephant in drag. He took the proffered smoke with something like reverence, placing it at a jaunty angle in the corner of his mouth. Amos popped a Lucifer match on his thumbnail and lit it for him before lighting his own. Gentleman Bob drew deeply on the cigarette, held it, and exhaled just as deeply, closing his eyes in apparent bliss.

"You have no idea how long it's been," he said, dragging on the cigarette between his lips as though he were trying to get molasses through a straw. Amos chuckled and the two men smoked in silence for some time.

"Where you hail from, Bob?" Amos asked. "Sounds like England, maybe bottom part o' Scotland."

"Been to Jolly Ole England, have you?" Bob asked, taking another deep drag.

"Naw, but I knew me some Limeys in the War. Most of 'em had a stick up they ass, but they's all right on the whole."

"Well, the ones from Southampton, at any rate," Bob said. "No, I believe I am what you would call 'exiled royalty.' I failed miserably at a particular task my Father set before me and can't return home until I make amends."

“Hmh,” Amos said. “Sounds familiar.”

“Really? We’re kindred spirits, then, I take it?”

“Guess so,” Amos said. “’cept my ol’ man don’t never wanna see me again, nor the rest of my family, neither.”

“Oh, come now,” Bob said. “Surely you’ve been home, tried to make amends.”

“Ain’t no goin’ home,” Amos said. “Not for me.”

Bob stared at him, then into the fire, and belched. “Well, I suppose Mr. Wolfe was right, then.”

“Who?” Amos asked.

“Ah,” said Bob, shaking his head. “No one you’ve heard of—not yet, at any rate.”

“I don’t—”

“No matter,” Bob said. “Listen to me, Amos,” he said, squatting by the fire to warm his hands. “You have to cut all that loose if you’re to survive the coming days. It’s a millstone that you can’t carry if you’re to finish your work here. It is a weakness your enemy will ruthlessly exploit.”

“What—?”

“Think of it this way, Amos. If God forgives transgressions and remembers them no more, what sort of hubris swells within the heart of a man who cannot—or *will* not—do the *same,* especially to himself?”

There was light in Bob’s eyes, a silvery shine that no amount of darkness could shroud. He spoke with fervor, as if trying to make a point but unable to find the right words.

“You… you wear your sorrow like a coat of many colors. It is a beacon that will attract certain… *parties* like moths to a flame. You cannot afford to be noticed, not yet. Go to the tent meeting tonight. See if what I tell you is true. Then find the guts to climb down off your cross, man. The world already *has* a Messiah, Amos. Never fool yourself otherwise.”

“Who are you, Bob?” Amos asked in wonder. “Who are you *really*?”

Bob gave a wan smile and tossed the soup can into the fire. Amos watched the label blacken and shrivel in the flames.

“Someone who’s in the same boat, paddling upstream on the same creek,” Bob replied.

There was a sudden gust of wind and a noise like sheets flapping on a clothesline.

Amos looked back at Bob, but he was alone.

In the distance, a pipe organ began to play "Nearer My God to Thee," accompanied by the gathered choir of the lost.

And then the big boat sank, Amos thought, staring out into the dark.

* * * *

The massive tent that housed Brother Guidry's Church of Hope and Restoration for All People was alive with the trapped heat of the day and a congregation of souls numbering in the hundreds. The air was stifling and redolent with sour body odor mingled with cinnamon-scented candles that burned in sconces placed at intervals throughout the portable church.

Row after row of picnic benches were filled with upturned faces that shone with both hope and desperation beneath thin veneers of dust and grime that would not wash off. Some held crying infants, others the hands of the elderly and infirm who were seated in wheelchairs down the aisles between the makeshift pews. The rows themselves fanned out from a pinewood plank stage, upon which stood a miniature pipe organ and the lectern where Brother Guidry dispensed the Word to the huddled masses. A microphone was attached to the lectern, spider-webbed by a brass halo with lightning bolts arcing away from the mouthpiece. This was where the rest of the Great Unwashed across the nation got their weekly dose of spirituality.

The small choir of a bass, two tenors, an alto and two sopranos had finished the last three bars of "Nearer My God to Thee" and were filing off the stage when Amos came through the entrance. He was directed behind the last pew along with the rest of the latecomers and wandering drop-ins, so as not to disturb the worshippers if they decided to wander out again.

From his viewpoint, he could barely make out the row of five ornately-carved chairs behind the lectern, that were filled with five men dressed to the nines. Four were most likely deacons, but the one who sat in their center was undoubtedly the great man himself.

He was broad-shouldered and tall, as his knees were bent up at an angle as he leaned forward on them, hands clasped together, head resting on his arms. His posture was that of a penitent pleading for his sins before an angry God, as if to show he was no different than the hundreds around him.

As the crowd waited for Guidry to finish his preparatory prayer, Amos noticed a sixth man off to the left, near the edge of the stage. He was thin, almost emaciated, and his head was hung low, as if he, too, were deep in the passion of prayer. A pristine black suit hung from his frame, the kind that country doctors wore in the Old West. A Texas string tie hung in black loops from his starched collar and long, white hair hung in tresses from beneath a flat-top, wide-brimmed black hat that cowled his face.

Amos assumed the man was most likely another deacon or usher, or maybe what was called a howler, a man who would 'amen' everything that came out of the pastor's mouth in order to work the crowd into a religious fervor, hoping to loosen wallets and purse strings in the process.

Finally, Guidry gave his clasped hands one good shake, rose from his chair, and walked to the lectern. He stood clasping each side of the lectern, surveying his flock.

He was luminous, Amos thought. There was no other word for it.

Older than Amos had expected, Guidry had a smile that was infectious, dazzling, and seemingly genuine, and maybe what had made him youthful in Amos's mind. His features were tanned like chestnut hulls on an open flame, as if he had seen some time in the fields tilling God's earth until he'd heard the call to ministry. His hair was flaxen, combed in waves, a spit curl hanging boyishly across his broad forehead. His eyes were cobalt blue and pierced the dust and gloom of the tent like beams of sunlight through a cloudbank, and even the most hardhearted of the roughnecks, hobos and tramps in the tent wiped more than dust away from their eyes when his gaze met their own.

Brother Arlen Guidry fairly radiated goodwill and sincerity. He was everything to everyone, and the crowd, having arrived at their spiritual oasis in the midst of a dying wasteland, drank him in long and slow and deep, never truly getting their fill, and always wanting more.

Amos couldn't help noticing that Guidry didn't have a Bible in his hands.

"Friends," he began softly. "There is a devil in the land." The tent was silent, except for the murmurs of hungry babies and the occasional snuffling of noses.

"I don't have to tell you all that. Many, if not all of you, are acquainted with this fiend. He strides the plains with a grim purpose. He climbs the Rockies as if they were no more than anthills in his sight. He claims the coasts as his own, poisoning the seas and slaying the innocent in their beds like chattel."

Heads nodded. They were with him every step.

"Yes, you all know him. He has been intimate with your family, your friends, even with total strangers. He is the houseguest that refuses to leave, the stray animal at your doorstep. His hunger is insatiable, his appetite knows no bounds."

Women clutched their husbands or held their young ones tight to their breasts. A moan escaped someone's lips in the dim.

"He is called by many names, but only truly known by one. His name is *Death*!"

Guidry gestured wildly to his right, at the thin man in the black suit. All heads whipped in that direction, gasps forming out of the crowd like geysers of anguish and fear.

The thin man never moved, never lifted his head. He merely stood, hands clasped in front of him, staring at the floor.

"Yes, children! Yes! *He* is the one! *He* is the one responsible for your ills! *He* is the one to blame for the state we find ourselves in, the misery of the tribulation that has befallen God's people! Look at him! See him, my people, but *fear* him no longer."

The congregation began to whisper among themselves, stricken and confused. They looked to their shepherd for answers. He readily gave them.

"Does he rave? Does he spit and growl in anger? Does he swing his scythe to take the lives of those not meant to be taken? Does he, children?" Guidry was in ecstasy, the ball rolling along nicely.

"No! And do you know why, good people? Why does he stand there, impotent and befuddled? It is because he has been *shackled* by the power of the Lord God Almighty!"

A great cheer arose from the crowd, filled with relief and a blessed assurance that things weren't as bad as they seemed. The balloon of terror Guidry had slowly blown up seemed to deflate and the room became quiet once more.

Of course, Amos thought. *All part of the show.* Looking closer, the thin man, most likely a transient Guidry had hired as part of the ceremony, was wearing manacles around his wrists, the cuffs all but hidden in the folds of his sleeves.

"Death no longer holds sway over the kingdom of God! He has been cast down and bound into the service of Jehovah! Impossible, you might say. I say to you that *nothing* in Heaven or on earth is impossible where the God of Israel lays His hand!" Guidry looked out into the crowd, peering past the stage lights into the gloom.

"You!" He pointed toward Amos, and for a second, Amos almost answered.

"You, there, ma'am. With the young lad. Bring him forward."

The crowd had turned around and was eyeing the woman in question, a gray-haired, frail thing wearing a blue bonnet and a faded dress with crocheted blue hyacinths that had been bleached gray by the sun. In her arms slept a boy of no more than four years. His young body was light as a feather, not an ounce over twenty pounds. His dark hair was matted to his forehead with sweat, and as the woman rose and carried him down the aisle, those on the end seats would later swear they felt the heat coming off him like a smithy's forge.

The crowd parted for them like the Red Sea. Helping hands reached out and supported the boy's head as the woman carefully made her way to the stage where Brother Guidry waited, smiling his beatific smile, as if that alone could hold death at bay.

The woman staggered, not under the weight of the boy, but under a terrific burden, one that had seen her life ripped away before her eyes, one that proclaimed itself in her shuffling gait. It was a burden that those around her knew all too well, and shared. The concern in their eyes seemed to buoy her and carry her along. She wept silently and without tears, for they had all dried up long ago, along with every hope.

Brother Guidry stepped down the top steps and lifted her and the boy effortlessly onto the stage. His arm around her shoulders, he guided them to stand before the thin man, and gently lifted the woman's chin to stare directly at him.

"You know him, do you not?" he asked her.

"Y-yes…" she said. "I know him." She dropped her head, unable to look upon the thin man.

"No. No. Look at him," Guidry said, guiding her chin once more. He cannot harm you or yours anymore. Do you believe that?"

"I-I w-*want* to believe it. I *do*," she replied shakily.

"Then believe it, sister. Believe it like Abraham believed the Lord God and have that belief counted to you as righteousness."

The woman looked at the thin man, who had not moved, much less breathed. He might have been a mannequin for all anyone knew. "I believe," she said. "I *believe*."

"Lay down your Isaac then, woman. Lay him down and be saved from all doubt and fear. This is what the Lord asks of you."

The woman looked uncertainly at Guidry, who nodded encouragingly, and laid the boy, shivering, on the ground at the thin man's feet. She remained on the floor, kneeling, hands clasped, her silent sobs wracking her feeble frame.

Guidry turned, raising his arms wide, calling the attention of he flock. "Now, brothers and sisters…now you shall see the power of God over Death. You will witness the eternal might of God, from everlasting to everlasting!"

He turned to the thin man. "Let loose your bond on this creature, demon! He does not belong to you, but to the One who created him! Turn him loose and trouble him no more! DEPART, I SAY! FLEE FROM HIM! GOD COMMANDS YOU! *I* COMMAND YOU!"

The thin man's back arched suddenly, wracking pain seeming to course through his body. A brilliant white light emanated from his person, blinding all who looked directly into it, and driving all shadows from the tent.

The woman threw herself over the boy's inert body, shielding him from what could only in her mind be the wrath of God for her presumption on His will. Guidry stood, arms outstretched, bellowing at the thin man, whose own arms were akimbo, and whose body was flailing from side to side.

"THE CIRCLE IS BROKEN! YOUR POWER IS DIMINISHED! YOU HAVE NO PLACE HERE ANY LONGER!

BEGONE, AND BY THE LORD GOD'S WILL, RETURN NO MORE!"

The light grew impossibly brighter, stabbing out into the darkness of the desert night. Amos squeezed his eyes until they began to water, the light passing through his eyelids, knifing into his brain. The churchgoers wailed in fear, cowering behind the pews, clutching themselves and waiting for the end to claim them.

All of a sudden the light dimmed to a bearable luster, then winked out just as quickly as it had appeared. People began to pick themselves up, helping each other to their feet, few daring to look toward the stage.

Brother Guidry had collapsed on the stage floor, barely holding himself up on his hands and knees. He was retching violently, the pool of his sick spreading outward between his hands. The four deacons rushed to his side and grasped him under his arms, helping him to stand. He regained his feet and wobbled over to the woman and her son.

"Rise, woman," he said. He helped her up and reached down to the boy, who opened his eyes at Guidry's touch, and took his hand.

"Come, child. Death has fled. The morning has come." The boy rose to his feet, sweat running down his face.

Guidry turned to the woman. "Go your way," he said, "and sin no more." The woman looked from Guidry to her son and back again. Her mouth worked but no sound would come. The boy looked up into his mother's face, his brown eyes focusing as if just waking from a bad dream.

"Mama? Mama, can we go home, now? I'm…I'm awful hungry."

Shouts of 'Hallelujah!' and 'Praise God!' erupted from the congregation, along with laughter and tears could have been heard clear to Arizona. Brother Guidry walked to the edge of the stage, soaking up their ardor and undying love, arms raised above his head, giving benediction and absolution away like dime-store candy.

"The Lord God is mighty, indeed!" he shouted. "OH, GRAVE WHERE IS THY VICTORY? OH, DEATH, WHERE IS THY STING?"

Amos was pushed and shoved as the crowd began frenzied around him. He had not known such a clamor since the artillery shells fell at

Verdun and trench dirt mingled with young men's blood had rained down on his steel pot for unending hours.

He ambled to his right, making for the door of the tent. Over shoulders and waving arms he glimpsed the deacons descending the stairs, each carrying a gilded offering plate and dispersing in the crowd.

"Children of God!" Guidry shouted. "Show your love for the Almighty and your deliverance at His hands! Give back to God what is his, and be *damned* to Caesar!"

It was all every hand in the place could do to fish into pockets, wallets, and purses to hurl what little money they had into the plates, all but mobbing the ushers and deacons who passed them by, shouting Guidry's name and praising God in the same breath.

Amos hurried to the rear of the tent and stumbled out into the night, breathing heavily, and reached for his hip flask. He made his way over to a nearby pickup truck, unscrewed the cap, and settled with a thump onto the lowered tailgate. He took a moment to gather his wits and then took a hard hit, the sour mash burning his throat and scalding his insides with welcome warmth.

"Helluva show, ain't it?" The voice belonged to a bearded man leaning against the truck's rear fender and smoking a corncob pipe. "Supposed to have done it sixteen times in as many states, to hear folks tell."

Amos took another pull before answering. "He rile 'em up like that every time?"

"Oh, yeah. Damn near had to call in the law back in Lincoln, Nebraska, so I hear."

Amos shrugged. "Well, I s'pose he put on a light show like that every time, he gonna make the nickels. That woman prolly a plant, too. Seen a bunch like that down South. Work like a charm."

"Plant? Hell, she ain't no plant, bubba. That's Thelma Hopkins. She been livin' here 'bout twenty some-odd years, I reckon. Her old man got chewed up in a wheat thresher 'bout six years a-gone. Then her oldest girl got the scarlet fever and up and died. Ol' Doc Collins give her boy Thad 'bout 'nother three weeks to live in that coma, then he'd be deader than Judas Iscariot."

Amos stared open-mouthed, the flask forgotten.

"Yeah, poor ol' Thelma," the man said, tapping out his pipe on the truck bed. "Don't reckon the ol' gal coulda stood another death in the family, what before she'd a-joined 'em in Paradise her own self."

Amos looked over his shoulder at the tent where the crowd was letting out. Thad Hopkins and his mother were leaving, surrounded by friends and strangers alike, all patting her on the back and ruffling the boy's hair.

He absentmindedly screwed the cap back on the flask and staggered out into the darkness, his mind awhirl, his task here unsure.

"Hey, friend," the man called. "Where you goin'?"

* * * *

"See what I mean?"

Amos stared into the fire, its embers dying like his resolve. The black dog sat at the edge of the fire's light, its tail twitching when stray sparks came too near.

"I ain't sure *what* I seen," Amos said, "and that's the trouble."

Gentleman Bob shook his head and laughed mirthlessly, tearing off bits of a stick and tossing them into the fire.

"What's so damn funny?" Amos asked, edgy.

"Oh, nothin'," Bob replied, "just that all this time and effort is being spent on a no-account boozer with a martyr complex."

"Say that again," Amos said, rising indignantly. "An' this time, get the collard greens out yo' mouth."

Bob shrugged, tossing another twig in the flames. "I'm saying that it's a cryin' shame that the fate of the free world rests on the shoulders of a hedonist and a thumbsucker that can't stop feelin' sorry for himself long enough to see the big picture."

A fire kindled in Amos's breast, burning white-hot in seconds. He felt himself giving in to the beast that continually clawed and scratched at his heart, looking for an easy exit—a beast that Amos normally put to sleep with whiskey or whatever was convenient in a bottle.

"I mean," Bob said between chuckles, "you can't believe yer four-legged friend there brung you all the way to Bakersfield for the climate?" Amos started. Fear, confusion, and wonder all jockeyed for a place on his face.

"What… *what* did you say?" Amos breathed.

"Oh, I get it. I bet you been thinkin' it was the drink, or that sliver of Kraut grenade behind your left eyeball. That sound about right?"

Actually, it did. Amos had wondered that for most of his adult life, but not in recent years. Only one other had ever seen the dog, and he wasn't sure if *that* person had been real *herself.* Amos began to look at Gentleman Bob in a new light, and it scared him.

"See, the question ain't *how*, Amos, but *why*. An' that's an easy answer, too. You been askin' 'why me?' but for all the wrong reasons."

Amos glared at Bob. "You better start makin' some sense, Limey, or there's gonna be another poor bastard needs some healin'."

Bob laughed out loud, looked heavenward, then back at Amos. "Can you *believe* this? It's a miracle 'e's still breathin', yet. And this is the shite I'm supposed t' work with. Bugger *me*." Figger it out fer yerself, 'Black Dog,'" he said.

Amos growled inarticulately and launched himself at the smug Brit, only to grab empty air and spill over the log where Bob had been seconds before.

"Oh, the Black Dog has *teeth*, does he?" laughed Bob, who sat on the log Amos had vacated, tossing more sticks into the fire. "Pathetic," he said, shaking his head, smirking.

Amos gathered himself and lunged again for Bob, grabbing his tattered lapels, only to find himself on the ground, the wind rushing out of his lungs in whoosh, and Bob's worn-out dress shoe planted firmly on his chest.

"I'm just about through dickin' around with you, Harlow," Gentleman Bob hissed, the silver fire flaring from his eyes once more.

Amos felt an electric current run through his body, jolting him stiff. He tried to grab the man's foot, but found he was unable to move. His hands, arms, feet, even toes were full of pins and needles, as though he'd slept on them for days. His mouth, however, was as good as ever.

"Let me up, shit-heel, or you gonna be sorry as hell when I *do* get up!"

Bob canted his head, studying Amos as a cat would a mouse it had pinned by the tail. "Are you worth my time, Amos? Are you worth *theirs*?" he asked, nodding toward the shantytown and the revival tent.

Amos glowered at the man who he was convinced now was *not* a man. "I'll listen," he said. "But it damn-well better be *good*."

"Oh, it's good, all right," Bob said. "'Greatest story ever told', and all that." He lifted his foot and sat on his log again and resumed picking apart his stick.

Amos felt all the blood flow back into his limbs and found that he could move again. He rubbed his fingers and arms, the feeling slowly flooding back.

"So *talk*," he growled.

Bob squatted by the fire, peering into its depths like a gypsy reading tea leaves.

"What did you see?" he said.

"Whatchu mean, 'what'd I see?' Same ol' song *all* them hucksters play. The preacher called up somebody and healed 'em, then passed the plate."

"Wrong," said Bob, still staring at the flames. "What did you *see*?"

"I done *tol'* you what I seen, smartass. The man called up a boy an' his mama and healed the boy." Amos was getting riled again.

"What *else* did you see?" Bob asked.

Amos thought for a minute. "There was this light show after the preacher commanded the man to let loose the boy and—"

"What did the man look like?" Bob interrupted.

Amos thought again. "Like anyone else I 'spect. Tall, thin, long hair. Had 'im a hat that covered his face. Couldn't see much else."

"And did the man do anything out of the ordinary ?"

"Well, he damn near exploded."

"What do you mean 'exploded?'"

"What the hell do it sound like? Preacher-man yelled at 'im and he lit up like a Christmas tree. Couldn't see a damn thing after, not even the man next to me."

Bob nodded, grimacing. "That's him all right, well—at least *some* of the time."

"That's *who*?"

"Death, Amos," Bob said, staring into the fire. "Death."

* * * *

At the exact moment little Thad Hopkins opened his eyes out of the fever-induced coma that would have killed him not a week later, a man in Schenectady, New York clutched at his chest, dying less than a second after.

The body would be found almost twelve hours later on a bench in Riverside Park overlooking the Mohawk River, a bag of roasted peanuts and half a loaf of bread beside it. Squirrels had eaten most of the nuts and birds had all but finished off the bread. The county coroner would spend half an hour wiping the bird feces from the body before the autopsy could begin in earnest.

The deceased's name was Gerard Ackerman—U.S. Senator Gerard Ackerman. His wife reported him missing after he failed to show for supper. Senator Ackerman had long been an advocate of the Constitution but had openly and vehemently opposed Reverend Arlen Guidry and his cause, indicting the minister as a rabble-rouser and an anarchist, a viable threat to the freedom of the nation.

The post-mortem indicated a healthy physique; no apparent cause of death.

* * * *

Three weeks before the Church of Hope and Restoration for All People had come to Bakersfield, a Las Vegas bookie and made-man by the name of Archibald "Sharkey" Watson began to have seizures while counting the day's take. Watson normally left strict instructions not to be disturbed while counting and locked himself in the back room of the gin joint he illegally operated off West Flamingo.

As a consequence, no one knew he had bled to death out of every pore in his body until the following afternoon, when the bar-back came in to prepare for the night crowd and saw a dark, viscous pool of fluid under the crack in Sharkey's office door, at which point he began to yell to the colored help for a crowbar.

Brother Arlen Guidry had been into Sharkey for thirty-large.

* * * *

The previous year, a young prostitute named Eileen McNamara in Ann Arbor who had known Brother Arlen Guidry as a regular john, and whom he had tried to silence with a diamond necklace and copious amounts of cash, was found in an alley half-naked, apparently frozen to death by the arctic winds whipping off the waters of Lake Erie—even though the temperature topped out in the low eighties that day, with only a slight chance of afternoon showers. Pretty average for a summer's day in southeast Michigan.

The child in her womb had been barely four months along.

* * * *

And so it continued. The leader of a teamsters organization in Philly. A beat cop in Charleston, South Carolina. A journalist in Kansas City. The mayor of a small mountain town in the Rockies. A congressman, a waitress, a minister, a dockworker, an accountant.

All had crossed the good Reverend at one time or another, and all had finally caught the bus. Brother Guidry's Church of Hope and Restoration for All People had cut a swath across the fruited plains and purple mountains' majesty and left a trail of blood and silent tongues in its wake.

And it wasn't half-finished.

* * * *

"It's called the *Ars Goetia*," Gentleman Bob explained, as he and Amos sat beneath a small stand of scrub pines at the edge of town, smoking butts they'd found outside the revival tent.

The sun had begun to rise in the east, painting the skyline with rust-colored hues of blood, a bad omen for sailors and landlubbers alike, Amos thought.

"The what?" he said.

"The *Ars Goetia*. Least that's what it's been called on earth. It's a book—a very *old* book. Older than the world, in fact. Legend says that it contains the true names of every demon in Hell and every angel in Heaven."

"Uh- *huh*, Amos said. "And?"

"'*And*'," Bob said, exhaling blue smoke, "it ain't no legend."

"It's a grimoire, then? A spellbook?" Amos asked.

Bob shook his head. "More like a ledger, or a roll-book." He hunkered down, flicking ashes into the dirt.

"See, before the world was created, the angels of Heaven thrived and watched over the universe. Now this was a big task, y' see, and a right honor. So it was given to one angel to write down every name of every angel for posterity mostly, but also to ensure that every one of them was on the straight and narrow. If one fell out of line, he was cast down, sent burning to earth, exiled forever from Paradise."

Amos thought a moment. "Then all them angels fell with Lucifer—"

"—their names, along with his, got written on a *different* page," Bob finished. "Sort of a 'naughty and nice' list."

"So what's so special about this book? It ain't no spellbook, ain't nobody can use it, right?"

"True, but with the right translation, and the right ritual, it can be the worst weapon on the earth."

"I don't follow," Amos said, confused.

"One's true name holds immense power. Once someone discovers it, he can use it to hold sway over that person. In this case, we're talking about celestial beings, each with the power of an entire army, all being controlled by one person."

Amos felt his bowels cramp. This was way beyond his pay-grade.

"That's not all," Bob said. "There were certain angels—four to be exact—that were given certain tasks and power far beyond even the archangels. They were held under tight reign until God saw that their… *talents,* were needed. This man you saw, the one on stage with the preacher? He's one of them. Maybe the worst of the lot."

"Death," Amos whispered.

"This Guidry is a shyster, but a dangerous one. Somehow, he got his hands on the *Ars Goetia.* It went missing from Heaven centuries ago, right around the time of the Black Plague."

"How do *you* know it went missing?" Amos asked.

Bob smirked, looking away from him. "Who do you think lost it?"

Amos shot a wide-eyed stare at Bob, stunned.

"Listen, boyo. I know it's a lot to take, but you need to hold it together, now. You have to get that book. Guidry's using it to control Death. He forces Death to relinquish his hold on the ones whose time has come so's to make a fortune for himself. But Death *has* to take a life; that's what he was *created* to do. So the preacher directs him at other targets like a guided missile."

"A what?"

"Never mind. The point is that man was never meant to have power over death. That belongs to another, and I think you know *who.* If this man isn't stopped, it could well mean the end of the world. And that ain't no metaphor."

Amos couldn't think straight, couldn't put it all together. He had long accepted that there were other things in the world, that the world was stranger that it let on, and he had looked some of those things in the eyeteeth. But *this…*

"Why cain't *you* go get the damn thing?" Amos cried.

"I can't. I've been in the tent. Death is bound up in a cage when he's not on stage. His cage is warded, as is the book. Guidry's ain't stupid; he knew we'd come for it sooner or later. If I tried to turn my brother loose or take the book, I'd be burnt to dust like that!" He snapped his fingers. "The ward is a sigil, a sign -- something that looks like this."

Bob scrawled a geometric symbol in the dirt. It had many hard lines, as well as flourishes and soft edges. It reminded Amos of some of the hobo signs he and others used to communicate on the open road.

"It's called a devil box," Bob said. "King Solomon once used these to trap a host of demons that was plaguing Israel. He got it from the book, same as Guidry. Most likely, it's on the floor of the cage and all over its bars, and probably burned into the stage floor. Grab the book, or it's all for naught. He keeps it locked in a desk drawer etched with the devil box. You gotta break the devil's box. It only has to be scratched, defaced even slightly. That's why it *has* to be you, don't you see? Only a human can cross the sigil."

"Amos," Bob said, fixing him with those silvery, haunted eyes. "I've hunted this book for over seven hundred years, and this is the closest I've gotten to reclaiming it. I *need* you to do this. This is the task you were prepared for, old son. You may be my last hope—the *world's* last hope."

Amos scowled at him. "Yeah? Well maybe if you'd-a taken better care of it, we wouldn't *be* in this fix."

"Now you sound like my *Father*," Bob muttered, pitching his cigarette butt into the weeds.

* * * *

Arlen Guidry was a self-made man, or so he thought of himself. Of course, he'd had to learn it the hard way, hadn't he? His was a life of toil, of back-breaking, soul-bleeding labor that had borne fruit of the sweetest stripe. Maybe it wasn't the kind of labor that came at the back of a plow, and maybe it wasn't completely *honest*, but he'd never had trouble sleeping.

A mattress stuffed to the brim with other people's money made sure of that.

That pious ass of a senator had called him an actor, a flimflam man, a busker. So what if he was? Didn't actors need to eat, too? Didn't they perform their craft to the reverberation of thunderous applause at the end of Act Three? Weren't they rewarded with fame, adulation, and roses at the curtain call?

But Guidry didn't care about the fame and adulation; they were mere stepping stones to the greatest of all dividends.

Power.

Power was what redirected rivers, redrew borders, carved tunnels through mountains and shaped destinies of entire nations. Renown and respect, hell, even money, were all just happy side effects. Those with power and the vision to guide it, *those* were the ones who were worshipped as *gods*.

Godhood. Was that what he was after? Maybe, but in his experience, it didn't pay to get too ahead of oneself. That was when the floor caved in and all one's best-laid plans were swallowed up by the earth.

No, he would continue to play it safe. That didn't mean he would abandon his timetable, oh, no. There were still obstacles in his way, hurdles to be leaped. For a man to rise to power—*true* power—there must be blood, and lots of it, before he could finally rise and take his rightful place.

He wasn't fixated on the Oval Office. That was a sucker bet. He didn't want to be the king; his place was at the king's ear, whispering wisdom and suggesting the courses of action that would place him in an unassailable position. And from *that* lofty perch, he would rule.

Guidry stretched his legs and placed them on the desk, crossing his feet. The night's take sat near his feet, all stacked and counted. He drew deeply on the Cuban cigar that cost more than one of these shitkickers made in a week, even when times were good.

But times *were* good, for *him* at any rate, ever since that snake-oil shyster Walton had met with an unfortunate—and very premature—stroke at the age of fifty. It had been easy enough to take over the reigns of his ministry, to put it back in the black and then some. Now it was *Guidry's* vision, *his* dream that would soon become a reality. Let those like the late Senator make their accusations and try to drag him through the mud. They'd all end up with their cables cut and their elevators shooting right through the basement.

The people of God, that's who *he* served. And in turn, they served him. Soon, he would have all the support he needed; he would have his army—the Army of Jehovah—and then this crusty old nag of a country would *really* feel the pillars of the earth shake. He had the golden ring in his grasp and he would ride and ride until he was ready to get off. And if Brother Arlen Guidry could help it, such a time would never come.

He considered the being in the tarp-covered cage across the room as he smoked. What was it thinking right now? What did it *ever* think? Was it planning escape? Was it calling out to a deity that was impotent to deliver it from it bonds? Or was it docile now, waiting to be called to perform again? Had it finally accepted its new master, a human who had done what only One other had ever done in the history of the world?

He reached into his vest pocket and removed a small brass key. He unlocked the bottom drawer of his desk and removed the book. Its fittings were gold, but the bindings and cover were worn. He ran his fingers over the cover, wondering if the fingers of creatures on the Other Side had touched those very same spots, invisible fingerprints of eternity.

Two dollars from a junk dealer in Pittsburgh who had no idea that he carried the very key to the gates of Hell itself.

A movement from the cage. Guidry smiled.

"You want this, don't you?" he cooed, tapping the book lightly.

No reply.

"Sorry, friend. You got a little more steppin'and fetchin' to do before the whistle blows," he said, crushing out the cigar in a glass ashtray. He replaced the book and locked the drawer.

Guidry could barely make out a whispered muttering from beneath the tarp.

"Don't worry. No need to pray, if one such as you *can* pray." He leapt to his feet, crossing the distance to the cage in two steps. He leaned close to the tarp.

"Because no one can hear you," he whispered.

The muttering stopped. Guidry smiled. He walked to the flap of the tent and turned before exiting.

"You rest up, now, hear? Showtime's at six sharp. And *do* be punctual, won't you?" He smiled again, laughed, and left the tent.

Two heartbeats.

Then the muttering resumed.

* * * *

It was high noon when Amos finished scoping out the great tent. He sat under the tailgate of a ministry truck to hide from the sun. His guitar sat on his lap, his hands hanging listlessly over its scarred finish.

He'd sat playing hymns and humming, watching the ministry workers come and go until he'd deciphered their schedule. Two of the deacons were helping a group of women unload a city truck full of food for the potluck supper that was to be held before the night's service. The men toted steel kegs of lemonade dappled with moisture to picnic tables set up under a small stand of live oaks.

Another two sat outside of the tent's rear entrance, across from which lay the entrance to Brother Guidry's office and living quarters. Every half-hour or so, one of them would step away from the tent to grab a smoke or to talk to one of the pretty girls that seemed to flit around the tent night and day. Every so often, one would offer his arm and lead the girl away, chatting her up, to more private environs.

Amos figured he'd have about five minutes inside Guidry's tent. If he wasn't out by then, he was burned. He'd already concocted a story in which he pleaded to the great man to heal his bad eye. Amos could play the poor unfortunate if he had to; he'd done it a thousand times for less. He was hoping it wouldn't come to that, but it wasn't Guidry and his cronies that had Amos quaking inside and wondering if this weren't the most hair-brained scheme he ever pulled.

It was the tall, thin man inside that cage that had him *really* worried. Was he really going to set him loose upon the world once more? Did he have the courage to *do* it? And worse yet, he thought, maybe—just maybe—did Arlen Guidry have the right idea?

Would a world without death be such a bad thing?

Amos knew he was whistling past the graveyard. Death was a fact of life, as a man once said. It wasn't natural to keep death like a genie in a lamp, forcing it into service that was the most heinous of sacrilege against the One who ordained it.

Still, Amos thought, still…

His fingers moved of their own accord, lightly strumming out a tune. It was a full minute before he realized it was "Nearer My God to Thee." Amos clamped his left hand tight on the frets, his right slapping the sound box, cutting the music. Why had he played that? He shook it off; the implications were too ominous to think about.

"Pretty tune," said a voice behind him. "You playin' to the crowd tonight?" Amos turned, squinting into the noonday sun. It was the man with the pipe from the night before.

Amos turned back to the tent. The two deacons were wandering away from the entrance with the women, carrying covered dishes and stacks of folded linen tablecloths.

"Somethin' like that," Amos said, watching them disappear into the shantytown.

* * * *

Two hours later, Brother Guidry was regaling a bevy of church women with some pulpit humor, all of them tittering and clucking like hens, hanging on his every word.

Just as he delivered the punch-line to his favorite anecdote, a weary-looking black man in a worn suit stumbled through the crowd of ladies, crashing into Guidry, causing him to spill his lemonade.

The women gasped at this outrage, but true to form, Brother Guidry reached down and helped the poor man up. The man had obviously been into his cups, and Guidry smiled wide and bright as he helped him stand.

"Whoa, there, brother," he said. "Come, now. Get yourself some food," he said.

"Yessir; I'm sorry, Reverend. I—I just been down so long, cain't rightly find my way *up*."

Guidry laughed a genuine belly laugh, which set the ladies ate ease. They giggled dutifully along.

"Well, you know," Guidry lowered his voice conspiratorially, "the Lord turned water into wine, but He knew when to *stop*, eh?"

The man laughed nervously, holding his hat in his hands. "Yessir," he said, "I s'pose He *did*."

They all laughed a moment longer and the black man donned his hat, never meeting the preacher's eye, made his manners, and shambled off.

Guidry watched him go. The man swerved left, barely avoiding a collision with another man carrying a platter of pulled pork.

He turned back to his audience with a stern, mock stare.

"Now, *ladies*," Guidry said, admonishingly. "Which one of you spiked the lemonade?"

The maniacal tittering that followed scared magpies from the trees overhead.

* * * *

The potluck supper was on in full swing by sundown. The city of Bakersfield had come together and produced more food and drink than the revelers had seen in a month of Sundays.

Children laughed and chased each other in the dying light. Men ate their fill of fried chicken and sliced ham, and the women marveled over paper cups of lemonade at Brother Guidry, who had brought all of this wonder to pass.

The sight was so moving, it almost made Amos ashamed to be about his chore.

Almost.

He had eaten well, because he'd learned in the Army that a man had to eat when he could. He had stopped before he got logy because his night was just starting, and he needed all his wits about him for the task ahead.

Amos had become somewhat of an expert at becoming invisible over the years. He found that if one looked needy and pathetic enough, even in a crowd of needy and pathetic people, that those more fortunate tended to become nearsighted and generally ignored his presence. That suited him just fine.

He dropped his paper cup into a wastebasket and sidled off to the edges of the gathering. He passed other hobos like himself, but as a rule they kept to themselves and barely noticed his passing, preferring instead to gnaw their way through another chicken thigh or slice of watermelon.

The shadows lengthened as he made his way to the entrance of Guidry's tent. He moved as fast as he dared, trying to look as inconspicuous as possible. The crowd had thinned out and pretty soon, he found himself trotting at a pace.

He paused at the entrance to the tent, hearing voices from within.

"I don't care if it takes *all* of you, just get the damn thing onstage! And for shit's sake, get it in the *center* of the circle this time! We don't need another Peekskill. You get me?"

"Sure, sure, Arlen," said another voice. "It's just that…"

"Just that *what*?"

"Well, me and the boys been thinkin'—"

"Dangerous pastime for the uninitiated."

"Yeah, ha! Right, well, um..."

"Lemme guess. You and the boys are scared shitless, am I right? You're all titty-babies when it comes to our friend here in the cage, that it?"

"Well, hell *yeah*, Arlen. We— "

"WELL YOU FUCKING-WELL *SHOULD* BE!"

Amos could hear the other man draw a sudden breath that he didn't release. Little choking sounds came from the tent.

"One mistake," said Guidry, softly, evenly. "One mistake you mouth-breathers make with that thing could wipe us off the map. What do you think'll happen if he gets loose? You ever have your atoms scattered all over Creation? Ever wonder what it's like to die slow only to be brought back and die again, over and over 'til you go crazy from the pain? We'll sure as shit find out if we ain't careful. He's got our scent, now. He knows us, Reggie. He *knows* us. For better or worse, that thing's with us for the long-haul, you get me? You *get* me?"

An affirmative gag.

"Then get your head out of your ass and into your job. Tell those other pus-buckets to do the same. I've got the Book to protect *me*, Reg. What do *you* have?"

A sudden, gasping intake of air.

"Now get out of my sight."

Amos pulled back into the shadows of the doorway just as Reggie stumbled out, massaging his throat. He stood for moment rubbing his throat and gathering his wits, then went through the rear entrance of the great tent, yelling for the others.

An eternal minute later, Guidry emerged from the tent, smoking a cigar, its tip flaring like a meteor. He stood inches from Amos, so close that Amos could have reached out and tied the man's shoelaces together.

Then Guidry turned to stare directly at Amos's hiding place.

Amos dared not breathe in the slightest. He was suddenly all too aware of the thunderous pounding of his own heartbeat, like a giant's metronome.

Guidry's head tilted to one side, as if considering a new suit. His brow furrowed as he peered into the darkness by the tent.

Amos wished beyond words that he could curl into the tiniest of balls and burrow beneath the pebbles at his feet.

Then Guidry abruptly turned and walked toward the field where the feast was winding down. He pitched the stub of his cigar into the shadows behind him, hitting Amos square on the nose, scorching him. Amos almost bit clean through his tongue to cut off the yelp that would have followed.

Guidry strolled around the great tent, out of sight. Amos bent and retrieved the cigar butt, snuffing it out in the dirt, and slipped it into his coat pocket. He watched and waited until he was sure he was alone, then eased through the tent flap.

The first thing to register in Amos's mind was the cold. The temperature had dropped at least ten degrees inside the tent. Outside, people were in short sleeves, sweating the day's heat away. In the tent, one could hang meat and not worry.

Amos turned and was face to face with the cage, the tarp stirring in the evening breeze. Against all reason, he slowly pulled the tarp back an inch, revealing the bars beneath.

They were wrought iron and covered with a thin veneer of frost, giving them the appearance of porcelain. The strange symbols Bob mentioned were etched into the bars—whorls and swirls, circles with crosses intersecting them, all unidentifiable, all unpronounceable by man since the dawn of time. Amos realized that the symbols must be the thing's true name to keep him trapped so.

The interior of the cage was entirely devoid of light; the light from the kerosene desk lamp stopped just short of the edge. It was almost as if the light was *swallowed* somehow.

A white puff of breath slid between the bars and hit Amos in the face. He reeled at the stench. It was the odor of an unearthed coffin, of maggots and decay. A guttural muttering followed it, shaking Amos to the core.

Amos tripped over his own feet in an effort to escape it. He stumbled and caught himself on the edge of the desk.

The desk.

He had to get back on track.

Eyeing the cage warily, he moved around behind the desk and began pulling drawers until he found one that was locked.

He reached into his pants pocket and withdrew the little brass key he'd palmed off of Guidry earlier in the day when he'd pulled his drunk act.

The key twisted in the lock with a loud pop, and Amos jerked his head toward the tent flap, sure someone had heard. He eased the drawer open and pulled the lamp over for light.

The book sat in the drawer, seemingly innocuous but with a quiet menace, surrounded by stacks of paper money and coin, like a dragon in the midst of its treasure hoard.

Amos hesitated, afraid to touch it for fear it would come to life and burn him with the cold fire of the seventh heaven. He gingerly brushed his fingertips over the cover.

Nothing happened. Even so, he lifted it from the drawer like he was holding a live cottonmouth.

There was nothing special about the book, nothing to make him do what he did next, but suddenly Amos felt far away from himself, floating in a vast reach of remoteness, of which there was no boundary, no horizon.

His hands, moving of their own accord, opened the book and began turning pages.

In the back of his mind, the part where he screamed at his body to stop what the hell it was doing, he could hear the muttering from the cage growing in volume and intensity.

In the front of his mind, he read the strange, esoteric symbols as though they were a child's book, the grammar and syntax coming easily to his mind. His hands flashed at the speed of thought, turning pages in a continuous blur.

The history of all things played out before his mind's eye. He saw the birth of the universe, first utter darkness, then the immeasurable reaches of space filling with the most glorious and penetrating of lights in a bare instant.

He saw planets whirling in their orbits, comets reeling through the starry void, galaxies spawning in milliseconds, spinning like cosmic tops.

He saw, in the briefest of moments, a great war being waged in the most beautiful, perfect battleground one could scarcely imagine. Winged beings zipped and flitted among each other, haloes of pure white casting their features into silhouette. They ran long spears of light though their enemies, and swords with blades of pure flame left afterimages in his vision as they struck home into inhuman flesh. Shrieks not quite human filled the air as wings of the dying burned to ash, their feathers fluttering to the ground like dead moths, and the hopeless moans of the walking wounded called for someone to end their torment.

From his vantage point outside the world, Amos saw a great, burning star fall from the battle, streaking through ether like a renegade comet, hurtling toward what he knew instinctively was Earth. A great shout of victory rose from the host on the battlefield, followed by the sorrow-filled cries of the vanquished as they followed the great star to perdition.

Then all at once, Amos felt as though a great hook was affixed to his belly and was pulling him backwards, back into himself, back to the present, and as he became aware of his surroundings, he looked down and saw that the book was open to the last page, the back cover hanging limply from the edge of the desk.

He grabbed the book and fled the tent, reaching the grounds just in time to vomit his lunch into the dirt. He fell to his hands and knees, clutching the book under his right arm, and heaved until he had nothing left but bile.

He heard voices coming from the great tent and hurried back inside, closing the drawer, locking it, and tossing the key on the floor. He lay down and rolled under the edge of the tent and out, just as Guidry walked in, Reggie and the other deacons close behind.

He heard them preparing to move the cage, yammering and backbiting with each other, trying to fill the nervous void all of them felt.

"The damn key was in my pocket! I *never* go anywhere without it! NEVER!" he heard Guidry yell. "Look all around! *Find* it, dammit!"

Amos didn't wait around to hear the rest. He took off at a brisk trot to the front entrance of the tent.

Everyone was loading up the remainder of the potluck, rinsing out pans and wrapping what little food was left. No one paid him any mind. He glanced into the great tent. Empty. With a last look around, he slipped inside.

The interior of the tent was brightly lit, kerosene lanterns casting a warm white glow into every corner. He moved to the stage where the thin man had stood.

A Persian runner rug covered the steps leading up to the spot and disappeared into the walkway behind the stage. Amos lifted the edge of the rug, gently, like it was the lid on a basket of angry cobras.

The devil's box was burned into the wood of the stage floor beneath, its mystical characters and arcs blackened in the center and rust-colored along the edges. It stared up at him from the dim past, a monument to the unknown perils of lost ages.

Amos removed his Old Timer pocketknife that had once belonged to his grandfather and had become his on his tenth birthday. It was the one remainder of his past that held no bad memory.

He drew the keenly-honed blade across the hardwood, making one thin cut, almost invisible to the naked eye, straight through the outer circle of the pictogram.

To his astonishment, the slice in the wood began to seal up as if it had never been there in the first place. He cut it again.

Same thing; the cut disappeared.

He cut again, and again, and again. His knife couldn't make the slightest nick in the mystical circle.

He heard voices from behind the great tent.

Oh, Lord, he thought. He rummaged frantically through his coat pockets for something, anything from his usual bag of tricks that would help. He had no idea what could cut—

Then he reached down and pulled Mean Sally from his old work boot— the bone-handled nightmare some had called the Devil's Tooth. Amos had a love/hate relationship with Sally. She'd saved his ass more than few times in his travels, but he knew the blade was wicked and wished sometimes he's never found the damned thing in that old shop in New York City. He'd tried to be rid of her several times, but Sally always found him on her own, God only knew how. But right then, wicked and damned was what he needed.

Right then, Mean Sally was the only dance partner on Amos's card.

He flicked the straight razor open and Sally shined in the candlelight, kissing his cheek with her reflection. Amos drew the blade across the circle from center to edge, a long, wafer-thin cut, and waited.

The voices were getting closer.

Amos waited, his breath galloping form his lungs like a prize stallion.

The cut remained.

Amos damn near cheered. He picked up the *Ars Goetia*, ran for the front flaps of the tent, and out into the night.

And straight into Brother Arlen Guidry.

The preacher smiled sadly, like the shepherd he pretended to be, finally having caught up to one of his wayward flock.

"My, my," he said. "So sad. You know, all you had to do was ask. I would have shown you what you sought. I'll take that, now." He extended his hand, palm up.

Amos dropped the Book and lunged at Guidry, who stood his ground, smiling. Two of Guidry's deacons grabbed Amos from behind, each pinning one of his arms behind his back. Amos struggled fruitlessly and watched as two other deacons flanked him, cutting off any means of escape.

Guidry stood, patiently holding his hand out.

One of the men stepped forward and picked up the Book, dusted it off and handed it to Guidry. Amos scowled, hoping his fear didn't show.

"Thank you, Reggie. So," Guidry said, turning to Amos, "this is the part of our little drama where you tell me that I won't get away with it, isn't it? That I shouldn't be 'meddling with powers beyond my control'?" Guidry flipped through the book, satisfied himself all was well, then closed it with a snap.

Amos said nothing.

"That was pretty clever finger-work with the key out there today," Guidry said. "I should have been more careful."

"How careful can a man be, pointin' the Angel of Death at folks like a loaded gun?" Amos growled.

Guidry angled his head and peered at Amos. "Who *are* you?"

"Nobody," Amos muttered, glaring at the preacher.

"Oh, come now," Guidry said, "everybody's *some*body. Who sent you? Was it Daniels? Or Wellington? Or are you just a simple thief?"

Amos was silent, fuming.

"No, no," Guidry said, thinking aloud. "You're not a thief, or else you'd've taken the money. You only took the Book. So once again—"

Guidry hit Amos hard in the breadbasket. Amos doubled over in pain, gagging and coughing. Guidry moved forward like a jungle cat and grabbed his chin and jerked it upward. He was close enough to touch noses with Amos.

"Who *are* you?"

Amos coughed up a wad of blood and phlegm and spat it into Guidry's face. "Somebody's who's endin' your dog-and-pony show forever, shit-bag. Somebody who's gonna laugh you all the way to Hell."

Guidry's face filled with sudden, vicious anger, and Amos thought he was dead for sure. Then Guidry softened and assumed the pastoral smile for which he was best known. He removed a handkerchief from his coat pocket and wiped his face.

"I don't know who you are," he whispered malevolently, "or how you know about me or my work, but I assure you, you'll find out firsthand in just a very short while. Boys?"

The men behind Amos forced his arms at an awkward upward angle, wrenching an agonized moan from his lips. The other two men circled around Guidry and moved toward him. The one named Reggie drew back a meaty fist which filled Amos's vision a split second before white light filled his head. He reeled from the blow into the arms of the men behind him.

"Tie him up backstage and prep him for the service. Little change in the show tonight, boys." He turned and walked toward the rear of the tent, the book under his arm.

"And make the knots tight," he called, exiting the tent.

Reggie drew back his meaty fist again, and Amos knew nothing but darkness.

* * * *

Amos came around to the sound of the church organ droning out "Blessed Be the Tie that Binds." His neck hurt from being in one position too long, but it was nothing next to the fifty-float parade in his skull. His right eye was swollen shut, and the right side of his face felt like an inner tube.

Beneath the muted sound of the organ, he could hear a flicking sound, like fingernails tapping rhythmically on a window pane.

He tried to reach up and touch his face, but found his hands were firmly secured to the hand rests of Guidry's desk chair. He was groggy, more so than usual from a beating. Amos had taken blows to the head before and been in scraps that were the stuff of legend, but that was when he was younger and had drowned the pain in whiskey and the warm thighs of willing women.

This was different. His tongue was thick in his mouth and dry like sandpaper. His thought processes came slow and plodding, and the vision in his one good eye was bleary, unfocused. Still, the flicking sound persisted.

He concentrated on the desk lamp and the shape of a man began to resolve itself. It was one of Guidry's men. He was greasy and unshaven, his hair slicked back with a fistful of pomade. He was flicking a metallic syringe half-full of an amber fluid. Amos could see the bubbles rising to the top of the plunger.

"Well, well, sleepyhead. Y'all up already?"

Amos tried to speak, but his bloated tongue wouldn't let him.

"Damn, son. I shot you up with enough morphine to drop a bull rhino. That's some kind of stamina you got, there."

Drugged. So that was how they'd play it, Amos thought. He couldn't move, couldn't cry out. All he could do was sit there and wait to die however the Reaper chose. Dimly, he wondered what that would be. Heart attack? Boiling blood? Either way, someone would find his corpse in the fields. His death would be chalked up to that of a drunkard and a junkie, especially after his performance today in front of the church crowd. Just another wino bound for Potter's Field.

No doubt Brother Guidry would say some kind words over his unmarked grave for the man whom no one knew but God, and Guidry's ministry of death would continue to wander the countryside, its congregation—its *army*— growing day by day.

Amos struggled in a sudden fit of strength against his bonds.

"Whoa, now," the man said, rising from the desk. "Hang on there, podna. Won't do no good to fight it. Them knots is tight. Used to be a Navy man, you know. A medic. Got discharged for stealin' this here good stuff from the ship's stores. But ol' Arlen found me and give me a place when the world wouldn't even spit in my t'roat when I was thirsty."

He moved closer holding the syringe, its needle gleaming wetly in the low light.

"Oh, yes, indeed," the man said. "He seen my talent for getting things outta folks that don't want to give 'em up."

The man slid Amos's sleeve up, pressing his thumb against Amos's forearm in search of a vein.

"I got to admit, though," he said, "you're one tough hombre. You ain't said nary a word all evenin', so now I just got to make sure you don't say shit at *all*. Wouldn't do to have folks hearin' a call for help while the good Reverend is doin' his thing, now would it?"

He slid the needle into Amos's arm and pushed the plunger. A warm fluid sensation flowed up Amos's arm, into his brainpan, and down to his extremities in seconds. The pain ebbed in his head and he could no longer feel the bite of the hemp ropes around his hands and feet.

"Tha's it," the man said soothingly. "Tha's it. Nice and easy, see? Not too much, now. Don't want you croakin' before it's time, do we?"

The man's leering face went hazy and indistinct again, and Amos teetered on the edge of a coma.

Can't, he thought. *Gotta stay awake, gotta get out this chair.*

His last thought before he slid into dreamless sleep was of the devil's box, and whether he'd done enough damage to make up for losing the book.

His head fell back into the same uncomfortable position as before, but to Amos, it might have been a feather pillow.

* * * *

"Amos!"

The voice maybe belonged to his mother, waking him for school, or maybe it was his doomed nephew Clarence, who he'd inadvertently knocked into a table-saw and killed in a drunken fit long ago.

Or maybe it was Lily, sweet Lily, calling him from the mists between here and the Beyond, telling him that all was forgiven.

"Amos! Fer God's sake, man, snap the hell out of it!"

It was a harsh whisper, and an even harsher slap that brought him around.

"He's got the book! I can't get near him! We have to get out of here!"

It took another hard slap before Amos recognized Gentleman Bob.

"Whu… what's goin' on?" asked Amos, shaking his head to clear the cobwebs.

"We gotta make tracks. C'mon, up we go." Bob pulled the last of ropes from Amos's legs.

Amos took stock of his surroundings. The greaser lay in a heap on the floor, his corpse twisted into angles foreign to the human body. His head was turned completely around so that he stared at them from between his shoulder blades. The sight jolted Amos awake. He turned away in disgust.

"We cain't leave yet," Amos said, "Guidry got the Book!"

"The book's dust any minute now, same as us, we don't hoof it out of here. C'mon, man! Move yer ass!"

Bob pulled Amos to his feet, throwing an arm around Amos's shoulder and led him to the back of the tent. Amos resisted.

"Hold on, now. What's the hurry? I wanna see the preacher-man get egg on his face."

Bob grabbed him by the collar, steadying him, and spoke in measured words.

"Amos, Death—Death *incarnate*—has been trapped for the last *year*, forced kill against his own will."

"I know," said Amos. "Be nice to see a sumbitch get *his* for a change."

Bob shook his head in frustration. "Are you *daft*, man? Don't you *see*?"

"See what?"

"You marred the devil's box, yeah?"

"Yeah, like you tol' me," Amos said. "Wasn't much, just a scratch."

"He's *free*, now. Just what kind of shite do ye think's comin' down the pike? It's gonna make Krakatoa look like a bleedin' Roman candle."

Amos stared at him, gaping, realization dawning.

"Where's my hat?"

* * * *

Brother Arlen Guidry sat on his gilded throne as the organist wound down, not in his normal, contemplative state, but wringing his hands in agitation.

The nigger's name was Harlow. That's all they managed to squeeze out of him. He was of no consequence, just a drifter, one of a thousand pieces of flotsam washed up on the shores of the west from the Dead Sea that the east had become.

So why was he so uneasy?

It was the timing, of course. Why was he here? Why *now*? How did he know about the book? Harlow had palmed the key off him in the crowd, had gone right to the drawer. Was there a Judas in Guidry's circle of disciples, plotting against him even now as he sat in his own Gethsemane?

Nothing added up, especially the money. It was piled all around the book in the drawer. No drifter would leave all that cash for an old book that had no significance for him.

Maybe the old coon had been right, he thought. Maybe he *had* dallied once too often with the Other Side. Maybe it was time to pack up and lay low, maybe build that cabin he'd always wanted in the Smokies.

But as he surveyed the crowd before him, he knew he wouldn't walk away. Guidry had been too much of a gambler before his "conversion," a sin that he'd often touted to his congregation. And a true gambler knew when to hedge his bets and when to roll them bones, and right then, Guidry was blowing on the dice. He smiled wide, thinking of the future.

He felt a gentle hand patting his shoulder. He looked up into Reggie's face, who was motioning him to the podium with his chin. He shook off his concern, rose, and strode to the lectern.

The crowd had tripled. It was the biggest crowd he'd drawn yet. They usually doubled after a healing, word of mouth being the best advertisement. But *this*... he could practically *hear* the money hitting the plates. The sides of the tent had been furled to allow extra seating, and men women and children stood four-deep on its sides, watching with expectant sheep's eyes, and waiting for their moment to be woven into the tapestry that God would weave here tonight.

He cleared his throat. "Good people," he began. "Beloved of God above, we have gathered to look death in the eye, once again. And once again, to see the might of God pitted against that which He has already conquered. You need not fear him here tonight. Merely watch and witness the power and majesty of God's promise to us all.

"Bring the afflicted forward."

The afflicted was Avery Durrence, an eighty-year old tuberculosis victim and local wealthy retired industrialist with no chance of living beyond the week. In the final stages of his disease, he'd turned to the ministry and Brother Guidry, with a promise of a hefty donation to the cause, which of course had gotten him bumped to the top of the list.

To Guidry, the only thing that was sweeter than the sound of coin money on brass plates was the solid *thump* of the silent kind.

Durrence was rolled forward to the stage in his wheelchair, a portable iron lung attached to its side. The whirr of the machine was loud as a cyclone in the tent. He was bleary-eyed and red-faced. He coughed and spat a wad of mucus, containing more than a bit of lung tissue, into the dirt.

Guidry reached down and helped the millionaire to his feet and up on the stage. He led Durrence, who shuffled his slippered feet, over to stand before the thin man, who stood as always, head down, features cast into shadow by the brim of his hat and silent, save for the even breathing and the soft rise and fall of his chest.

"Stand, brother. Stand before Death and spit in his eyes! He no longer holds sway over you!"

As if taking Guidry literally, Durrence hacked up another blood-tinged wad of phlegm. It shot from his mouth and hit the thin man in the chest. Guidry watched with barely-concealed amusement as it rolled down his prisoner's starched shirt, dripped off his coattails and onto his dusty boots.

His mirth turned instantly to stark terror.

The bottom half of the devil's box he'd so carefully inscribed into the plywood stage poked out from beneath the rug, which had become askew when his lackeys had moved the cage.

A single, thin cut in the wood ran from the outer circle, bisecting it neatly, its edges burned as if cut with a hot poker. He toed the rug with his shoe, revealing the cut's path all the way to the center of the protective sigil.

He looked up at the prisoner, and for the first time, locked eyes with him.

Death smiled back.

A sluggish, pale gray light seeped out of the thin man's eyes, arching out into the air and splitting into dozens tentacles that caressed the air above the congregation's heads like a lover.

Then the screams began.

* * * *

Amos whipped around at the first scream.

"What the hell was that?" he said.

"My brother, doing his job," Bob replied, tugging violently at Amos.

Amos stared at the tent in horror. Silvery flashes of light arced behind the canvas, illuminating the silhouettes of the doomed congregation, whose screams were male and female, but so awful that neither was distinguishable from the other.

"We have to go back," Amos said, unable to look away, to even move.

"Are ye *mental?*" Bob yelled. "Ever hear of Sodom and Gomorrah? And *that* was just another day on the *job* for him. We don't even want t' be on the same *continent* tonight!"

"All them people," Amos breathed. "They ain't asked for this. They was hurtin', and stupid, maybe, but they don't deserve *this*. And I *done* it to 'em. I set that that monster loose again."

"Had to be done, boyo." Bob said. "I ever get 'round to startin' another book, the record will reflect that, for sure."

Amos jerked his arm from Bob's grasp. "Screw yo' book, and screw you, too, if you ain't gonna help! I done yo' dirty work an' this is how I get paid?" He began trot back across the parking area toward the tent.

"Go on, then!" Bob yelled after him. "Die with the rest of 'em! He'll show you no mercy! You can believe that!"

But Amos was gone.

Bob slapped his hat against his knee, dust billowing out in a cloud.

"Dad's gonna be pissed," he said.

* * * *

Arlen Guidry had never known true fear, but he was quickly becoming acquainted.

He held his stomach, lying curled in the fetal position on the stage floor. His bowels had long given way, but he didn't even register the wet spot that grew by the second on his suit pants. The tableau of terror laid out before him preoccupied even those thoughts.

The congregation was in a dozen states of death. Blood poured from all orifices—eyes, ears, nostrils. Heads shriveled like raisins in the sun in seconds. Abdomens exploded with such force the pews were bathed in offal as far as the eye could see, turning the house of God into an abattoir. Most just curled up and died, their bodies instantly shutting off like light switches whenever the silver tendrils licked against them.

And above it all, the thin man, the ancient of days, Death personified and prisoner no more, hovered in midair, his body alight with the ruddy pale glow of his namesake.

Run.

That was the one thought Guidry's catatonic mind would allow. Run, run, and don't look back. Never look back.

It was a plan with which Brother Arlen Guidry could swing.

He crawled at first, then somehow got to his feet and bolted for the rear of the tent. True to his plan, he never looked back. A fraud he may be, but he knew enough about Scripture to remember what happened to Lot's wife. He didn't slow down, not even when the foothills of the Sierra Nevada loomed before him like a bulwark against the darkness.

Not even when the first explosions ripped though the night like the sounding of Gabriel's horn.

* * * *

The explosion would play on Amos's retinas for months.

The concussion blew him at least thirty feet and landed him in a heap. He scrambled to his feet and watched as the tent burned like a sacrifice, the flames reaching up to the heavens in something like supplication.

A second explosion rocked the night, then a third, and Amos wondered fleetingly what could be catching in there, then decided he never wanted to know. The heat from the furnace that the great revival tent had become was blistering his face, even at that distance. He could feel his beard catch fire in places and he absently brushed them out, the smell of burning hair in his nostrils.

He had no notion of how long he'd stood there, watching the handiwork of something beyond his ken perform the vocation for which it was specifically created. He longed to feel something—anything—for the ones inside, but was incapable of anything but numbness.

Something stirred at the edges of his vision, something moving *inside* the conflagration, slowly resolving itself as it left the flames.

It was the thin man. He strode through the flames as if they were nothing more than a rain shower. Flames leapt from his clothes, dancing along the length of his tall frame, then one by one puffed out, trailing smoke, until that, too, vanished.

He was myth made concrete, majestic and terrible, silhouetted in the flames, and Amos realized that he was walking toward *him.*

Thunder rolled in the distance. Lightning flickered and died in the clouds above the distant mountains. Amos could not pull his gaze away from the man striding inexorably toward him.

The thin man stopped a foot away, looking Amos up and down. Amos felt all the blood freeze in his veins and the desert night became twelve degrees colder.

"You are the one who freed me." It wasn't a question. His voice was that of a sarcophagus lid scraping open.

"Y-yes, sir."

He looked Amos over again with those eyes, still flickering with the pale glow of his rage.

"My thanks," he said, looking into the west. "That has not happened to me for a long, long time. Not since the Lamb."

Amos shuddered, unable to think straight. How he managed to speak would be unknown to him for the rest of his days.

"W-what you gonna do t-to m-me?"

Death turned to face him again a spark of dark hilarity in his eyes. "'*Do*' to you? Why nothing, I suppose. You freed me, after all. And," he said, "it is not your time."

"Yeah?" Amos said, drawing on nerve he never knew he had. "And what about all them folks inside? Was it *their* time?"

Death looked him squarely in the eye and blinked. In that moment, a village in Borneo died to a man.

"Imagine," he said, "that you are an ant, climbing a mountain. It may take days, weeks, months, perhaps even years for you to reach the summit.

"When you *do* finally reach it, a man walks out of his home and steps on you, crushing the life from your tiny form. All that effort, all that struggle, counts for naught."

Amos tried to wet his mouth, but there wasn't enough spit in the world to do the job.

"You speak to a being that has ridden the black spaces between stars. A being that has known the names of countless worlds and their all inhabitants and laid waste to all of them with but a thought."

He lowered his face to Amos's. "Do *not* presume to speak of philosophy and righteousness to *me... ant.*"

Amos shook uncontrollably, his eyes wide in terror.

"You are afraid," the thin man said. "Why do you all fear death? Death is merely another part of life, a natural end to a natural beginning. Yet you all tremble." He shook his head. "Death isn't to be feared, Amos Harlow. If you must fear something, fear a life ill-spent, never standing for what is right and true. *That* is a thing worthy of your fear. If you can do the opposite, then when the end comes, you can stand and face it with courage and a song in your heart."

A horse's whinny broke the moment, and the thin man looked off into the west again. Amos followed his gaze.

At the crest of a small hillock, silhouetted in the rising full moon, stood three mounted riders. The third held the reins to a fourth, riderless horse. They all wore hats and trail gear and seemed to be waiting.

"Ah," the thin man said. "My brothers. They heard my call after all."

Amos dimly remembered strange mutterings behind warded iron bars.

"You-you're leavin'? Jus' like that?"

The thin man stared off to the east, into an approaching storm. "I've been away too long," he sighed. His breath was a dense fog in the cool desert air. He returned a steely gaze to Amos.

"And I've got a lot of work to do out there."

He turned and strode toward the waiting riders, raising a hand in silent farewell.

Amos watched him go. His legs were trembling, and not from the night chill. He wondered if such a being felt anything at all. Did he have fears and doubts, hopes and dreams? Or was he just a machine, created to do a job and nothing more? If so, Amos pitied him almost as much as he feared him.

He jumped as another explosion ripped through the tent, mingling with the low rumble of thunder from the east.

He turned back to the hill.

The riders were gone, for good or ill, leaving nothing but swirling clouds of trail dust in the moonlight to speak of their passing.

* * * *

Arlen Guidry knew nothing but pain and fear. Pain from the scorching he'd received when his prisoner decided to bring Hell to earth; fear that his prisoner would find him and bring him to a full reckoning.

He flopped in the rain gulley, trying to drown the screaming in his skin. Blisters the size of half-dollars had blossomed all over his body, oozing pus. His suit had actually *melted*, fused to his body in places like a second skin. He had long stopped trying to peel it off after receiving white hot lances of pain, the new reddened skin exposed to the elements.

Rain had begun to fall, slowly at first, then increasing in tempo until its drumming on the hardpan drowned out the world. He didn't know the car was there until the headlights washed over him.

Someone got out of the car and ran through the storm to his side. He felt strong arms lift him from the washout, drag him to the car, and throw him in the backseat. He lay there dazed, listening to the staccato rhythm of the rain on the car roof.

"Dammit, Arlen. Dammit, oh, *hell*! What we gonna do, Arlen? What we gonna *do*?"

Guidry muttered from the backseat.

"What? What'd you say, Arlen?"

"Drive," he managed.

"What? Drive *where*?"

"Just... *DRIVE!"* Guidry began coughing, unable to stop.

Reggie glanced over the seat. "Okay, okay...! You all right, there, Arlen?"

No, thought Arlen Guidry. *I am most definitely* NOT "*all right,*" *you prick.*

"Oh, Arlen. That...that bastard killed 'em all! He killed 'em *all*! What we gonna do, huh? What in the hell are we gonna *do*?"

Grunting in agony, Guidry managed to sit up.

It wasn't over, he thought. Not by a mile. Any good leader has a backup plan. Any good leader thinks around corners. Any good leader is crafty, smart, and always has strength in reserves. If Arlen Guidry was anything, he was a leader.

"First," he said, "we hole up for a few days. Get drunk. Get laid. Get our heads together. Then we go see a man I know in Kentucky and get the ball rollin' again."

The car jolted, hitting something heavy in the road. Reggie clung to the wheel, barely keeping the car on four wheels. He righted the car, and then, in a flash of lightning, his breath lodged in his throat. He swung the car left and right, the headlights washing over the land in front of them, his mind unable to take in what he was seeing.

The road was littered with the corpses of deer, wildcats, coyotes, groundhogs, and every stripe of wildlife to be found in a hundred-mile radius. Death as far as the eye could see, and beyond.

"Oh... *damn*," he breathed. "Oh, *damn*, Arlen! What are we gonna *do*? For God's sake, man, what are we gonna *do*?"

"We're gonna find that nigger," Guidry said in a voice that belonged more to the creature that they had trapped, used, and unleashed on an unsuspecting world.

"We're gonna find Amos Harlow and make him rue the day he dropped outta his mama's *womb*."

The car rolled on through the storm. Thunder rolled, and lighting flashed, revealing the dead and blackened landscape from which nothing would ever grow again.

* * * *

Amos woke early, the last vestiges of the storm having passed. He crawled out of his bedroll, snuffed the fire that had kept him warm through the night, and ambled out of the cave.

He'd tried to put as many miles between himself and the town of Bakersfield as he could before the storm drove him into the hills. There were many caves in this area of the Sierra Nevada range and providence had provided him one for shelter.

He stretched out, listening to his joints pop and staring at the early morning purple sky in which the moon still hung like a jack-o'-lantern, grinning at his plight.

Regardless of the events the night before, Amos had slept the best he'd ever slept in his life. He woke refreshed in mind and body, if not in spirit. That part may never again be restored. Not after Bakersfield.

He realized now, gathering his meager belongings and hoisting his guitar case, that he was a player on the board. He knew that he could no longer go unnoticed, could no longer enjoy the anonymity of his past life. He knew for a certainty that he would meet Brother Arlen Guidry again, somewhere on that great and secret battlefield that the United States had become. He had no idea what form that confrontation would take, or what would result from that meeting, but he knew for one of them--maybe *both* of them--it would be the last time.

"Fine mornin' for a walk, ain't it?"

Amos didn't bother to turn.

"Done skulkin' in the shadows now that the hard part's done?" he asked.

"Come, now, Amos. You knew the deal. I told ye why things had ta go down the way they did. No reason to get nasty, is it?"

Amos turned to face Gentleman Bob, scowling.

"Musta been, four, five hunnerd people at that meetin'," Amos said. "How's that for 'nasty'?"

"There were ten times that at Sodom; ten times *that* at Babylon," Bob said, as if that explained everything. "The whole *world* drowned at one point, Amos. It was a small price to pay."

Amos just gaped, his pulse a war drum.

"*Small* price? You call that *small*?"

Bob shook his head, laughing. "Ye still don't get it, do ye?" he said. "They were his bleedin' *army*, Amos. They were damned before they even set foot in that tent!"

"They thought they was goin' to *church*, you sumbitch! There was women and kids in there! Wasn't no damned *army*, it was *families*! Hopeless bunch of lost people!"

Bob glared at Amos. "Lost is *exactly* what they were," he said. "They were thralls, Amos. Tools of the Enemy, and they didn't know it—didn't *have* to know it—but they were tools all the same."

Amos spat on the ground at Bob's feet.

"You know," Bob said, "I ain't one to question the way of things, but I'm beginnin' to feel you ain't the man for the job."

"See, that's the difference between you an' your brother and me," Amos said. "Y'all ain't *got* to feel nothin'. You ain't got no *clue* what it means to feel anything at *all*. And you talkin' at me about *tools*."

Bob's face tightened. "Do you have any *idea* how painful it is for me to even *be* here? For seven centuries, no less? It's like a constant toothache that grows with each second. This cesspool, this mudhut you all call a world, it used to be Paradise, but you all screwed that up, didn't you? An' it's guys like me and my brothers got to clean up the mess."

"About that," Amos said. "I read the book, don't never forget that. I seen it. I seen it all, jes' like you wrote down."

"Yeah? So?" Bob said. "You weren't the first one to see the book. Fella by the name of John saw everything you saw. I showed it to him so's he could write Revelation."

"Bet I seen some things he *ain't*," Amos said. "Some I'd like to forget, some I won't never.

"Like your true name."

Bob stared at him, agape.

Amos picked at his teeth. "Why you think Mr. Skin-and-Bones didn't try to take me off the board back there? Got his, too."

"You're bluffin'," Bob breathed.

"Ain't but one way to find out, I reckon."

"Now, listen, Amos—" Bob began.

"No *you* listen. I'm gonna do whatever it is I'm supposed to, but I'm gonna do it *my* way, hear? I'm done bein' a ' *tool.*'"

Amos walked over and stood chest to chest with the angel, poking a finger in his chest. "An' if I ever see *you* again, Heaven gonna need a new secretary, you readin' me, asshole?"

Amos held Bob's gaze, then bent to pick up his guitar case. He looked up and Bob was gone.

"Damn right," he muttered.

Amos surveyed the countryside, looking east. He made his way down the narrow path from the cave and picked up a game trail he knew would put him on the highway before noon.

He decided he would head to Virginia, or Tennessee, maybe. Yeah, Memphis.

Look up some old friends. Drink until he couldn't see straight and try to drown the screams he knew would never be silent, even in his waking hours.

And across the world, bombs fell, babies starved, widows wept, crops failed, and plague spread like a prairie fire.

Amos heard none of it, save for a whirring sound on the desert wind, like that of a scythe shearing through golden stalks, separating the wheat from the chaff.

AFTERWORD

As I said in the introduction, this isn't the end of Amos Harlow's tale. It's a story that could only be told in two volumes, and even then, only the crux of his story.

The next and final collection will be coming soon, believe me. I feel an obligation to a man who gave the world so much and went into history no more than a buried footnote. The second volume will tell the tale of Amos's background, of who he was before he took the first step on his long, dark road. We will see his childhood, the horror he faced in the Great War, his escape from an insane asylum with dark purpose, a battle of wits with an ancient Faerie lord, the terrible vengeance of a murdered policeman, the hateful seeds of an old man's prejudice bear terrible fruit, and the fate of Amos's lost love Lily.

In a greater sense, the book will describe Amos's arduous and perilous journey across the Dust Bowl in pursuit of the Doorway Man—the serial killer Herod—and the unscrupulous false preacher Arlen Guidry, both of whom we've only briefly met in this collection, and both of whom Amos must face with the fate of the world hanging in the balance. I believed that story deserved its own space for the telling, as it is what Amos was born to accomplish.

I hope that you've enjoyed Amos Harlow's exploits thus far and will follow him and the black dog further down the road, bindle slung over one shoulder, and humming a tune to keep the dark at bay.

Don't worry; we'll be right there together.

Thanks so very much for reading,

Matt Coleman
Pearland, TX
March, 2012

ABOUT THE AUTHOR

Matt Coleman was born in Savannah, GA—a place where ghosts and other weird beings are known to hang out—and raised on a steady diet of the pulps, comic books, horror stories, the Twilight Zone, Kolchak: The Night Stalker, and Coca-Cola and peanuts.

He lives in Pearland, Texas with his wife and daughter, where an entirely *different* set of weird beings reside.

CPSIA information can be obtained at www.ICGtesting.com
Printed in the USA
LVOW072349261112

308871LV00014B/1335/P

9 781475 246698